BLASPHEMY

Also by Sherman Alexie

Fiction

War Dances
The Absolutely True Diary of a Part-Time Indian
Flight
Ten Little Indians
The Toughest Indian in the World
Indian Killer
Reservation Blues
The Lone Ranger and Tonto Fistfight in Heaven

Screenplays

The Business of Fancydancing
Smoke Signals

Poetry

Face
Dangerous Astronomy
Il powwow della fine del mondo
One Stick Song
The Man Who Loves Salmon
The Summer of Black Widows
Water Flowing Home
Seven Mourning Songs for the Cedar Flute I Have Yet
    to Learn to Play
First Indian on the Moon
Old Shirts & New Skins
I Would Steal Horses
The Business of Fancydancing

BLASPHEMY

Sherman Alexie

Grove Press
New York

"Green World" appeared in slightly different form in the June 2009 issue of *Harper's Magazine*.

"Cry Cry Cry" appeared in slightly different form in *The Speed Chronicles*, ed. Joseph Matson, Akashic Books.

"Idolatry" appeared in slightly different form in *Narrative*.

"Fame" appeared in slightly different form in *The Stranger*.

Published simultaneously in Canada
Printed in the United States of America

FIRST EDITION

ISBN-13: 978-0-8021-2039-7

Grove Press
an imprint of Grove/Atlantic, Inc.
841 Broadway
New York, NY 10003

Distributed by Publishers Group West

www.groveatlantic.com

12 13 14 15 16   10 9 8 7 6 5 4 3 2 1

For Red Group, you know who you are.

CONTENTS

BLASPHEMY

CRY CRY CRY

Forget crack, my cousin, Junior, said, meth is the new war dancer.

World Champion, he said.

Grand Entry, he said.

Five bucks, he said, give me five bucks and I'll give you enough meth to put you on a Vision Quest.

For a half-assed Indian, Junior talked full-on spiritual. Yeah, he was a born-again Indian. At the age of twenty-five, he war-danced for the first time. Around the same day he started dealing drugs.

I'm traditional, Junior said.

Whenever an Indian says he's traditional, you know that Indian is full of shit.

But, not long after my cousin started dancing, the pow-wow committee chose him as Head Man Dancer because he was charming and popular. Powwow is like high school, except with more feathers and beads.

Before he sold drugs, Junior used them. He started with speed and it made him dance for hours. Little fucker did somersaults. I've seen maybe three somersaulting war dancers.

You war-dance that good, Junior said, and the Indian women will line up to braid your hair.

No, I don't wear rubbers, he said. I want to be God and repopulate the world.

I wondered, since every Indian boy either looks like a girl or like a chicken with a big belly and skinny legs, how he could tell which kids were his.

He was all sexed up from the cradle.

He used to go to the Assembly of God, but when he was fifteen, he made a pass at the preacher's wife. Grabbed her tit and said, I'll save you.

Preacher man punched my cousin in the face.

I thought you were supposed to forgive me, Junior said.

Preacher man packed up his clothes, books, and wife and left the rez forever. I felt sorry for the wife—who'd made good friends among the Indian women—but was happy the preacher man was gone.

I didn't like him teaching us how to speak tongues.

Anyway, after the speed came the crack and it took hold of my cousin and made him jitter and shake the dust. Earthquake—his Indian name should have changed to Earthquake. Saddest thing: Powwow regalia looks great on a too-skinny Indian man.

Then came the meth.

Indian Health Service had already taken Junior's top row of teeth and the meth took the bottom row.

Use your drug money to buy some false teeth, I said.

I was teasing him, but he went out and bought new choppers. Even put a gold tooth in front like some kind of gangster rapper wannabe. He led a gang full of reservation-Indians-who-listened-to-hardcore-rap-so-much-they-pretended-to-be-inner-city-black. Shit, we got fake Bloods fake-fighting fake Crips. But they aren't brave or crazy enough to shoot at one another with real guns. No, they mostly yell out car windows. Fuckers are drive-by cursing.

I heard some fake gangsters had taken to throwing government commodity food at one another.

Yeah, my cousin was deadly as a can of cling peaches.

And this might have gone on forever if he'd only dealt drugs on the rez and only to Indians. But he crossed the border and found customers in the white farm towns that circled us.

Started hooking up the Future Farmers of America.

And then he started fucking the farmers' daughters.

So they charged him for possession, intent to sell, and statutory rape. And I figured he deserved whatever punishment he'd get during the trial.

Hey, Cousin, he said to me when I visited him in jail, they're going to frame me.

You're guilty, I said, you did all of it, and if the cops ever ask me, I'll tell them everything I know about your badness.

He was mad at first. Talked about betrayal. But then he softened and cried.

You're the only one, he said, who loves me enough to tell the truth.

But I could tell he was manipulating me. Putting the Jedi shaman mind tricks on me. But I didn't fall for his magic.

I do love you, I said, but I don't love you enough to save you.

While the lawyers and judges and jury were deciding my cousin's future, some tribal members showed up at the court-house to protest. They screamed and chanted about racism. They weren't exactly wrong. Plenty of Indians have gone to jail for no good reason. But plenty more have gone to jail for the exact right reasons.

Of course, it didn't help that I knew half of those protestors were my cousin's loyal customers.

So I felt sorry for the protestors who believed in what they were doing. They were good-hearted people looking to change the system. But when you start fighting for every Indian, you end up defending the terrible ones, too.

That's what being tribal can do to you. It traps you in the tipi with the murderers and rapists and drug dealers. It seems everywhere you turn, some felon-in-buckskin elbows you in the rib cage.

After a few days of trial and testimony, when things were looking way bad for my cousin, Junior plea-bargained his way to a ten-year prison sentence in Walla Walla State Penitentiary.

Maybe out in six with good behavior. Yeah, like my cousin was capable of good behavior.

And, oh, man was he terrified.

You're right to be scared, I said, but just find all the Indians and they'll keep you safe.

But what did I know? The only thing I'd learned about prison was what I'd seen on HBO, A&E, and MSNBC documentaries.

Halfway through his first day in prison, my cousin got into a tussle with the big boss Indian.

Why did you fight him? I asked.

Because he was a white man, Junior said, as fucking pale as snow.

My cousin wasn't too dark himself but I guess he was dark enough.

That fucker had blue eyes, Junior said, and you know Indians can't be blue-eyed.

My cousin wasn't smart enough to know about recessive genes, but he was speaking some truth.

But no matter how Junior felt about that white Indian, he should have kept the peace. He should have looked for the Indian hidden behind those blue eyes.

I tried to explain myself, Junior said. I told him I was just punching the white guy in him.

Like an exorcism, I said when Junior called me collect from the prison pay phone. I think jail is the only place where you can find pay phones anymore.

Yeah, Junior said, I'm a devil-killer.

But here's the saddest thing: My cousin's late mother was white. A blonde and blue-eyed Caucasian beauty. Yeah, my cousin is half white. He just won the genetic lottery when he got the black hair and brown eyes. His late brother had the light skin and pale eyes. We used to call them Sunrise and Sundown.

Anyway, my cousin lost his tribal protection damn quick, and halfway through his second day in prison, he was gang-raped by black guys. And halfway through his third day, those black guys sold Junior to an Aryan dude for five cartons of cigarettes.

One thousand cigarettes.

5

It's cruel to say, but that doesn't seem near enough to buy somebody. If it's going to happen to you, it should cost a lot more, right?

But what do I know about prison economics? Maybe that was a good price. I hoped that it was a good price.

My cousin was pretty. He had the long, black hair and the skinny legs and ass. It didn't take much to make him look womanly. Just some mascara, lipstick, and prison pants scissored into short shorts.

Suddenly, Junior said, I am Miss Indian USA.

But I'm not gay, he said.

It's not about being gay, I said, it's about crazy guys trying to fill you with their pain.

Jesus, Junior said, all these years since Columbus landed and now he's finally decided to fuck me in the ass.

Yeah, we could laugh about it. What else were we going to do? If you sing the first note of a death song while you're in prison, you'll soon be singing the whole damn song every damn day.

For the next three years, I drove down to Walla Walla to visit Junior. At first, it was once or twice a month. Then it became every few months. Then I stopped driving there at all. I accepted his collect calls for the first five years, but then I stopped doing that. And he stopped calling. He disappeared from my life.

Some things happen. Some things don't.

My cousin served his full ten-year sentence, was released on a Monday, and had to hitchhike back to the reservation.

He showed up at the tribal cafe as I was eating an overcooked hamburger and too-greasy fries. He sat in the chair across the table from me and smiled big and shiny. New false teeth. Looked like he got one good thing out of prison.

Hey, Cousin, he said.

He was way casual for a guy who'd been in prison for ten years and hadn't heard from me in five.

So, I said, are you really free or did you break out?

It was a hot summer day, but Junior was wearing long sleeves to cover his track marks. He'd graduated from meth to heroin.

We restarted our friendship You could call us cousin-brothers or cousin–best friends. Either works. Both work. He never mentioned my absence from his prison life and I wasn't about to bring it up.

He got a job working forestry. It was easy work for decent money. Nobody on the rez was interested in punishing the already-punished.

It's a good job, he said, I drive through all the deep woods on the rez and mark trees that I think should be cut down.

Thing is, he said, we never cut down any trees, so my job is really just driving through the most beautiful place in the world while carrying a box full of spray paint.

He fell in love, too, with Jeri, a white woman who worked as a nurse at the Indian Health Service Clinic. She was round and red-faced, but funny and cute and all tender in the heart, and everybody on the rez liked her. So it felt like a slice of redemption pie.

She listens to me, Junior said. You know how hard that is to find?

Yeah, I said, but do you listen to her?

Junior shrugged his shoulders. Of course he didn't listen to her. He'd been forced to keep his mouth shut for ten years in prison. It was his turn to talk. And talk he did.

He told me everything about how he sexed her up. Half of me wanted to hear the stories and half of me wanted to close my ears. But I couldn't stop him. I felt guilty for abandoning him in prison. I owed him patience and grace.

But it was so awful sometimes. He was already sex-drunk and half-mean when he went into prison, but being treated as a fuck-slave for ten years turned him into something worse. I don't have a name for it, but he talked about sex like he talked about speed and meth and crack and heroin.

She's my pusher, he said about Jeri, and her pussy is my drug.

He reduced Jeri all the way down to the sacred parts of her anatomy. And those parts stop being sacred when you talk blasphemy about them.

Maybe he wasn't in love with Jeri, I thought. Maybe he was time-traveling her back to prison with him.

But I also wondered what Jeri was doing with him. From the outside, she looked solid and real, but I think she was broken inside and, for some crazy reason, thought that broken men could fix her.

Things went on like that for a couple of years. He started punching her in the stomach. She hid those bruises beneath her clothes. And she punched him and gave him black eyes that Junior carried around like war paint.

We are Romeo and Juliet, he said.

Yeah, like he'd ever read the book or watched any of those movies more than ten minutes through.

Then, one day, Jeri disappeared.

Rumor had it she went into a battered women's shelter. Rumor also had it she was hiding in Spokane. Which, if true, was stupid. How can you hide in the City of Spokane from a Spokane Indian?

Six months after she went missing, Junior found her in a 7-Eleven in the Indian part of town.

Yeah, scared as she was of one Indian, she was hiding among other Indians. Yeah, we Indians are addicting. You have to be careful around us because we'll teach you how to cry epic tears and you'll never want to stop.

Anyway, you might think he wanted to kill her. Or break some bones. But, no, he was crazy in a whole different way. In the aisle of that 7-Eleven, he dropped to his knees and asked for her hand in marriage.

So, yes, they got married and I was the best man.

In the parking lot after the ceremony, Junior and Jeri smoked meth with a bunch of toothless wonders.

Fucking zombies walking everywhere on the rez.

Monster movie all the time.

A thousand years from now, archaeologists are going to be mystified by all the toothless skulls they find buried in the ancient reservation mud.

Junior and Jeri couldn't afford a honeymoon so they spent a night in the tribal casino hotel. That's free for any Indian newly-weds. Mighty generous, I guess, letting tribal members sleep free in the casino they're supposed to own.

They moved into a trailer house down near Tshimakain Creek and they got all happy and safe for maybe six months.

Then, one night, after she wouldn't have sex with him, he punched her so hard that he knocked out her front teeth.

That was it for her.

She left him and lived on the rez in plain sight. All proud for leaving, she mocked him by carrying her freedom around like her own kind of war paint. And I loved her for it.

Stand up, woman, I thought, stand up and kick out your demons.

Junior seemed to accept it okay. I should've known better, but he talked a good line.

The world is an imperfect place, he said. I don't know where he got that bit of philosophy but he seemed to believe it.

Then Jeri fell in love with Dr. Bob. He was the general practitioner who also worked at the Indian clinic and was counting the days until he paid off his scholarship and could flee the rez. In the meantime, he'd found a warm body to keep him company during the too-damn-many-Indians night.

Everybody deserves love. Well, almost everybody deserves love. And Jeri certainly needed some brightness, but Dr. Bob was all dark and bitter and accelerated. He punched her in the face on their eleventh date.

Ten minutes after we heard the news, Junior and I were speeding toward Dr. Bob's house, located right next to the rez border down near the Spokane River. Yeah, he had to live on the rez, but he'd only live fifteen feet past the border.

I'm going to fuck him up, Junior said. You can't be hitting my woman.

I knew Junior was going to do something very bad. And I should have stopped him. I probably could have stopped him. Instead, I held on to my silence hard. I was a mute man riding shotgun for a bad man looking to hurt another bad man.

All the while he was driving, Junior was snorting whatever he could find within arm's reach. I think he snorted up spilled sugar and salt. Any powder was good. So he was all feedback and static when we arrived at Dr. Bob's door.

Junior raced ahead of me and rhino-charged into the house. And, once inside, he pulled a pistol from somewhere and whipped Dr. Bob across the face.

A fucking .45. I'd seen tons of hunting rifles on the rez, but never a pistol like that.

Junior whipped Dr. Bob maybe five times across the face and then kicked him in the balls and threw him against the wall. And Dr. Bob, the so-called healer, slid all injured and bloody to the floor.

You do not fuck with my possessions, Junior said.

There it was. The real reason for all of it. It was hatred and revenge, not love. Maybe at that point, all Junior could see was the Aryan who'd raped him a thousand times. Maybe Junior could only see the white lightning of colonialism. I don't mean to get so intellectual, but I'm trying to understand. I'm trying to explain what happened. I'm trying to explain myself to myself.

I watched Junior lean over and backhand Dr. Bob. Then again. And again.

He's had enough, I said, let's get out of here.

Junior laughed.

Yeah, he said, this fucker will never hit another woman again.

Junior and I walked toward the door together. I thought it was over. But Junior turned back, pressed that pistol against Dr. Bob's forehead, and pulled the trigger.

I will never forget how that head exploded. It was like a comet smashing through a planet.

I couldn't move. It was the worst thing I'd ever seen. But then Junior did something worse. He flipped over the doctor's body, pulled down his pants and underwear, and shoved that pistol into Dr. Bob's ass.

Even then, I knew there was some battered train track stretching between Junior's torture in prison and that violation of Dr. Bob's body.

No more, I said, no more.

Junior stared at me with such hatred, such pain, that I thought he might kill me, too. But then his eyes filled with something worse: logic.

We have to get rid of the body, he said.

I shook my head. At least, I think I shook my head.

You owe me, he said.

That was it. I couldn't deny him. I helped him clean up the blood and bone and brain, and wrap Dr. Bob in a blanket, and throw him into the trunk of the car.

I know where to dump him, Junior said.

So we drove deep into the forest, to the end of a dirt road that had started, centuries ago, as a game trail. Then we carried Dr. Bob's body through the deep woods toward a low canyon that Junior had discovered during his tree-painting job.

Nobody will ever find the body, Junior said.

As we trudged along, mosquitoes and flies, attracted by the blood, swarmed us. I must have gotten bit a hundred times or more. Soon enough, Junior and I were bleeding onto Dr. Bob's body.

Blood for blood. Blood with blood.

After a few hours of dragging that body through the wilderness, we reached Junior's canyon. It was maybe ten feet across and choked with brush and small trees.

He's going to get caught up in the branches, I said.

Jesus, I thought, I'm terrified of my own logic.

Just throw him real hard, Junior said.

So we somehow found the strength to lift Dr. Bob over our heads and hurl him into the canyon. His body crashed through the green and came to rest, unseen, somewhere below us.

Maybe you want to say a few words, Junior said.

Don't be so fucking mean, I said, we've done something awful here.

Junior laughed.

You should throw that gun down there, too, I said.

I paid five hundred bucks for this, Junior said. I'm keeping it.

He stuffed the gun down the back of his jeans. I didn't like it but I didn't want to piss him off.

As we slogged back toward the car, Junior started talking childhood memories. He and I, as babies, had slept in the same crib, and we'd lost our virginities at the same time in the same bedroom with a pair of sisters. And now we had killed together, so we were more than cousins, more than best friends, and more than brothers. We were the same person.

Of course, I kept reminding myself that I didn't touch Dr. Bob. I didn't pistol-whip him or punch him or slap him. And I certainly didn't shoot him. But I'd helped Junior dispose of the body and that made me a criminal.

When we made it back to the car, Junior stopped and stared at the stars, newly arrived in the sky.

Then he pulled out the pistol and pointed it at the ground.

You're going to keep quiet about this, he said.

I stared at the gun. He saw me staring at the gun. I knew he was deciding whether to kill me or not. And I guess his love for me, or whatever it was that he called love, won him over. He turned and threw the pistol as far as he could into the dark.

We silently drove back down that dirt road. As he dropped me at my house, he cried a little, and hugged me.

You owe me, he said.

After he drove away, I climbed onto the roof of my house. It seemed like the right thing to do. Folks would later me call me

Snoopy, and I would love laughing with them, but at the time, it seemed like a serious act.

I wanted to be in a place where I'd never been before and think about the grotesquely new thing that I'd just done, and what I needed to do about it. But I was too exhausted for much thought or action, so I closed my eyes and fell asleep.

The next morning, I woke wet and cold, climbed off the roof, and went to the Tribal Police. A couple hours after I told them the story, the Feds showed up. And a few hours after that, I led them to Dr. Bob's body.

Later that night, as the police laid siege to his trailer house, Junior shot himself in the head.

He'd chosen death over a return to prison.

I wasn't charged with any crime. I could have been, I suppose, and maybe should have been. But I guess I'd done the right thing, or maybe something close enough to the right thing.

And Jeri? She left the rez. I hear she's working on another rez in Arizona. I pray that she never falls in love again. I'm not blaming her for what happened. I just think she's better off alone. Who isn't better off alone?

I didn't go to Junior's funeral. I figured somebody might shoot me if I did. Most everybody thought I was evil for turning against Junior. Yeah, I was the bad guy because I betrayed another Indian.

And, yes, it's true that I betrayed Junior. But if betrayal can be righteous, then I believe I was righteous. But who knows except God?

Anyway, in honor of Junior, I started war-dancing. I had to buy my regalia from a Sioux Indian who didn't care about my troubles, but that was okay. I think the Sioux make the best outfits anyway.

So I danced.

I practiced dancing first in front of a mirror. I'd put a pow-wow CD in my computer and I'd stumble in circles around my living room. After a few months of that, I felt confident enough to make my public debut.

It was a minor powwow in the high school gym. Just another social event during a boring early December.

At first, nobody recognized me. I'd war-painted my whole face black. I wanted to look like a villain, I guess.

Anyway, as I danced, a few people recognized me and started talking to everybody around them. Soon enough, the whole powwow knew it was me swinging my feathers. A few folks jeered and threw curses my way. But most just watched me. I felt like crying. But then one of the elders, a great-grandmother named Agnes, trilled like a bird. She said my name quietly but everybody heard it anyway. Indians stand to honor people, so she stood for me. Then another elder woman trilled and said my name. And then a third. Soon enough, a dozen elder women were standing for me. I wept. I realized that I wasn't dancing for Junior. No, I was dancing for the old women. I was dancing for all of the dead. And all of the living. But I wasn't dancing for war. I was dancing for my soul and for the soul of my tribe. I was dancing for what we Indians used to be and who we might become again.

GREEN WORLD

In a little town on an Indian reservation, whose name I don't want to mention, there lived a man, a Native American, who owned a shotgun. This was forty or so years ago, in the early part of the twenty-first century, just before the government hired thousands of hungry, desperate people to build the windmills. How many windmills did they build? I suppose there is a bureaucrat willing to apply for the grant that would pay her to do the extensive research that would yield a number, but one might as well try to count all of the grains of rice in the world. But, wait, before I continue, let me make something clear: I am not afraid of large numbers. Just write down a number, any number, and follow it with more numbers, and keep writing numbers for a week. You will find, in that strange exercise, more patterns than you'd ever imagine. And you'll find mysteries, too. There is beauty and magic in numbers. Take, for instance, the windmills spinning off the Southern California coast. I've been there and I've seen them, with their huge white wings slowly rotating and their long legs buried deep in the ocean floor. On the most blustery of days, they look like an infinite flock of giant birds lifting into flight, forever caught in that moment of leaving the water for the sky.

But please, as I speak of infinity, don't worry that I am trying to tell you an infinite tale. I cannot tell you about every windmill; I can only tell you about the twelve windmills that were built a few miles outside of the little town on that unnameable Indian reservation. I don't know who built those windmills; I was hired to dispose of the dead birds.

As you know, windmills kill birds. Each windmill kills hundreds of birds a year. Perhaps thousands. It's hard to say. Since the birds are chopped into pieces, it is impossible to count individuals. One can only weigh a shovel-, wheelbarrow-, or truckload of bird parts and estimate the death count. Of course, due to personal and political bias, environmentalists overestimate the carnage while energy companies underestimate. It was that way with the first windmills and it is that way with all of our current windmills. As with most things, the truth, or the most accurate possible measure of the truth, exists somewhere in the in-between.

It is still my job, even as an old man, to collect the dead birds, and I share this work with tens of thousands of men and women. But, I must repeat, this story is not about any of those windmills. Or any of those dead birds. No, this story is only about the twelve windmills—my first windmills—that churned on a bluff overlooking one of the world's great rivers. No, this story is about that unnamed Indian man. And his shotgun. No. Let me be more honest. This story is about me.

I was lucky to get the job. The tribe had wanted to hire an Indian. I am not an Indian. But they hired me because nobody else wanted the job. Or rather, three or four Indians had been hired but had soon quit because of the terrible amounts of blood and gore. Frankly speaking, if one comes near enough dead birds, one begins to smell like dead birds. It is not an odor that can be easily washed away.

Of course, I did not know about the more difficult aspects of the job when I was hired. I only knew that I had found a job, and a well-paying job at that, in the midst of our country's Second Great Depression. And while I was not happy with the work—who could be happy doing such a thing?—I labored with great discipline and, dare I say it, passion. It was not a job I wanted to lose.

Each day, just before sunrise, I arrived at the tribal garage, procured my official vehicle—a flatbed truck—and drove the short distance to the twelve windmills. Arranged in two rows of six, those windmills were rather simple and lovely but became glorious at sunrise, when the golden light struck those golden windmills rising like wooden giants in the wild and golden fields. Still, as physically beautiful as the windmills were, I found myself falling in love with their music, the rhythmic hum of wood meeting metal.

But then, each day, after admiring the windmills, I would have to back the truck up to the base of a windmill, step out, grab my shovel, and pick up pieces of bird. And, each day, as I bent my back and calloused my hands, I would think—or try not to think—Dead bird, dead bird, dead bird, dead bird.

I vomited, often, during my first few weeks of that work. One could not be a thinking, feeling person and not be made sick. One would not be human if one were not overcome with sadness and pity. But in order to continue working—in order to keep the job—I became immune to such emotions. And so, three months into the job, on an early October morning, I realized that I had acquired enough self-control to keep disposing of dead birds forever.

The first snow came early that year. It wasn't a big storm. There was only an inch or two of snow on the ground. It didn't prevent me from driving the truck the short distance from the garage to the windmills. And so it was that I came to see the windmills, those wooden giants, standing ankle-deep in twelve ponds of blood.

They weren't ponds of blood, of course. I can be a fantasist; forgive me. Rather, the windmills had sliced dozens of birds and scattered the bloody pieces into twelve distinct circles around their foundations.

It was a particularly disturbing sight, and I might have driven away had I not seen that Indian man walking toward the windmills. The windmills and those bloody circles stood between the Indian man and me. He was singing a tribal song, and though I understood none of the words or rhythms, I can promise you that he was singing a death song.

And so, for reasons I still cannot explain, I stepped out of the truck and walked toward that Indian man. I walked between the windmill rows and through those bloody circles and that Indian man did the same from the opposite direction, until we stood just ten feet apart. It was only then that I noticed he was carrying a shotgun.

He kept singing his death song as he raised his weapon and pointed it at me. I remember thinking that he was singing my death song.

19

"Please," I said.

The Indian man kept singing as he stepped closer to me and pressed the shotgun against my forehead.

"Please," I said again.

He was singing so loudly that it hurt my ears. And as his song reached a crescendo, I closed my eyes, sure that I was about to become my own bloody circle in the snow.

But then he stopped singing.

I opened my eyes and watched him lower the shotgun and walk over to a circle and kneel in the bloody snow. He dropped the shotgun into the snow and picked up a carcass so ravaged and mutilated that I cannot even tell you what kind of bird he was holding. He hugged that corpse close to his chest, as if he were holding something of his own, and wept for some long moments.

I watched him.

He stopped weeping and held the dead bird toward me. "My tribe built these windmills," he said.

"I know," I said.

"We started this," he said.

"I suppose," I said.

"This is just the beginning," he said.

"I don't know," I said.

"It's never going to stop," he said.

"I guess not," I said. But I wanted to tell him that it was necessary and predictable. We humans have to kill in order to live. No, every living thing on earth kills in order to survive. But I didn't say anything. I knew that my opinion might put my life in more danger.

The Indian studied my face for a while. Then he made some judgment about me. I could see him make his decision. He set down the dead bird, picked up the shotgun, walked close to one of the windmills, and shot it.

He stepped forward and closely studied the shotgun blast in the windmill, as if he expected the machine to bleed. Then he stepped back and shot the windmill again. He reloaded, shot, reloaded, shot, reloaded, shot, and then stepped back and looked up at the windmill. It was still moving, working, and ready to kill birds. It was impervious.

After a while, he turned and walked away. I watched him go over the slight rise and disappear. Indians are good at walking away.

I stood in the cold for a while. I'm not a religious man. I'm not even sure that I believe in God, but I knelt in the snow and prayed.

SCARS

On Mike's right forearm, a lightning-shaped scar.

"Hurrying for a job interview," he said. "Trying to make my white shirt crisp. Reached across the ironing board for the starch bottle and dragged my arm over the tip of the hot iron."

On Mike's left forearm, a keloid scar that looks like Pac-Man.

"Got that job," he said. "Waiting tables at that pancake house on Aurora. First shift. First ten minutes. First time I tried to pour coffee, I spilled some on my arm. At first, the burn was just a mess of red skin and blisters, but then, as it healed, it shrank up, got all thick and ugly, and turned into Pac-Man, if Pac-Man got his face all burned to shit in a pizza oven."

On Mike's forehead, a white scar running from temple to temple like the horizon.

"Only worked that job long enough to buy me a snowboard," he said. "Hitchhiked to Stevens Pass. Hitchhiked up a mountain. How crazy is that? Anyway, my first run, I plow into this old dude. And we tumble and slide down the hill together and somehow his ski slices my forehead. Took seventy-five stitches to sew it up. Old dude broke his leg, but wasn't too freaked about it. Said it was just the way skiing goes sometimes. Cool old dude."

Mike's right ear was cauliflowered like a boxer's.

"It looks like an alien is fucking my earhole," he said. "But people don't mess with me because of it. They think I'm some mixed-martial artist who will spinning-backfist them into the hospital.

"My father did it," he said. "First time, I was maybe seven, and I dropped my orange juice on the kitchen floor, and he slapped me on the side of my head. Knocked me out. Woke up, my ear swollen and all bloody and funny-color bruised. You know what I said to my mom? I told her my ear had a black eye.

"Yeah, my mom knew my dad hit me," he said. "She never did anything about it. But that's okay. Nobody else did anything about it, either.

"Dad kept hitting the same ear," he said. "He kept hitting me whenever he was pissed. And he was pissed all the time. Hit me maybe fifty times over the years.

"It's my right ear," he said, "because my dad was left-handed.

23

"Last time he hit me was the night I graduated from high school," he said. "He was drunk and kept pushing at me. Kept asking me if I thought I was too good for him now. Kept saying I thought I'd taken a shit on the moon. And then I told him I was going to community college and he hit me. But I was bigger than I used to be. Same size as him. And I was younger and sober. So, yeah, I just kicked his ass out the front door and onto the lawn. Had an audience after a while.

"And nobody stopped me, either," Mike said. "Not my mom. Not even Pastor Arnold. Because they all knew for years that dad was beating on me, and none of them did a thing to stop him. And now I was getting revenge. And they were okay with that. All they could do was call the ambulance after I was done.

"Got five years for manslaughter," he said. "Out early for good behavior. Got my bachelor's degree in education. I want to teach high school. But no way in hell they'll let an ex-con teach in a real school. No way they'll let me teach white kids. So I moved back to the rez. Back in with my mother.

"Sometimes," he said, "she asks me why I had to kill him. She still misses him.

"And sometimes," he said, "she rubs this lotion on my ear. It's some miracle medicine that's supposed to make scars go away. I don't tell her that shit might have worked when I was ten, but it ain't going to work now. This ear is going to look like this forever.

"And, yeah," Mike said, "prison was horrible at first. I got scars way deep inside. But things got better as soon as the other Indians realized I was Indian, too. They saw my blond hair and blue eyes, you know, and thought I was just another Aryan. The real Aryans thought I was one of them, too. But I speak my tribal language, man, and I play drum and sing. So I just walked up to the Indians gathered in the prison yard. And I clapped my hands together like a drum and I sang a powwow song, northern style, maybe a little too fast because I was nervous.

"And, man, oh, man," he said. "Did those Indians laugh and cheer and war-whoop it up when I was done. And this one elder, with these long, gray braids and about ten thousand tattoos, he calls for quiet. And all these hard-ass Indians shut up because they respect the elder. And he says to me and everybody else, he says, the Creator has gifted us with a half-breed who can sing full-blood.

"So Full-Blood became my prison name," Mike said. "Funny as shit, right? A blond Indian named Full-Blood. And, let me tell you, I sang ten thousand songs in prison, even sang for the governor, this tiny white woman, when she came to visit.

"Before I sang, she asked me what crime I'd committed," he said. "And that's a question you don't ask or answer in prison. But I figure, Hey, she's the Governor, so I tell her the truth. I tell her I manslaughtered my father. That I punched him to death because he punched me for years. And the governor leans in close to me, so close I could feel her breath on my ear, and she says, she says, she says, Good for you.

"Can you believe that shit?" Mike asked. "I couldn't even respond. But let me tell you this. If they ever let ex-cons vote, I'm going to vote for that governor. I'll vote for her no matter what she's running for. You see? I finally understand this damn country. I finally know who should lead us. It's got to be somebody who is equal parts revenge and forgiveness. Somebody who is equal parts love and blood.

"Do you know what I mean?" Mike asked. "Please tell me you know what I mean."

THE TOUGHEST INDIAN
IN THE WORLD

Being a Spokane Indian, I only pick up Indian hitchhikers.

I learned this particular ceremony from my father, a Coeur d'Alene, who always stopped for those twentieth-century aboriginal nomads who refused to believe the salmon were gone. I don't know what they believed in exactly, but they wore hope like a bright shirt.

My father never taught me about hope. Instead, he continually told me that our salmon—our hope—would never come back, and though such lessons may seem cruel, I know enough to cover my heart in any crowd of white people.

"They'll kill you if they get the chance," my father said. "Love you or hate you, white people will shoot you in the heart. Even after all these years, they'll still smell the salmon on you, the dead salmon, and that will make white people dangerous."

All of us, Indian and white, are haunted by salmon.

When I was a boy, I leaned over the edge of one dam or another—perhaps Long Lake or Little Falls or the great gray dragon known as the Grand Coulee—and watched the ghosts of the salmon rise from the water to the sky and become constellations.

For most Indians, stars are nothing more than white tombstones scattered across a dark graveyard.

But the Indian hitchhikers my father picked up refused to admit the existence of sky, let alone the possibility that salmon might be stars. They were common people who believed only in the thumb and the foot. My father envied those simple Indian hitchhikers. He wanted to change their minds about salmon; he wanted to break open their hearts and see the future in their blood. He loved them.

In 1975 or '76 or '77, driving along one highway or another, my father would point out a hitchhiker standing beside the road a mile or two in the distance.

"Indian," he said if it was an Indian, and he was never wrong, though I could never tell if the distant figure was male or female, let alone Indian or not.

If a distant figure happened to be white, my father would drive by without comment.

That was how I learned to be silent in the presence of white people.

The silence is not about hate or pain or fear. Indians just like to believe that white people will vanish, perhaps explode into smoke, if they are ignored enough times. Perhaps a thousand white families are still waiting for their sons and daughters to return home, and can't recognize them when they float back as morning fog.

"We better stop," my mother said from the passenger seat. She was one of those Spokane women who always wore a purple bandanna tied tightly around her head.

These days, her bandanna is usually red. There are reasons, motives, traditions behind the choice of color, but my mother keeps them secret.

"Make room," my father said to my siblings and me as we sat on the floor in the cavernous passenger area of our blue van. We sat on carpet samples because my father had torn out the seats in a sober rage not long after he bought the van from a crazy white man.

I have three brothers and three sisters now. Back then, I had four of each. I missed one of the funerals and cried myself sick during the other one.

"Make room," my father said again—he said everything twice—and only then did we scramble to make space for the Indian hitchhiker.

Of course, it was easy enough to make room for one hitchhiker, but Indians usually travel in packs. Once or twice, we picked up entire all-Indian basketball teams, along with their coaches, girlfriends, and cousins. Fifteen, twenty Indian strangers squeezed into the back of a blue van with nine wide-eyed Indian kids.

Back in those days, I loved the smell of Indians, and of Indian hitchhikers in particular. They were usually in some stage of drunkenness, often in need of soap and a towel, and always ready to sing.

Oh, the songs! Indian blues bellowed at the highest volumes. We called them "49s," those cross-cultural songs that combined Indian lyrics and rhythms with country-and-western and blues melodies. It seemed that every Indian knew all the lyrics to every Hank Williams song ever recorded. Hank was our Jesus, Patsy Cline was our Virgin Mary, and Freddy Fender, George Jones, Conway Twitty, Loretta Lynn, Tammy Wynette, Charley Pride, Ronnie Milsap, Tanya Tucker, Marty Robbins, Johnny Horton, Donna Fargo, and Charlie Rich were our disciples.

We all know that nostalgia is dangerous, but I remember those days with a clear conscience. Of course, we live in different days now, and there aren't as many Indian hitchhikers as there used to be.

Now, I drive my own car, a 1998 Toyota Camry, the best-selling automobile in the United States, and therefore the one most often stolen. *Consumer Reports* has named it the most reliable family sedan for sixteen years running, and I believe it.

In my Camry, I pick up three or four Indian hitchhikers a week. Mostly men. They're usually headed home, back to their reservations or somewhere close to their reservations. Indians hardly ever travel in a straight line, so a Crow Indian might hitchhike west when his reservation is back east in Montana. He has some people to see in Seattle, he might explain if I ever asked him. But I never ask Indians their reasons for hitchhiking. All that matters is this: They are Indians walking, raising their thumbs, and I am there to pick them up.

At the newspaper where I work, my fellow reporters think I'm crazy to pick up hitchhikers. They're all white and never stop to pick up anybody, let alone an Indian. After all, we're the ones who write the stories and headlines: hitchhiker kills husband and wife, missing girl's body found, rapist strikes again. If I really tried, maybe I could explain to them why I pick up any Indian, but who wants to try? Instead, if they ask I just give them a smile and turn back to my computer. My coworkers smile back and laugh loudly. They're always laughing loudly at me, at one another, at themselves, at goofy typos in the newspapers, at the idea of hitchhikers.

I dated one of them for a few months. Cindy. She covered the local courts: speeding tickets and divorces, drunk driving and embezzlement. Cindy firmly believed in the who-what-where-when-why-and-how of journalism. In daily conversation, she talked like she was writing the lead of her latest story. Hell, she talked like that in bed.

"How does that feel?" I asked, quite possibly the only Indian man who has ever asked that question.

"I love it when you touch me there," she answered. "But it would help if you rubbed it about thirty percent lighter and with your thumb instead of your middle finger. And could you maybe turn the radio to a different station? KYZY would be good. I feel like soft jazz will work better for me right now. A minor chord, a C or G-flat, or something like that. Okay, honey?"

During lovemaking, I would get so exhausted by the size of her erotic vocabulary that I would fall asleep before my orgasm, continue pumping away as if I were awake, and then regain consciousness with a sudden start when I finally did come, more out of reflex than passion.

Don't get me wrong. Cindy is a good one, cute and smart, funny as hell, a good catch no matter how you define it, but she was also one of those white women who date only brown-skinned guys. Indians like me, black dudes, Mexicans, even a few Iranians. I started to feel like a trophy, or like one of those entries in a personal ad. I asked Cindy why she never dated pale boys.

"White guys bore me," she said. "All they want to talk about is their fathers."

"What do brown guys talk about?" I asked her.

"Their mothers," she said and laughed, then promptly left me for a public defender who was half Japanese and half African, a combination that left Cindy dizzy with the interracial possibilities.

Since Cindy, I haven't dated anyone. I live in my studio apartment with the ghosts of two dogs, Felix and Oscar, and a laptop computer stuffed with bad poems, the aborted halves of three novels, and some three-paragraph personality pieces I wrote for the newspaper.

I'm a features writer, and an Indian at that, so I get all the shit jobs. Not the dangerous shit jobs or the monotonous shit jobs. No. I get to write the articles designed to please the eye, ear, and heart. And there is no journalism more soul-endangering to write than journalism that aims to please.

So it was with reluctance that I climbed into my car last week and headed down Highway 2 to write some damn pleasant story about some damn pleasant people. Then I saw the Indian hitchhiker standing beside the road. He looked the way Indian hitchhikers usually look. Long, straggly black hair. Brown eyes and skin. Missing a couple of teeth. A bad complexion that used to be much worse. Crooked nose that had been broken more than once. Big, misshapen ears. A few whiskers masquerading as a mustache.

Even before he climbed into my car I could tell he was tough. He had some serious muscles that threatened to rip through his blue jeans and denim jacket. When he was in the car, I could see his hands up close, and they told his whole story. His fingers were twisted into weird, permanent shapes, and his knuckles were covered with layers of scar tissue.

"Jeez," I said. "You're a fighter, enit?"

I threw in the "enit," a reservation colloquialism, because I wanted the fighter to know that I had grown up on the rez, in the woods, with every Indian in the world.

The hitchhiker looked down at his hands, flexed them into fists. I could tell it hurt him to do that.

"Yeah," he said. "I'm a fighter."

I pulled back onto the highway, looking over my shoulder to check my blind spot.

"What tribe are you?" I asked him, inverting the last two words in order to sound as aboriginal as possible.

"Lummi," he said. "What about you?"

"Spokane."

"I know some Spokanes. Haven't seen them in a long time."

He clutched his backpack in his lap like he didn't want to let it go for anything. He reached inside a pocket and pulled out a piece of deer jerky. I recognized it by the smell.

"Want some?" he asked.

"Sure."

It had been a long time since I'd eaten jerky. The salt, the gamy taste. I felt as Indian as Indian gets, driving down the road in a fast car, chewing on jerky, talking to an indigenous fighter.

"Where you headed?" I asked.

"Home. Back to the rez."

I nodded my head as I passed a big truck. The driver gave us a smile as we went by. I tooted the horn.

"Big truck," said the fighter.

I haven't lived on my reservation for twelve years. But I live in Spokane, which is only an hour's drive from the rez. Still, I hardly ever go home. I don't know why not. I don't think about it much, I guess, but my mom and dad still live in the same house where I grew up. My brothers and sisters, too. The ghosts of my two dead siblings share an apartment in the converted high school. It's just a local call from Spokane to the rez, so I talk to all of them once or twice a week. Smoke signals courtesy of U.S. West Communications. Sometimes they call me up to talk about the stories they've seen that I've written for the newspaper. Pet pigs and support groups and science fairs. Once in a while, I used to fill in for the obituaries writer when she was sick. Then she died, and I had to write her obituary.

"How far are you going?" asked the fighter, meaning how much closer was he going to get to his reservation than he was now.

"Up to Wenatchee," I said. "I've got some people to interview there."

"Interview? What for?"

"I'm a reporter. I work for the newspaper."

"No," said the fighter, looking at me like I was stupid for thinking he was stupid. "I mean, what's the story about?"

"Oh, not much. There's two sets of twins who work for the fire department. Human-interest stuff, you know?"

"Two sets of twins, enit? That's weird."

He offered me more deer jerky, but I was too thirsty from the salty meat, so I offered him a Pepsi instead.

"Don't mind if I do," he said.

"They're in a cooler on the backseat," I said. "Grab me one, too."

He maneuvered his backpack carefully and found room enough to reach into the backseat for the soda pop. He opened my can first and handed it to me. A friendly gesture for a stranger. I took a big mouthful and hiccupped loudly.

"That always happens to me when I drink cold things," he said.

We sipped slowly after that. I kept my eyes on the road while he stared out the window into the wheat fields. We were quiet for many miles.

"Who do you fight?" I asked as we passed through another anonymous small town.

"Mostly Indians," he said. "Money fights, you know? I go from rez to rez, fighting the best they have. Winner takes all."

"Jeez, I never heard of that."

"Yeah, I guess it's illegal."

He rubbed his hands together. I could see fresh wounds.

"Man," I said. "Those fights must be rough."

The fighter stared out the window. I watched him for a little too long and almost drove off the road. Car horns sounded all around us.

"Jeez," the fighter said. "Close one, enit?"

"Close enough," I said.

He hugged his backpack more tightly, using it as a barrier between his chest and the dashboard. An Indian hitchhiker's version of a passenger-side air bag.

"Who'd you fight last?" I asked, trying to concentrate on the road.

"Some Flathead," he said. "In Arlee. He was supposed to be the toughest Indian in the world."

"Was he?"

"Nah, no way. Wasn't even close. Wasn't even tougher than me."

He told me how big the Flathead kid was, way over six feet tall and two hundred and some pounds. Big buck Indian. Had hands as big as this and arms as big as that. Had a chin like a damn buffalo. The fighter told me that he hit the Flathead kid harder than he ever hit anybody before.

"I hit him like he was a white man," the fighter said. "I hit him like he was two or three white men rolled into one."

But the Flathead kid would not go down, even though his face swelled up so bad that he looked like the Elephant Man. There were no referees, no judge, no bells to signal the end of the round. The winner was the Indian still standing. Punch after punch, man, and the kid would not go down.

"I was so tired after a while," said the fighter, "that I just took a step back and watched the kid. He stood there with his arms down, swaying from side to side like some toy, you know? Head bobbing on his neck like there was no bone at all. You couldn't even see his eyes no more. He was all messed up."

"What'd you do?" I asked.

"Ah, hell, I couldn't fight him no more. That kid was planning to die before he ever went down. So I just sat on the ground while they counted me out. Dumb Flathead kid didn't even know what was happening. I just sat on the ground while they raised his hand. While all the winners collected their money and all the losers cussed me out. I just sat there, man."

"Jeez," I said. "What happened next?"

"Not much. I sat there until everybody was gone. Then I stood up and decided to head for home. I'm tired of this shit. I just want to go home for a while. I got enough money to last me a long time. I'm a rich Indian, you hear? I'm a rich Indian."

The fighter finished his Pepsi, rolled down his window, and pitched the can out. I almost protested, but decided against it. I kept my empty can wedged between my legs.

"That's a hell of a story," I said.

"Ain't no story," he said. "It's what happened."

"Jeez," I said. "You would've been a warrior in the old days, enit? You would've been a killer. You would have stolen everybody's goddamn horses. That would've been you. You would've been it."

I was excited. I wanted the fighter to know how much I thought of him. He didn't even look at me.

"A killer," he said. "Sure."

We didn't talk much after that. I pulled into Wenatchee just before sundown, and the fighter seemed happy to be leaving me.

"Thanks for the ride, cousin," he said as he climbed out. Indians always call each other cousin, especially if they're strangers.

"Wait," I said.

He looked at me, waiting impatiently.

I wanted to know if he had a place to sleep that night. It was supposed to get cold. There was a mountain range between Wenatchee and his reservation. Big mountains that were dormant volcanoes, but that could all blow up at any time. We wrote about it once in the newspaper. Things can change so quickly. So many emergencies and disasters that we can barely keep track. I wanted to tell him how much I cared about my job, even if I had to write about small-town firemen. I wanted to tell the fighter that I pick up all Indian hitchhikers, young and old, men and women, and get them a little closer to home, even if I can't get them all the way. I wanted to tell him that the night sky was a graveyard. I wanted to know if he was the toughest Indian in the world.

"It's late," I finally said. "You can crash with me, if you want."

He studied my face and then looked down the long road toward his reservation.

"Okay," he said. "That sounds good."

We got a room at the Pony Soldier Motel, and both of us laughed at the irony of it all. Inside the room, in a generic watercolor hanging above the bed, the U.S. Cavalry was kicking the crap out of a band of renegade Indians.

"What tribe you think they are?" I asked the fighter.

"All of them," he said.

The fighter crashed on the floor while I curled up in the uncomfortable bed. I couldn't sleep for the longest time. I listened to the fighter talk in his sleep. I stared up at the water-stained ceiling. I don't know what time it was when I finally drifted off, and I don't know what time it was when the fighter got into bed with me. He was naked and his penis was hard. I felt it press against my back as he snuggled up close to me, reached inside my underwear, and took my penis in his hand. Neither of us said a word. He continued to stroke me as he rubbed himself against my back. That went on for a long time. I had never been that close to another man, but the fighter's callused fingers felt better than I would have imagined if I had ever allowed myself to imagine such things.

"This isn't working," he whispered. "I can't come."

Without thinking, I reached around and took the fighter's penis in my hand. He was surprisingly small.

"No," he said. "I want to be inside you."

"I don't know," I said. "I've never done this before."

"It's okay," he said. "I'll be careful. I have rubbers."

Without waiting for my answer, he released me and got up from the bed. I turned to look at him. He was beautiful and scarred. So much brown skin marked with bruises, badly healed wounds, and tattoos. His long black hair was unbraided and hung down to his thin waist. My slacks and dress shirt were folded and draped over the chair near the window. My shoes were sitting on the table. Blue light filled the room. The fighter bent down to his pack and searched for his condoms. For reasons I could not explain then and cannot explain now, I kicked off my underwear and rolled over on my stomach. I could not see him, but I could hear him breathing heavily as he found the condoms, tore open a package, and rolled one over his penis. He crawled onto the bed, between my legs, and slid a pillow beneath my belly.

"Are you ready?" he asked.

"I'm not gay," I said.

"Sure," he said as he pushed himself into me. He was small but it hurt more than I expected, and I knew that I would be sore for days afterward. But I wanted him to save me. He didn't say anything. He just pumped into me for a few minutes, came with a loud sigh, and then pulled out. I quickly rolled off the bed and went into the bathroom. I locked the door behind me and stood there in the dark. I smelled like salmon.

"Hey," the fighter said through the door. "Are you okay?"

"Yes," I said. "I'm fine."

A long silence.

"Hey," he said. "Would you mind if I slept in the bed with you?"

I had no answer to that.

"Listen," I said. "That Flathead boy you fought? You know, the one you really beat up? The one who wouldn't fall down?"

In my mind, I could see the fighter pummeling that boy. Punch after punch. The boy too beaten to fight back, but too strong to fall down.

"Yeah, what about him?" asked the fighter.

"What was his name?"

"His name?"

"Yeah, his name."

"Elmer something or other."

"Did he have an Indian name?"

"I have no idea. How the hell would I know that?"

I stood there in the dark for a long time. I was chilled. I wanted to get into bed and fall asleep.

"Hey," I said. "I think, I think maybe—well, I think you should leave now."

"Yeah," said the fighter, not surprised. I heard him softly singing as he dressed and stuffed all of his belongings into his pack. I wanted to know what he was singing, so I opened the bathroom door just as he was opening the door to leave. He stopped, looked at me, and smiled.

"Hey, tough guy," he said. "You were good."

The fighter walked out the door, left it open, and walked away. I stood in the doorway and watched him continue his walk down the highway, past the city limits. I watched him rise from earth to sky and become a new constellation. I closed the door and wondered what was going to happen next. Feeling uncomfortable and cold, I went back into the bathroom. I ran the shower with the hottest water possible. I stared at myself in the mirror. Steam quickly filled the room. I threw a few shadow punches. Feeling stronger, I stepped into the shower and searched my body for changes. A middle-aged man needs to look for tumors. I dried myself with a towel too small for the job. Then I crawled naked into bed. I wondered if I was a warrior in this life and if I had been a warrior in a previous life. Lonely and laughing, I fell asleep. I didn't dream at all, not one bit. Or perhaps I dreamed but remembered none of it. Instead, I woke early the next morning, before sunrise, and went out into the world. I walked past my car. I stepped onto the pavement, still warm from the previous day's sun. I started walking. In bare feet, I traveled upriver toward the place where I was born and will someday die. At that moment, if you had broken open my heart you could have looked inside and seen the thin white skeletons of one thousand salmon.

WAR DANCES

1. My Kafka Baggage

A few years ago, after I returned from a trip to Los Angeles, I unpacked my bag and found a dead cockroach, shrouded by a dirty sock, in a bottom corner. "Shit," I thought. "We're being invaded." And so I threw the unpacked clothes, books, shoes, and toiletries back into the suitcase, carried it out onto the driveway, and dumped the contents onto the pavement, ready to stomp on any other cockroach stowaways. But there was only the one cockroach, stiff and dead. As he lay on the pavement, I leaned closer to him. His legs were curled under his body. His head was tilted at a sad angle. Sad? Yes, sad. For who is lonelier than the cockroach without his tribe? I laughed at myself. I was feeling empathy for a dead cockroach. I wondered about its story. How had it got into my bag? And where? At the hotel in Los Angeles? In an airport baggage system? It didn't originate in our house. We've kept those tiny bastards away from our place for fifteen years. So what had happened to this little vermin? Did he smell something delicious in my bag—my musky deodorant or some crumb of chocolate Power Bar—and climb inside, only to be crushed by the shifts of fate and garment bags? As he died, did he feel fear? Isolation? Existential dread?

2. Symptoms

Last summer, in reaction to various allergies I was suffering from, defensive mucous flooded my inner right ear and confused, frightened, untied, and unmoored me. Simply stated, I could not fucking hear a thing from that side, so I had to turn my head to understand what my two sons, ages eight and ten, were saying.

"We're hungry," they said. "We keep telling you."

They wanted to be fed. And I had not heard them.

"Mom would have fed us by now," they said.

Their mother had left for Italy with her mother two days ago. My sons and I were going to enjoy a boys' week, filled with unwashed socks, REI rock wall climbing, and ridiculous heaps of pasta.

"What are you going to cook?" my sons asked. "Why haven't you cooked yet?"

I'd been lying on the couch reading a book while they played and I had not realized that I'd gone partially deaf. So I, for just a moment, could only weakly blame the silence—no, the contradictory roar that only I could hear.

Then I recalled the man who went to the emergency room because he'd woken having lost most, if not all, of his hearing. The doctor peered into one ear, saw an obstruction, reached in with small tweezers, and pulled out a cockroach, then reached into the other ear, and extracted a much larger cockroach. Did you know that ear wax is a delicacy for roaches?

I cooked dinner for my sons—overfed them out of guilt—and cleaned the hell out of our home. Then I walked into the bathroom and stood close to my mirror. I turned my head and body at weird angles, and tried to see deeply into my congested ear. I sang hymns and prayed that I'd see a small angel trapped in the canal. I would free the poor thing, and she'd unfurl and pat dry her tiny wings, then fly to my lips and give me a sweet kiss for sheltering her metamorphosis.

3. The Symptoms Worsen

When I woke at three a.m., completely unable to hear out of my clogged right ear, and positive that a damn swarm of locusts was wedged inside, I left a message for my doctor, and told him that I would be sitting outside his office when he reported to work.

This would be the first time I had been inside a health-care facility since my father's last surgery.

4. Blankets

After the surgeon cut off my father's right foot—no, half of my father's right foot—and three toes from the left, I sat with him in the recovery room. It was more like a recovery hallway.

There was no privacy, not even a thin curtain. I guessed it made it easier for the nurses to monitor the postsurgical patients, but still, my father was exposed—his decades of poor health and worse decisions were illuminated—on white sheets in a white hallway under white lights.

"Are you okay?" I asked. It was a stupid question. Who could be okay after such a thing? Yesterday, my father had *walked* into the hospital. Okay, he'd shuffled while balanced on two canes, but that was still called walking. A few hours ago, my father still had both of his feet. Yes, his feet and toes had been black with rot and disease but they'd still been, technically speaking, feet and toes. And, most important, those feet and toes had belonged to my father. But now they were gone, sliced off. Where were they? What did they do with the right foot and the toes from the left foot? Did they throw them in the incinerator? Were their ashes floating over the city?

"Doctor, I'm cold," my father said.

"Dad, it's me," I said.

"I know who are you. You're my son." But considering the blankness in my father's eyes, I assumed he was just guessing at my identity.

"Dad, you're in the hospital. You just had surgery."

"I know where I am. I'm cold."

"Do you want another blanket?" Another stupid question. Of course, he wanted another blanket. He probably wanted me to build a fucking campfire or drag in one of those giant propane heaters that NFL football teams used on the sidelines.

I walked down the hallway—the recovery hallway—to the nurses' station. There were three women nurses, two white and one black. Being Native American-Spokane and Coeur d'Alene Indian, I hoped my darker pigment would give me an edge with the black nurse, so I addressed her directly.

"My father is cold," I said. "Can I get another blanket?"

The black nurse glanced up from her paperwork and regarded me. Her expression was neither compassionate nor callous.

"How can I help you, sir?" she asked.

"I'd like another blanket for my father. He's cold."

"I'll be with you in a moment, sir."

She looked back down at her paperwork. She made a few notes. Not knowing what else to do, I stood there and waited.

"Sir," the black nurse said. "I'll be with you in a moment."

She was irritated. I understood. After all, how many thousands of times had she been asked for an extra blanket? She was a nurse, an educated woman, not a damn housekeeper. And it was never really about an extra blanket, was it? No, when people asked for an extra blanket, they were asking for a time machine. And, yes, she knew she was a health care provider, and she knew she was supposed to be compassionate, but my father, an alcoholic, diabetic Indian with terminally damaged kidneys, had just endured an incredibly expensive surgery for what? So he could ride his motorized wheelchair to the bar and win bets by showing off his disfigured foot? I know she didn't want to be cruel, but she believed there was a point when doctors should stop rescuing people from their own self-destructive impulses. And I couldn't disagree with her but I could ask for the most basic of comforts, couldn't I?

"My father," I said. "An extra blanket, please."

"Fine," she said, then stood and walked back to a linen closet, grabbed a white blanket, and handed it to me. "If you need anything else—"

I didn't wait around for the end of her sentence. With the blanket in hand, I walked back to my father. It was a thin blanket, laundered and sterilized a hundred times. In fact, it was too thin. It wasn't really a blanket. It was more like a large beach towel. Hell, it wasn't even good enough for that. It was more like the world's largest coffee filter. Jesus, had health care finally come to this? Everybody was uninsured and unblanketed.

"Dad, I'm back."

He looked so small and pale lying in that hospital bed. How had that change happened? For the first sixty-seven years of his life, my father had been a large and dark man. And now, he was just another pale and sick drone in a hallway of pale and sick drones. A hive, I thought, this place looks like a beehive with colony collapse disorder.

"Dad, it's me."

"I'm cold."

"I have a blanket."

As I draped it over my father and tucked it around his body, I felt the first sting of grief. I'd read the hospital literature about this moment. There would come a time when roles would reverse and the adult child would become the caretaker of the ill parent. The circle of life. Such poetic bullshit.

"I can't get warm," my father said. "I'm freezing."

"I brought you a blanket, Dad, I put it on you."

"Get me another one. Please. I'm so cold. I need another blanket."

I knew that ten more of these cheap blankets wouldn't be enough. My father needed a real blanket, a good blanket.

I walked out of the recovery hallway and made my way through various doorways and other hallways, peering into the

47

rooms, looking at the patients and their families, looking for a particular kind of patient and family.

I walked through the ER, cancer, heart and vascular, neurology, orthopedic, women's health, pediatrics, and surgical services. Nobody stopped me. My expression and posture were that of a man with a sick father and so I belonged.

And then I saw him, another Native man, leaning against a wall near the gift shop. Well, maybe he was Asian; lots of those in Seattle. He was a small man, pale brown, with muscular arms and a soft belly. Maybe he was Mexican, which is really a kind of Indian, too, but not the kind that I needed. It was hard to tell sometimes what people were. Even brown people guessed at the identity of other brown people.

"Hey," I said.

"Hey," the other man said.

"You Indian?" I asked.

"Yeah."

"What tribe?"

"Lummi."

"I'm Spokane."

"My first wife was Spokane. I hated her."

"My first wife was Lummi. She hated me."

We laughed at the new jokes that instantly sounded old.

"Why are you in here?" I asked.

"My sister is having a baby," he said. "But don't worry, it's not mine."

"Ayyyyyy," I said—another Indian idiom—and laughed.

"I don't even want to be here," the other Indian said. "But my dad started, like, this new Indian tradition. He says it's a thousand years old. But that's bullshit. He just made it up to impress himself. And the whole family just goes along, even when we know it's bullshit. He's in the delivery room waving eagle feathers around. Jesus."

"What's the tradition?"

"Oh, he does a naming ceremony right in the hospital. Like, it's supposed to protect the baby from all the technology and shit. Like hospitals are the big problem. You know how many babies died before we had good hospitals?"

"I don't know."

"Most of them. Well, shit, a lot of them, at least."

This guy was talking out of his ass. I liked him immediately.

"I mean," the guy said. "You should see my dad right now. He's pretending to go into this, like, fucking trance and is dancing around my sister's bed, and he says he's trying to, you know, see into her womb, to see who the baby is, to see its true nature, so he can give it a name—a protective name—before it's born."

The guy laughed and threw his head back and banged it on the wall.

"I mean, come on, I'm a loser," he said and rubbed his sore skull. "My whole family is filled with losers."

The Indian world is filled with charlatans, men and women who pretended—hell, who might have come to believe—that they were holy. Last year, I had gone to a lecture at the University of Washington. An elderly Indian woman, a Sioux writer and scholar and charlatan, had come to orate on Indian sovereignty and literature. She kept arguing for some kind of separate indigenous literary identity, which was ironic considering that she was speaking English to a room full of white professors. But I wasn't angry with the woman, or even bored. No, I felt sorry for her. I realized that she was dying of nostalgia. She had taken nostalgia as her false idol—her thin blanket—and it was murdering her.

"Nostalgia," I said to the other Indian man in the hospital.

"What?"

"Your dad, he sounds like he's got a bad case of nostalgia."

"Yeah, I hear you catch that from fucking old high school girlfriends," the man said. "What the hell you doing here anyway?"

"My dad just got his feet cut off," I said.

"Diabetes?"

"And vodka."

"Vodka straight up or with a nostalgia chaser?"

"Both."

"Natural causes for an Indian."

"Yep."

There wasn't much to say after that.

"Well, I better get back," the man said. "Otherwise, my dad might wave an eagle feather and change my name."

"Hey, wait," I said.

"Yeah?"

"Can I ask you a favor?"

"What?"

"My dad, he's in the recovery room," I said. "Well, it's more like a hallway, and he's freezing, and they've only got these shitty little blankets, and I came looking for Indians in the hospital because I figured—well, I guessed if I found any Indians, they might have some good blankets."

"So you want to borrow a blanket from us?" the man asked.

"Yeah."

"Because you thought some Indians would just happen to have some extra blankets lying around?"

"Yeah."

"That's fucking ridiculous."

"I know."

"And it's racist."

"I know."

"You're stereotyping your own damn people."

"I know."

"But damn if we don't have a room full of Pendleton blankets. New ones. Jesus, you'd think my sister was having, like, a dozen babies."

Five minutes later, carrying a Pendleton Star Blanket, the Indian man walked out of his sister's hospital room, accompanied by his father, who wore Levi's, a black T-shirt, and eagle feathers in his gray braids.

"We want to give your father this blanket," the old man said. "It was meant for my grandson, but I think it will be good for your father, too."

"Thank you."

"Let me bless it. I will sing a healing song for the blanket. And for your father."

I flinched. This guy wanted to sing a song? That was dangerous. This song could take two minutes or two hours. It was impossible to know. Hell, considering how desperate this old man was to be seen as holy, he might sing for a week. I couldn't let this guy begin his song without issuing a caveat.

"My dad," I said. "I really need to get back to him. He's really sick."

"Don't worry," the old man said and winked. "I'll sing one of my short ones."

Jesus, who'd ever heard of a self-aware fundamentalist? The son, perhaps not the unbeliever he'd pretended to be, sang backup as his father launched into his radio-friendly honor song, just three-and-a-half minutes, like the length of any Top 40 rock song of the last fifty years. But here's the funny thing: the old man couldn't sing very well. If you were going to have the balls to sing healing songs in hospital hallways, then you should logically have a great voice, right? But, no, this guy couldn't keep the tune. And his voice cracked and wavered. Does a holy song lose its power if its singer is untalented?

"That is your father's song," the old man said when he was finished. "I give it to him. I will never sing it again. It belongs to your father now."

Behind his back, the old man's son rolled his eyes and walked back into his sister's room.

"Okay, thank you," I said. I felt like an ass, accepting the blanket and the old man's good wishes, but silently mocking them at the same time. But maybe the old man did have some power, some real medicine, because he peeked into my brain.

"It doesn't matter if you believe in the healing song," the old man said. "It only matters that the blanket heard."

"Where have you been?" my father asked when I returned. "I'm cold."

"I know, I know," I said. "I found you a blanket. A good one. It will keep you warm."

I draped the Star Blanket over my father. He pulled the thick wool up to his chin. And then he began to sing. It was a healing song, not the same song that I had just heard, but a healing song nonetheless. My father could sing beautifully. I wondered if it was proper for a man to sing a healing song for himself. I wondered if my father needed help with the song. I hadn't sung for many years, not like that, but I joined him. I knew this song would not bring back my father's feet. This song would not repair my father's bladder, kidneys, lungs, and heart. This song would not prevent my father from drinking a bottle of vodka as soon as he could sit up in bed. This song would not defeat death. No, I thought, this song is temporary, but right now, temporary is good enough. And it was a good song. Our voices filled the recovery hallway. The sick and healthy stopped to listen. The nurses, even the remote black one, unconsciously took a few steps toward us. The black nurse sighed and smiled. I smiled back. I knew what she was thinking. Sometimes, even after all of these years, she could still be surprised by her work. She still marveled at the infinite and ridiculous faith of other people.

5. Doctor's Office

I took my kids with me to my doctor, a handsome man—a reservist—who'd served in both Iraq wars. I told him I could not hear. He said his nurse would likely have to clear wax and fluid, but when he scoped inside, he discovered nothing.

"Nope, it's all dry in there," he said.

He led my sons and me to the audiologist in the other half of the building. I was scared, but I wanted my children to remain calm, so I tried to stay measured. More than anything, I wanted my wife to materialize.

During the hearing test, I heard only 30 percent of the clicks, bells, and words—I apparently had nerve and bone conductive deafness. My inner ear thumped and thumped.

How many cockroaches were in my head?

My doctor said, "We need an MRI of your ear and brain, and maybe we'll find out what's going on."

Maybe? That word terrified me.

What the fuck was wrong with my fucking head? Had my hydrocephalus come back for blood? Had my levees burst? Was I going to flood?

6. Hydrocephalus

Merriam-Webster's dictionary defines hydrocephalus as "an abnormal increase in the amount of cerebrospinal fluid within the cranial cavity that is accompanied by expansion of the cerebral ventricles, enlargement of the skull and especially the forehead, and atrophy of the brain." I define hydrocephalus as "the obese, imperialistic water demon that nearly killed me when I was six months old."

In order to save my life, and stop the water demon, I had brain surgery in 1967 when I was six months old. I was supposed to die. Obviously, I didn't. I was supposed to be severely mentally disabled. I have only minor to moderate brain damage. I was supposed to have epileptic seizures. Those I did have, until I was seven years old. I was on phenobarbital, a major league antiseizure medication, for six years.

Some of the side effects of phenobarbital—all of which I suffered to some degree or another as a child—include sleepwalking, agitation, confusion, depression, nightmares, hallucinations, insomnia, apnea, vomiting, constipation, dermatitis, fever, liver and bladder dysfunction, and psychiatric disturbance.

How do you like them cockroaches?

And now, as an adult, thirty-three years removed from phenobarbital, I still suffer—to one degree or another—from sleepwalking, agitation, confusion, depression, nightmares, hallucinations, insomnia, bladder dysfunction, apnea, and dermatitis.

Is there such a disease as post-phenobarbital traumatic stress syndrome?

Most hydrocephalics are shunted. A shunt is essentially brain plumbing that drains away excess cerebrospinal fluid. Those shunts often fuck up and stop working. I know hydrocephalics who've had a hundred or more shunt revisions and repairs. That's over a hundred brain surgeries. There are ten fingers on any surgeon's hand. There are two or three surgeons working on any particular brain. That means certain hydrocephalics have had their brains fondled by three thousand fingers.

I'm lucky. I was only temporarily shunted. And I hadn't suffered any hydrocephalic symptoms since I was seven years old.

And then, in July 2008, at the age of forty-one, I went deaf in my right ear.

7. Conversation

Sitting in my car in the hospital parking garage, I called my brother-in-law, who was babysitting my sons.

"Hey, it's me. I just got done with the MRI on my head."

My brother-in-law said something unintelligible. I realized I was holding my cell to my bad ear. And switched it to the good ear.

"The MRI dude didn't look happy," I said.

"That's not good," my brother-in-law said.

"No, it's not. But he's just a tech guy, right? He's not an expert on brains or anything. He's just the photographer, really.

And he doesn't know anything about ears or deafness or anything, I don't think. Ah, hell, I don't know what he knows. I just didn't like the look on his face when I was done."

"Maybe he just didn't like you."

"Well, I got worried when I told him I had hydrocephalus when I was a baby and he didn't seem to know what that was."

"Nobody knows what that is."

"That's the truth. Have you fed the boys dinner?"

"Yeah, but I was scrounging. There's not much here."

"I better go shopping."

"Are you sure? I can do it if you need me to. I can shop the shit out of Trader Joe's."

"No, it'll be good for me. I feel good. I fell asleep during the MRI. And I kept twitching. So we had to do it twice. Otherwise, I would've been done earlier."

"That's okay; I'm okay; the boys are okay."

"You know, before you go in that MRI tube, they ask you what kind of music you want to listen to—jazz, classical, rock, or country—and I remembered how my dad spent a lot of time in MRI tubes near the end of his life. So I was wondering what kind of music he always chose. I mean, he couldn't hear shit anyway by that time, but he still must have chosen something. And I wanted to choose the same thing he chose. So I picked country."

"Was it good country?"

"It was fucking Shania Twain and Faith Hill shit. I was hoping for George Jones or Loretta Lynn, or even some George Strait. Hell, I would've cried if they'd played Charley Pride or Freddy Fender."

"You wanted to hear the alcoholic Indian father jukebox."

"Hey, that's my line. You can't quote me to me."

"Why not? You're always quoting you to you."

"Kiss my ass. So, hey, I'm okay, I think. And I'm going to the store. But I think I already said that. Anyway, I'll see you in a bit. You want anything?"

"Ah, man, I love Trader Joe's. But you know what's bad about them? You fall in love with something they have—they stock it for a year—and then it just disappears. They had those wontons I loved and now they don't. I was willing to shop for you and the boys, but I don't want anything for me. I'm on a one-man hunger strike against them."

8. World Phone Conversation, 3 A.M.

After I got home with yogurt and turkey dogs and Cinnamon Toast Crunch and my brother-in-law had left, I watched George Romero's *Diary of the Dead*, and laughed at myself for choosing a movie that featured dozens of zombies getting shot in the head.

When the movie was over, I called my wife, nine hours ahead in Italy.

"I should come home," she said.

"No, I'm okay," I said. "Come on, you're in Rome. What are you seeing today?"

"The Vatican."

"You can't leave now. You have to go and steal something. It will be revenge for every Indian. Or maybe you can plant an eagle feather and claim that you just discovered Catholicism."

"I'm worried."

"Yeah, Catholicism has always worried me."

"Stop being funny. I should see if I can get Mom and me on a flight tonight."

"No, no, listen, your mom is old. This might be her last adventure. It might be your last adventure with her. Stay there. Say Hi to the Pope for me. Tell him I like his shoes."

That night, my sons climbed into bed with me. We all slept curled around one another like sled dogs in a snowstorm. I woke, hour by hour, and touched my head and neck to check if they had changed shape—to feel if antennae were growing. Some insects "hear" with their antennae. Maybe that's what was happening to me.

9. Valediction

My father, a part-time blue collar construction worker, died in March 2003, from full-time alcoholism. On his deathbed, he asked me to "Turn down that light, please."

"Which light?" I asked.

"The light on the ceiling."

"Dad, there's no light."

"It burns my skin, son. It's too bright. It hurts my eyes."

"Dad, I promise you there's no light."

"Don't lie to me, son, it's God passing judgment on Earth."

"Dad, you've been an atheist since '79. Come on, you're just remembering your birth. On your last day, you're going back to your first."

"No, son, it's God telling me I'm doomed. He's using the brightest lights in the universe to show me the way to my flame-filled tomb."

"No, Dad, those lights were in your delivery room."

"If that's true, son, then turn down my mother's womb."
We buried my father in the tiny Catholic cemetery on
our reservation. Since I am named after him, I had to stare at a
tombstone with my name on it.

10. Battle Fatigue

Two months after my father's death, I began research on a
book about our family's history with war. I had a cousin who had
served as a cook in the first Iraq war in 1991; I had another cousin
who served in the Vietnam War in 1964–65, also as a cook; and my
father's father, Adolph, served in WWII and was killed in action
on Okinawa Island, on April 5, 1946.

During my research, I interviewed thirteen men who'd
served with my cousin in Vietnam but could find only one surviving
man who'd served with my grandfather. This is a partial transcript
of that taped interview, recorded with a microphone and an iPod
on January 14, 2008:

Me: Ah, yes, hello, I'm here in Livonia, Michigan, to
interview—well, perhaps you should introduce yourself, please?

Leonard Elmore: What?

Me: Um, oh, I'm sorry, I was asking if you could perhaps
introduce yourself.

LE: You're going to have to speak up. I think my hearing
aid is going low on power or something.

Me: That is a fancy thing in your ear.

LE: Yeah, let me mess with it a bit. I got a remote control
for it. I can listen to the TV, the stereo, and the telephone with

this thing. It's fancy. It's one of them Bluetooth hearing aids. My grandson bought it for me. Wait, okay, there we go. I can hear now. So what were you asking?

Me: I was hoping you could introduce yourself into my recorder here.

LE: Sure, my name is Leonard Elmore.

Me: How old are you?

LE: I'm eighty-five-and-a-half years old (laughter). My great-grandkids are always saying they're seven-and-a-half or nine-and-a-half or whatever. It just cracks me up to say the same thing at my age.

Me: So, that's funny, um, but I'm here to ask you some questions about my grandfather—

LE: Adolph. It's hard to forget a name like that. An Indian named Adolph and there was that Nazi bastard named Adolph. Your grandfather caught plenty of grief over that. But we mostly called him "Chief," did you know that?

Me: I could have guessed.

LE: Yeah, nowadays, I suppose it isn't a good thing to call an Indian "Chief," but back then, it was what we did. I served with a few Indians. They didn't segregate them Indians, you know, not like the black boys. I know you aren't supposed to call them boys anymore, but they were boys. All of us were boys, I guess. But the thing is, those Indian boys lived and slept and ate with us white boys. They were right there with us. But, anyway, we called all them Indians "Chief." I bet you've been called "Chief" a few times yourself.

Me: Just once.

LE: Were you all right with it?

Me: I threw a basketball in the guy's face.

LE: (laughter)

Me: We live in different times.

LE: Yes, we do. Yes, we do.

Me: So, perhaps you could, uh, tell me something about my grandfather.

LE: I can tell you how he died.

Me: Really?

LE: Yeah, it was on Okinawa, and we hit the beach, and, well, it's hard to talk about it—it was the worst thing—it was Hell—no, that's not even a good way to describe it. I'm not a writer like you—I'm not a poet—so I don't have the words—but just think of it this way—that beach, that island—was filled with sons and fathers—men who loved and were loved—American and Japanese and Okinawan—and all of us were dying—were being killed by other sons and fathers who also loved and were loved.

Me: That sounds like poetry—tragic poetry—to me.

LE: Well, anyway, it was like that. Fire everywhere. And two of our boys—Jonesy and O'Neal—went down—were wounded in the open on the sand. And your grandfather—who was just this little man—barely five feet tall and maybe one hundred and thirty pounds—he just ran out there and picked up those two guys—one on each shoulder—and carried them to cover. Hey, are you okay, son?

Me: Yes, I'm sorry. But, well, the thing is, I knew my grandfather was a war hero—he won twelve medals—but I could never find out what he did to win the medals.

LE: I didn't know about any medals. I just know what I saw. Your grandfather saved those two boys, but he got shot in the back doing it. And he laid there in the sand—I was lying right beside him—and he died.

Me: Did he say anything before he died?

LE: Hold on. I need to—

Me: Are you okay?

LE: It's just—I can't—

Me: I'm sorry. Is there something wrong?

LE: No, it's just—with your book and everything—I know you want something big here. I know you want something big from your grandfather. I knew you hoped he'd said something huge and poetic, like maybe something you could have written, and, honestly, I was thinking about lying to you. I was thinking about making up something as beautiful as I could. Something about love and forgiveness and courage and all that. But I couldn't think of anything good enough. And I didn't want to lie to you. So I have to be honest and say that your grandfather didn't say anything. He just died there in the sand. In silence.

11. Orphans

I was worried that I had a brain tumor. Or that my hydrocephalus had returned. I was scared that I was going to die and orphan my sons. But, no, their mother was coming home from Italy. No matter what happened to me, their mother would rescue them.

"I'll be home in sixteen hours," my wife said over the phone.

"I'll be here," I said. "I'm just waiting on news from my doctor."

12. Coffee Shop News

While I waited, I asked my brother-in-law to watch the boys again because I didn't want to get bad news with them in the room.

Alone and haunted, I wandered the mall, tried on new clothes, and waited for my cell phone to ring.

Two hours later, I was uncomposed and wanted to murder everything, so I drove south to a coffee joint, a spotless place called Dirty Joe's.

Yes, I was silly enough to think that I'd be calmer with a caffeinated drink.

As I sat outside on a wooden chair and sipped my coffee, I cursed the vague, rumbling, ringing noise in my ear. And yet, when my cell phone rang, I held it to my deaf ear.

"Hello, hello," I said and wondered if it was a prank call, then remembered and switched the phone to my left ear.

"Hello," my doctor said. "Are you there?"

"Yes," I said. "So, what's going on?"

"There are irregularities in your head."

"My head's always been wrong,"

"It's good to have a sense of humor," my doctor said. "You have a small tumor that is called a meningioma. They grow in the meninges membranes that lie between your brain and your skull."

"Shit," I said. "I have cancer."

"Well," my doctor said. "These kinds of tumors are usually noncancerous. And they grow very slowly, so in six months or so, we'll do another MRI. Don't worry. You're going to be okay."

"What about my hearing?" I asked.

"We don't know what might be causing the hearing loss, but you should start a course of prednisone, the steroid, just to go with the odds. Your deafness might lessen if left alone, but we've had success with the steroids in bringing back hearing. There *are* side effects, like insomnia, weight gain, night sweats, and depression."

"Oh, boy," I said. "Those side effects might make up most of my personality already. Will the 'roids also make me quick to pass judgment? And I've always wished I had a dozen more skin tags and moles."

The doctor chuckled. "You're a funny man."

I wanted to throw my phone into a wall but I said goodbye instead and glared at the tumorless people and their pretty tumorless heads.

13. Meningioma

Mayoclinic.com defines "meningioma" as "a tumor that arises from the meninges—the membranes that surround your brain and spinal cord. The majority of meningioma cases are noncancerous (benign), though rarely a meningioma can be cancerous (malignant)."

Okay, that was a scary and yet strangely positive definition. No one ever wants to read the word "malignant" unless one is reading a Charles Dickens novel about an evil landlord, but "benign" and "majority" are two things that go great together.

From the University of Washington Medical School Web
site I learned that meningioma tumors "are usually benign, slow
growing and do not spread into normal brain tissue. Typically, a
meningioma grows inward, causing pressure on the brain or spinal
cord. It may grow outward toward the skull, causing it to thicken."

So, wait, what the fuck? A meningioma can cause pressure on the brain and spinal fluid? Oh, you mean, just like fucking
hydrocephalus? Just like the water demon that once tried to crush
my brain and kill me? Armed with this new information—with
these new questions—I called my doctor.

"Hey, you're okay," he said. "We're going to closely monitor
you. And your meningioma is very small."

"Okay, but I just read—"

"Did you go on the Internet?"

"Yes."

"Which sites?"

"Mayo Clinic and the University of Washington."

"Okay, so those are pretty good sites. Let me look at them."

I listened to my doctor type.

"Okay, those are accurate," he said.

"What do you mean by accurate?" I asked. "I mean, the
whole pressure on the brain thing, that sounds like hydrocephalus."

"Well, there were some irregularities in your MRI that
were the burr holes from your surgery and there seems to be some
scarring and perhaps you had an old concussion, but other than
that, it all looks fine."

"But what about me going deaf? Can't these tumors make
you lose hearing?"

"Yes, but only if they're located near an auditory nerve.
And your tumor is not."

"Can this tumor cause pressure on my brain?"

"It could, but yours is too small for that."

"So, I'm supposed to trust you on the tumor thing when you can't figure out the hearing thing?"

"The MRI revealed the meningioma, but that's just an image. There is no physical correlation between your deafness and the tumor. Do the twenty-day treatment of prednisone and the audiologist and I will examine your ear, and your hearing. Then, if there's no improvement, we'll figure out other ways of treating you."

"But you won't be treating the tumor?"

"Like I said, we'll scan you again in six to nine months—"

"You said six before."

"Okay, in six months we'll take another MRI, and if it has grown significantly—or has changed shape or location or anything dramatic—then we'll talk about treatment options. But if you look on the Internet, and I know you're going to spend a lot of time obsessing on this—as you should—I'll tell you what you'll find. About 5 percent of the population has these things and they live their whole lives with these undetected meningiomas. And they can become quite large—without any side effects—and are only found at autopsies conducted for other causes of death. And even when these kinds of tumors become invasive or dangerous they are still rarely fatal. And your tumor, even if it grows fairly quickly, will not likely become an issue for many years, decades. So that's what I can tell you right now. How are you feeling?"

"Freaked and fucked."

I wanted to feel reassured, but I had a brain tumor. How does one feel any optimism about being diagnosed with a brain tumor? Even if that brain tumor is neither cancerous nor interested in crushing one's brain?

14. Drugstore Indian

In Bartell's Drugs, I gave the pharmacist my prescription for prednisone.

"Is this your first fill with us?" she asked.

"No," I said. "And it won't be the last."

I felt like an ass, but she looked bored.

"It'll take thirty minutes," she said, "more or less. We'll page you over the speakers."

I don't think I'd ever felt weaker, or more vulnerable, or more absurd. I was the weak antelope in the herd—yeah, the mangy fucker with the big limp and a sign that read, "Eat me! I'm a gimp!"

So, for thirty minutes, I walked through the store and found myself shoving more and more useful shit into my shopping basket, as if I were filling my casket with the things I'd need in the afterlife. I grabbed toothpaste, a Swiss Army knife, moisturizer, mouthwash, non-stick Band-Aids, antacid, protein bars, and extra razor blades. I grabbed pen and paper. And I also grabbed an ice scraper and sunscreen. Who can predict what weather awaits us in Heaven?

This random shopping made me feel better for a few minutes but then I stopped and walked to the toy aisle. My boys needed gifts: Lego cars or something, for a lift, a shot of capitalistic joy. But the selection of proper toys is art and science. I have been wrong as often as right and heard the sad song of a disappointed son.

Shit, if I died, I knew my sons would survive, even thrive, because of their graceful mother.

I thought of my father's life: he was just six when his father was killed in World War II. Then his mother, ill with tuberculosis, died a few months later. Six years old, my father was cratered. In most ways, he never stopped being six. There was no religion, no magic tricks, and no song or dance that helped my father.

Jesus, I needed a drink of water, so I found the fountain and drank and drank until the pharmacist called my name.

"Have you taken these before?" she asked.

"No," I said, "but they're going to kick my ass, aren't they?"

That made the pharmacist smile, so I felt sadly and briefly worthwhile. But another customer, some nosy hag, said, "You've got a lot of sleepless nights ahead of you."

I was shocked. I stammered, glared at her, and said, "Miss, how is this any of your business? Please, just fuck all the way off, okay?"

She had no idea what to say, so she just turned and walked away and I pulled out my credit card and paid far too much for my goddamn steroids, and forgot to bring the toys home to my boys.

15. Exit Interview for My Father

- True or False?: when a reservation-raised Native American dies of alcoholism it should be considered death by natural causes.
- Do you understand the term *wanderlust*, and if you do, can you please tell us, in twenty-five words or less, what place gave you wanderlust the most?
- Did you, when drunk, ever get behind the tattered wheel of a '76 Ford three-speed van and somehow drive your family one thousand miles on an empty tank of gas?
- Is it true that the only literary term that has any real meaning in the Native American world is *road movie*?

- During the last road movie you saw, how many times did the characters ask, "Are we there yet?"
- How many times, during any of your road trips, did your children ask, "Are we there yet?"
- In twenty-five words or less, please define *there*.
- Sir, in your thirty-nine years as a parent, you broke your children's hearts, collectively and individually, 612 times and you did this without ever striking any human being in anger. Does this absence of physical violence make you a better man than you might otherwise have been?
- Without using the words *man* or *good*, can you please define what it means to be a good man?
- Do you think you will see angels before you die? Do you think angels will come to escort you to Heaven? As the angels are carrying you to Heaven, how many times will you ask, "Are we there yet?"
- Your son distinctly remembers stopping once or twice a month at that grocery store in Freeman, Washington, where you would buy him a red-white-and-blue Rocket Popsicle and purchase for yourself a pickled pig foot. Your son distinctly remembers the feet still had their toenails and little tufts of pig fur. Could this be true? Did you actually eat such horrendous food?
- Your son has often made the joke that you were the only Indian of your generation who went to Catholic school on purpose. This is, of course, a tasteless joke that makes light of the forced incarceration and subsequent physical, spiritual, cultural, and sexual abuse of tens of thousands of Native American children in Catholic and Protestant boarding schools. In consideration of your son's

SHERMAN ALEXIE

questionable judgment in telling jokes, do you think there
should be any moral limits placed on comedy?

- Your oldest son and your two daughters, all over thirty-six
  years of age, still live in your house. Do you think this is
  a lovely expression of tribal culture? Or is it a symptom of
  extreme familial codependence? Or is it both things at the
  same time?

- F. Scott Fitzgerald wrote that the sign of a superior mind "is
  the ability to hold two opposing ideas at the same time."
  Do you believe this is true? And is it also true that you once
  said, "The only time white people tell the truth is when
  they keep their mouths shut"?

- A poet once wrote, "Pain is never added to pain. It multi-
  plies." Can you tell us, in twenty-five words or less, exactly
  how much we all hate mathematical blackmail?

- Your son, in defining you, wrote this poem to explain one
  of the most significant nights in his life:

Mutually Assured Destruction

When I was nine, my father sliced his knee
With a chain saw. But he let himself bleed
And finished cutting down one more tree
Before his boss drove him to EMERGENCY.
Late that night, stoned on morphine and beer,
My father needed my help to steer
His pickup into the woods. "Watch for deer,"
My father said. "Those things just appear
Like magic." It was an Indian summer
And we drove through warm rain and thunder,

> Until we found that chain saw, lying under
> The fallen pine. Then I watched, with wonder,
> As my father, shotgun-rich and impulse-poor,
> Blasted that chain saw dead. "What was that for?"
> I asked. "Son," my father said, "here's the score.
> Once a thing tastes blood, it will come for more."

- Well, first of all, as you know, you did cut your knee with a chain saw, but in direct contradiction to your son's poem:

  A) You immediately went to the emergency room after injuring yourself.

  B) Your boss called your wife, who drove you to the emergency room.

  C) You were given morphine but even you were not alcoholically stupid enough to drink alcohol while on serious narcotics.

  D) You and your son did not get into the pickup that night.

  E) And even if you had driven the pickup, you were not injured seriously enough to need your son's help with the pedals and/or steering wheel.

  F) You never in your life used the word, *appear,* and certainly never used the phrase, *like magic.*

  G) You also think that Indian summer is a fairly questionable seasonal reference for an Indian poet to use.

  H) What the fuck is "warm rain and thunder"? Well, everybody knows what warm rain is, but what the fuck is warm thunder?

  I) You never went looking for that chain saw because it belonged to the Spokane tribe of Indians and what

71

kind of freak would want to reclaim the chain saw that had just cut the shit out of his knee?

J) You also think that the entire third stanza of this poem sounds like a Bruce Springsteen song and not necessarily one of the great ones.

K) And yet, "shotgun-rich and impulse-poor" is one of the greatest descriptions your son has ever written and probably redeems the entire poem.

L) You never owned a shotgun. You did own a few rifles during your lifetime, but did not own even so much as a pellet gun during the last thirty years of your life.

M) You never said, in any context, "Once a thing tastes blood, it will come for more."

N) But you, as you read it, know that it is absolutely true and does indeed sound suspiciously like your entire life philosophy.

O) Other summations of your life philosophy include: "I'll be there before the next teardrop falls."

P) And: "If God really loved Indians, he would have made us white people."

Q) And: "Oscar Robertson should be the man on the NBA logo. They only put Jerry West on there because he's a white guy."

R) And: "A peanut butter sandwich with onions. Damn, that's the way to go."

S) And: "Why eat a pomegranate when you can eat a plain old apple. Or peach. Or orange. When it comes to fruit and vegetables, only eat the stuff you know how to grow."

T) And: "If you really want a woman to love you, then you have to dance. And if you don't want to dance, then you're going to have to work extra hard to make a woman love you forever, and you will always run the risk that she will leave you at any second for a man who knows how to tango."

U) And: "I really miss those cafeterias they use to have in Kmart. I don't know why they stopped having those. If there is a Heaven then I firmly believe it's a Kmart cafeteria."

V) And: "A father always knows what his sons are doing. For instance, boys, I knew you were sneaking that *Hustler* magazine out of my bedroom. You remember that one? Where actors who looked like Captain Kirk and Lieutenant Uhura were screwing on the bridge of the *Enterprise*. Yeah, that one. I know you kept borrowing it. I let you borrow it. Remember this: men and pornography are like plants and sunshine. To me, porn is photosynthesis."

W) And: "Your mother is a better man than me. Mothers are almost always better men than men are."

16. Reunion

After she returned from Italy, my wife climbed into bed with me. I felt like I had not slept comfortably in years.

I said, "There was a rumor that I'd grown a tumor but I killed it with humor."

"How long have you been waiting to tell me that one?" she asked.

"Oh, probably since the first time some doctor put his fingers in my brain."

We made love. We fell asleep. But I, agitated by the steroids, woke at two, three, four, and five a.m. The bed was killing my back so I lay flat on the floor. I wasn't going to die anytime soon, at least not because of my little friend, Mr. Tumor, but that didn't make me feel any more comfortable or comforted. I felt distant from the world—from my wife and sons, from my mother and siblings—from all of my friends. I felt closer to those who've always had fingers in their brains.

And I didn't feel any closer to the world six months later when another MRI revealed that my meningioma had not grown in size or changed its shape.

"You're looking good," my doctor said. "How's your hearing?"

"I think I've got about 90 percent of it back."

"Well, then, the steroids worked. Good."

And I didn't feel any more intimate with God nine months later when one more MRI made my doctor hypothesize that my meningioma might only be more scar tissue from the hydrocephalus.

"Frankly," my doctor said. "Your brain is beautiful."

"Thank you," I said, though it was the oddest compliment I'd ever received.

I wanted to call up my father and tell him that a white man thought my brain was beautiful. But I couldn't tell him anything. He was dead. I told my wife and sons that I was okay. I told my mother and siblings. I told my friends. But none of them laughed as hard about my beautiful brain as I knew my father would have. I miss him, the drunk bastard. I would always feel closest to the man who had most disappointed me.

THIS IS WHAT IT MEANS TO SAY PHOENIX, ARIZONA

Just after Victor lost his job at the BIA, he also found out that his father had died of a heart attack in Phoenix, Arizona. Victor hadn't seen his father in a few years, only talked to him on the telephone once or twice, but there still was a genetic pain, which was soon to be pain as real and immediate as a broken bone.

Victor didn't have any money. Who does have money on a reservation, except the cigarette and fireworks salespeople? His father had a savings account waiting to be claimed, but Victor needed to find a way to get to Phoenix. Victor's mother was just as poor as he was, and the rest of his family didn't have any use at all for him. So Victor called the Tribal Council.

"Listen," Victor said. "My father just died. I need some money to get to Phoenix to make arrangements."

"Now, Victor," the council said. "You know we're having a difficult time financially."

"But I thought the council had special funds set aside for stuff like this."

"Now, Victor, we do have some money available for the proper return of tribal members' bodies. But I don't think we have enough to bring your father all the way back from Phoenix."

"Well," Victor said. "It ain't going to cost all that much. He had to be cremated. Things were kind of ugly. He died of a heart attack in his trailer and nobody found him for a week. It was really hot, too. You get the picture."

"Now, Victor, we're sorry for your loss and the circumstances. But we can really only afford to give you one hundred dollars."

"That's not even enough for a plane ticket."

"Well, you might consider driving down to Phoenix."

"I don't have a car. Besides, I was going to drive my father's pickup back up here."

"Now, Victor," the council said. "We're sure there is somebody who could drive you to Phoenix. Or is there somebody who could lend you the rest of the money?"

"You know there ain't nobody around with that kind of money."

"Well, we're sorry, Victor, but that's the best we can do."

Victor accepted the Tribal Council's offer. What else could he do? So he signed the proper papers, picked up his check, and walked over to the Trading Post to cash it.

While Victor stood in line, he watched Thomas Builds-the-Fire standing near the magazine rack, talking to himself. Like he always did. Thomas was a storyteller that nobody wanted to listen to. That's like being a dentist in a town where everybody has false teeth.

Victor and Thomas Builds-the-Fire were the same age, had grown up and played in the dirt together. Ever since Victor could remember, it was Thomas who always had something to say.

Once, when they were seven years old, when Victor's father still lived with the family, Thomas closed his eyes and told Victor this story: "Your father's heart is weak. He is afraid of his own family. He is afraid of you. Late at night he sits in the dark. Watches the television until there's nothing but that white noise. Sometimes he feels like he wants to buy a motorcycle and ride away. He wants to run and hide. He doesn't want to be found."

Thomas Builds-the-Fire had known that Victor's father was going to leave, knew it before anyone. Now Victor stood in the Trading Post with a one-hundred-dollar check in his hand, wondering if Thomas knew that Victor's father was dead, if he knew what was going to happen next.

Just then Thomas looked at Victor, smiled, and walked over to him.

"Victor, I'm sorry about your father," Thomas said.

"How did you know about it?" Victor asked.

"I heard it on the wind. I heard it from the birds. I felt it in the sunlight. Also, your mother was just in here crying."

"Oh," Victor said and looked around the Trading Post. All the other Indians stared, surprised that Victor was even talking to

Thomas. Nobody talked to Thomas anymore because he told the same damn stories over and over again. Victor was embarrassed, but he thought that Thomas might be able to help him. Victor felt a sudden need for tradition.

"I can lend you the money you need," Thomas said suddenly. "But you have to take me with you."

"I can't take your money," Victor said. "I mean, I haven't hardly talked to you in years. We're not really friends anymore."

"I didn't say we were friends. I said you had to take me with you."

"Let me think about it."

Victor went home with his one hundred dollars and sat at the kitchen table. He held his head in his hands and thought about Thomas Builds-the-Fire, remembered little details, tears and scars, the bicycle they shared for a summer, so many stories.

Thomas Builds-the-Fire sat on the bicycle, waited in Victor's yard. He was ten years old and skinny. His hair was dirty because it was the Fourth of July.

"Victor," Thomas yelled. "Hurry up. We're going to miss the fireworks."

After a few minutes, Victor ran out of his house, jumped the porch railing, and landed gracefully on the sidewalk.

"And the judges award him a 9.95, the highest score of the summer," Thomas said, clapped, laughed.

"That was perfect, cousin," Victor said. "And it's my turn to ride the bike."

Thomas gave up the bike and they headed for the fairgrounds. It was nearly dark and the fireworks were about to start.

"You know," Thomas said. "It's strange how us Indians celebrate the Fourth of July. It ain't like it was *our* independence everybody was fighting for."

"You think about things too much," Victor said. "It's just supposed to be fun. Maybe Junior will be there."

"Which Junior? Everybody on this reservation is named Junior."

And they both laughed.

The fireworks were small, hardly more than a few bottle rockets and a fountain. But it was enough for two Indian boys. Years later, they would need much more.

Afterwards, sitting in the dark, fighting off mosquitoes, Victor turned to Thomas Builds-the-Fire.

"Hey," Victor said. "Tell me a story."

Thomas closed his eyes and told this story: "There were these two Indian boys who wanted to be warriors. But it was too late to be warriors in the old way. All the horses were gone. So the two Indian boys stole a car and drove to the city. They parked the stolen car in front of the police station and then hitchhiked back home to the reservation. When they got back, all their friends cheered and their parents' eyes shone with pride. *You were very brave*, everybody said to the two Indian boys. *Very brave*."

"Ya-hey," Victor said. "That's a good one. I wish I could be a warrior."

"Me, too." Thomas said.

They went home together in the dark, Thomas on the bike now, Victor on foot. They walked through shadows and light from streetlamps.

"We've come a long ways," Thomas said. "We have outdoor lighting."

79

"All I need is the stars," Victor said. "And besides, you still think about things too much."

They separated then, each headed for home, both laughing all the way.

Victor sat at his kitchen table. He counted his one hundred dollars again and again. He knew he needed more to make it to Phoenix and back. He knew he needed Thomas Builds-the-Fire. So he put his money in his wallet and opened the front door to find Thomas on the porch.

"Ya-hey, Victor," Thomas said. "I knew you'd call me."

Thomas walked into the living room and sat down on Victor's favorite chair.

"I've got some money saved up," Thomas said. "It's enough to get us down there, but you have to get us back."

"I've got this hundred dollars," Victor said. "And my dad had a savings account I'm going to claim."

"How much in your dad's account?"

"Enough. A few hundred."

"Sounds good. When we leaving?"

When they were fifteen and had long since stopped being friends, Victor and Thomas got into a fistfight. That is, Victor was really drunk and beat Thomas up for no reason at all. All the other Indian boys stood around and watched it happen. Junior was there and so were Lester, Seymour, and a lot of others. The beating might have gone on until Thomas was dead if Norma Many Horses hadn't come along and stopped it.

"Hey, you boys," Norma yelled and jumped out of her car. "Leave him alone."

If it had been someone else, even another man, the Indian boys would've just ignored the warnings. But Norma was a warrior. She was powerful. She could have picked up any two of the boys and smashed their skulls together. But worse than that, she would have dragged them all over to some tipi and made them listen to some elder tell a dusty old story.

The Indian boys scattered, and Norma walked over to Thomas and picked him up.

"Hey, little man, are you okay?" she asked.

Thomas gave her a thumbs-up.

"Why they always picking on you?"

Thomas shook his head, closed his eyes, but no stories came to him, no words or music. He just wanted to go home, to lie in his bed and let his dreams tell his stories for him.

Thomas Builds-the-Fire and Victor sat next to each other in the airplane, coach section. A tiny white woman had the window seat. She was busy twisting her body into pretzels. She was flexible.

"I have to ask," Thomas said, and Victor closed his eyes in embarrassment.

"Don't," Victor said.

"Excuse me, miss," Thomas asked. "Are you a gymnast or something?"

"There's no something about it," she said. "I was first alternate on the 1980 Olympic team."

"Really?" Thomas asked.

"Really."

"I mean, you used to be a world-class athlete?" Thomas asked.

"My husband still thinks I am."

Thomas Builds-the-Fire smiled. She was a mental gymnast, too. She pulled her leg straight up against her body so that she could've kissed her kneecap.

"I wish I could do that," Thomas said.

Victor was ready to jump out of the plane. Thomas, that crazy Indian storyteller with ratty old braids and broken teeth, was flirting with a beautiful Olympic gymnast. Nobody back home on the reservation would ever believe it.

"Well," the gymnast said. "It's easy. Try it."

Thomas grabbed at his leg and tried to pull it up into the same position as the gymnast. He couldn't even come close, which made Victor and the gymnast laugh.

"Hey," she asked. "You two are Indian, right?"

"Full-blood," Victor said.

"Not me," Thomas said. "I'm half magician on my mother's side and half clown on my father's."

They all laughed.

"What are your names?" she asked.

"Victor and Thomas."

"Mine is Cathy. Pleased to meet you all."

The three of them talked for the duration of the flight. Cathy the gymnast complained about the government, how they screwed the 1980 Olympic team by boycotting.

"Sounds like you all got a lot in common with Indians," Thomas said.

Nobody laughed.

After the plane landed in Phoenix and they had all found their way to the terminal, Cathy the gymnast smiled and waved good-bye.

"She was really nice," Thomas said.

"Yeah, but everybody talks to everybody on airplanes," Victor said. "It's too bad we can't always be that way."

"You always used to tell me I think too much," Thomas said. "Now it sounds like you do."

"Maybe I caught it from you."

"Yeah."

Thomas and Victor rode in a taxi to the trailer where Victor's father died.

"Listen," Victor said as they stopped in front of the trailer. "I never told you I was sorry for beating you up that time."

"Oh, it was nothing. We were just kids and you were drunk."

"Yeah, but I'm still sorry."

"That's all right."

Victor paid for the taxi and the two of them stood in the hot Phoenix summer. They could smell the trailer.

"This ain't going to be nice," Victor said. "You don't have to go in."

"You're going to need help."

Victor walked to the front door and opened it. The stink rolled out and made them both gag. Victor's father had lain in that trailer for a week in hundred-degree temperatures before anyone found him. And the only reason anyone found him was because of the smell. They needed dental records to identify him. That's exactly what the coroner said. They needed dental records.

"Oh, man," Victor said. "I don't know if I can do this."

"Well, then don't."

"But there might be something valuable in there."

"I thought his money was in the bank."

"It is. I was talking about pictures and letters and stuff like that."

"Oh," Thomas said as he held his breath and followed Victor into the trailer.

When Victor was twelve, he stepped into an underground wasp nest. His foot was caught in the hole, and no matter how hard he struggled, Victor couldn't pull free. He might have died there, stung a thousand times, if Thomas Builds-the-Fire had not come by.

"Run," Thomas yelled and pulled Victor's foot from the hole. They ran then, hard as they ever had, faster than Billy Mills, faster than Jim Thorpe, faster than the wasps could fly.

Victor and Thomas ran until they couldn't breathe, ran until it was cold and dark outside, ran until they were lost and it took hours to find their way home. All the way back, Victor counted his stings.

"Seven," Victor said. "My lucky number."

Victor didn't find much to keep in the trailer. Only a photo album and a stereo. Everything else had that smell stuck in it or was useless anyway.

"I guess this is all," Victor said. "It ain't much."

"Better than nothing," Thomas said.

"Yeah, and I do have the pickup."

"Yeah," Thomas said. "It's in good shape."

"Dad was good about that stuff."

"Yeah, I remember your dad."

"Really?" Victor asked. "What do you remember?"

Thomas Builds-the-Fire closed his eyes and told this story: "I remember when I had this dream that told me to go to Spokane, to stand by the Falls in the middle of the city and wait for a sign. I knew I had to go there but I didn't have a car. Didn't have a license. I was only thirteen. So I walked all the way, took me all day, and I finally made it to the Falls. I stood there for an hour waiting. Then your dad came walking up. *What the hell are you doing here?* he asked me. I said, *Waiting for a vision.* Then your father said, *All you're going to get here is mugged.* So he drove me over to Denny's, bought me dinner, and then drove me home to the reservation. For a long time I was mad because I thought my dreams had lied to me. But they didn't. Your dad was my vision. *Take care of each other* is what my dreams were saying. *Take care of each other.*"

Victor was quiet for a long time. He searched his mind for memories of his father, found the good ones, found a few bad ones, added it all up, and smiled.

"My father never told me about finding you in Spokane," Victor said.

"He said he wouldn't tell anybody. Didn't want me to get in trouble. But he said I had to watch out for you as part of the deal."

"Really?"

"Really. Your father said you would need the help. He was right."

"That's why you came down here with me, isn't it?" Victor asked.

"I came because of your father."

Victor and Thomas climbed into the pickup, drove over to the bank, and claimed the three hundred dollars in the savings account.

Thomas Builds-the-Fire could fly.

Once, he jumped off the roof of the tribal school and flapped his arms like a crazy eagle. And he flew. For a second, he hovered, suspended above all the other Indian boys who were too smart or too scared to jump.

"He's flying," Junior yelled, and Seymour was busy looking for the trick wires or mirrors. But it was real. As real as the dirt when Thomas lost altitude and crashed to the ground.

He broke his arm in two places.

"He broke his wing," Victor chanted, and the other Indian boys joined in, made it a tribal song.

"He broke his wing, he broke his wing, he broke his wing," all the Indian boys chanted as they ran off, flapping their wings, wishing they could fly, too. They hated Thomas for his courage, his brief moment as a bird. Everybody has dreams about flying. Thomas flew.

One of his dreams came true for just a second, just enough to make it real.

Victor's father, his ashes, fit in one wooden box with enough left over to fill a cardboard box.

"He always was a big man," Thomas said.

Victor carried part of his father and Thomas carried the rest out to the pickup. They set him down carefully behind the seats, put a cowboy hat on the wooden box and a Dodgers cap on the cardboard box. That's the way it was supposed to be.

"Ready to head back home?" Victor asked.

"It's going to be a long drive."

"Yeah, take a couple days, maybe."

"We can take turns," Thomas said.

"Okay," Victor said, but they didn't take turns. Victor drove for sixteen hours straight north, made it halfway up Nevada toward home before he finally pulled over.

"Hey, Thomas," Victor said. "You got to drive for a while."

"Okay."

Thomas Builds-the-Fire slid behind the wheel and started off down the road. All through Nevada, Thomas and Victor had been amazed at the lack of animal life, at the absence of water, of movement.

"Where is everything?" Victor had asked more than once.

Now when Thomas was finally driving they saw the first animal, maybe the only animal in Nevada. It was a long-eared jackrabbit.

"Look," Victor yelled. "It's alive."

Thomas and Victor were busy congratulating themselves on their discovery when the jackrabbit darted out into the road and under the wheels of the pickup.

"Stop the goddamn car," Victor yelled, and Thomas did stop, backed the pickup to the dead jackrabbit.

"Oh, man, he's dead," Victor said as he looked at the squashed animal.

"Really dead."

"The only thing alive in this whole state and we just killed it."

"I don't know," Thomas said. "I think it was suicide."

Victor looked around the desert, sniffed the air, felt the emptiness and loneliness, and nodded his head.

"Yeah," Victor said. "It had to be suicide."

"I can't believe this," Thomas said. "You drive for a thousand miles and there ain't even any bugs smashed on the windshield. I drive for ten seconds and kill the only living thing in Nevada."

"Yeah," Victor said. "Maybe I should drive."

"Maybe you should."

Thomas Builds-the-Fire walked through the corridors of the tribal school by himself. Nobody wanted to be anywhere near him because of all those stories. Story after story.

Thomas closed his eyes and this story came to him: "We are all given one thing by which our lives are measured, one determination. Mine are the stories which can change or not change the world. It doesn't matter which as long as I continue to tell the stories. My father, he died on Okinawa in World War II, died fighting for this country, which had tried to kill him for years. My mother, she died giving birth to me, died while I was still inside her. She pushed me out into the world with her last breath. I have no brothers or sisters. I have only my stories which came to me before I even had the words to speak. I learned a thousand stories before I took my first thousand steps. They are all I have. It's all I can do."

Thomas Builds-the-Fire told his stories to all those who would stop and listen. He kept telling them long after people had stopped listening.

Victor and Thomas made it back to the reservation just as the sun was rising. It was the beginning of a new day on earth, but the same old shit on the reservation.

"Good morning," Thomas said.

"Good morning."

The tribe was waking up, ready for work, eating breakfast, reading the newspaper, just like everybody else does. Willene Le-Bret was out in her garden wearing a bathrobe. She waved when Thomas and Victor drove by.

"Crazy Indians made it," she said to herself and went back to her roses.

Victor stopped the pickup in front of Thomas Builds-the-Fire's HUD house. They both yawned, stretched a little, shook dust from their bodies.

"I'm tired," Victor said.

"Of everything," Thomas added.

They both searched for words to end the journey. Victor needed to thank Thomas for his help, for the money, and make the promise to pay it all back.

"Don't worry about the money," Thomas said. "It don't make any difference anyhow."

"Probably not, enit?"

"Nope."

Victor knew that Thomas would remain the crazy story-teller who talked to dogs and cars, who listened to the wind and pine trees. Victor knew that he couldn't really be friends with Thomas, even after all that had happened. It was cruel but it was real. As real as the ashes, as Victor's father, sitting behind the seats.

"I know how it is," Thomas said. "I know you ain't going to treat me any better than you did before. I know your friends would give you too much shit about it."

Victor was ashamed of himself. Whatever happened to the tribal ties, the sense of community? The only real thing he shared with anybody was a bottle and broken dreams. He owed Thomas something, anything.

"Listen," Victor said and handed Thomas the cardboard box which contained half of his father. "I want you to have this."

Thomas took the ashes and smiled, closed his eyes, and told this story: "I'm going to travel to Spokane Falls one last time and toss these ashes into the water. And your father will rise like a salmon, leap over the bridge, over me, and find his way home. It will be beautiful. His teeth will shine like silver, like a rainbow. He will rise, Victor, he will rise."

Victor smiled.

"I was planning on doing the same thing with my half," Victor said. "But I didn't imagine my father looking anything like a salmon. I thought it'd be like cleaning the attic or something. Like letting things go after they've stopped having any use."

"Nothing stops, cousin," Thomas said. "Nothing stops."

Thomas Builds-the-Fire got out of the pickup and walked up his driveway. Victor started the pickup and began the drive home.

"Wait," Thomas yelled suddenly from his porch. "I just got to ask one favor."

Victor stopped the pickup, leaned out the window, and shouted back. "What do you want?"

"Just one time when I'm telling a story somewhere, why don't you stop and listen?" Thomas asked.

"Just once?"

"Just once."

Victor waved his arms to let Thomas know that the deal was good. It was a fair trade, and that was all Victor had ever wanted from his whole life. So Victor drove his father's pickup toward home while Thomas went into his house, closed the door behind him, and heard a new story come to him in the silence afterwards.

MIDNIGHT BASKETBALL

During a regular pickup game at St. Jerome University's outdoor court, Big Ed head-faked once, twice, three times—despite the fact that nobody was guarding him—and wildly missed a three-pointer.

"Come on, Ed," Joey said. "Stop shooting that crap. You're O-for-ten tonight."

"I had a good look," Big Ed said. That was always his excuse. If he'd driven over a bicycle but missed the bicyclist, Big Ed would have said, "I had a good look."

"Just move the ball," Joey said. "And set a damn pick."

On the next possession, Big Ed intercepted a pass meant for Joey and took a three-on-one fast-break running jump shot that completely missed the rim and backboard. Hell, it missed *the earth.*

"My bad," Big Ed said.

Joey howled and spun circles.

Two weeks earlier, at their favorite pub, Ed had confided to Joey that he'd been working on his jump shot.

"How's that?" Joey asked.

"No big changes," Ed said. "I don't need big changes. My shot—my form—is pretty good as it is. I just need to make some minor adjustments."

"Yeah, that's exactly what you need. *Minor* adjustments."

"I've been studying Obama—"

"No, not that shit again. Obama can't play ball—"

"Yes he can, he's got a first quick step—"

"No he doesn't. That's all public relations bullshit."

"Well, he's got hops—"

"No, no, no, don't bring up that damn photo again."

Ed loved the *New York Times* front-page photograph of President Obama shooting a running jump over some short and skinny white dude who was probably a Vermont congressman and former ninth man on his high school basketball team.

"It's photographic evidence," Ed said. "It could be used in a courtroom—"

"Those aren't hops. He's got his legs tucked up and splayed out behind him, like *a frog,* so it looks like he's high in the air. But it's an optical illusion. He's actually only three inches off the ground."

"No, man, you can tell. Obama's got style. He's got so much style, I'm just going to call him the Big O—"

"You can't call him O. Oscar Robertson is the Big O."

"Oh, I forgot."

"You can't forget Oscar Robertson. He should be on the NBA logo instead of Jerry West."

"I just know I want to play ball like Obama."

"Come on, Ed. I like Obama. I voted for him. I'm a damn commie bastard. But you don't want to play basketball like him."

"Have you seen the videos? That one where he dribble-drives through a bunch of guys?"

"Those are Secret Service dudes he's running with. They'd take a bullet for him. They're not supposed to stop him; they're trained to stop *other people* from getting to him."

"You see him hit that scoop shot over that North Carolina dude—"

"God, it's North Carolina, Ed. It's Division I basketball. Do you have any idea how great those guys are? Shit, in a real game against real players like that, Obama wouldn't score in ten thousand *years*."

"Well, he's scoring in that video."

"That guy wasn't guarding him. Obama is POTUS. He is mother-effing POTUS. And even if he wasn't POTUS, Obama still had that ball hanging out so far that *anybody* could have blocked it. *You* could have blocked it, Ed. That shit was as weak as the public option in health care. If Obama pulled that on me, I'd block it like some racist-ass redneck senator from Alabama."

Ed didn't laugh. He was incapable of finding any humor in basketball—not in the game in general and certainly not in his game in particular. The thing is: Ed thought he was good. No, it was worse than that. Ed believed he was *underrated.*

"You know," Ed often said. "I'm not great at any one thing, but I feel like I'm a positive force on the court. My teammates are better because of me, you know? I can feel it."

Joey had always marveled at Ed's basketball delusions. The guy might have been blind and deaf on the court but he still believed in his talent. No matter how poorly he played—and he always played poorly—he thought he'd been the all-star of the evening.

"No!" Joey screamed as Ed shot and missed another jumper.

"I'll get the next one," Ed said.

"No, you won't get the next one," Joey said. "You'll never get the next one. There has never once been a next one for you."

Ed smiled. Joey was furious. He wanted to punch Big Ed, but they'd been friends for twenty-seven years. They'd met on their first day of college. Big Ed had almost married Joey's sister and had eventually married and divorced one of Joey's cousins. Joey was godfather to Big Ed's middle son. Joey and Big Ed loved each other with the kind of straight-boy-devotion that started wars, terror attacks, and video game companies.

"Why do you shoot that shit?" Joey asked. "You haven't made a three-pointer in, like—wait, no, you've never made a three-pointer. Not *ever.*"

"I had a good look," Big Ed said again. He smiled. He was always so damn handsome and genial, even though he was a basketball *sociopath.* Yep, Big Ed was the Ted Bundy of the Saturday afternoon basketball crowd and murdered the hopes and dreams of his teammates forty-seven times a day.

Of course, one might wonder why people kept throwing the ball to Big Ed. Well, Joey and his fellow hoopsters were good players, so they always threw the correct pass. The open man always got the ball. And since Big Ed's true shooting percentage was in the single digits, he was always left open by his defender and thus, due to the immutable laws of teamwork, always got the ball. Big Ed didn't need a cut or pick to get open. He didn't need to move. He could stand in place—and often did stand in one place for entire possessions—and would still get touches. And after Big Ed missed some horrific bukakke jumper, the man who'd thrown him the ball would think, I had to give it to him because the basketball gods demand that I play with honor and trust.

"Come on, Ed!" Joey screamed at his friend—his best friend. "Move the ball!"

Moments later, Big Ed drove into the key and missed a finger roll—no, it wasn't a roll; it was a week-old *croissant*.

Joey didn't howl. He didn't make a sound. He just shook his head, walked off the court, grabbed his bag, and began his twelve-block walk home. As he walked, he removed his shirt, shorts, and boxers and tossed them aside. He also removed his knee braces, magnetic back warmer, and mouth guard and threw them into the street. He was forty-five years old and he was walking mostly naked—he was still wearing his socks and shoes—through his Seattle neighborhood. Strangers gawked and giggled; two of his neighbors smiled and waved. Joey ignored all of them. He wasn't sure why he was doing this. He knew somebody had done the same thing during a hockey movie, and soccer players were always tearing off their clothes. Joey only knew he was engaged in some kind of political protest—perhaps the most minor political protest in human history—but it felt important to him.

At his doorstep, Joey sat on his welcome mat—it was sur-prisingly comfortable on his bare ass—and removed his shoes and socks. Then, completely naked, Joey walked into his living room, slumped into his recliner, stared at his blank television, and pre-tended he was watching Stockton-and-Malone run the pick-and-roll on an endless highlight reel.

Twenty minutes later, his wife, Sharon, pulled into the driveway. She walked up to the front porch and stared at her hus-band's socks and shoes. She cradled them in her arms, opened the door, and discovered her naked husband still daydreaming about high-percentage basketball.

She regarded him. She certainly knew all of the curves and angles, and the parallel and perpendicular lines, of his body, and she'd memorized his half-damned soul.

"Big Ed again?" she asked.

"He tried a finger roll," Joey said. "Can you believe that? A *finger roll*."

"Oh," she said. "That's tragic."

"The thing is, I don't know how much more of this I can take. I'm *old*. Truly. How many years of hoops do I have left? And I want it to be good ball, you know? I don't want to tear my damn ACL or Achilles because I'm trying to chase down some shitty Big Ed jump shot."

"Why do you keep playing with him?"

"I don't know, honey. It's so *demoralizing*. And I feel trapped. It's a terrible, destructive, and endless circle."

"Just like poverty," she said.

"It's oppression and slavery," he said. "Ed is, like, England, circa 1363."

"Well, Braveheart," she said. "If there's a revolution, if you kill him, I'll help you hide the body."

They laughed.

"Hey," she said, and checked her watch. "The boys won't get home for forty-three minutes."

Nineteen minutes later, after they'd made love, after he'd kissed her belly and thighs and moved his tongue and hips in the same way he'd moved them for nineteen years, and after she'd chewed on his collarbone and pulled his hair and sucked on his lips in the same way she had for those same nineteen years, and after they'd had the most recent orgasms of a one-thousand-orgasm marriage, they laughed again.

"Damn," she said. "That was efficient."

"Teamwork," Joey said.

Later that night, unable to sleep, Joey tried to sneak out of bed.

"Hey," she said. "Are you okay?"

"No," Joey said.

"What's wrong?" she asked.

"I keep thinking about Ed. I was pretty hard on him today. I want to apologize."

"It's three in the morning. You can't call him this late."

"I'm not going to call him. I'm going over to see him."

"You're crazy," she said. "He's crazy. Basketball just makes you guys crazy."

"Yeah, yeah, yeah," Joey said. But she was right. Ed's ex-wife, Joey's cousin, had actually claimed that Ed's hoops habit—he played at least three times a week—was an irreconcilable differ-ence. And the judge had mockingly agreed.

"Just don't divorce me because of ball," Joey said.

"Just don't wake up the boys," Sharon said.

She rolled over and went back to sleep. Joey got dressed, warmed up his car, and drove toward Big Ed's apartment building. Divorced for two years, Ed lived in a studio apartment with his plasma television. It was a much better relationship than the one he'd had with his wife.

"I don't miss her," Ed had said more than once. "But I miss seeing my son every day. And I miss seeing us all together, you know?"

Joey knew.

On his way to Ed's place, Joey noticed a lone figure shooting hoops on the St. Jerome basketball court. It was too dark and far for Joey to be sure, but the night-shift hoopster was approximately the same size and shape as Big Ed.

Joey pulled over, turned off the car, and watched the may-be-Ed shoot and miss jump shot after jump shot. Joey kept score.

Miss. Off the front rim.

Miss. Off the side of the backboard.

Miss. Front rim.

Miss. Off the top of the backboard.

Miss. Front rim.

Air ball.

Joey watched the man, unguarded and alone on the court, miss twenty-one jump shots in a row. In the dark, in such a large but quiet city, it was an eerie display of ineptitude.

Then maybe-Ed dribbled left and right and took a running jump shot and scudded it off the bottom of the rim. Maybe-Ed angrily grabbed the rebound and threw the ball as hard and far as he could. It flew maybe fifty feet through the air, bounced through a parking lot, rolled across the manicured grass, and came to a rest at the base of a pine tree.

"Nice shot," Joey said to himself.

Maybe-Ed walked to center court, perhaps in initial pursuit of the ball, but he stopped and stood still for an impossibly long time. Joey wondered how a person could stand so motionless for— yes, Joey kept checking his watch—twenty-three damn minutes. Joey wondered if this maybe-Ed needed help but, Jesus, what could he do to help anyway? Maybe this guy was some schizophrenic transient who was stuck in some dreamworld. Maybe this homeless hoopster was dangerous.

Two or three times, Joey told himself to start the car and drive away. What kind of sad bastard, homeless or not, plays basketball in the middle of the night? But worse, what kind of hoopster turns himself into a goddamn statue in the middle of that night?

And then, finally, this maybe-Ed—Screw that, Joey decided, it had to be Ed; yes, it was Ed—walked off the court, away from the basketball, and disappeared into the dark.

"Jesus," Joey said aloud, and made the Sign of the Cross. He wasn't Catholic—he wasn't a Christian at all—but he knew he'd watched something unbeatific happen on a Catholic basketball court.

"Jesus," Joey said again, just to be sure.

Soon after that, Joey started his car and drove back home. Inside the house, he took off his clothes—he was naked for the fourth time that day—and crawled back into bed with his wife.

"How'd it go?" she asked.

"What?"

"With Ed?" she asked. "How is he?"

"Okay, I guess," Joey said.

"Do you want to talk about it?" she asked.

"No," he said.

She kissed him and quickly fell back to sleep. Awake for hours more, Joey promised himself that he would never ask Big Ed about his late-night hoops practice. Every man must have his secrets, right? And every man was supposed to ignore every other man's secrets. That's how the game was supposed to be played.

IDOLATRY

Marie waited for hours. That was okay. She was Indian and everything Indian—powwows, funerals,
and weddings—required patience. This audition wasn't Indian,
but she was ready when they called her name.

"What are you going to sing?" the British man asked.

"Patsy Cline," she said.

"Let's hear it."

She'd only sung the first verse before he stopped her.

"You are a terrible singer," he said. "Never sing again."

She knew this moment would be broadcast on national
television. She'd already agreed to accept any humiliation.

"But my friends, my voice coaches, *my mother*, they all say I'm great."

"They lied."

How many songs had Marie sung in her life? How many lies had she been told? On camera, Marie did the cruel math, rushed into the green room, and wept in her mother's arms.

In this world, we must love the liars or go unloved.

PROTEST

My friend Jimmy was a pale Indian, though all of his brothers and sisters were dark. You might have wondered if Jimmy's real father was a white guy. Some tribal members did wonder, but Jimmy had the same widow's peak cowlick as his browner siblings. When he was little and living on the rez, Jimmy got teased a bunch. Other Indians called him Salt or Vanilla or Snow White, so yeah, he was insecure about his pigment. But he never would have admitted to that insecurity. Instead, he pretended to embrace it. He insisted on being called White Eagle Feather, or Eagle for short, like that was his real Indian name. But you don't get to give yourself an Indian name, so most people ignored his wishes and still called him Jimmy. I was his best friend so I called him Eagle once in a while, but I usually called him Ego.

Yeah, Jimmy caught a lot of shit, even from me. But I was also the one who convinced him to go to Spokane Community College.

We shared a studio apartment in Hillyard, a poor neighborhood near the college, and went to class more often than not. Jimmy and I were studying auto repair and planned on opening a garage after we graduated. It was a small dream, I guess, but Jimmy acted like it was a supertraditional Indian thing.

"A car won't be a car after we work on it," he said. "It won't have horsepower. It will be a powerful horse."

It was a goofy thing to say, but Jimmy took it seriously. Almost overnight, Jimmy got political. It happens all the time in the Indian world, especially among the pale warriors. I think their radicalism becomes inversely proportional to their skin color. But Jimmy's transformation was sadder than most. He became a *community college* rebel and started showing up to auto repair class shirtless and barefoot.

"Shoes were invented by the white man," he said.

"Come on, Ego," I said. "I like shoes. Everybody likes shoes."

But he stopped listening to my advice. He got all weird and fundamental. He became so Indian that he jaywalked constantly. He refused to obey traffic signals and would not defer to moving vehicles.

"My tribal sovereignty isn't only about the land," he said. "As an Indian man, it's also about the sovereignty of my body. And the space around my body. Because I am indigenous, I always get the right of way."

He also started challenging any white man in a uniform—
security guards, cops, and firemen. He gave shit to postal workers.

"Fuck them," he said. "And their Nazi fucking shorts."

While running along the Spokane River, he spotted a sher-
iff's cruiser in a parking lot and flipped off the two cops inside.
The cops recognized the shirtless, barefoot guy slogging along the
jogging path.

One cop leaned out and shouted, "Run, Forrest, run."

The other cop yelled, "Go, Dog, go."

Jimmy wanted to be taken seriously—he wanted to be
feared—so he ran up to the cop car and kicked the driver's door.
Then kicked it again.

The cops scrambled out of their seats, chased and tackled
Jimmy.

"You racist bastards," Jimmy yelled at the confused cops.
They couldn't figure out why a white man was calling two white
cops racists. Yeah, Jimmy was feeling oppressed but the cops didn't
even realize he was Indian. They thought he was just another
white-trash Hillyard redneck.

A few hours later, Jimmy called me from jail.

"I resisted," he said. "I've started a resistance movement."

"Come on, Ego," I said. "And I am not bailing you out."

"Don't want bail," he said. "I'm a political prisoner."

"You're an asshole is what you are."

Then, a day after that, the television told me that a cop
had shot and killed a homeless Indian named Harold in downtown
Spokane.

"He had a knife," the cop said.

A carving knife, we learned, about three inches long. The
murdered Indian, Harold, trying to reconnect with his culture, had

been taking carving lessons at the Indian Center. He came from a tribe that made totem poles. They made canoes. Most of the tribe drank; some drank themselves to death.

"He had a threatening look on his face," the cop said.

I knew Harold a little bit. Every Indian pretty much knows every other Indian. Harold wasn't an angry man. That was his face.

I phoned Jimmy to talk about the shooting. But I got his voice mail.

"Damn it," I said. "Indians are still prey animals, enit? When are they going to stop shooting at us?"

I was so mad at the world that I had to make a joke. I wanted to make Jimmy laugh.

"You see, Ego," I said, "looking as white as you can be is a good thing. Ain't no cop going to shoot you because he thinks you're an angry redskin."

Later, I realized it had been a terrible thing to say, so I called him back and apologized to his machine. A few days after that, I called and apologized to his machine again. After a few months of silence, I called him but his phone was disconnected. I asked around town about him, but nobody knew where he was. I never heard from him or of him again.

Jimmy's last act was to disappear, and that was probably the most Indian thing he had ever done.

WHAT EVER HAPPENED TO
FRANK SNAKE CHURCH?

Frank's heart fibrillated as he walked along a tree-line trail on the northern slope of Mount Rainier. He staggered, leaned against a small pine tree for balance, but tumbled over it instead, rolled for twenty or thirty yards down the slope, and fell over a small cliff onto the scree below. A moment later, Frank's arrhythmic heart corrected itself and resumed beating normally, but he wondered if he was going to die on the mountain. He was only thirty-nine years old and weighed only eleven more pounds than he had when he graduated from high school, but he'd been smoking too many unfiltered Camels, and his cholesterol level was a dangerous 344, exactly the same as Ted Williams's career batting average. But damn it, Frank thought, he was a Spokane Indian, and Indians are supposed to die young. Thirty-nine years is old for a Spokane. Old enough to join the American Association of Retired Indians. Frank laughed. Bloody and hurt on this mountain, his heart maybe scarred and twisted beyond repair, and he was still making jokes. How indigenous, Frank thought, how wonderfully aboriginal, applause, applause, applause, applause for me and my people. Still laughing, Frank pushed himself to his hands and knees and sat on a flat rock. His heart beat slow and steady. He breathed easily. He felt no tingling pain in his chest, arms, or legs. He wasn't lightheaded or nauseated. He seemed to be fine. Maybe his heart was okay; maybe it had missed only one dance step in a lifetime of otherwise lovely coronary waltzes. He was cut and scraped, a nasty gash on his arm would probably need stitches, but none of his wounds seemed to be too serious. He didn't have any broken bones or sprains. So there was the diagnosis: His heart had played a practical joke on him—how terribly amusing, ha, ha, ha, ha, ha, ha, ha, ha—and he was bruised and battered and had one hell of a headache, but he'd live.

Carefully, painfully, Frank crawled back up the slope to the trail. Once there, while still on his hands and knees, he took a few deep breaths and promised himself that he'd visit a superhero cardiologist as soon as he got off the mountain. He'd promise to see an organic nutritionist, aromatherapist, deep-tissue masseuse, feng shui consultant, yoga master, and Mormon stand-up comedian if those promises would help him get off this mountain. Frank stood, tested his balance, and found it to be true enough, so he resumed his rough trek along the trail. He felt stronger with each step. He was now convinced he was going to be okay. Yes, he was going to be fine. But after a few more steps, an electrical charge jolted him.

Damn, Frank thought, I have a heart attack, fall down a damn mountain, and then I crawl back only to get struck by lightning. Frank imagined the newspaper headline: HEART-DISEASED FOREST RANGER STRUCK BY LIGHTNING. Frank was imagining the idiot readers laughing at the idiot park ranger when another electrical bolt knocked him back ten feet and dropped him to the ground, where a third lightning strike shocked him again. Damn, Frank thought, this lightning has a personal vendetta against me. He felt a fourth electrical charge shoot up his spine and into his brain. He convulsed and vomited. He kicked and punched at the air, and then he couldn't move at all. As he lay paralyzed on the trail, Frank thought: This is it, now I'm really dead, and I have crapped my pants; I'm going to die with half-digested pieces of mushroom and sausage pizza stuck to my ass; humiliation, degradation, sin, and mortal shame. But Frank didn't die. Instead, as the electricity fired inside his brain, Frank saw an image of his father, Harrison Snake Church, as the old man lay faceup on the floor of his kitchen in Seattle. Harrison's eyes were open, but there was no light behind them; blood dripped from his nose and ears. In great pain, Frank understood that he hadn't suffered a heart attack or been struck by lightning. No, he'd been gifted and cursed with the first real vision of his life, and though Frank was one of the very few Indian agnostics in the world, he accepted this vision as a simple and secular truth: His father was dead.

How much can one son love one father? Frank loved his father enough to stand and stagger five miles to the logging road where he'd parked his truck. He knew he should get on the radio and call for help. He was exhausted and in no safe shape to drive. But he also knew that his father was lying dead on the kitchen floor. Covered with blood and food, half naked in a ratty bathrobe that his father called a valuable antique, Jerry Springer or Dr. Phil lecturing on the television. Frank needed to be the first on the scene. He needed to restore his father's dignity before the proper authorities were called. Perhaps his father's spirit was waiting for him. But Frank didn't believe in spirits, in souls, in the afterlife. Why was he thinking about his father's soul? Mr. Death, Frank thought, you have entered my house and rearranged the furniture. But it didn't matter what Frank believed. With or without soul and spirit, Harrison was lying dead on the kitchen floor and should be lifted, cleaned, and covered with old quilts. Frank needed to perform burial ceremonies. Harrison needed to have his honor restored, and Frank was the only one who could, or should, do the restoration.

So Frank drove his truck dangerously fast along fifteen miles of logging and undeveloped roads. He didn't need a map; he'd been a forest ranger at Mount Rainier for ten years and had driven thousands of miles on these roads. As he drove, Frank thought of his father and wondered how the old man should be remembered. As he traveled toward his father's dead body, Frank composed the eulogy: "Thank you all for coming here today to say good-bye to my father. For those of you who know me, you know I'm not a man of words. But I do have a few things I'd like to say about my father. Harrison was a beloved man. Beloved. I guess you're supposed to use words like that at a funeral. Fancy words. But I guess I should just say it simple. Most people liked my dad, and quite a few loved him. He was an active member of St. Therese Church. He was always a good Catholic, maybe the only Indian of his generation who went to Catholic boarding school on purpose. That was a joke. I don't know if it was funny or not. But I'm an Indian, and Indians are supposed to be funny at funerals. At least that's what it says in the *Indian Funeral Handbook*. That was another joke.

"Here at St. Therese, my dad volunteered for the youth programs, and he was one of the most dependable readers and Eucharistic ministers. He read the gospels with more passion and pride than the Jesuits. Ay, jokes. Sorry about that, Father Terry, but you know it's true. Ay, jokes.

"My dad, Harry, he was fond of telling people how he would've become a priest if he hadn't loved the ladies so much. And there were always a few ladies who would have loved him back, and you know who you are. You're the ones crying the most. Ay, jokes. But of course my loyal dad has been chaste since his wife, my mother, Helen, died of brain cancer twenty-one years ago. So maybe my dad was like a Jesuit, except he didn't have sex, unlike most of the Jesuits. Ay, jokes.

"My mom died only three days after I graduated from high school. It was a terrible, ugly death. And my dad was never really happy again and never looked to be loved again by another woman, but he stayed active like a shark: *Don't stop moving or you die*. Ha, he was the Great Red Whale, my dad. Ay, jokes. Maybe my dad and I were the Great Red Whale together. We were always together. I've lived in the same house with him all of my life. I guess, in some real way, my father became my mother. Harrison was Helen. He adopted some of her mannerisms, you know, like he scratches his head whenever he's frustrated, just like she does.

"Listen to me. I keep talking about them in the present tense. And then I talk about them in the past tense. And I was never any good at English grammar anyway. So you can blame my high school English teacher for that. Sorry about that, Ms. Balum. Ay, jokes.

"After he got old, my dad was the crossing guard at Thirty-fourth and Union and knew the names of all of his kids. Since they were all Catholic kids, they only had twelve names. Or maybe eleven, since nobody has named their kid Judas since Judas was named Judas by his folks. Ay, jokes.

"My old man was strong for an old man, you know, and he could still hit ten or twelve of those long-range set shots in a row. Basketball was always my dad's passion. He was Idaho State High School Basketball Player of the Year in 1952. He loved the Lakers when they played in Minneapolis, and he loved them more after they moved to Los Angeles. Elgin Baylor. Gail Goodrich. Jerry West. Wilt Chamberlain. Happy Hairston. Those guys won thirty-three in a row in 1973.

"After my mother died, my dad and I watched thousands of basketball games on television and in person. Sometimes, on cold Saturday nights, he and I would drive for hours to watch small-town high school teams, not because we knew any of the players but because they were playing a small-town version of basketball, and it was ragged and beautiful and passionate and clumsy and perfect. Davenport Gorillas. Darrington Loggers. Selkirk Rangers. Neah Bay Red Devils. Toutle Lake Fighting Ducks.

"And now my father is gone, and my mother is gone, and they're gone together, and I'm a thirty-nine-year-old orphan. I didn't even say good-bye to my father before I left the house on the day he died. I never really said good-bye to my mother before she died. I will have to live the rest of my life with a failed son's regrets. I don't even know what I'm going to do now."

As he drove off Mount Rainier and through the park, Frank knew his eulogy was inadequate, incomplete, and improvisational. He knew he would have to sit and write a real eulogy. He would fill a dozen notebooks with draft after draft. Every word would perfectly capture how much love and pain he felt for his father and mother. Harrison and Helen Snake Church deserved poetry, not the opening monologue of an indigenous talk show. Mr. Death, Frank thought, you are a funnyman, but I will not laugh. Frank sped out of the park. Ignoring the risk of speeding tickets, he drove west on two-lane highways, north on Interstate 5 through Tacoma into Seattle, east off the James Street exit, and ran red lights twenty blocks into the Central District, where he and Harrison lived on Thirty-seventh Avenue. Frank drove his government truck onto the front lawn, leaped out and raced up the front steps, struggled with the front door, threw it open, rushed into the kitchen, and saw his father sitting at the table. Harrison was drinking coffee and eating Grape-Nuts. He ate breakfast for every meal.

"You're alive," said Frank, completely surprised by the fact.

"Yes, I am," Harrison said as he studied his bloody, panicked son. "But you look half dead."

"I had a vision," Frank said.

Harrison sipped his coffee.

"I saw you in my head," Frank said. "You're supposed to be dead. I saw you dead."

"You have blurry vision," said Harrison.

One year and four days later, Harrison died of a heart attack in the QFC supermarket on Broadway and Pike. When he heard the news, Frank wondered if his previous year's vision had been accurate, if he'd foreseen his father's death. But there must be a statute of limitations for visions, Frank thought, there must be an expiration date for ESP. Beyond all that, Frank didn't believe anyone could predict the future. His supposedly psychic vision of his father's death bore some general resemblance to his real death, but the details were different. Harrison was shopping in the produce department when he coughed once, rubbed his tingling left arm, and died. "Probably dead before he hit the floor," the coroner had said. When Harrison fell, he knocked over an artfully arranged display of bananas, which was appropriate and funny, since Harrison had always hated the taste of what he called "the devil's evil yellow penis." Frank buried his father beside his mother's grave in the same Seattle graveyard where Bruce and Brandon Lee were also buried. So, hey, Frank figured his father was lying with damn good company, and if there was an afterlife, then Harrison was probably learning jeet kune do and making love to his wife, Helen, for all of eternity.

At his father's graveside, overlooking Lake Washington, Frank stood to give the eulogy he'd carefully written but found he couldn't read the words on the page. Grief turned him into an illiterate. He tried to remember what he'd written so he could recite his eulogy by memory, but he discovered he couldn't speak at all. Grief turned him into a mute. Finally, after five minutes of silence, as the assembled mourners shook with collective embarrassment, Frank finally remembered how to say four words: "I love my father."

Afterward, Frank shook the hands and accepted the hugs of dozens of his father's friends and family. He couldn't remember any of their names. Grief turned him into a stranger in his own tribe. Finally, Frank recognized an older woman, his mother's aunt Margaret Marie, who kissed him hard on the lips. She tasted like salt.

"Your father was a ballplayer," she said. "He could have played in college, you know? You should have said something about that."

Frank laughed. What kind of person offered constructive criticism at a funeral? What kind of literate mourner had the nerve to deconstruct a eulogy?

Harrison had been a very good basketball player, but he'd never been good enough to play college hoops, not even at the community-college level. He'd been a great shooter but was never much of an athlete—too short and slow and tentative—but Frank, a genetic freak at six feet six (making him the seventeenth tallest Spokane Indian in tribal history), had always been a truly supernatural baller, the kind of jumper and runner who ignored physics when he played. He'd averaged forty-one points a game during his senior year at Seattle's Garfield High School and had received 114 scholarship offers from colleges all over the country. He'd signed a letter of intent with the University of Washington and had planned to major in environmental science. But then his mother died. To honor her and keep her memory sacred, Frank knew he had to give up something valuable. He had to bury with her one of his most important treasures. So he buried his basketball dreams. On the morning of her funeral, Frank walked to the local park and shot one hundred jump shots and made eighty-five of them. He left the ball at the park, helped bury his mother that afternoon, and had not played the game since. For the first few years, Frank had almost died whenever he thought about basketball, but the acute pain turned chronic, and then it was a dull and distant ache, and then it was the phantom itch of an amputated limb, and then it was gone.

Now he was forty years old, and his life could be divided into two almost equal halves: He'd been a star basketball player for eighteen years—he was a hooper right out of the womb—and a non-basketball player for twenty-two years.

After his father's burial, Frank went home alone and stood in the quiet house. He had not yet cried for his father, and he wondered if he would ever cry, but his grief grew so suddenly huge that it pushed him to the floor. He lay on the living room carpet and wept huge and gasping tears. He screamed and wailed for ten minutes or more. He didn't know how to sing and drum, but he pounded the floor and wailed tribal vocals: *Father, way, ya, way, ha, Father, way, ya, way, ha, Father, way, ya, way, ha.* He sang himself hoarse and fell asleep on the carpet. When he woke, he crawled upstairs to his father's bedroom and lay in his father's bed. The sheets still smelled like Harrison. Frank pressed his face into the pillow and breathed in his father's scent. And then Frank gathered his father's hair, so different than Frank's graying crew cut. His father's hair was still black and two feet long on the day he died. Frank found long black hair on the pillow, in the sheets, tangled in a comb, stuck to the bathtub porcelain, clumped into a wet ball in the drain stops, and scattered in every corner of the house. Frank gathered all of the hair, rolled it into a ball, and ate it. He felt split in two, one crazy man eating hair and one rational man watching a crazy man eat hair. He chewed and swallowed the last pieces of his father's life. He felt like he was building a museum of pain, a freak show, where he was the only visitor viewing the only mutant screaming the only prayer he knew: *Come back, Daddy. Come back, Daddy.*

Come back, Daddy. Come back, Daddy. Come back, Daddy. Come back, Daddy. Come back, Daddy.

Frank howled. He slept. Woke and howled again. Slept again. Woke and howled until his lips and tongue were bloody. Slept again. Woke and wondered if his grief would ever end. He didn't know what to do, but he needed to love and be loved, so he opened his father's closet and stared at the basketball waiting inside. A couple times a week for many years, Harrison had gone alone to the neighborhood park to shoot baskets, so the ball was worn and comfortable, low on air. Trying to move exactly like his father, to honor his father through muscle memory, Frank picked up the ball, dribbled it around his back, between his legs, bobbled it, and knocked over a chair. Clumsy and stupid with grief, he grabbed the ball, left the house, and walked then ran to the neighborhood park. Once there, he stood at the free-throw line on the northern end of the basketball court. He stared at the iron rim with its chain net. He had not taken a shot in over two decades. He'd given up this game to honor his mother, and now he was reclaiming it to honor his father. He wanted both of them to rise from the dead. Frank dribbled the ball once, twice, three times, stepped back to the three-point line, and rose into the air for a jump shot. He missed the basket completely. Frank watched the sacrilegious air ball bounce away from him and roll quickly across the manicured grass, until it finally slowed to a stop at the tennis court on the other side of the park.

A week after he buried his father, Frank quit his job as a forest ranger. He'd saved tens of thousands of dollars over the years, and the house was completely paid for, so he wasn't worried about money. But he was worried about being alone. For most of his life, he'd loved solitude. Walking through the deep woods, he often imagined he was the only person left in the world, the only survivor of a nuclear war or a smallpox epidemic. During these fantasies, Frank lived alone for fifty years until the day when he curled into a ball at the base of a beautiful pine and died like an old dog, whereby the human race ceased to exist. Inside and outside of this fantasy, Frank knew he was guilty of arrogance and misanthropy, but he compensated by being kind to strangers and tipping really well at restaurants. He didn't have any close friends and had probably shared more conversations with the redheaded clerk at the university bookstore and the blond cashier at the QFC supermarket than he did with anyone other than his father. As for romance, Frank had dated a few women over the years but found them to be too inconsistent and illogical, so he dated a few men and found them to be even more random and frightening. For a while, he had paid for sex with men and women, then women only, but he eventually grew disgusted with the desperation of such acts and, for many years, had lived as chastely as his father had lived. All along, Frank understood that he was suffering from a quiet sickness, a sort of emotional tumor that never grew or diminished but prevented him from living a full and messy life. At the end of every day, Frank thoroughly washed away the human funk of the world, but now, with his father's death, he worried that he would never feel clean again. He needed to take control of his life. He needed to organize his grief; he needed to compose a mournful to-do list: *Bury your father, visit your mother's grave, cry, eat hair, play basketball again, lose weight.* Of course he felt banal. In a time of extraordinary pain, why was he worried about something as ordinary as his body-fat percentage? He only knew for sure that he needed to keep moving, get stronger, build, and connect.

So he picked up the Yellow Pages, looked up personal trainers, and dialed the first one on the list.

"Athletes, Incorporated, this is Russell."

The next day, he walked thirty blocks into downtown Seattle (why not start training immediately?) and met with Russell, a thin and muscular black man who looked more like a long-distance runner than a weight lifter.

"So," said Russell as he sat across the desk from Frank.

"So," Frank said.

"What can we do for you?"

"I'm not sure. I've never done this before."

"Well, why don't we start with your name."

"I'm Frank Snake Church."

"Damn, that's impressive. A man with a name like that is destined for greatness."

"If my name was John Smith, you'd tell me I was destined for greatness, right?"

"Well, I'm supposed to help you be great. That's my job. Stronger body, stronger mind, stronger spirit. That's our motto."

Frank stared at Russell. Silently studied him. A confident man, Russell was comfortable with the silence.

"Are you a serious man?" Frank asked him.

"I'm not sure I understand your question."

Frank stood and walked around the desk. He knelt beside Russell and spoke to him from inches away. Russell didn't mind this closeness.

"Listen," Frank said, "I know this is your job, and I know you need to make money. And I know a large part of what you do

119

here is sales. You're a salesman. And that's okay. You need to make a living. We all need to make a living. And hey, this job you have is a great way to make money, right? You get to wear T-shirts and shorts all year long. And you've probably helped a lot of people get healthy, right?"

Russell could feel Frank's desperation and sense of purpose, the religious fervor that needed to be directed. Russell had met a thousand desperate people, all looking to rescue or be rescued, but this Indian man was especially radiant with need.

"I keep a scrapbook of the clients who've meant the most to me," Russell said. He'd never told anybody about that scrapbook and how he studied it. If exercise was his religion, then the scrapbook was his bible, and every one of his clients was a prophet. Russell never spoke aloud of how proud he was of the woman who lost five hundred pounds and kept it off, of the man who recovered from a triple bypass and now ran marathons, of the teenager paralyzed in a car wreck who now played professional wheelchair basketball. Russell fixed broken people, and sometimes the repairs lasted a lifetime. But he could not say these things aloud. In order to be taken seriously, Russell knew he had to pretend to be less than serious about his job, his *calling*. He could not tell his clients that he thought his gym was a church. He'd sound like a crazy fundamentalist, an idiot parody of a personal trainer. He couldn't express sentiment or commitment; he was forced to be ironic and cynical. He couldn't tell people he cried whenever clients failed or quit or trained too inconsistently for the work to make a difference. So he simply repeated the tired and misleading mantra whenever asked about his work: *It's better than having a real job*. But now, after all these years, Russell somehow understood that he could tell the truth to this sad and desperate stranger.

"I remember everybody I've worked with," Russell said. "I remember their names, their weights, their goals. I remember the exact day when the quitters quit. I keep a running count of the total weight my clients have lost."

"What is it?"

"I can't tell you that. It's just for me. It's a sacred number."

"Okay," Frank said. "I think it's good to remember things that way. Very good. I admire that. So, with my admiration clearly expressed, I want you to answer my question. Are you a serious man?"

"If I said this aloud to most of the world, they'd laugh at me," said Russell. "But I think I have one of the most important jobs in the world. That's how serious I am about what I do. So yes, in answer to your question, when it comes to this work, I am a very serious man."

Frank stood and looked out the window at the Seattle skyline. With his back to Russell, he spoke. It was the only way he could say what he needed to say.

"My father died a week ago," Frank said.

Russell had often heard these grief stories before. He knew five people who'd come directly to the gym from funerals and immediately signed up for full memberships.

"What about your mother?" Russell asked.

"She died when I was eighteen."

"My mother died of sickle cell last year," Russell said. "My father was killed when I was twelve. He was a taxi driver. Guy held him up and shot him in the head."

Frank honored that story—those tragic deaths—with his silence.

"How did your father die?" Russell asked.

"Heart attack."

Frank and Russell were priests and confessors.

"Listen to me," Frank said. "I used to be a basketball player, a really good basketball player, the best in the city and maybe the best in the state, and maybe I could have become one of the best in the country. But I haven't played in a long, long time."

"What do you need from me?" Russell asked.

Frank turned from the window. "I want to be good again," he said.

Russell studied the man and his body, visually estimated his fitness levels, and emotionally guessed at his self-discipline and dedication.

"Give me a year," Russell said.

For the next twelve months, Frank trained five days a week. He lifted free weights, ran miles on the treadmill, climbed hundreds of stories on the stair stepper, jumped boxes until he vomited from the lactic acid buildup, and climbed ropes until his hands bled. He quit smoking. He measured his food, kept track of all of the calories and the fat, protein, and carbohydrate grams. He drank twelve glasses of water a day. Mr. Death, Frank thought, I am going to drown you before you drown me. Frank's body-fat percentage, heart rate, and blood pressure all lowered. Every three months, he bought new clothes to fit his new body.

During the course of the year, Frank also cleaned his house. He removed the art from the walls and sold it through want ads and garage sales. Without ceremony, he piled up all of the old blankets and quilts, a few of them over eighty years old, and gave them one by one to the neighbors. He gathered financial records, wills, tax returns, old magazines, photograph albums, and scrapbooks, and stored them in a large safe-deposit box at the bank. After that, he scooped all of the various knickknacks and sentimental souvenirs into cardboard boxes and left them on the corner for others to cart away. One day after the movers carried away all of the old-fashioned and overstuffed furniture, other movers brought in the new, sleek, and simple pieces, so there was only one bed, one dresser, one coffee table, one dining table, one wardrobe, one stove, one refrigerator freezer, and four chairs in the entire house. He pulled up the rugs, hired a local teenager to haul them to the dump, and sanded the hardwood until the floors glowed golden and sepia. Near the end of the year, he found enough courage to give away his father's clothes and the boxes of his mother's clothes his father had saved. Frank gave away most of his clothes as well, until he owned only black T-shirts, blue jeans, black socks, black boxers, and black basketball shoes.

Frank kept all of the books, three thousand novels, histories, biographies, and essays, and neatly organized them on bookshelves he built into the walls. He read one book a day. After he disconnected the telephone and permanently stopped the mail, his family and friends worried about him and came to see him, but he turned away all visitors, treating loved ones, strangers, salespeople, religious crusaders, and political activists as if they were all the same.

Frank knew his behavior was obsessive and compulsive, and perhaps he was seriously disturbed, in need of medical care and strong prescriptions, but he didn't want to stop. He needed to perform this ceremony, to disappear into the ritual, to methodically change into something new and better, into someone stronger.

"Make me hurt," he said to Russell before every training session.

"All right," said Russell every few weeks. "I want one thousand sit-ups and one thousand push-ups, and you're not leaving here until I get them."

Sometimes Frank overtrained, ran too many miles or lifted too much weight, and injured himself. Russell would chase him out of the gym, tell him to lay off for a week or even two or three, give his body a chance to recover, to heal, but Frank kept pushing, tore muscles and dislocated joints, broke fingers and twisted vertebrae. He stopped training only when he couldn't get out of bed, and if he found the strength to crawl into a hot shower, he'd warm his muscles enough to lift what he could. At his strongest, he bench-pressed 350 and leg-pressed a thousand pounds. At his weakest, when he was injured, he could lift only paperbacks or pencils, but he'd still do three sets of ten repetitions.

"You can't keep doing this to yourself," Russell said to him again and again. "I can't keep doing this to you. It's malpractice, man. If you get hurt again, I'm quitting. I'm banning you from the gym forever."

But Russell never quit on him, and Frank never quit on Russell. Joined, they were not twins or friends; they were not lovers or brothers; they were not teachers or students; they were not mentors or apprentices; they were not monks or sinners. They remained mutable and variable, sacred and profane. Mr. Death, Frank thought, we are your contraries, your opposites and contradictions, your X factors and missing links, your self-canceling saints and self-flagellating monks, your Saint Francis and the other Saint Francis, and we have come to blaspheme your name.

Away from Russell and the gym, Frank played basketball.

Seven days a week, Frank drove the city and searched for games. He traveled from the manicured intramural courts at the University of Washington to the broken-asphalt courts of the Central District; from the violent and verbose games in Green Lake Park to the genial and clumsy games at the YMCA; from the gladiator battles under the I-5 freeway to the hyperorganized leagues at Sound Mind & Body Gym. He played against black men who believed it was their tribal right to dominate the court. He played against white men who wanted to be black men. He played against brown men who hated black and white men. He played against black, brown, and white men who didn't care about any color other than the green-money bets placed on every point and game. He played against Basketball Democrats who came to the court alone and ran with anybody, and Basketball Republicans who traveled in groups of five and ran only with one another. He played against women who endured endless variations of the same dumb joke: *Hey, girl, you can play, but it's shirts and skins, and you're running skins*. He played against former football players who still wanted to play football, and former wrestlers who wanted only to wrestle. He played against undisciplined young men who couldn't run a basic pick-and-roll, and against elderly men who never missed their two-handed set shots. He played against trash talkers and polite gentlemen. He played against sociopathic ball hogs, wild gunners, rebound hounds, and assist-happy magicians. He played games to seven, nine, eleven, and twenty-one points. He played winner-keeps-ball and alternate possessions. He played one-on-one, two-on-two, three-on-three, four-on-four, five-on-five, and mob rules, improvisational, every-baller-for-himself, anarchist, free-for-all, death-cage matches. He played against cheaters who constantly changed the score, and honest freaks who called fouls on themselves. He played against liars who bragged about how good they used to be, and dreamers who would never be as good as they wanted to be. He played against Basketball Presbyterians who refused to fast-break, and Basketball Pagans who refused to slow down. He played against the vain Allen-Iverson-wanna be punks who dribbled between their legs, around their backs, and missed 99 percent of the ridiculous, driving, triple-pump, reverse-scoop shots they hoisted up but talked endless and pornographic trash whenever they happened to make even one shot. He played against the vain Larry-Bird-wanna be court lawyers who argued every foul call and planted themselves at three-point lines and constantly called for the ball because they were open, damn it, more open than any outsider shooter in the history of the damn game, so pass the freaking rock!

Frank played so well that he earned (and re-earned) a playground reputation and was known by a variety of nicknames: Shooter, Old Man, Chief, and Three. Frank's favorite nickname was Oh Shit, given to him in July by a teenage Chicano kid in MLK, Jr. Park.

"Every time the old Indio shoots and makes one of those crazy thirty-footers," the Chicano kid had said, "his man be yelling, 'Oh shit, oh shit, oh shit!'"

Frank was making a comeback, though he hated that word as much as Norma Desmond had hated it, and just like her, he preferred to call it his return. After all, over the course of the year, a few older players had recognized Frank and remembered him as the supernatural Indian kid who'd disappeared from the basketball world two decades ago.

On the basketball courts of Seattle, Frank was the love child of Sasquatch and D. B. Cooper; he was the murder of Charles Lindbergh's baby, the building of Noah's Ark, and the flooding of Atlantis; he was the mystery and the religion and the outright lies.

During one legendary game at the University of Washington Intramural Activities Building, Frank caught the ball in the low post and turned to face Double O, the Huskies' power forward. He was a Division I stud slumming among the gym rats, a future second-round draft pick destined to be eleventh man for the Cleveland Cavaliers, which didn't sound glamorous but still made him one of the thousand best basketball players in the world.

"Oh Shit, you better give up the rock," Double O taunted. "I ain't letting you win this game."

Frank faked the jumper and dribbled right, but Double O, five inches taller and seventy-five pounds heavier, easily pushed Frank away from the key.

"Oh Shit, you're an old man," taunted Double O. "Why you coming after me? I ain't got your social security check."

Frank dribbled the ball between his legs, behind his back, then between his legs again. He didn't know why he was bouncing the ball like a madman. There was no point to it, but he wanted to challenge the trash-talking black kid.

"Oh Shit, you got yourself some skills!" shouted Double O. "Come on, come on, show me the triple-threat position. That's it. That's it. I am so bedazzled, I cannot tell if you're going to shoot, pass, or drive. Oh man, you got them fun-da-men-tals. Bet you learned those with the Original Celtics!"

Distracted by the insulting rant, by its brilliant and racist poetry, Frank laughed and almost lost the ball.

"Better make your move, Old Milk," taunted Double O. "Your expiration date is long past due."

Frank faked right, dribbled left, and scored the game-winning hoop on an archaic rolling left-handed hook shot that barely made it over Double O's outstretched hands.

Frank screamed in triumph and relief as Double O howled with disbelief and fell backward to the floor. All the other players in the gym—the eyewitnesses to a little miracle—shouted curses and promises, screamed in harmony with Frank, slapped one another's hands and backs and butts, and spun in delirious circles. People laughed until they were nauseated. Nobody held anything back. Because he had no idea what else to do with his excitement, one skinny black kid nicknamed Skinny, a sophomore in electrical engineering, ran out of the gym and twenty-four blocks to his house to tell his father and younger brother what he had just seen. Skinny's father and little brother never once asked why he'd run so far to tell the story of one hoop in one meaningless game. They understood why the story had to be immediately told. In basketball, there is no such thing as "too much" or "too far" or "too high." In basketball, enough is never enough. At its best and worst, basketball is all about excess. Every day is Fat Tuesday on a basketball court.

"Did you see that? Did you see that?" screamed Double O as he lay on the floor and flailed his arms and legs. He laughed and hooted and cursed. Losing didn't embarrass him; he was proud of playing a game that could produce such a random, magical, and ridiculous highlight. There was no camera crew to record the event for *SportsCenter*, but it had happened nonetheless, and it would become a part of the basketball mythology at the University of Washington: *Do you remember the time that Old Indian scored on Double O? Do I remember? I was there. Old Chief scored seven straight buckets on Double O and won the game on a poster dunk right in O's ugly mug. O's feelings hurt so bad, he needed stitches. Hell, O never recovered from the pain. He's got that post-traumatic stress illness, and it's getting worse now that he plays ball in Cleveland. Playing hoops for the Cavaliers is like fighting in Vietnam.*

In that way, over the years, the story of Frank's game-winning bucket would change with each telling. Every teller would add his or her personal details; every biographer would turn the story into autobiography. But the original story, the aboriginal hook shot, belonged to Frank, and he danced in fast circles around the court, whooping and celebrating like a spastic idiot. I sound like some Boy Scout's idea of an Indian warrior, Frank thought, like I'm a parody, but a happy parody.

The other ballplayers laughed at Frank's display. He'd always been a quiet player, rarely speaking on or off the court, and now he was emoting like a game-show host.

"Somebody give Oh Shit a sedative!" shouted Double O from the floor. "The Old Indian has gone spastic!"

Still whooping with joy, Frank helped Double O to his feet. The old man and the young man hugged each other and laughed.

"I beat you," Frank said.

"Old man," said Double O, "you gave me a trip on your time machine."

If smell is the memory sense, as Frank once read, then he was most nostalgic about the spicy aroma of Kentucky Fried Chicken. Whenever Frank smelled Kentucky Fried Chicken, and not just any fried chicken but the very particular and chemical scent of the Colonel's secret recipe, he thought of his mother. Because he was a child who could not separate his memories of his mother and his father and sometimes confused their details, Frank thought of his mother and father together. And when he thought about his mother and father and the smell of Kentucky Fried Chicken, Frank remembered one summer day when his parents

129

took him to the neighborhood park to picnic with a twenty-piece bucket of mixed Kentucky Fried Chicken, and a ten-piece box of legs and wings only, along with a cooler filled with Diet Pepsi and store-bought potato salad and apples and bananas and potato chips and a chocolate cake. Harrison and Frank had fought over which particular basketball to bring, but they had at last agreed on an ABA red-white-and-blue rock.

"Can't you ever leave that ball at home?" Helen asked Harrison. She always asked him that question. After so many years of hard-worked marriage, that question had come to mean *I love you, but your obsessions irritate the hell out of me, but I love you, remember that, okay?*

On that day, Frank was eleven years old, young enough to sit on his mother's lap and be only slightly embarrassed by their shared affection, and old enough to need his father and be completely unable to tell him about that need.

"Let's play ball," Frank said to Harrison, though he meant to say, *Prove your love for me.*

"Eat first," Helen said.

"If I eat now, I'll throw up," Frank said. "I'll eat after we play."

"You'll eat now, and if you throw up, you'll just have to eat again, and then you'll play again, and then you'll throw up, so you'll have to eat again. It might go on for days that way. You'll be trapped in a vicious circle."

"You're weird, Mom."

"Yes, I am," she said. "And weirdness is hereditary."

"I'm weird, too," Harrison said. "So you got it coming from both sides. You don't have a chance."

"I can't believe you're my parents. Did you adopt me?"

"Honey, we certainly did not adopt you," Helen said. "We stole you from a pack of wolves, so eat your meat, you darling little carnivore."

Laughing, feeling like an adult because his parents treated him with respect and satire, Frank sat between his mother and father and almost cried with happiness. His chest tightened, and his mouth tasted bitter. He cried too easily, he knew, and sometimes had to fight school-yard bullies who teased him about his quick tears. He usually won the fights and usually cried about his victory.

Sitting with his parents, Frank closed his eyes against his tears, blinked and blinked and thought of the utter hilarity of a dog farting in its sleep, and that made him laugh a little. Soon enough, he felt normal, like a kid made of steel and oak, and he could breathe easily, and he quickly ate his lunch of Kentucky Fried Chicken, but only wings and legs.

"Okay, I'm done," he said. "Let's play ball, Dad."

"I'm too tired," Harrison said. "I'm going to lie down in the grass and fall asleep in some dog poop."

His father was always trying to be funny. He was funny sometimes, maybe most of the time, but nobody could be funny all of the time. And being funny was sometimes a way of being dishonest.

A few years back, Harrison had told Frank's third-grade teacher that Indians didn't believe in using numbers, that the science of mathematics was a colonial evil.

"Well," the mystified teacher had asked, "then how do Indians count?"

"We guess," Harrison had said with as much profundity as he could fake.

Okay, so maybe Harrison was funny because funny was valuable. Maybe being funny was usually a way of being honest.

"Come on, let's play ball," Frank pleaded with his father, who had flopped onto the grass with a chicken leg and a banana.

"I'm going to eat and sleep and fart," Harrison said.

"Dad, you said you'd show me something new."

"Did I promise you I would show you something new?"

"Well, no."

"Did I sign something that said I would show you something new?"

"No."

"That means we don't have an oral or written contract. We don't have an implied contract, either, because you don't even know how to spell 'implication.' So that means I'm going to eat chicken until I pass out from a grease overdose."

"Mom, he's talking like a lawyer again."

"Yeah," she said. "I hate it when he does that."

"And I can, too, spell 'implication,'" Frank said.

"Okay," Harrison said. "If you can spell 'implication,' your mother will play ball with you."

"I don't want to play ball with Mom, I want to play with somebody good."

"Hey, your mom is great. Why do you think I fell in love with her?"

"Mom, he's lying again."

"I'm not lying. Our dear Helen was a cannibal on the basketball court."

"Is that true, Mom?"

"I used to play," she said.

Frank looked at his mother. Sure, she was tall (five feet eight or so, the same height as Harrison), and she was strong (she grew up bucking hay bales), but Frank had never seen her touch a basketball except to toss it in a closet or down the stairs or into a room or out the door, or anywhere to get that dang thing out of her way.

"Mom, are you lying?"

"Have I ever lied to you?"

"You told me I was raised by wolves."

"Okay, have I ever lied to you twice in one day?"

"Mom, be serious."

"She is being serious," Harrison said. "She used to play those girls' rules. Three girls on defense, three on offense. Your mom was the shooter. Damn, I saw her score fifty-two points once. And then the coaches decided to play boys' rules. They didn't have to, but they wanted to see what your mom could do in a real game. And she scored seventy-three. I missed that one. If I'd seen that game, I would have proposed to her on the spot."

"I love you, too, sweetie," Helen said to her husband.

Frank couldn't believe it. He looked at his mother in her denim skirt and frilly blue top, with her lipstick and her beaded earrings and her scarf all matching perfectly, all of her life and spirit and world color-coordinated and alphabetically organized. How could his mother, who washed her hands twelve times a day, ever have played a game so fundamentally sweaty and messy?

"Mom, did you really play ball?"

"It was girls' basketball," she said, "so it doesn't really count."

She was being sarcastic, Frank knew, because she'd taught him how to be sarcastic.

"For the rest of your academic life," she'd told him on his first day of kindergarten, "whenever any teacher tells you that Columbus discovered America, I want you to run up to him or her, jump on his or her back, and scream, 'I discovered you!'"

He'd never been courageous enough to do it, but he always considered it. He always almost did it. He almost always ran home and told Helen how close he'd been to doing it, how he was sure he could do it the next time, and she hugged him and told him how smart and good and handsome he was. Helen was loving and crazy and unpredictable and gentle and voluble and bitter and funny and a thousand other good and bad and indefinable things, but she was certainly not a liar.

"Are you telling the truth?" Frank asked her. "Were you really a good basketball player?"

"People said I was good," she said and shrugged. "If enough people say you're good at something, then you're probably good at it."

"Okay, cool," Frank said. "Do you want to play ball with me?"

"Remember, you have to spell 'implication' first," Harrison said.

"It's spelled 'D-A-D I-S A J-E-R-K,'" Frank said.

All three of them laughed. They were always laughing. That was what people said about the Snake Churches. People said the Snake Churches were good at laughing.

"Okay, okay," Helen said. "Let's play ball. But I'm not making any guarantees. It's been a long time."

So mother and son took to the court and played basketball. At first, she practiced shots while he rebounded her makes and misses and passed the ball back to her. She had a funny shot, a one-handed push, and she missed the first ten or twelve before her body remembered the game, and then she rarely missed. From ten feet away, then fifteen, then twenty, and twenty-five feet, she shot and made it and shot and made it and shot and made it and shot and missed it and then shot and made it and shot and made it and shot many times and made many more than she missed.

"Wow," Frank said to his mother as she shot. He kept saying it. It was all he could think to say. This was a new ceremony for them, for this mother and son. They'd created and shared other ceremonies. They baked cookies together; they told stories to each other at night; they made up love songs while she drove him to school; they gave silly nicknames to strangers in shopping malls; they made up stupid knock-knock jokes and laughed until milk sprayed out of their noses. But they'd never played a sport together, had never been this physical, this strong and competitive. Frank looked at his mother, and he saw a new woman, a different person, a mysterious stranger, and a romantic figure.

"Mom," Frank said. "You're a ballplayer."

Oh man, he loved her, and he felt like crying yet again. Oh, he was young and worshipful and sentimental, and he didn't know it, but his mother would always want her son to be young and worshipful and sentimental. She prayed that the world, filled with its cruel people and crueler philosophies, would not punish her son too harshly for being so kind and so receptive to kindness.

"Mom," Frank said. "Show me something new."

So Helen dribbled the ball toward the hoop, dribbled across the key, and shot a rolling left-handed hook that bounced around the rim and dropped in.

"Oh, sweetie! I love you!" Harrison shouted from the grass and sprayed chicken and banana into the air. "That was her favorite move, son, she never missed that one! And nobody ever stopped it. Hell, I never stopped it!"

"Do it again," Frank said.

So Helen shot the left-handed hook again. She shot it twenty times and made nineteen of them.

"She's beautiful!" Harrison shouted and ran to join his wife and son on the court. "Isn't she beautiful?"

Frank wondered if this was the best day of his whole life so far, if he would ever be this happy again. Those were extreme thoughts for an eleven-year-old, and Frank, though he was that eleven-year-old, understood he was being extreme, but it was the only way he knew how to be. It was the only way he'd been taught to be.

So mother, father, and son played basketball for hours, until it got dark enough for the streetlights to blink on, until it was too dark for even the streetlights to make any difference, until Frank could barely keep his eyes open, until Helen and Harrison took their exhausted son home and put him to bed and watched him sleep and breathe, and inhale and exhale and inhale and exhale.

On the first anniversary of his father's death, Frank stepped outside to see what kind of day it was. He cursed the rain, stepped back inside to grab his windbreaker, and walked to the covered courts over on Rainier Avenue. On a sunny day, fifty guys played at Rainier, but on that rainy day, Preacher was shooting hoops all by himself; he was always shooting hoops by himself. Two or three hundred set shots a day. One day a month, he closed his eyes and shot blindly and would never reveal why he performed such an eccentric ceremony.

"Honey, honey, honey," Preacher always said when asked. "Just let the mystery be."

On that day, Preacher's eyes were wide open when Frank joined him for a game of Horse.

"Hey, Frank Snake Church, what ever happened to you?" Preacher asked. He always asked variations of the same question when he saw Frank. "Tell me, tell me, tell me, what ever happened to Frank Snake Church, what the hell happened to Benjamin Franklin Snake Church?"

Preacher hit a thirty-foot bank shot, but Frank missed it. Preacher hit a left-handed hook shot from half-court, but Frank threw the ball over the basket.

"Look at me," said Preacher. "I'm a senior citizen and I've given Frank the 'H' and the 'O.' Ho, ho, ho, Merry Christmas. But wait, I must stop and ponder this existential dilemma. How could I, a retired blue-collar worker, a fixed-income pensioner, a tattered coat upon a stick, how could I be defeating the legendary Frank Snake Church? What the hell is wrong with this picture? What the hell ever happened to Frank Snake Church?"

"I am Frank Snake Church in the here and now and forever," Frank said and laughed. He loved to listen to Preacher rant and rave. A retired railroad engineer, Preacher was a gray-haired black man with a big belly. He stood at the top of the key, bounced the ball off the free-throw line, and off the board into the hoop.

"That was a garbage shot," Frank said. "You'd never take that shot in a real game. Never."

"Every game is real, every game is real, every game is real," Preacher chanted as Frank missed the trick shot.

"That's a screaming scarlet 'R' for you," said Preacher and called out his next shot. "This one is all net all day."

Preacher hit the fifteen-foot swish, and Frank also swished it.

"Oh, a pretty little shot by the Indian stranger," said Preacher.

"I ain't no stranger, I am Frank Snake Church."

"Naw, you ain't no Frank Snake Church," Preacher said. "I saw Frank Snake Church score seventy-seven against the Ballard Beavers in 1979. I saw Frank Snake Church shoot twenty-eight for thirty-six from the field and twenty-one for twenty-two from the line. I saw Frank Snake Church grab nineteen rebounds that same night and hand out eleven dimes. Yeah, I knew Frank Snake Church. Frank Snake Church was a friend of basketball, and believe me, you ain't no Frank Snake Church."

"My driver's license says I'm Frank Snake Church."

"Your social security card, library card, unemployment check, and the tattoo on your right butt cheek might say Frank Snake Church," Preacher said, "but you, sir, are an imposter; you are a doppelgänger; you are a body snatcher; you are a pod person; you are Frank Snake Church's evil and elderly twin is what you are."

Preacher closed his eyes and hit a blind shot from the corner. Frank closed his eyes and missed by five feet.

"That's an 'S' for you, as in Shut Up and Learn How to Play Another Game," said Preacher. "God could pluck out my eyes, and you could play with a microscope, and I'd still beat you. Man, you used to be somebody."

"I am now what I always was," Frank said.

"You now and you then are two entirely different people. You used to be Frank the Snake, Frank the Hot Dog, but now you're just a plain Oscar Mayer wiener, just a burned-up frankfurter without any damn mustard to make you taste better, make you easier to swallow. I watch you toss up one more of those ugly jumpers, and I'm going to need the Heimlich to squeeze your ugliness out of my throat."

"Nope, Frank now and Frank then are exactly the same. I am a tasty indigenous sausage."

"You were young and fresh, and now you're prehistoric, my man, you're only about two and a half hours younger than the Big Bang, that's how old you are. And I know you're old because I'm old. I smell the old on you like I smell the old on me. And it reeks, son, it reeks of stupid and desperate hope."

Preacher hit a Rick Barry two-handed scoop-shot free throw.

"I can't believe you took that white-boy shot," Frank said. "I'm going to turn you in to the NAACP for that sinful thing."

"Honey, I believe in the multicultural beauty of this diverse country."

"But that Anglo crap was just plain ugly."

"Did it go in?" Preacher asked.

"Well, it went in, but it didn't go in pretty."

"All right, pretty boy, let's see what you got."

Frank clanged the shot off the rim.

"My shot might've been ugly," Preacher said, "but your shot is missing chromosomes. You want me to prove it, or you want to lose this game all by yourself?"

"Here begins my comeback," said Frank as he took the shot and missed again.

"Spell it out, honey, that's 'H-O-R-S' and double 'E.' Game over."

"Man, I can't believe I lost on that old-fashioned antique."

"Sweetheart, I might be old-fashioned, but you're just plain old."

Frank felt hot and stupid. He tasted bitterness—that awful need to cry—and he was ashamed of his weakness, and then he was ashamed of being ashamed.

"Age don't mean anything," Frank said. "I walk onto any court in this city, and I'm the best baller. Other guys might be faster or stronger, maybe they jump higher, but I'm smarter. I've got skills and I've got wisdom."

Frank's heart raced. He wondered if he was going to fall again; he wondered if lightning was going to strike him again.

"You might be the wisest forty-year-old ballplayer in the whole city," Preacher said. "You might be the Plato, Aristotle, and Socrates of Seattle street hoops, but you're still forty years old. You should be collecting your basketball pension."

"You're twenty years older than me," Frank said. "Why are you giving me crap about my age?"

Frank could hear the desperation in his own voice, so he knew Preacher could also hear it. In another time, in other, less civilized places, desperate men killed those who made them feel desperation. Who was he kidding? Frank knew, and Preacher should have known, that desperate men are fragile and dangerous at all times and places. Frank wanted to punch Preacher in the face. Frank wanted to knock the old man to the ground and kick and kick and kick and kick him and break his ribs and drive bone splinters into the old man's heart and lungs.

"I know I'm old," Preacher said. "I know it like I know the feel of my own sagging ball sack. I know exactly how old I am in my brain, in my mind. And my basketball mind is the same age as my basketball body. Old, old, ancient, King Tut antique. But you, son, you're in denial. Your mind is stuck somewhere back in 1980, but your eggshell body is cracking here in the twenty-first century."

"I'm only forty years old," Frank said. He bounced the ball between his legs, around his back, thump, thump, between his legs,

140

around his back, thump, thump, again and again, thump, thump, faster and faster, thump, thump, thump, thump, thump.

"Basketball years are like dog years," Preacher said. "You're truly about two hundred and ninety-nine years old."

Thump, thump, thump, thump, thump.

"I'm still a player," Frank said. "I'm still playing good and hard."

Thump, thump, thump, thump, thump.

"But why are you still playing so hard?" Preacher asked. "What are you trying to prove? You keep trying to get all those years back, right? You're trying to time-machine it, trying to alternate-universe it, but one of these days, you're going to come down wrong on one of your arthritic knees, and it will be over. What will you do then? You've bet your whole life on basketball, and playground basketball at that, and what do you have to show for it? Look at you. You're not some sixteen-year-old gangster trying to play your way out of the ghetto. You ain't even some reservation warrior boy trying to shoot your way off the reservation and into some white-collar job at Microsoft Ice Cream. You're just Frank the Pretty Good Shooter for an Old Fart. Nobody's looking to recruit you. Nobody's going to draft you. Ain't no university alumni lining up to financially corrupt your naive ass. Ain't no pretty little Caucasian cheerleaders looking to bed you down in room seven of the Delta Delta Delta house. Ain't no ESPN putting you in the Plays of the Day. You ain't as cool as the other side of the pillow. You're hot and sweaty, like an orthopedic support. You're one lonely Chuck Taylor high-top rotting in the ten-cent pile at Goodwill. Your game is old and ugly and misguided, like the Salem witch trials. You're committing injustice every time you step on the court. I think I'm going to organize a march against your ancient ass. I'm going to boycott you. I'm going to boycott your corporate sponsors. But wait, you ain't got any corporate sponsors, unless Nike has come out with a shoe called Tired Old Bastard. So why don't you just give up the full-court game and the half-court game and enjoy the fruitful retirement of shooting a few basketballs and drinking a few glasses of lemonade."

Frank stopped bouncing the ball and threw it hard at Preacher, who easily caught it and laughed.

"Man oh man," Preacher said. "I'm getting to you, ain't I? I'm hurting your ballplaying heart, ain't I?"

Preacher threw the ball back at Frank, who also caught it easily, and resumed the trick dribbling, the thump, thump, thump, and thump, thump.

"I play ball because I need to play," Frank said.

Thump, thump.

"And I need yearly prostate exams," Preacher said, "so don't try to tell me nothing about needing nothing."

Thump, thump.

"I'm playing to remember my mom and dad," Frank said.

Preacher laughed so hard he sat on the court.

"What's so funny?" Frank asked. He dropped the ball and let it roll away.

"Well, I just took myself a poll," Preacher said. "And I asked one thousand mothers and fathers how they would feel about a forty-year-old son who quit his high-paying job to pursue a full-time career as a playground basketball player in Seattle, Washington, and all one thousand of them mothers and fathers cried in shame."

"Preacher," Frank said, "it's true. I'm not kidding. This is, like, a mission or something. My mom and dad are dead. I'm playing to honor them. It's an Indian thing."

Preacher laughed harder and longer. "That's crap," he said. "And it's racist crap at that. What makes you think your pain is so special, so different from anybody else's pain? You look up death in the medical dictionary, and it says everybody's going to catch it. So don't lecture me about death."

"Believe me, I'm playing to remember them."

"You're playing to remember yourself. You're playing because of some of that nostalgia. And nostalgia is a cancer. Nostalgia will fill your heart up with tumors. Yeah, yeah, yeah, that's what you are. You're just an old fart dying of terminal nostalgia."

Frank moaned—a strange, involuntary, and primal noise—and turned his back on Preacher. Frank wept and furiously wiped the tears from his face.

"Oh man, are you crying?" Preacher asked. He was alarmed and embarrassed for Frank.

"Leave me alone," Frank said.

"Oh, come on, man, I'm just talking."

"No, you're not just talking. You're talking about my whole failed life."

"You ain't no failure. I'm just trying to distract you. I'm just trying to win."

"Don't you condescend to me. Don't. Don't you look inside me and then pretend you didn't look inside me."

Preacher felt the heat of Frank's mania, of his burning.

"Listen, brother," Preacher said. "Why don't we go get some decaf and talk this out? I had no idea this meant so much to you. Why don't we go talk it out?"

Frank walked in fast circles around Preacher, who wondered if he could outrun the younger man.

"Listen," said Frank. "You can't take something away from me, steal from me, and then just leave me. You have to replace what you've broken. You have to fix it."

"All right, all right, tell me how to fix it."

"I don't know how to fix it. I didn't know it could be broken. I thought I knew what I was doing. I thought I was doing what I was supposed to do."

"Hey, brother, hey, man, this is too heavy for me and you, all right? Why don't we head over to the church and talk to Reverend Billy?"

"You're a preacher."

"That's just my name. They call me Preacher because I talk too much. I ain't spiritual. I just talk. I don't know anything."

"You're a preacher. Your name is Preacher."

"I know my name is Preacher, but that's like, that's just, it's, you know, it's nothing but false advertising."

Frank stepped quickly toward the old man, who raised his fists in defense. But Frank only hugged him hard and cried into the black man's shoulder. Preacher didn't know what to do. He was pressed skin-to-skin with a crazy man, maybe a dangerous man, and how the hell do you escape such an embrace?

"I'm sorry, brother," Preacher said. "I didn't know."

Frank laughed. He released Preacher. He turned in circles and walked away. And he laughed. He stood on the grass on the edge of the basketball court and spun in circles. And he laughed. Preacher couldn't believe what he was witnessing. He'd known quite a few crazy people in his life. A man doesn't grow up black in the USA without knowing a lot of crazy black folks, without being born to and giving birth to the breakable and broken. But Preacher had never seen this kind of crazy, and he'd certainly never seen the exact moment when a crazy man went completely crazy.

"Hey, Frank, man, I don't like what I'm seeing here. You're hurting really bad here. You maybe want me to call somebody for you?"

Frank laughed and ran. He ran away from Preacher and the basketball court. Frank ran until he fell on somebody's green, green lawn, and then Frank stood and ran again.

After Preacher's devastating sermon, Frank didn't play basketball for two weeks. He didn't leave the house or answer the telephone or the door. He ate all of the food in the house and then drank only water and fruit juice. He was on his own personal hunger strike. Mr. Death, you are an obese bastard, Frank thought, and I'm going to starve you down until I can fit my hands around your throat and choke you. Frank lost fifteen pounds in fifteen days. He wondered how long he could live without food. Forty, fifty, sixty days? He wondered who would find his body.

Three weeks after Preacher's sermon, and after dozens of unanswered phone calls, Russell found Frank's address in his files, drove to the house, crawled through an unlocked window, and found Frank dead in bed. Well, he thought Frank was dead.

"You're breaking and entering," Frank said and opened his eyes.

"You scared me," Russell said. "I thought you were dead."

"Black man, you keep crawling through windows in this gentrified neighborhood, and you're going to get shot in your handsome African head."

"I was worried about you."

"Well, aren't you the full-service personal trainer? You should be charging me more." Frank sat up in bed. He was pale and clammy and far too thin.

"You look terrible, Frank. You're really sick."

"I know."

"I'm going to call for help, okay? We need to get you help, all right?"

"Okay."

Russell walked into the kitchen to use the telephone and hurried back.

"They'll be here soon," he said.

"What would you have done if you'd come too late?" Frank asked. "You know, part of me wishes you'd waited too long."

"I did wait too long. You're sick. And I helped you get sick. I'm sorry. I just wanted to believe in what you believed."

"You're not going to hug me now, are you?" Frank asked.

Both men laughed.

"No, I'm not going to hug you, I'm not going to kiss you, I'm not going to recite poetry to you," Russell said. "And I'm not going to crawl under these nasty sheets with you, either."

An ambulance siren wailed in the distance.

"Because, well," Frank said, "I know you're gay and all, and I care about you a bunch, but not in that way. If we were stuck on a deserted island or something, or if we were in prison, then maybe we could be Romeo and Juliet, but in the real world, you're going to have to admire me from afar."

"Yeah, let me tell you," Russell said, "I've always been very attracted to straight, suicidal, bipolar anorexics."

"And I've always been attracted to gay, black, narcissistic codependents."

146

Both men laughed again because they were good at laughing.

One year after Russell saved Frank's life, after four months of residential treatment and eight months of inpatient counseling, Frank walked into the admissions office at West Seattle Community College. He'd gained three extra pounds for every twelve of the steps he'd taken over the last year, so he was fat. Not unhappy and fat, not fat and happy, but fat and alive, and hungry, always hungry.

"Can I help you? Is there anything I can do?" the desk clerk asked. She was young, blonde, and tentative. A work-study student or scholarship kid, Frank thought, smart and pretty and poor.

"Yeah," he said, feeling damn tentative as well. "I think, well, I want to go to school here."

"Oh, that's good. That's really great. I can help. I can help you with that."

She ducked beneath the counter, came back up with a thick stack of paper, and set it on the counter.

"Here you go, this is it," she said. "You have to fill these out. Fill them out, and sign them, and bring them back. These are admission papers. You fill them out and you can get admitted."

Frank stared at the thick pile of paper, as mysterious and frightening to him as Stonehenge. The young woman recognized the fear in his eyes. She came from a place where that fear was common.

"What's your name?" she asked.

"Frank," he said. "Frank Snake Church."

"Are you Native American?"

"Why do you ask?"

"Well, they have a Native American admissions officer here. Her name is Stephanie. She works with the Native Americans. She can help you with admissions. You're Native American, right?"

"Yes, I'm Indian."

"If you don't mind me asking, it's a personal question, but how old are you?"

"I'm forty-one."

"You know, they also have a program here for older students, you know, for the people who went to college when you were young—when you were younger—and come back."

"I never went to college before."

"Well, the program is for all older students, you know? They call it Second Wind."

"Second Wind? That sound like a bowel condition you have when you're old."

The young woman laughed. "That's funny. You're funny. It does sound sort of funny, doesn't it? But it's a really good program. And they can help you. The Second Wind program can help you."

She reached beneath the counter again, pulled out another stack of paper, and set it beside the other stack of paper. So much paper, so much work. He didn't know why he was here; he'd come here only because his therapist had suggested it. Frank felt stupid and inadequate. He'd made a huge mistake by quitting his Forest Service job, but he could probably go back. He didn't want to go to college; he wanted to walk the quiet forests and think about nothing as often as he could.

"Hey, listen," Frank said, "I've got another thing to go to. I'll come back later."

"No, listen," she said, because she was poor and smart and had been poorer and was now smarter than people assumed she was. "I know this is scary. I was scared to come here. I'll help you. I'll take you to Stephanie."

She came around the counter and took his hand. She was only eighteen, and she led him by the hand down the hallway toward the Native American Admissions Office.

"My name is Lynn," she said as they walked together, as she led him by the hand.

"I'm Frank."

"I know, you already told me that."

He was scared, and she knew it and didn't hate him for it. She wasn't afraid of his fear, and she wouldn't hurt him for it. She was so young and so smart, and she led him by the hand.

Lynn led him into the Native American Admissions Office, Room 21A at West Seattle Community College in Seattle, Washington, a city named after a Duwamish Indian chief who died alone and drunk and poor and forgotten, only to be remembered decades after his death for words of wisdom he'd supposedly said, but words that had been written by the mayor's white assistant. Mr. Death, Frank thought, if a lie is beautiful, then is it truly a lie?

Lynn led Frank into the simple office. Sitting at a metal desk, a chubby Indian woman with old-fashioned eyeglasses looked up at the odd pair.

"Dang, Lynn," the Indian woman said. "I didn't know you like them old and dark."

"Old and dark and bitter," Lynn said. "Like bus-station coffee."

The women laughed together. Frank thought they were smart and funny, too smart and funny for him to compete with, too smart and funny for him to understand. He knew he wasn't smart and funny enough to be in their presence.

"This is Mr. Frank Snake Church," Lynn said with overt formality, with respect. "He is very interested in attending our beloved institution, but he's never been to college before. He's a Native American and a Second Winder."

The young woman spoke with much more confidence and power than she had before. How many people must underestimate her, Frank thought, and get their heads torn off.

"Hello, Mr. Frank Snake Church," the Indian woman said, "I'm Stephanie. Why don't you have a seat and we'll set you up."

"I told you she was great," Lynn said. She led him by the hand to a wooden chair across the desk from Stephanie. Lynn sat him down and kissed him on the cheek. She came from a place, from a town and street, from a block and house, where all of the men had quit, had surrendered, had simply stopped and lay down in the street to die before they were fifteen years old. And here was an old man, a frightened man the same age as her father, and he was beautiful like Jesus, and scared like Jesus, and rising from the dead like Jesus. She kissed him because she wanted to pray with him and for him, but she didn't know if he would accept her prayers, if he even believed in prayers. She kissed him, and Frank wanted to cry because this young woman, this stranger, had been so kind and generous. He knew he would never have another conversation with Lynn apart from hurried greetings and smiles and quick hugs and exclamations. She would soon graduate and transfer to a four-year university, taking her private hopes and dreams to a private college. After that, he would never see her again but would always remember her, would always associate the smell of chalk and new books and floor polish and sea-salt air with her memory. She kissed him on the cheek, touched his shoulder, and hurried out the door, back to the work that was paying for school that was saving her life.

"So, Mr. Snake Church," Stephanie said. "What tribe are you?"

"I'm Spokane," he said, his voice cracking.

"Are you okay?" she asked.

"Yes," he said. But he wasn't. He covered his face and cried. She came around the table and knelt beside him.

"Frank," she said. "It's okay, it's okay. I'm here, I'm here."

With Stephanie's help, Frank enrolled in Math 99, English 99, History 99, Introduction to Computer Science, and Physical Education.

His first test was in math.

The first question was a story problem: "Bobby has forty dollars when he walks into the supermarket. If Bobby buys three loaves of bread for ten dollars each, and he buys a bottle of orange juice for three dollars, how much money will he have left?"

Frank didn't have to work the problem on paper. He did the math in his head. Bobby would have seven bucks left, but he'd paid too much for the bread and not enough for the juice. Easy cheese, Frank thought, confident he could do this.

With one question answered, Frank moved ahead to the others.

Three weeks into his first quarter, Frank walked across campus to the athletic center and knocked on the basketball coach's door.

"Come in," the coach said.

Frank stepped inside and sat across the desk from the coach, a big white man with curly blond hair. He was maybe Frank's age or a little older.

"How can I help you?" the coach asked.

"I want to play on your basketball team."

The coach smiled and leaned toward Frank. "How old are you?" he asked.

"Forty-one," Frank said.

"Do you have any athletic eligibility left?"

"This is my first time in college. So that means I have all my eligibility, right?"

"That's right."

"I thought so. I looked it up."

"I bet you did. Not a whole lot of forty-one-year-old guys are curious about their athletic eligibility."

"How old are you?" Frank asked.

"Forty-three. But my eligibility is all used up."

"I know, you played college ball at the University of Washington. And high school ball at Roosevelt."

"Did you look that up, too?"

"No, I remember you. I played against you in high school. And I was supposed to play with you at UW."

The coach studied Frank's face for a while, and then he remembered. "Snake Church," he said.

"Yes," Frank said, feeling honored.

"You were good. No, you were great. What happened to you?"

"That doesn't matter. My history isn't important. I'm here now, and I want to play ball for you."

"You don't look much like a ballplayer anymore."

"I've gained a lot of weight in the last year. I've been in residential treatment for some mental problems."

"You don't have to tell me this."

"No, I need to be honest. I need to tell you these things. Before I got sick, I was in the best shape of my life. I can get there again."

The coach stood. "Come on," he said. "I want to show you something."

He led Frank out of the office and to the balcony overlooking the basketball court. The community-college team ran an informal scrimmage. Ten young and powerful black men ran the court with grace and poetry. It was beautiful. Frank wanted to be a part of it.

"Hey!" the coach yelled down to his players. "Run a dunk drill!"

Laughing and joking, the black men formed two lines and ran the drill. All of them could easily dunk two-handed, including the five-foot-five point guard.

"That's pretty good, right?" the coach asked.

"Yes," Frank said.

"All right!" the coach yelled down to his players. "Now run the real dunk drill!"

Serious now, all of the young men ripped off reverse dunks, 360-degree dunks, alley-oops, bounce-off-the-floor-and-off-the-backboard dunks, and one big guy dunked two balls at the same time.

"I've built myself a great program here," the coach said. "I've had forty players go Division One in the last ten years. All ten guys down there have Division One talent. It's the best team I've ever had."

"They look great," Frank said.

"Do you really think you can compete with them? Twenty years ago, maybe. But now? I'm happy you're here, Frank, I'm proud of you for coming back to college, but I think you're dreaming about basketball."

"Let me down there," Frank said. "And I'll show you something."

The coach thought it over. What did he have to lose? If basketball was truly a religion, as he believed, then he needed to practice charity in order to be a truly spiritual man.

"All right," the coach said. "Let's see how much gas you have left in the tank."

Frank and the coach walked down to the court and greeted the players.

"Okay, men," the coach said. "I've got a special guest today."

"Hey, Coach, is that your chiropractor?" the big guy asked.

They laughed.

"No, this is Frank Snake Church. He's going to run a little bit with you guys."

Wearing black jeans, a black T-shirt, and white basketball shoes, Frank looked like a coffee-shop waiter.

"Hey, Coach, is he going to run in his street clothes?"

"He can talk," Coach said. "Ask him."

"Yo, old-timer," said the point guard. "Is this one of those Make-A-Wish things? Are we your dying request?"

They laughed.

"Yes," Frank said.

They stopped laughing.

"Shit, man," the point guard said. "I'm sorry. I didn't mean no harm. What you got, the cancer?"

"No, I'm not dying. It's for my father and mother. They're dead, and I'm trying to remember them."

Uncomfortable, the players shuffled their feet and looked to their coach for guidance.

"Frank, are you okay?" asked the coach, wishing he hadn't let this nostalgic stunt go so far.

"I want to be honest with all of you," Frank said. "I'm a little crazy. Basketball has made me a little crazy. And that's probably a little scary to you guys. I know you all grew up with tons of crazy, and you're playing ball to get away from it. But I don't mean to harm anybody. I'm a good man, I think, and I want to be a better man. The thing is, I don't think I was a good son when my mother and father were alive, so I want to be a good son now that they're dead. I think I can do that by playing ball with you guys. By playing on this team."

"You think you're good enough to make the team?" the point guard asked. He tried to hide his smile.

Frank smiled and laughed. "Hey, I know I'm a fat old man, but that just means your feelings are going to be really hurt when a fat old man kicks your ass."

The players and Coach laughed.

"Old man," the point guard said. "I didn't know they trash-talked in your day. Man, what did they do it with? Cave paintings?"

"Just give me the ball and we'll run," Frank said.

The point guard tossed the ball to Frank.

"Check it in," Frank said and tossed it back.

"All right," said the point guard. "I'll take the bench, and you can have the other starters. Make it fair that way."

"One of you has to sit."

"I'll sit," the big guy said and stood with his coach.

155

"We got our teams," the point guard said and tossed the ball back to Frank. "Check."

Frank dribbled the ball to the top of the key, turned, and discovered the point guard five feet away from him.

"Are you going to guard me?" Frank asked.

"Do I need to guard you?" the point guard asked.

"I don't want no charity," Frank said.

"I'll guard you when you prove I need to guard you."

"All right, guard this," Frank said and shot a jumper that missed the rim and backboard by three feet.

"Man oh man, I don't need to guard you," the point guard said. "Gravity is going to take care of you."

The point guard took the inbound pass and dribbled down-court. Frank tried to stay in front of the little guard, but he was too quick. He burned past Frank, tossed a lazy pass to a forward, and pointed at Frank when the forward dunked the ball.

"Were you guarding me?" he asked Frank. "I just want to be sure you know you're guarding me. I'm your man. Do you understand that? Do you understand the basic principles of defense?"

Frank didn't respond. Twice up and down the court, he was already breathing hard and needed to conserve his energy.

Frank set a back pick for his center, intending to free him for a shot, but Frank was knocked over instead and hit the ground hard. By the time Frank got to his feet, the point guard had stolen the ball and raced down the court for an easy layup.

"Hey, Coach," the point guard shouted as he ran by Frank. "It's only four on five out here. We need another player. Oh, wait! There is another player out here. I just didn't see him until right now."

"Shut up," Frank said.

"Oh, am I getting to you?" The point guard turned to jaw with his teammates, and Frank broke for the hoop. He caught a bounce pass, stepped past a forward, and hit a five-footer.

"Two for Snake Church," said Coach from the sidelines.

"That's the only hoop you're getting," the point guard said and hurried the ball down the court. He spun and went for the crossover dribble, but Frank reached in and knocked the ball away. One of Frank's teammates picked up the loose ball and tossed it back to Frank.

"Come on, come on, come on," the point guard shouted in Frank's ear as he ran alongside him.

Frank was slower than the young man, but he was stronger, so he dug an elbow into the kid's ribs, pushed him away, and rose up for a thirty-foot jumper, an impossible shot. And bang, he nailed it!

"Three points!" shouted Coach.

"You fouled me twice," the point guard said as he brought the ball back toward Frank.

"Call it, then."

"No, man, I don't need it," the point guard said and spun past Frank and drove down the middle of the key. Frank was fooled, but he dove after the point guard, hit the ball from behind, and sent it skidding toward one of his teammates, a big guard, who raced down the court for an easy layup.

"What's the score?" the point guard shouted out. He was angry now.

"Five to four, for Snake Church."

"What are we playing to?" Frank asked. He struggled for oxygen. Lactic acid burned holes in his thighs.

"Eleven," said the point guard.

Frank hoped he could make it that far.

"All right, all right, you can play ball for an old man," the point guard said. "But you ain't touching the rock again. It's all over for you."

He feinted left, feinted right, and Frank got his feet all twisted up and fell down again as the point guard raced by him and missed a ten-foot jumper. As his forward grabbed the rebound, Frank staggered to his feet and ran down the court on the slowest fast break in the history of basketball. He caught a pass just inside the half-court line and was too tired to dribble any farther, so he launched a thirty-five-foot set shot.

"Three!" shouted the coach, suddenly loving this sport more than he had ever loved it before. "That's eight to four, another three and Frank wins."

"I can't believe this," the point guard said. He'd been humiliated, and he sought revenge. He barreled into Frank, sending him staggering back, and pulled up for his own three-pointer. Good! Eight to seven!

"It's comeback time, baby," the point guard said as he shadowed Frank down the court. Frank could barely move. His arms and legs burned with pain. His back ached. He figured he'd torn a muscle near his spine. His lungs felt like two sacks of rocks. But he was happy! He was joyous! He caught a bounce pass from a teammate and faced the point guard.

"No, no, no, old man, you're not winning this game on me."

Smiling, Frank head-faked, dribbled right, planted for a jumper, and screamed in pain as his knee exploded. He'd never felt pain this terrible. He grabbed his leg and rolled on the floor.

Coach ran over and held him down. "Don't move, don't move," he said.

"It hurts, it hurts," Frank said.

"I know," Coach said. "Just let me look at it."

As the players circled around them, Coach examined Frank's knee.

"Is it bad?" Frank asked. He wanted to scream from the pain.

"Really bad," Coach said. "It's over. It's over for this."

Frank rolled onto his face and screamed. He pounded the floor like a drum and sang: Mother, Father, way, ya, hi, yo, good-bye, good-bye. Mother, Father, way, ya, hi, yo, good-bye, good-bye. Mother, Father, way, ya, hi, yo, good-bye, good-bye. Mother, Father, way, ya, hi, yo, good-bye, good-bye. Mother, Father, way, ya, hi, yo, good-bye, good-bye.

Coach and the players stared at Frank. What could they say?

"Hey, old man," the point guard said. "That was a good run."

Yes, it was, Frank thought, and he wondered what he was going to do next. He wondered if this pain would ever subside. He wondered if he'd ever step onto a basketball court again.

"I'm going to call an ambulance," Coach said. "Get him in the training room."

As Coach ran toward his office, the point guard and the big guy picked up Frank and carried him across the gym.

"You're going to be okay," the point guard said. "You hear me, old man? You're going to be fine."

"I know it," Frank said. "I know."

THE LONE RANGER
AND TONTO FISTFIGHT
IN HEAVEN

Too hot to sleep so I walked down to the Third Avenue 7-Eleven for a Creamsicle and the company of a graveyard-shift cashier. I know that game. I worked graveyard for a Seattle 7-Eleven and got robbed once too often. The last time the bastard locked me in the cooler. He even took my money and basketball shoes.

The graveyard-shift worker in the Third Avenue 7-Eleven looked like they all do. Acne scars and a bad haircut, work pants that showed off his white socks, and those cheap black shoes that have no support. My arches still ache from my year at the Seattle 7-Eleven.

"Hello," he asked when I walked into his store. "How you doing?"

I gave him a half-wave as I headed back to the freezer. He looked me over so he could describe me to the police later. I knew the look. One of my old girlfriends said I started to look at her that way, too. She left me not long after that. No, I left her and don't blame her for anything. That's how it happened. When one person starts to look at another like a criminal, then the love is over. It's logical.

"I don't trust you," she said to me. "You get too angry."

She was white and I lived with her in Seattle. Some nights we fought so bad that I would just get in my car and drive all night, only stop to fill up on gas. In fact, I worked the graveyard shift to spend as much time away from her as possible. But I learned all about Seattle that way, driving its back ways and dirty alleys.

Sometimes, though, I would forget where I was and get lost. I'd drive for hours, searching for something familiar. Seems like I'd spent my whole life that way, looking for anything I recognized. Once, I ended up in a nice residential neighborhood and somebody must have been worried because the police showed up and pulled me over.

"What are you doing out here?" the police officer asked me as he looked over my license and registration.

"I'm lost."

"Well, where are you supposed to be?" he asked me, and I knew there were plenty of places I wanted to be, but none where I was supposed to be.

"I got in a fight with my girlfriend," I said. "I was just driving around, blowing off steam, you know?"

"Well, you should be more careful where you drive," the officer said. "You're making people nervous. You don't fit the profile of the neighborhood."

I wanted to tell him that I didn't really fit the profile of the country but I knew it would just get me into trouble.

"Can I help you?" the 7-Eleven clerk asked me loudly, searching for some response that would reassure him that I wasn't an armed robber. He knew this dark skin and long, black hair of mine was dangerous. I had potential.

"Just getting a Creamsicle," I said after a long interval. It was a sick twist to pull on the guy, but it was late and I was bored. I grabbed my Creamsicle and walked back to the counter slowly, scanned the aisles for effect. I wanted to whistle low and menacingly but I never learned to whistle.

"Pretty hot out tonight?" he asked, that old rhetorical weather bullshit question designed to put us both at ease.

"Hot enough to make you go crazy," I said and smiled. He swallowed hard like a white man does in those situations. I looked him over. Same old green, red, and white 7-Eleven jacket and thick glasses. But he wasn't ugly, just misplaced and marked by loneliness. If he wasn't working there that night, he'd be at home alone, flipping through channels and wishing he could afford HBO or Showtime.

"Will this be all?" he asked me, in that company effort to make me do some impulse shopping. Like adding a clause onto a treaty. *We'll take Washington and Oregon and you get six pine trees and a brand-new Chrysler Cordoba.* I knew how to make and break promises.

"No," I said and paused. "Give me a Cherry Slushie, too."

"What size?" he asked, relieved.

"Large," I said, and he turned his back to me to make the drink. He realized his mistake but it was too late. He stiffened, ready for the gunshot or the blow behind the ear. When it didn't come, he turned back to me.

"I'm sorry," he said. "What size did you say."

"Small," I said and changed the story.

"But I thought you said large."

"If you knew I wanted a large, then why did you ask me again?" I asked him and laughed. He looked at me, couldn't decide if I was giving him serious shit or just goofing. There was something about him I liked, even if it was three in the morning and he was white.

"Hey," I said. "Forget the Slushie. What I want to know is if you know all the words to the theme from 'The Brady Bunch'?"

He looked at me, confused at first, then laughed.

"Shit," he said. "I was hoping you weren't crazy. You were scaring me."

"Well, I'm going to get crazy if you don't know the words."

He laughed loudly then, told me to take the Creamsicle for free. He was the graveyard-shift manager and those little demonstrations of power tickled him. All seventy-five cents of it. I knew how much everything cost.

"Thanks," I said to him and walked out the door. I took my time walking home, let the heat of the night melt the Creamsicle all over my hand. At three in the morning I could act just as young as I wanted to act. There was no one around to ask me to grow up.

163

*   *   *

In Seattle, I broke lamps. She and I would argue and I'd break a lamp, just pick it up and throw it down. At first she'd buy replacement lamps, expensive and beautiful. But after a while she'd buy lamps from Goodwill or garage sales. Then she just gave up the idea entirely and we'd argue in the dark.

"You're just like your brother," she'd yell. "Drunk all the time and stupid."

"My brother don't drink that much."

She and I never tried to hurt each other physically. I did love her, after all, and she loved me. But those arguments were just as damaging as a fist. Words can be like that, you know? Whenever I get into arguments now, I remember her and I also remember Muhammad Ali. He knew the power of his fists but, more importantly, he knew the power of his words, too. Even though he only had an IQ of 80 or so, Ali was a genius. And she was a genius, too. She knew exactly what to say to cause me the most pain.

But don't get me wrong. I walked through that relationship with an executioner's hood. Or more appropriately, with war paint and sharp arrows. She was a kindergarten teacher and I continually insulted her for that.

"Hey, schoolmarm," I asked. "Did your kids teach you anything new today?"

And I always had crazy dreams. I always have had them, but it seemed they became nightmares more often in Seattle.

In one dream, she was a missionary's wife and I was a minor war chief. We fell in love and tried to keep it secret. But the missionary caught us fucking in the barn and shot me. As I lay dying, my tribe learned of the shooting and attacked the whites all across the reservation. I died and my soul drifted above the reservation.

Disembodied, I could see everything that was happening. Whites killing Indians and Indians killing whites. At first it was small, just my tribe and the few whites who lived there. But my dream grew, intensified. Other tribes arrived on horseback to continue the slaughter of whites, and the United States Cavalry rode into battle.

The most vivid image of that dream stays with me. Three mounted soldiers played polo with a dead Indian woman's head. When I first dreamed it, I thought it was just a product of my anger and imagination. But since then, I've read similar accounts of that kind of evil in the old West. Even more terrifying, though, is the fact that those kinds of brutal things are happening today in places like El Salvador.

All I know for sure, though, is that I woke from that dream in terror, packed up all my possessions, and left Seattle in the middle of the night.

"I love you," she said as I left her. "And don't ever come back."

I drove through the night, over the Cascades, down into the plains of central Washington, and back home to the Spokane Indian Reservation.

When I finished the Creamsicle that the 7-Eleven clerk gave me, I held the wooden stick up into the air and shouted out very loudly. A couple lights flashed on in windows and a police car cruised by me a few minutes later. I waved to the men in blue and they waved back accidentally. When I got home it was still too hot to sleep so I picked up a week-old newspaper from the floor and read.

There was another civil war, another terrorist bomb exploded, and one more plane crashed and all aboard were presumed dead. The crime rate was rising in every city with populations larger than 100,000, and a farmer in Iowa shot his banker after foreclosure on his 1,000 acres.

A kid from Spokane won the local spelling bee by spelling the word *rhinoceros*.

When I got back to the reservation, my family wasn't surprised to see me. They'd been expecting me back since the day I left for Seattle. There's an old Indian poet who said that Indians can reside in the city, but they can never live there. That's as close to truth as any of us can get.

Mostly I watched television. For weeks I flipped through channels, searched for answers in the game shows and soap operas. My mother would circle the want ads in red and hand the paper to me.

"What are you going to do with the rest of your life?" she asked.

"Don't know," I said, and normally, for almost any other Indian in the country, that would have been a perfectly fine answer. But I was special, a former college student, a smart kid. I was one of those Indians who was supposed to make it, to rise above the rest of the reservation like a fucking eagle or something. I was the new kind of warrior.

For a few months I didn't even look at the want ads my mother circled, just left the newspaper where she had set it down.

After a while, though, I got tired of television and started to play basketball again. I'd been a good player in high school, nearly great, and almost played at the college I attended for a couple years. But I'd been too out of shape from drinking and sadness to ever be good again. Still, I liked the way the ball felt in my hands and the way my feet felt inside my shoes.

At first I just shot baskets by myself. It was selfish, and I also wanted to learn the game again before I played against anybody else. Since I had been good before and embarrassed fellow tribal members, I know they would want to take revenge on me. Forget about the cowboys versus Indians business. The most intense com-petition on any reservation is Indians versus Indians.

But on the night I was ready to play for real, there was this white guy at the gym, playing with all the Indians.

"Who is that?" I asked Jimmy Seyler.

"He's the new BIA chief's kid."

"Can he play?"

"Oh, yeah."

And he could play. He played Indian ball, fast and loose, better than all the Indians there.

"How long's he been playing here?" I asked.

"Long enough."

I stretched my muscles, and everybody watched me. All these Indians watched one of their old and dusty heroes. Even though I had played most of my ball at the white high school I went to, I was still all Indian, you know? I was Indian when it counted, and this BIA kid needed to be beaten by an Indian, any Indian.

I jumped into the game and played well for a little while. It felt good. I hit a few shots, grabbed a rebound or two, played enough defense to keep the other team honest. Then that white kid took over the game. He was too good. Later, he'd play college ball back East and would nearly make the Knicks team a couple years on. But we didn't know any of that would happen. We just knew he was better that day and every other day.

The next morning I woke up tired and hungry, so I grabbed the want ads, found a job I wanted, and drove to Spokane to get it. I've been working at the high school exchange program ever since, typing and answering phones. Sometimes I wonder if the people on the other end of the line know that I'm Indian and if their voices would change if they did know.

One day I picked up the phone and it was her, calling from Seattle.

"I got your number from your mom," she said. "I'm glad you're working."

"Yeah, nothing like a regular paycheck."

"Are you drinking?"

"No, I've been on the wagon for almost a year."

"Good."

The connection was good. I could hear her breathing in the spaces between our words. How do you talk to the real person whose ghost has haunted you? How do you tell the difference between the two?

"Listen," I said. "I'm sorry for everything."

"Me, too."

"What's going to happen to us?" I asked her and wished I had the answer for myself.

"I don't know," she said. "I want to change the world."

* * *

These days, living alone in Spokane, I wish I lived closer to the river, to the falls where ghosts of salmon jump. I wish I could sleep. I put down my paper or book and turn off all the lights, lie quietly in the dark. It may take hours, even years, for me to sleep again. There's nothing surprising or disappointing in that.

I know how all my dreams end anyway.

THE APPROXIMATE SIZE
OF MY FAVORITE TUMOR

A fter the argument that I had lost but pretended to
win, I stormed out of the HUD house, jumped into
the car, and prepared to drive off in victory, which was also known
as defeat. But I realized that I hadn't grabbed my keys. At that
kind of moment, a person begins to realize how he can be fooled
by his own games. And at that kind of moment, a person begins
to formulate a new game to compensate for the failure of the first.

"Honey, I'm home," I yelled as I walked back into the house.

My wife ignored me, gave me a momentary stoic look that
impressed me with its resemblance to generations of television
Indians.

"Oh, what is that?" I asked. "Your Tonto face?"

She flipped me off, shook her head, and disappeared into the bedroom.

"Honey," I called after her. "Didn't you miss me? I've been gone so long and it's good to be back home. Where I belong."

I could hear dresser drawers open and close.

"And look at the kids," I said as I patted the heads of imagined children. "They've grown so much. And they have your eyes."

She walked out of the bedroom in her favorite ribbon shirt, hair wrapped in her best ties, and wearing a pair of come-here boots. You know, the kind with the curled toe that looks like a finger gesturing *Come here, cowboy, come on over here.* But those boots weren't meant for me: I'm an Indian.

"Honey," I asked. "I just get back from the war and you're leaving already? No kiss for the returning hero?"

She pretended to ignore me, which I enjoyed. But then she pulled out her car keys, checked herself in the mirror, and headed for the door. I jumped in front of her, knowing she meant to begin her own war. That scared the shit out of me.

"Hey," I said. "I was just kidding, honey. I'm sorry. I didn't mean anything. I'll do whatever you want me to."

She pushed me aside, adjusted her dreams, pulled on her braids for a jumpstart, and walked out the door. I followed her and stood on the porch as she jumped into the car and started it up.

"I'm going dancing," she said and drove off into the sunset, or at least she drove down the tribal highway toward the Powwow Tavern.

"But what am I going to feed the kids?" I asked and walked back into the house to feed myself and my illusions.

After a dinner of macaroni and commodity cheese, I put on my best shirt, a new pair of blue jeans, and set out to hitchhike down the tribal highway. The sun had gone down already so I decided that I was riding off toward the great unknown, which was actually the same Powwow Tavern where my love had escaped to an hour earlier.

As I stood on the highway with my big, brown, and beautiful thumb showing me the way, Simon pulled up in his pickup, stopped, opened the passenger door, and whooped.

"Shit," he yelled. "If it ain't little Jimmy One-Horse! Where you going, cousin, and how fast do you need to get there?"

I hesitated at the offer of a ride. Simon was world famous, at least famous on the Spokane Indian Reservation, for driving backward. He always obeyed posted speed limits, traffic signals and signs, even minute suggestions. But he drove in reverse, using the rearview mirror as his guide. But what could I do? I trusted the man, and when you trust a man you also have to trust his horse.

"I'm headed for the Powwow Tavern," I said and climbed into Simon's rig. "And I need to be there before my wife finds herself a dance partner."

"Shit," Simon said. "Why didn't you say something sooner? We'll be there before she hears the first note of the first goddamned song."

Simon jammed the car into his only gear, reverse, and roared down the highway. I wanted to hang my head out the window like a dog, let my braids flap like a tongue in the wind, but good manners prevented me from taking the liberty. Still, it was so tempting. Always was.

"So, little Jimmy Sixteen-and-One-Half-Horses," Simon asked me after a bit. "What did you do to make your wife take off this time?"

"Well," I said. "I told her the truth, Simon. I told her I got cancer everywhere inside me."

Simon slammed on the brakes and brought the pickup sliding to a quick but decidedly cinematic stop.

"That ain't nothing to joke about," he yelled.

"Ain't joking about the cancer," I said. "But I started joking about dying and that pissed her off."

"What'd you say?"

"Well, I told her the doctor showed me my X-rays and my favorite tumor was just about the size of a baseball, shaped like one, too. Even had stitch marks."

"You're full of shit."

"No, really. I told her to call me Babe Ruth. Or Roger Maris. Maybe even Hank Aaron 'cause there must have been about 755 damn tumors inside me. Then, I told her I was going to Cooperstown and sit right down in the lobby of the Hall of Fame. Make myself a new exhibit, you know? Pin my X-rays to my chest and point out the tumors. What a dedicated baseball fan! What a sacrifice for the national pastime!"

"You're an asshole, little Jimmy Zero-Horses."

"I know, I know," I said as Simon got the pickup rolling again, down the highway toward an uncertain future, which was, as usual, simply called the Powwow Tavern.

We rode the rest of the way in silence. That is to say that neither of us had anything at all to say. But I could hear Simon breathing and I'm sure he could hear me, too. And once, he coughed.

"There you go, cousin," he said finally as he stopped his pickup in front of the Powwow Tavern. "I hope it all works out, you know?"

I shook his hand, offered him a few exaggerated gifts, made a couple promises that he knew were just promises, and waved wildly as he drove off, backwards, and away from the rest of my life. Then I walked into the tavern, shook my body like a dog shaking off water. I've always wanted to walk into a bar that way.

"Where the hell is Suzy Boyd?" I asked.

"Right here, asshole," Suzy answered quickly and succinctly.

"Okay, Suzy," I asked. "Where the hell is my wife?"

"Right here, asshole," my wife answered quickly and succinctly. Then she paused a second before she added, "And quit calling me *your wife*. It makes me sound like I'm a fucking bowling ball or something."

"Okay, okay, Norma," I said and sat down beside her. I ordered a Diet Pepsi for me and a pitcher of beer for the next table. There was no one sitting at the next table. It was just something I always did. Someone would come along and drink it.

"Norma," I said. "I'm sorry. I'm sorry I have cancer and I'm sorry I'm dying."

She took a long drink of her Diet Pepsi, stared at me for a long time. Stared hard.

"Are you going to make any more jokes about it?" she asked.

"Just one or two more, maybe," I said and smiled. It was exactly the wrong thing to say. Norma slapped me in anger, had a look of concern for a moment as she wondered what a slap could do to a person with terminal cancer, and then looked angry again.

"If you say anything funny ever again, I'm going to leave you," Norma said. "And I'm fucking serious about that."

I lost my smile briefly, reached across the table to hold her hand, and said something incredibly funny. It was maybe the best one-liner I had ever uttered. Maybe the moment that would have made me a star anywhere else. But in the Powwow Tavern, which was just a front for reality, Norma heard what I had to say, stood up, and left me.

Because Norma left me, it's even more important to know how she arrived in my life.

I was sitting in the Powwow Tavern on a Saturday night with my Diet Pepsi and my second-favorite cousin, Raymond.

"Look it, look it," he said as Norma walked into the tavern. Norma was over six feet tall. Well, maybe not six feet tall but she was taller than me, taller than everyone in the bar except the basketball players.

"What tribe you think she is?" Raymond asked me.

"Amazon," I said.

"Their reservation down by Santa Fe, enit?" Raymond asked, and I laughed so hard that Norma came over to find out about the commotion.

"Hello, little brothers," she said. "Somebody want to buy me a drink?"

"What you having?" I asked.

"Diet Pepsi," she said and I knew we would fall in love.

"Listen," I told her. "If I stole 1,000 horses, I'd give you 501 of them."

"And what other women would get the other 499?" she asked.

And we laughed. Then we laughed harder when Raymond leaned in closer to the table and said, "I don't get it."

Later, after the tavern closed, Norma and I sat outside on my car and shared a cigarette. I should say that we pretended to share a cigarette since neither of us smoked. But we both thought the other did and wanted to have all that much more in common.

After an hour or two of coughing, talking stories, and laughter, we ended up at my HUD house, watching late-night television. Raymond was passed out in the backseat of my car.

"Hey," she said. "That cousin of yours ain't too smart."

"Yeah," I said. "But he's cool, you know?"

"Must be. Because you're so good to him."

"He's my cousin, you know? That's how it is."

She kissed me then. Soft at first. Then harder. Our teeth clicked together like it was a junior high kiss. Still, we sat on the couch and kissed until the television signed off and broke into white noise. It was the end of another broadcast day.

"Listen," I said then. "I should take you home."

"Home?" she asked. "I thought I was at home."

"Well, my tipi is your tipi," I said, and she lived there until the day I told her that I had terminal cancer.

I have to mention the wedding, though. It was at the Spokane Tribal Longhouse and all my cousins and her cousins were there. Nearly two hundred people. Everything went smoothly until my second-favorite cousin, Raymond, drunk as a skunk, stood up in the middle of the ceremony, obviously confused.

"I remember Jimmy real good," Raymond said and started into his eulogy for me as I stood not two feet from him. "Jimmy was always quick with a joke. Make you laugh all the damn time.

I remember once at my grandmother's wake, he was standing by the coffin. Now, you got to remember he was only seven or eight years old. Anyway, he starts jumping up and down, yelling, *She moved, she moved.*"

Everyone at the wedding laughed because it was pretty much the same crowd that was at the funeral. Raymond smiled at his newly discovered public speaking ability and continued.

"Jimmy was always the one to make people feel better, too," he said. "I remember once when he and I were drinking at the Powwow Tavern when all of a sudden Lester FallsApart comes running in and says that ten Indians just got killed in a car wreck on Ford Canyon Road. *Ten Skins?* I asked Lester, and he said, *Yeah, ten.* And then Jimmy starts up singing, *One little, two little, three little Indians, four little, five little, six little Indians, seven little, eight little, nine little Indians, ten little Indian boys.*"

Everyone in the wedding laughed some more, but also looked a little tense after that story, so I grabbed Raymond and led him back to his seat. He stared incredulously at me, tried to reconcile his recent eulogy with my sudden appearance. He just sat there until the preacher asked that most rhetorical of questions:

"And if there is anyone here who has objections to this union, speak now or forever hold your peace."

Raymond staggered and stumbled to his feet, then staggered and stumbled up to the preacher.

"Reverend," Raymond said. "I hate to interrupt, but my cousin is dead, you know? I think that might be a problem."

Raymond passed out at that moment, and Norma and I were married with his body draped unceremoniously over our feet.

* * *

Three months after Norma left me, I lay in my hospital bed in Spokane, just back from another stupid and useless radiation treatment.

"Jesus," I said to my attending physician. "A few more zaps and I'll be Superman."

"Really?" the doctor said. "I never realized that Clark Kent was a Spokane Indian."

And we laughed, you know, because sometimes that's all two people have in common.

"So," I asked her. "What's my latest prognosis?"

"Well," she said. "It comes down to this. You're dying."

"Not again," I said.

"Yup, Jimmy, you're still dying."

And we laughed, you know, because sometimes you'd rather cry.

"Well," the doctor said. "I've got other patients to see."

As she walked out, I wanted to call her back and make an urgent confession, to ask forgiveness, to offer truth in return for salvation. But she was only a doctor. A good doctor, but still just a doctor.

"Hey, Dr. Adams," I said.

"What?"

"Nothing," I said. "Just wanted to hear your name. It sounds like drums to these heavily medicated Indian ears of mine."

And she laughed and I laughed, too. That's what happened.

Norma was the world champion fry bread maker. Her fry bread was perfect, like one of those dreams you wake up from and say, *I didn't want to wake up.*

178

"I think this is your best fry bread ever," I told Norma one day. In fact, it was January 22.

"Thank you," she said. "Now you get to wash the dishes."

So I was washing the dishes when the phone rang. Norma answered it and I could hear her half of the conversation.

"Hello."

"Yes, this is Norma Many Horses."

"No."

"No!"

"*No!*" Norma yelled as she threw the phone down and ran outside. I picked the receiver up carefully, afraid of what it might say to me.

"Hello," I said.

"Who am I speaking to?" the voice on the other end asked.

"Jimmy Many Horses. I'm Norma's husband."

"Oh, Mr. Many Horses. I hate to be the bearer of bad news, but, uh, as I just told your wife, your mother-in-law, uh, passed away this morning."

"Thank you," I said, hung up the phone, and saw that Norma had returned.

"Oh, Jimmy," she said, talking through tears.

"I can't believe I just said *thank you* to that guy," I said. "What does that mean? Thank you that my mother-in-law is dead? Thank you that you told me that my mother-in-law is dead? Thank you that you told me that my mother-in-law is dead and made my wife cry?"

"Jimmy," Norma said. "Stop. It's not funny."

But I didn't stop. Then or now.

*   *   *

Still, you have to realize that laughter saved Norma and me from pain, too. Humor was an antiseptic that cleaned the deepest of personal wounds.

Once, a Washington State patrolman stopped Norma and me as we drove to Spokane to see a movie, get some dinner, a Big Gulp at 7-Eleven.

"Excuse me, officer," I asked. "What did I do wrong?"

"You failed to make proper signal for a turn a few blocks back," he said.

That was interesting because I had been driving down a straight highway for over five miles. The only turns possible were down dirt roads toward houses where no one I ever knew had lived. But I knew to play along with this game. All you can hope for in these little wars is to minimize the amount of damage.

"I'm sorry about that, officer," I said. "But you know how it is. I was listening to the radio, tapping my foot. It's those drums, you know?"

"Whatever," the trooper said. "Now, I need your driver's license, registration, and proof of insurance."

I handed him the stuff and he barely looked at it. He leaned down into the window of the car.

"Hey, chief," he asked. "Have you been drinking?"

"I don't drink," I said.

"How about your woman there?"

"Ask her yourself," I said.

The trooper looked at me, blinked a few seconds, paused for dramatic effect, and said, "Don't you even think about telling me what I should do."

"I don't drink, either," Norma said quickly, hoping to avoid any further confrontation. "And I wasn't driving anyway."

"That don't make any difference," the trooper said. "Washington State has a new law against riding as an inebriated passenger in an Indian car."

"Officer," I said. "That ain't new. We've known about that one for a couple hundred years."

The trooper smiled a little, but it was a hard smile. You know the kind.

"However," he said. "I think we can make some kind of arrangement so none of this has to go on your record."

"How much is it going to cost me?" I asked.

"How much do you have?"

"About a hundred bucks."

"Well," the trooper said. "I don't want to leave you with nothing. Let's say the fine is ninety-nine dollars."

I gave him all the money, though, four twenties, a ten, eight dollar bills, and two hundred pennies in a sandwich bag.

"Hey," I said. "Take it all. That extra dollar is a tip, you know? Your service has been excellent."

Norma wanted to laugh then. She covered her mouth and pretended to cough. His face turned red. I mean redder than it already was.

"In fact," I said as I looked at the trooper's badge. "I might just send a letter to your commanding officer. I'll just write that Washington State Patrolman D. Nolan, badge number 13746, was polite, courteous, and above all, legal as an eagle."

Norma laughed out loud now.

"Listen," the trooper said. "I can just take you both in right now. For reckless driving, resisting arrest, threatening an officer with phyiscal violence."

"If you do," Norma said and jumped into the fun, "I'll just tell everyone how respectful you were of our Native traditions, how much you understood about the social conditions that lead to the criminal acts of so many Indians. I'll say you were sympathetic, concerned, and intelligent."

"Fucking Indians," the trooper said as he threw the sandwich bag of pennies back into our car, sending them flying all over the interior. "And keep your damn change."

We watched him walk back to his cruiser, climb in, and drive off, breaking four or five laws as he flipped a U-turn, left rubber, crossed the center line, broke the speed limit, and ran through a stop sign without lights and siren.

We laughed as we picked up the scattered pennies from the floor of the car. It was a good thing that the trooper threw that change back at us because we found just enough gas money to get us home.

After Norma left me, I'd occasionally get postcards from powwows all over the country. She missed me in Washington, Oregon, Idaho, Montana, Nevada, Utah, New Mexico, and California. I just stayed on the Spokane Indian Reservation and missed her from the doorway of my HUD house, from the living room window, waiting for the day that she would come back.

But that's how Norma operated. She told me once that she would leave me whenever the love started to go bad.

"I ain't going to watch the whole thing collapse," she said. "I'll get out when the getting is good."

"You wouldn't even try to save us?" I asked.

"It wouldn't be worth saving at that point."

"That's pretty cold."

"That's not cold," she said. "It's practical."

But don't get me wrong, either. Norma was a warrior in every sense of the word. She would drive a hundred miles round-trip to visit tribal elders in the nursing homes in Spokane. When one of those elders died, Norma would weep violently, throw books and furniture.

"Every one of our elders who dies takes a piece of our past away," she said. "And that hurts more because I don't know how much of a future we have."

And once, when we drove up on a really horrible car wreck, she held a dying man's head in her lap and sang to him until he passed away. He was a white guy, too. Remember that. She kept that memory so close to her that she had nightmares for a year.

"I always dream that it's you who's dying," she told me and didn't let me drive the car for almost a year.

Norma, she was always afraid; she wasn't afraid.

One thing that I noticed in the hospital as I coughed myself up and down the bed: A clock, at least one of those old-style clocks with hands and a face, looks just like somebody laughing if you stare at it long enough.

The hospital released me because they decided that I would be much more comfortable at home. And there I was, at home, writing letters to my loved ones on special reservation stationery that read: FROM THE DEATHBED OF JAMES MANY HORSES, III.

But in reality, I sat at my kitchen table to write, and DEATH TABLE just doesn't have the necessary music. I'm also the only

James Many Horses, but there is a certain dignity to any kind of artificial tradition.

Anyway, I sat there at the death table, writing letters from my deathbed, when there was a knock on the door.

"Come in," I yelled, knowing the door was locked, and smiled when it rattled against the frame.

"It's locked," a female voice said and it was a female voice I recognized.

"Norma?" I asked as I unlocked and opened the door.

She was beautiful. She had either gained or lost twenty pounds, one braid hung down a little longer than the other, and she had ironed her shirt until the creases were sharp.

"Honey," she said. "I'm home."

I was silent. That was a rare event.

"Honey," she said. "I've been gone so long and I missed you so much. But now I'm back. Where I belong."

I had to smile.

"Where are the kids?" she asked.

"They're asleep," I said, recovered just in time to continue the joke. "Poor little guys tried to stay awake, you know? They wanted to be up when you got home. But, one by one, they dropped off, fell asleep, and I had to carry them off into their little beds."

"Well," Norma said. "I'll just go in and kiss them quietly. Tell them how much I love them. Fix the sheets and blankets so they'll be warm all night."

She smiled.

"Jimmy," she said. "You look like shit."

"Yeah, I know."

"I'm sorry I left."

"Where've you been?" I asked, though I didn't really want to know.

"In Arlee. Lived with a Flathead cousin of mine."

"Cousin as in cousin? Or cousin as in I-was-fucking-him-but-don't-want-to-tell-you-because-you're-dying?"

She smiled even though she didn't want to.

"Well," she said. "I guess you'd call him more of that second kind of cousin."

Believe me: nothing ever hurt more. Not even my tumors which are the approximate size of baseballs.

"Why'd you come back?" I asked her.

She looked at me, tried to suppress a giggle, then broke out into full-fledged laugher. I joined her.

"Well," I asked her again after a while. "Why'd you come back?"

She turned stoic, gave me that beautiful Tonto face, and said, "Because he was so fucking serious about everything."

We laughed a little more and then I asked her one more time, "Really, why'd you come back?"

"Because someone needs to help you die the right way," she said. "And we both know that dying ain't something you ever done before."

I had to agree with that.

"And maybe," she said, "because making fry bread and helping people die are the last two things Indians are good at."

"Well," I said. "At least you're good at one of them."

And we laughed.

INDIAN COUNTRY

Low Man Smith stepped off the airplane in Missoula, Montana, walked up the humid jetway, and entered the air-conditioned terminal. He was excited that he was about to see her, Carlotta, the Navajo woman who lived on the Flathead Indian Reservation. All during the flight from Seattle, he'd been wondering what he would first say to her, this poet who taught English at the Flathead Indian College, and had carried on a fierce and exhausting internal debate on the matter. He'd finally decided, just as the plane touched down, to begin his new life with a simple declaration: "Thank you for inviting me."

He practiced those five words in his head—*thank you for inviting me*—and chastised himself for not learning to say them in her language, in Navajo, in Dine.

He was a Coeur d'Alene Indian, even though his mother was white. He'd been born and raised in Seattle, didn't speak his own tribal language, and had visited his home reservation only six times in his life. His mother had often tried to push Low Man toward the reservation, toward his cousins, aunts, and uncles—all of those who had survived one war or another—but Low Man just wasn't interested, especially after his Coeur d'Alene father died of a heart attack while welding together one of the last great ships in Elliott Bay. More accurately, Low Man's father had drowned after his heart attack had knocked him unconscious and then off the boat into the water.

Low Man believed the Coeur d'Alene Reservation to be a monotonous place—a wet kind of monotony that white tourists saw as spiritual and magic. Tourists snapped off dozens of photographs and tried to capture it—the wet, spiritual monotony—before they climbed back into their rental cars and drove away to the next reservation on their itineraries.

The tourists didn't know, and never would have guessed, that the reservation's monotony might last for months, sometimes years, before one man would eventually pull a pistol from a secret place and shoot another man in the face, or before a group of women would drag another woman out of her house and beat her left eye clean out of her skull. After that first act of violence, rival families would issue calls for revenge and organize the retaliatory beatings. Afterward, three or four people would wash the blood from their hands and hide in the hills, causing white men to write editorials, all of this news immediately followed by capture, trial, verdict, and bus ride to prison. And then, only then, would the long silence, the monotony, resume.

Walking through the Missoula airport, Low Man wondered if the Flathead Reservation was a dangerous place, if it was a small country where the king established a new set of laws with every sunrise.

Carrying a suitcase and computer bag, Low Man searched for Carlotta's face, her round, purple-dark face, in the crowd of people—most of them white men in cowboy hats—who waited at the gate. Instead, he saw an old Indian man holding a hardcover novel above his head.

"I wrote that book," Low Man said proudly to the old man, who stood with most of his weight balanced on his left hip.

"You're him, then," said the old man. "The mystery writer."

"I am, then," said Low Man.

"I'm Carlotta's boss, Raymond. She sent me."

"It's good to meet you, Ray. Where is she?"

"My name is Raymond. And she's gone."

"Gone?"

"Yeah, gone."

Low Man wondered if *gone* carried a whole different meaning in the state of Montana. Perhaps, under the Big Sky, being *gone* meant that you were having lunch, or that your car had run out of gas, or that you'd broken your leg in a fly-fishing accident and were stranded in a hospital bed, doped up on painkillers, eagerly awaiting the arrival of the man you loved more than anything else in the world.

"Where, exactly, is gone?" asked Low Man.

The old man's left eye was cloudy with glaucoma. Low Man wondered about the quality of Raymond's depth perception.

"She got married yesterday," said the old man. "She and Chuck woke up before sunrise and drove for Flagstaff."

"Flagstaff?" asked Low Man, desperately trying to remember when he had last talked to Carlotta. When? Three days ago, for just a minute, to confirm the details of his imminent arrival.

"Arizona?" Low Man asked.

"Yeah, that's where she and Chuck grew up."

"Who is Chuck?"

"That's her husband," said Raymond.

"Obviously."

Low Man needed a drink. He'd been sober for ten years, but he still needed a drink. Not of alcohol, no, but of something. He never worried about falling off the wagon, not anymore. He had spent many nights in hotel rooms where the mini-bars were filled with booze, but had given in only to the temptations of the three-dollar candy bars.

"Ray," said Low Man. "Can we, please, just put a hold on this conversation while I go find me a pop?"

"Carlotta's been sober for six years," said the old man.

"Yes, I know. That's one of the reasons I came here."

"She told me you drank a lot of soda pop. Said it was your substitute addiction."

Shaking his head, Low Man found a snack bar, ordered a large soda, finished it with three swallows, and then ordered another.

When he was working on a book, when he was writing, Low Man would drink a six-pack of soda every hour or so, and then, hopped up on the caffeine, he'd pound the keyboard, chapter after chapter, until carpal tunnel syndrome fossilized the bones in his wrists. There it was, the central dilemma of his warrior life: repetitive stress. In his day, Crazy Horse had to worry about Custer and the patriotic sociopaths of the Seventh Cavalry.

"Okay," said Low Man. "Now, tell me, please, Raymond, how long has Carlotta been planning on getting married?"

"Oh, jeez," said Raymond. "She wasn't planning it at all. But Chuck showed up a couple days back, they were honeyhearts way back when, and just swept her off her feet. He's been sober for eleven years."

"One more than me."

"Oh, yeah, but I don't think that was the reason she married him."

"No, I imagine not."

"Well, I better get going. I got to pick up my grandchildren from school."

"Ray?"

"It's Raymond."

Low Man wondered what had happened to the Indian men who loved their nicknames, who earned their nicknames? His father had run around with indigenous legends named Bug, Mouse, Stubby, and Stink-Head.

"You're an elder, right?" Low Man asked Raymond.

"Elder than some, not as elder as others."

"Elders know things, right?"

"I know one or two things."

"Then perhaps, just perhaps, you could tell me what, what, what *thing* I'm supposed to do now?"

Raymond scratched his head and pursed his lips.

"Maybe," said the elder. "You could sign my book for me?"

Distracted, Low Man signed the book, but with his true signature and not with the stylized flourish he'd practiced for years. He signed it: *Peace.*

"You're a pretty good writer," Raymond said. "You should keep doing it."

"I'll try," said Low Man as he watched the old Indian shuffle away.

Low Man began to laugh, softly at first, but then with a full-throated roar that echoed off the walls. He laughed until tears ran down his face, until his stomach cramped, until he retched and threw up in a water fountain. He could not stop laughing, not even after three security officers arrived to escort him out of the airport, and not even after he'd walked three miles into town and found himself standing in a phone booth outside a 7-Eleven.

"Shit," he said and suddenly grew serious. "Who am I supposed to call?"

Then he laughed a little more and wondered how he was going to tell this story in the future. He'd change the names of those involved, of course, and invent new personalities and characters—and brand-new desires as well—and then he would be forced to invert and subvert the chronology of events, and the tone of the story would certainly be tailored to fit the audience. Whites and Indians laughed at most of the same jokes, but they laughed for different reasons. Maybe Low Man would turn himself into a blue-collar Indian, a welder who'd quit a good job, who'd quit a loyal wife, to fly to Missoula in pursuit of a crazy white woman.

And because he was a mystery writer, Low Man would have to throw a dead body into the mix.

Whose body? Which weapon?

Pistol, knife, poison, Low Man thought, as he stood in the phone booth outside the Missoula 7-Eleven.

"Chuck?" he asked the telephone. "Who the fuck is Chuck?"

The telephone didn't answer.

Low Man's last book, *Red Rain,* had shipped 125,000 copies in hardcover, good enough to flirt with the *New York Times* best-seller list, before falling into the Kingdom of Remainders. He belonged to seven frequent-flier clubs, diligently tossed money into his SEP-IRA, and tried to ignore the ulcer just beginning to open a hole in his stomach.

"Okay," said Low Man as he stood in the telephone booth. "Crazy Horse didn't need Tums. Okay? Think."

He took a deep breath. He wondered if the world was a cruel place. He checked the contents of his wallet. He carried two hundred dollars in cash, three credit cards, and a valid driver's license, all the ingredients necessary for renting a car and driving back to Seattle.

He doubted they were going to let him back into the airport, a thought that made him break into more uncontrolled laughter.

Jesus, he'd always wanted to be the kind of Indian who *didn't* get kicked out of public places. He played golf, for God's sake, with a single-digit handicap.

Opening the phone book, Low Man looked for the local bookstores. He figured a small town like Missoula might have a Waldenbooks or a B. Dalton's, but he needed something more intimate and eccentric, even sacred. Low Man prayed for a used bookstore, a good one, a musty church filled with bibles written by thousands of disciples. There, in that kind of place, he knew that he could buy somebody's novel or book of poems, then sit down in a comfortable chair to read, and maybe drink a cup of good coffee or a tall glass of the local water.

He found the listing for a bookstore called Bread and Books. Beautiful. He tore the page out of the directory and walked into the 7-Eleven.

"Hey," said Low Man as he slapped the yellow page on the counter. "Where is this place?"

The cashier, a skinny white kid, smiled.

"You tore that out of the phone book, didn't you?"asked the kid.

"Yes, I did," said Low Man.

"You're going to have to pay for that."

Low Man knew the telephone directory was free because merchants paid to advertise in the damn things.

"Fine," said Low Man and set his suitcase on the counter. "I'll trade you this yellow page for everything inside this suitcase. Hell, you can have the suitcase, too, if you tell me where to find this place."

"Breads?"

A good sign. It was a place popular enough to have a diminutive.

"Yeah, do you read?" asked Low Man.

"Of course."

"What do you read?"

"Comic books."

"What kind of comics?"

"Not comics," said the kid. "Comic books."

"Okay," said Low Man. "What kind of comic books?"

"Good ones. *Daredevil, Preacher, Love and Rockets, Astro City.*"

"Do you read mysteries?"

"You mean, like, murder mysteries?"

"That's exactly what I mean."

"No, not really."

"Well, I got a mystery for you anyway," said Low Man as he pushed the suitcase a few inches across the counter, closer to the cashier.

"This is a suitcase," said Low Man.

"I know it's a suitcase."

"I just want you to know," said Low Man as he patted the suitcase, as he tapped a slight rhythm against the lock. "I just need you to understand, understand this, understand that there are only two kinds of suitcase."

"Really?" asked the cashier. He was making only six bucks an hour, not enough to be speaking metaphysically with a total stranger, and an Indian stranger at that.

"There is the empty suitcase," said Low Man. "And there is the full suitcase. And what I have here is a full suitcase. And I want to give it to you."

"Mister," said the kid. "You don't have to give me your suitcase. I'll tell you where Breads is. Hell, Missoula is a small town. You could find it by accident."

"But the thing is, I need you to take me there."

"I'm working."

"I know you're working," said Low Man. "But I figure that car, that shit-bag Camaro out there is yours. So I figure you can close this place down for a few minutes and give me a ride. You give me a ride and I'll give you this suitcase and all of its contents."

There was a pistol, a revolver, sitting in a dark place beneath the cash register.

"I can't close," said the cashier. He believed in rules, in order. "This is 7-Eleven. We're supposed to be open, like, all the time. Look outside, the sign says twenty-four hours. I mean, I had to work last Christmas."

"Sweetheart," said Low Man. "I'm older than you, so I remember when 7-Eleven used to be open from seven in the morning until eleven at night. That's why they called it 7-Eleven. Get it? Open from seven to eleven? So, why don't you and I get nostalgic, and pretend it's 1973, and close the store long enough for you to drive me to the bookstore?"

"Mister," said the kid. "Even if this was 1973, and even if this store was only open from seven to eleven, it would still be three in the afternoon, like it is right now, and I would still not close down."

"Son, son, son," said Low Man, losing his patience. "What if I told you there was a dead body inside this suitcase?"

The cashier blinked, but remained calm. He had once shot a deer in the heart at two hundred yards, and bragged about it, though he'd been aiming for the head, the trophy hunter's greatest sin.

"That suitcase is too small. You couldn't fit a body in there," said the kid.

"Fair enough," said Low Man. "What if there's just a head?"

The cashier ran through the 7-Eleven employee's handbook in his memory, searching for the proper way to deal with a crazy customer, a man who may or may not have a dead man—or pieces of a dead man—in his suitcase, but who most definitely had a thing for bookstores. The cashier had always been a good employee; his work ethic was quite advanced for somebody so young. But there was no official company policy, no corporate ethic, when it came to dealing with a man—an Indian man—who had so much pain illuminating both of his eyes.

"Mister," said the cashier, forced to improvise. "This is Montana. Everybody's got a gun. Including me. And since you aren't from Montana, and I can tell that by looking at you, then you most likely don't have a gun."

"Your point being?"

"I'm going to shoot you in the ass if you don't exit the store immediately."

"Fine," said Low Man. "You can keep the damn bag anyway."

Leaving his suitcase behind, Low Man walked out of the store. He still carried his computer case and the yellow page with Bread and Books' address.

In the 7-Eleven, the cashier waited until the Indian was out of sight before he carefully opened the suitcase to find two pairs of shoes, a suit jacket, four shirts, two pairs of pants, and assorted socks and underwear. He also found a copy of *Red Rain* and discovered Low Man's photograph on the back of the book.

Away from that black-and-white image taken fifty pounds earlier, Low Man walked until he stumbled across the Barnes & Noble superstore filling up one corner of an ugly strip mall.

Fucking colonial clipper ships are everywhere, thought Low Man, *even in Missoula, Montana*. But he secretly loved the big green boats, mostly because they sold tons of his books.

Low Man stepped into the store, found the mystery section, gathered all the copies of his books, soft and hard, and carried them to the information desk.

"I want to sign these," he said to the woman working there.

"Why?"

"Because I wrote them."

"Oh," said the woman, immediately dropping into some highly trained and utterly pleasant demeanor. Perhaps everybody in Missoula, Montana, loved their jobs. "Please, let me get the manager. She'll be glad to help you."

"Hold on," said Low Man as he handed her the yellow page. "Do you know where this place is?"

"Breads?"

There it was again, the place with the nickname. Everybody must go there. At that moment, there could be dozens of people in Breads. Low Man wondered if there was a woman, a lovely woman in the bookstore, a lonely woman who would drag him back to her house and make love to him without removing any of her clothes.

"Is it a good store?" asked Low Man.

"I used to work there," she said. "It closed down a month ago."

Low Man wondered if her eyes changed color when she mourned.

"The kid at 7-Eleven didn't tell me that."

"Oh," said the woman, completely confused. She was young, just months out of some small Montana town like Wolf Point or Harlem or Ronan, soon to return. "Well, let me get the manager."

"Wait," said Low Man, handing her his computer case. "I found this over in the mystery section."

He'd purchased the computer case through a catalogue, and had regretted it ever since. The bag was bulky, heavy, poorly designed.

"Thank you. I'll put it in Lost and Found."

Low Man's computer was an outdated Apple, its hard drive stuffed to the brim with three unpublished mystery novels and hundreds of programs and applications that he'd never used after downloading them.

Free of his possessions, Low Man waited. He watched the men and women move through the bookstore.

He wondered what Missoula meant, if there'd been some cavalry soldier named Missoula who'd made this part of the world safe for white people. He wondered if he could kill somebody, an Indian or a white soldier, and what it would feel like. He wondered if he would cry when he had to wash blood from his hands.

He studied the faces of the white people in the store. He decided to choose the one that he would kill if he were forced to kill. Not the woman with the child, and certainly not the child, but maybe the man reading movie magazines, and, most likely, the old man asleep in the poetry-section chair.

Low Man stared at the gold band on the dead man's left hand. Low Man was still staring when the dead man woke up and walked out of the store.

Low Man had been married twice, to a Lummi woman and a Yakama woman, and had fathered three kids, one each with his ex-wives, the third the result of a one-night stand with a white woman in Santa Fe. He sent money and books to his Indian children, but he hadn't seen his white kid in ten years.

"Mr. Smith, Low Man Smith?" asked the Barnes & Noble manager upon her arrival in Low Man's world. She was blonde, blue-eyed, plain.

"Please," he said. "Call me Chuck."

"My name is Eryn."

Low Man wondered if he was going to sleep with her, this Eryn. He'd spent many nights in hotel rooms with various bookstore employees and literary groupies. That was one of the unpublicized perks of the job. He always wondered what the women saw in him, why they wanted to have sex with a stranger simply based on his ability to create compelling metaphors, or even when he failed to create compelling metaphors. The women were interested in him no matter what *The New York Times Book Review* had to say about his latest novel. Low Man was bored with his own writing, with his books, and to be honest, he'd grown bored with his literary life and the sexual promiscuity that seemed to go with it. Last year, after meeting Carlotta at the Native American Children of Alcoholics convention in Albuquerque, after sharing a bed with her for five nights, he'd vowed to remain faithful to her—and had been faithful to her and the idea of her—even though they'd made no promises to each other, even though she'd talked openly of the three men who were actively pursuing her, of the one man that she still loved, who had never been named Chuck.

"Mr. Smith, Chuck?" asked Eryn, the Barnes & Noble manager. "Are you okay?"

"Yes, sorry," said Low Man. "I'm very tired."

"I wish we'd known you were going to be in town," she said. "We would have ordered more copies of your books."

She smiled. Low Man decided that she was the kind of woman who lost sleep so that she could finish reading a good novel. He wondered if he was going to wake up before her the next morning and pass the time by scanning the titles of the books stacked on her nightstand.

"I didn't know I was going to be in Missoula," he said. "I was supposed to be spending a week up on the Flathead Reservation."

"Oh, I thought you might be here to see Tracy."

"Who?"

"Tracy," said the manager, and when that elicited no response from Low Man, she added, "Tracy Johnson. You went to college together, right?"

"She lives here?"

"Actually, she works here at the bookstore."

"Really?"

"Well, she's here part-time while she's getting her MFA at the university."

"She's a writer?"

"Yes. Didn't you know that?"

"I haven't seen Tracy in ten years," said Low Man.

He closed his eyes and when he opened them again two uniformed police officers were standing in front of him. One of the officers, the tall one with blue eyes, carried Low Man's suitcase.

"Mr. Smith," said the tall cop. "Are you Mr. Smith?"

"No, no," said Low Man. "You must be mistaken. My name is Crazy Horse."

Later, in the police station, Low Man paged through another telephone directory. He hoped that Tracy Johnson's number was listed.

He found her.

"This better be you," she said when she answered the phone, clearly expecting somebody else.

"Hi, Tracy, it's Low Man."

Low Man remembered, when it came to poetry, that a strategic pause was called a caesura.

"Bah," she said.

"No bah."

"Damn, Low, it's been forever. Are you still an Indian?"

"Yes, I am. Are you still a lesbian?"

They both remembered their secret language, their shared ceremonies.

"Definitely," she said. "In fact, I thought you were my partner. I'm supposed to pick her up after work. We've got a big date tonight."

"Well, you think maybe you could pick me up, too?"

"Are you in town?" she asked, her voice cracking with excitement. Low Man hoped it was excitement, though he feared it was something else. His chest ached with the memory of her. During college, when he was still drinking, he had once crawled through her apartment window and slept on her living room floor, though he'd made sure to wake up before dawn and leave before she'd ever known he was there. During the long walk home, he'd veered off the road into a shallow swamp, not because he was too drunk to properly navigate but because he wanted to do something self-flagellating and noble, or at least something that approximated nobility—a drunk twenty-year-old's idea of nobility. He'd wanted to be a drunk monk in love.

"Damn, Low," she said. "Why didn't you call me before? I would have gone out and bought a dress. I know how much you like me in dresses."

She remembered him so well. He liked that.

"I didn't know I was going to be here," he said. "And I didn't know you lived here."

"So, how'd you get my number?"

"Well, your manager at the bookstore told me you were getting an MFA."

"Eryn," she said. "I bet you were wondering if she was going to hop on you, right?"

Low Man couldn't answer.

"Damn, Low," she said, laughing loudly. Her laughter had always been too loud, impolite, and wonderful. "Eryn is a lesbian. You always fall for the lesbians."

Low Man had once kissed Tracy, though they each remembered it differently. She'd thought the kiss was a desperate attempt to change her mind about him in particular, and about men in general, but he believed that he'd kissed her only because he wanted to know how it felt, how she smelled and tasted, before he put his feelings into a strongbox and locked them away forever.

"Yeah, that's me," said Low. "The Dyke Mike. Now, can you pick me up?"

"Low, I can't, really," she said. "I mean, my partner's parents are coming over for dinner. They drove over here from Spokane Rez and, like, it's the first time I've met them, and they're not exactly happy their daughter has come roaring out of the closet on the motorcycle called Me."

"I really need you to pick me up."

"Low, I want to see you, I really do, but the time is so bad. How about tomorrow? Can't we do this tomorrow? Hell, we'll talk for three days straight, but I really need tonight, okay?"

"I'm in jail."

Low wondered if there was a word in Navajo that meant caesura.

"What did you do?"

"I broke my heart."

"I didn't realize that was illegal."

"Well," he said. "In Missoula, it seems to be a misdemeanor."

"Are you arrested?"

"No," said Low. "Not really. The police said they just don't want me to be alone tonight."

"Low, what happened?"

"I came here to see a woman. I was going to ask her to marry me."

"And she said no."

"Not exactly."

"What then?"

"She married Chuck yesterday and moved to Flagstaff."

"I hate Arizona."

She'd always known exactly what to say.

"Low, honey," she added. "I'll be right there."

Tracy Johnson drove a 1972 half-ton Chevrolet pickup. Red with long streaks of gray primer paint. Four good tires and one bad alternator. Hay-bale molding in the bed.

"This truck," said Low as he climbed in. "What stereotype are you trying to maintain?

"There are no stereotypes in Missoula, Montana," she said, appraising his face and body. "You've gained weight. A lot of weight."

"So have you," he said. "I love all of your chins."

Forty pounds overweight, she was beautiful, wearing a loose T-shirt and tight blue jeans. Her translucent skin bled light into her dark hair.

On the radio, Hank Williams sang white man blues.

"You're lovely," said Low. "Just lovely."

"Yes, I know," she said. "But don't get your hopes up."

"My hopes have never been up," he said, though he knew he was lying. "Your partner, what's her name?"

"Sara Polatkin," said Tracy. "She's Indian."

"Indian dot-in-the-head or Indian arrow-in-the-heart?"

"She's Spokane. From the rez. Unlike your lame urban Indian ass."

"Yes," said Low Man. "And you can say that, given you've spent so much time on reservations."

Tracy dropped the truck into gear and drove down a narrow street.

"Yeah," she said. "I'm freaking out her parents. Completely. Not only am I a lesbian but I'm also white."

"The double whammy."

"She's in law school," said Tracy. "She's smart. Even smarter than you."

"Good for you."

"We're getting married."

"Really?"

"Yeah, that's why Sara's parents are coming over. They're going to try to talk her out of it."

"Jesus," said Low Man, wondering why he had bothered to get on the flight from Seattle.

"Jesus has nothing to do with it," said Tracy as she stared ahead and smiled.

Ahead, on the right side of the street, Sara Polatkin was waiting outside the coffee joint. She was short, thin, very pretty, even with her bad teeth and eccentric clothes—a black dress with red stockings, and Chuck Taylor basketball shoes with Cat in the Hat socks.

Low Man couldn't look Sara in the eye when she climbed into the truck. He remembered how Crazy Horse—that great Indian warrior, that savior, that Christ-figure—was shot in the face by his lover's husband.

Low Man sat on the bench seat between Tracy and Sara. He watched as the women leaned over him to kiss each other. He could smell their perfumes.

"So, you're Low," said Sara, her voice inflected with a heavy singsong reservation accent. She probably had to work hard to keep that accent. Her black hair hung down past her waist.

"It's Low Man, both words, Low Man," he said. Only three people had ever been allowed to call him Low: his mother, his late father, and Tracy.

"Okay, Low Man, both words, Low Man," said Sara. "So, you're the one who is madly in love with my wife."

"Yes, I was," he said, careful with the tense. "And she's not your wife, yet."

"Details. Do you still love her?"

Low Man hesitated—*caesura*—and Tracy rushed to fill the silence.

"He just got his heart broken by an Indian woman," she said. "I don't think you want to be the second one today, huh, Sara?"

Sara's face went dark, darker.

"Did you ever fuck her?" Sara asked him, and Low Man heard the Spokane River in her voice, and heard the great Columbia as well, and felt the crash of their confluence.

"Sara, let it go," said Tracy, with some traces of laughter still in her voice.

"Do they talk like that in law school?" Low Man asked Sara.

"Yeah," she said. "Except it's in Latin."

Low Man could feel the Indian woman's eyes on him, but he didn't return the stare. He watched the road moving ahead of them.

"Sara, let it go," said Tracy, and there was something else in her voice then. "Remember, you're the one who used to sleep with guys."

Tracy put her hand on Low's knee.

"Sorry, Low," she said. "But these born-again dykes can be so righteous."

"Yeah, yeah, I'm sorry, Low Man," said Sara. "I'm just nervous about my ma and pa."

"So, you're a new lesbian, huh?" asked Low Man.

"I'm still in the wrapper," said Sara.

"She's still got that new-car smell," said Tracy.

"What made you change teams?" asked Low.

"I'm running away from the things of man," she said.

At dinner, Low Man sat at the small table between Tracy and Sara. Directly across from him, Sid Polatkin, longtime husband, held the hand of Estelle Polatkin, longtime wife. All five of them had ordered the salmon special because it had just seemed easier.

"Do you think the salmon will be good?" asked Estelle, her voice thick with a reservation accent, much thicker than her daughter's.

"It's the Holiday Inn," said her husband. He was president of the Spokane Indian Reservation VFW. "The Holiday Inn is dependable."

Sid's hair was pulled back in a gray ponytail. So was Estelle's. Both of their faces told stories. Sid's: the recovering alcoholic; the wronged son of a wronged son; the Hamlet of his reservation. Estelle's: the tragic beauty; the woman who stopped drinking because her husband did; the woman who woke in the middle of the night to wash her hands ten times in a row.

Now they were Mormons.

"Do you believe in God?" Sid had asked Low Man before they sat down.

"Sure," said Low Man, and he meant it.

"Do you believe in Jesus?" asked Sid as he unrolled his napkin and set it on his substantial lap.

"How do you mean?" asked Low Man.

"Do you believe that Jesus was crucified and rose from the dead?"

"Come on, Daddy, leave him alone," said Sara. She knew how her father's theological conversations usually began and how they often ended. He'd always been a preacher.

"No, Sara," said Low Man. "It's okay."

"I think Mr. Smith can speak for himself," said Sid. He leaned across the table and jabbed the air with a sharp index finger, a twenty-first century Indian's idea of a bow and arrow.

"Low speaks too much," said Tracy. Sure, it was a lame joke, but she was trying to change the tone of the conversation. Hey, she thought, everybody should laugh. Ha, ha, ha, ha, ha! Let's all clap hands and sing!

"Hey, Mr. Smith, Low Man," continued Sid. "Why don't you and I pretend we're alone here. Let's pretend this is a country of men."

Low Man smiled and looked at the three women: Estelle, Sara, and Tracy; two strangers and his unrequited love; two Indians and one white. If asked, as a man, to rush to their defense, what would Low Man do? How far would he go? If asked, as an Indian, to defend Jesus, what could he say?

"Please, Low, tell me what you think about Jesus," said Sid, moving from question to command somewhere in the middle of that sentence.

"I don't think it matters what I think," said Low Man. "I'm not a Christian. Let them have their Jesus."

"How vague," said Sid. "Tell me, then, what do you think their Jesus would say about lesbian marriage?"

Tracy and Sara sighed and leaned back in their chairs. How often had men sat around dinner tables and discussed women's lives, their choices, and the reasons why one woman reached across the bed to touch another woman?

"Mr. Polatkin," said Tracy. "If you want to talk about our relationship, then you should talk to Sara and me. Otherwise, it's just cowardly."

"You think I'm a coward?" asked Sid.

"Daddy, let's just order dinner," said Sara. "Mom, tell him to order dinner."

Estelle closed her eyes.

"Hey," said Sid. "Maybe I should order chicken, huh? But that would be cannibalism, right? Am I right, Tracy, tell me, am I right?"

"Mr. Polatkin," said Tracy. "I don't know you. But I love your daughter, and she tells me you're a good man, so I'm willing to give you a chance. I'm hoping you'll extend the same courtesy to me."

"I don't have to give you anything," said Sid as he tossed his napkin onto his plate.

"No," said Estelle, her voice barely rising above a whisper.

"What?" asked Sid. "What did you say?"

"We came here with love," said Estelle. "We came here to forgive."

"Forgive?" asked Tracy. "Forgive what? We don't need your forgiveness."

Low Man recognized the anger in Tracy's eyes and in her voice. *Low,* she'd said to him in anger all those years ago, *I'm never going to love you that way. Never. Can you please understand that? I can't change who I am. I don't want to change who I am. And if you ever touch me again, I swear I will hate you forever.*

"Hey, hey, Sid, sit down," said Low. "You want to talk Jesus, I'll talk Jesus."

Sid hesitated a moment—asserting his independence—and then nodded his head.

"That's good," said Low. "Now, let me tell you. Jesus was a fag."

Everybody was surprised, except Tracy, who snorted loudly and laughed.

"No, no, no," continued Low. "Just think about it. I mean, there Jesus was, sticking up for the poor, the disadvantaged, the disabled. Who else but a fag would be that liberal, huh? And damn, Jesus hung out with twelve guys wearing great robes and great hair and never, ever talked about women. Tell me, Sidney, what kind of guys never talk about women?"

"Fags!" shouted Tracy.

"This isn't funny," said Sid.

"No, it's not," said Sara. "Tracy, let's just go home. Let's just go. And Low Man, you just shut up, you shut up."

"No, Sara," said Tracy. "Let them talk. Let them be men. And God said, let them be men."

"I don't like you this way," Sara said to Tracy. "You've been different ever since Low showed up. You're different with him."

Low Man wondered if that was true; he wondered what it meant; he knew what he wanted it to mean.

"Please," said Sara. "Let's just go, Tracy, let's go."

"Nobody's going anywhere," said Sid. "Not until this is over."

Estelle's eyes glowed with tears.

"I'm being dead serious here, Sid," said Low. "I mean, Jesus was an incredibly decent human being and they crucified him for it. He sounds like a fag to me."

"Jesus *was* a human being," said Sid. "At least, you've got that much right. He didn't rise from the dead. He wasn't the Son of God. He was just a man."

"No, Sid, you and me, we're just men. Simple, stupid men."

"Yes, yes, I'm simple," said Sid. "I'm a man who is simply afraid of God. And next to God, we're all stupid. That much we can agree on."

"Fine, fine, Sid, we agree."

Sid stared at Low Man. The question: How does any father prove how much he loves his child? One answer: the father must hate his child's enemies. Another answer: the father must protect his child from all harm.

"Listen to me," said Sid. "I'm being terrible. I'm not being good. Not good at all. We're all hungry and angry and tired. Why don't we eat and then figure out whether we're going to stay or go? How does that sound?"

Because they all loved one another, in one form or another, in one direction or another, they agreed.

All five of them ordered soda pop, except for Tracy, the white woman, who ordered red wine. Low Man wondered what would happen when every drunk Indian quit drinking—and he truly believed it would someday happen—when Indians quit giving white people something to worry about besides which wine went with fish and which wine went with Indians.

"So, you're a writer?" Sid asked Low Man.

"Yes."

"You make a living at it?"

"Sid," said Low Man, leaning close to the table. "I make shitloads of money. I make so much money that white people think I'm white."

Nobody laughed.

"You're one of the funny Indians, enit?" Sid asked Low Man. "Always making the jokes, never taking it seriously."

"What is this *it* you're talking about?" asked Low Man.

"Everything. You think everything is funny."

Low knew for a fact that everything was funny. Homophobia? Funny! Genocide? Hilarious! Political assassination? Sidesplitting! Love? Ha, Ha, Ha!

"Low, honey," said Tracy. "Maybe you should get some coffee. Maybe you should shut up, huh?"

Low Man looked at Tracy, at Sara. He wanted to separate them.

Sara looked at Low and wondered yet again why Indian men insisted on being warriors. *Put down your bows and arrows,* she wanted to scream at Low, at her father, at every hypermasculine Injun in the world. *Put down your fucking guns and pick up your kids.*

"Sid," said Low Man. "How many women have you had in your life?"

"What do you mean?"

"I mean, counting lovely Estelle here, how many women have you slept with, bedded down, screwed, humped, did the nasty with?"

Estelle gasped and slapped her hand over her mouth—a strangely mannered gesture for a reservation Indian woman.

"I think we made a mistake here," said Sid, rising with his wife. "I think we should just go home. Whatever treaties we signed here are broken now."

"No, no, no," said Sara. "Please, Mom, Dad, sit down."

Sid and Estelle might have left then, might never have returned to their daughter's life, but the salmon arrived at that moment.

"Eat, eat," said Sara, with tears in her eyes. She turned her attention to Low Man.

"I think you should leave," she said, understanding that Indian men wanted to own the world just as much as white men did. They just wanted it for different reasons.

Low Man looked to Tracy. He wanted her to choose.

"I think she's right, Low," said Tracy. "Why don't you take the truck and drive back to our place?"

Low Man stared into her eyes. He stepped through her pupils and searched for some sign, some indication, some clue of what he was supposed to do.

"Low, go, just go," said Tracy.

"Mom," said Sara, as she held her mother's hand. "Please, stay."

Tracy said, "Go, Low, just go for a ride. Sid and Estelle can give us a ride back to our place, right?"

Sid nodded his head. He sliced into his salmon and shoved a huge piece into his mouth.

"Please, Low," said Tracy. "Go."

"Sid," said Low Man. "I was wondering why you came here. I mean, if you don't approve of this, of them, then why the hell are you here?"

Sid chewed on his salmon. The great fish was gone from the Spokane River. Disappeared.

"I love my daughter," said Sid. "And I don't want her to go to hell."

Estelle started weeping. She stared down at the salmon on her plate.

"Mom," said Sara. "Please."

Sid finished his salmon with two huge bites. He washed it down with water and leaned back in his chair. He stared at Low Man.

"Come on, boys," said Tracy. "No need for the testicle show, okay?"

"You have a filthy mouth," Sid said.

"Yeah, I guess I fucking do," she said.

"Whore."

"Dad, stop it," said Sara. Her mother lowered her chin onto her chest and wept like she was thirty years older.

"I raised my daughter to be better than this," said Sid.

"Better than what?" asked Low.

"My daughter wasn't, wasn't a gay until she met this, this white woman."

"Maybe I should go," said Tracy.

"No," said Sara. "Nobody's going anywhere."

In Sara's voice, the others heard something new: an adult-hood ceremony taking place between syllables.

"What's wrong with you?" Low asked Sid. "She's your daughter. You should love her no matter what."

213

Low Man wanted this father to take his daughter away.

"I don't think this is any of your business," said Sid. "You're not even supposed to be here."

"I'm not supposed to be anywhere," said Low. "But here I am."

Low Man smiled at himself. He sounded like a character out of film noir, like Lee Marvin or Robert Mitchum. Or maybe like Peter Lorre.

"What are you smiling at?" asked Sid.

"I'm going to the room," said Estelle as she stood up. Sara rose with her.

"Mom, Mom, I love you," said Sara as she hugged her.

Low Man wondered what would have happened if he had a pistol. He wondered if he would have shot Sid Polatkin in the face. No, of course not. Low Man probably would have raced out into the dark and tried to bring down one of the airplanes that kept passing over the motel.

"Do you know what I want?" Low asked Sid.

"No. Tell me."

"I want to take Tracy out of here. I want to take her back home with me. I want her to fall in love with me."

"Go ahead," said Sid. "And I'll take my daughter back home where she belongs."

"Sid," said Low. "These women don't belong to us. They live in whole separate worlds, man, don't you know that?"

Sid couldn't answer. His jaw worked furiously. When he was a young man, he used to fight Golden Gloves. Even at his advanced age, he could have beaten the crap out of Low Man. Both men knew this to be a fact.

Tracy stood up from the table. She took two steps away, then turned back.

"I'm leaving, Sara," she said. "Finally, I'm leaving."

Sara looked to her father and mother. Together, the three of them had buried dozens of loved ones. The three of them knew all of the same mourning songs. Two of them had loved each other enough to conceive the third. They'd invented her! She was their Monster; she was surely going to murder them. That's what children were supposed to do!

"Mom, Dad," she said. "I love you."

Sara stepped away from her mother, her father. She stepped away from the table, away from the salmon, and toward Tracy.

"If you leave now," said Sid. "Don't you ever call us. Don't you ever talk to us again."

Sara closed her eyes. She remembered the winter when her father fell from the roof of their house and disappeared into a snowbank. She remembered the dreadful silence after the impact, and then the wondrous noise, the joyful cacophony of his laughter.

Tracy took Sara's hand. They stood there in the silence.

"Sid," said Low Man. "These women don't need us. They never did."

"We're leaving," said Tracy and Sara together. Hand in hand, they walked away.

With surprising speed, Sid rose from the table and chased after them. He caught them just before they got to the restaurant exit. He pushed Tracy into a wall—pushed her into the plasterboard—and took his daughter by the elbow.

"You're coming with us," he said.

"No," said Sara.

Estelle couldn't move. "Help them," she said to Low Man. "Help them."

Low didn't know which "them" she was talking about. He rushed across the room just as Sid slapped his daughter once, then again. One Indian man raised his hand to slap an Indian woman, but a third Indian stepped between them.

"She's my daughter, she's mine," shouted Sid. He pushed against Low, as Sara fell back against a glass door, as she turned to hide her face.

Sid and Low grappled with each other. The old man was very strong.

At the table, Estelle covered her face with her hands.

"She's my daughter, she's my daughter," shouted Sid as he punched Low in the chest. Low staggered back and fell to one knee.

"She's my daughter," shouted Sid as he turned to attack Tracy. But she slapped him hard. Surprised, defeated, Sid dropped to the floor beside Low.

The two Indian men sat on the ground as the white woman stood above them.

Tracy turned away from the men and ran after Sara.

Sid climbed to his feet. He pointed an accusing finger at Low, who rose slowly to his feet. Sid turned and walked back toward his wife, back toward Estelle, who held her husband close and cried in his arms.

"What are you going to do?" Low called after him. "What are you going to do when she's gone?"

BECAUSE MY FATHER ALWAYS SAID HE WAS THE ONLY INDIAN WHO SAW JIMI HENDRIX PLAY "THE STAR-SPANGLED BANNER" AT WOODSTOCK

During the sixties, my father was the perfect hippie, since all the hippies were trying to be Indians. Because of that, how could anyone recognize that my father was trying to make a social statement?

But there is evidence, a photograph of my father demonstrating in Spokane, Washington, during the Vietnam war. The photograph made it onto the wire service and was reprinted in newspapers throughout the country. In fact, it was on the cover of *Time*.

In the photograph, my father is dressed in bell-bottoms and flowered shirt, his hair in braids, with red peace symbols splashed

217

across his face like war paint. In his hands my father holds a rifle above his head, captured in that moment just before he proceeded to beat the shit out of the National Guard private lying prone on the ground. A fellow demonstrator holds a sign that is just barely visible over my father's left shoulder. It reads MAKE LOVE NOT WAR.

The photographer won a Pulitzer Prize, and editors across the country had a lot of fun creating captions and headlines. I've read many of them collected in my father's scrapbook, and my favorite was run in the *Seattle Times*. The caption under the photograph read DEMONSTRATOR GOES TO WAR FOR PEACE. The editors capitalized on my father's Native American identity with other headlines like ONE WARRIOR AGAINST WAR and PEACEFUL GATHER-ING TURNS INTO NATIVE UPRISING.

Anyway, my father was arrested, charged with attempted murder, which was reduced to assault with a deadly weapon. It was a high-profile case so my father was used as an example. Convicted and sentenced quickly, he spent two years in Walla Walla State Peni-tentiary. Although his prison sentence effectively kept him out of the war, my father went through a different kind of war behind bars.

"There was Indian gangs and white gangs and black gangs and Mexican gangs," he told me once. "And there was somebody new killed every day. We'd hear about somebody getting it in the shower or wherever and the word would go down the line. Just one word. Just the color of his skin. Red, white, black, or brown. Then we'd chalk it up on the mental scoreboard and wait for the next broadcast."

My father made it through all that, never got into any serious trouble, somehow avoided rape, and got out of prison just in time to hitchhike to Woodstock to watch Jimi Hendrix play "The Star-Spangled Banner."

"After all the shit I'd been through," my father said, "I figured Jimi must have known I was there in the crowd to play something like that. It was exactly how I felt."

Twenty years later, my father played his Jimi Hendrix tape until it wore down. Over and over, the house filled with the rockets' red glare and the bombs bursting in air. He'd sit by the stereo with a cooler of beer beside him and cry, laugh, call me over and hold me tight in his arms, his bad breath and body odor covering me like a blanket.

Jimi Hendrix and my father became drinking buddies. Jimi Hendrix waited for my father to come home after a long night of drinking. Here's how the ceremony worked:

1. I would lie awake all night and listen for the sounds of my father's pickup.
2. When I heard my father's pickup, I would run upstairs and throw Jimi's tape into the stereo.
3. Jimi would bend his guitar into the first note of "The Star-Spangled Banner" just as my father walked inside.
4. My father would weep, attempt to hum along with Jimi, and then pass out with his head on the kitchen table.
5. I would fall asleep under the table with my head near my father's feet.
6. We'd dream together until the sun came up.

The days after, my father would feel so guilty that he would tell me stories as a means of apology.

"I met your mother at a party in Spokane," my father told me once. "We were the only two Indians at the party. Maybe the only two Indians in the whole town. I thought she was so beautiful. I figured she was the kind of woman who could make buffalo walk on up to her and give up their lives. She wouldn't have needed to hunt. Every time we went walking, birds would follow us around. Hell, tumbleweeds would follow us around."

Somehow my father's memories of my mother grew more beautiful as their relationship became more hostile. By the time the divorce was final, my mother was quite possibly the most beautiful woman who ever lived.

"Your father was always half crazy," my mother told me more than once. "And the other half was on medication."

But she loved him, too, with a ferocity that eventually forced her to leave him. They fought each other with the kind of graceful anger that only love can create. Still, their love was passionate, unpredictable, and selfish. My mother and father would get drunk and leave parties abruptly to go home and make love.

"Don't tell your father I told you this," my mother said. "But there must have been a hundred times he passed out on top of me. We'd be right in the middle of it, he'd say *I love you*, his eyes would roll backwards, and then out went his lights. It sounds strange, I know, but those were good times."

I was conceived during one of those drunken nights, half of me formed by my father's whiskey sperm, the other half formed by my mother's vodka egg. I was born a goofy reservation mixed drink, and my father needed me just as much as he needed every other kind of drink.

One night my father and I were driving home in a near-blizzard after a basketball game, listening to the radio. We didn't talk much. One, because my father didn't talk much when he was sober, and two, because Indians don't need to talk to communicate.

"Hello out there, folks, this is Big Bill Baggins, with the late-night classics show on KROC, 97.2 on your FM dial. We have a request from Betty in Tekoa. She wants to hear Jimi Hendrix's version of 'The Star-Spangled Banner' recorded live at Woodstock."

My father smiled, turned the volume up, and we rode down the highway while Jimi led the way like a snowplow. Until that night, I'd always been neutral about Jimi Hendrix. But, in that near-blizzard with my father at the wheel, with the nervous silence caused by the dangerous roads and Jimi's guitar, there seemed to be more to all that music. The reverberation came to mean something, took form and function.

That song made me want to learn to play guitar, not because I wanted to be Jimi Hendrix and not because I thought I'd ever play for anyone. I just wanted to touch the strings, to hold the guitar tight against my body, invent a chord, and come closer to what Jimi knew, to what my father knew.

"You know," I said to my father after the song was over, "my generation of Indian boys ain't ever had no real war to fight. The first Indians had Custer to fight. My great-grandfather had World War I, my grandfather had World War II, you had Vietnam. All I have is video games."

My father laughed for a long time, nearly drove off the road into the snowy fields.

"Shit," he said. "I don't know why you're feeling sorry for yourself because you ain't had to fight a war. You're lucky. Shit, all you had was that damn Desert Storm. Should have called it Dessert Storm because it just made the fat cats get fatter. It was all sugar and whipped cream with a cherry on top. And besides that, you didn't even have to fight it. All you lost during that war was sleep because you stayed up all night watching CNN."

We kept driving through the snow, talked about war and peace.

"That's all there is," my father said. "War and peace with nothing in between. It's always one or the other."

"You sound like a book," I said.

"Yeah, well, that's how it is. Just because it's in a book doesn't make it not true. And besides, why the hell would you want to fight a war for this country? It's been trying to kill Indians since the very beginning. Indians are pretty much born soldiers anyway. Don't need a uniform to prove it."

Those were the kinds of conversations that Jimi Hendrix forced us to have. I guess every song has a special meaning for someone somewhere. Elvis Presley is still showing up in 7-Eleven stores across the country, even though he's been dead for years, so I figure music just might be the most important thing there is. Music turned my father into a reservation philosopher. Music had powerful medicine.

"I remember the first time your mother and I danced," my father told me once. "We were in this cowboy bar. We were the only real cowboys there despite the fact that we're Indians. We danced to a Hank Williams song. Danced to that real sad one, you know. 'I'm So Lonesome I Could Cry.' Except your mother and I weren't lonesome or crying. We just shuffled along and fell right goddamn down into love."

"Hank Williams and Jimi Hendrix don't have much in common," I said.

"Hell, yes, they do. They knew all about broken hearts," my father said.

"You sound like a bad movie."

"Yeah, well, that's how it is. You kids today don't know shit about romance. Don't know shit about music either. Especially you Indian kids. You all have been spoiled by those drums. Been hearing them beat so long, you think that's all you need. Hell, son, even an Indian needs a piano or guitar or saxophone now and again."

My father played in a band in high school. He was the drummer. I guess he'd burned out on those. Now, he was like the universal defender of the guitar.

"I remember when your father would haul that old guitar out and play me songs," my mother said. "He couldn't play all that well but he tried. You could see him thinking about what chord he was going to play next. His eyes got all squeezed up and his face turned all red. He kind of looked that way when he kissed me, too. But don't tell him I said that."

Some nights I lay awake and listened to my parents' lovemaking. I know white people keep it quiet, pretend they don't ever make love. My white friends tell me they can't even imagine their own parents getting it on. I know exactly what it sounds like when my parents are touching each other. It makes up for knowing exactly what they sound like when they're fighting. Plus and minus. Add and subtract. It comes out just about even.

Some nights I would fall asleep to the sounds of my parents' lovemaking. I would dream Jimi Hendrix. I could see my father standing in the front row in the dark at Woodstock as Jimi Hendrix played "The Star-Spangled Banner." My mother was at home with me, both of us waiting for my father to find his way back home to the reservation. It's amazing to realize I was alive, breathing and wetting my bed, when Jimi was alive and breaking guitars.

I dreamed my father dancing with all these skinny hippie women, smoking a few joints, dropping acid, laughing when the rain fell. And it did rain there. I've seen actual news footage. I've seen the documentaries. It rained. People had to share food. People got sick. People got married. People cried all kinds of tears.

But as much as I dream about it, I don't have any clue about what it meant for my father to be the only Indian who saw Jimi Hendrix play at Woodstock. And maybe he wasn't the only Indian there. Most likely there were hundreds but my father thought he was the only one. He told me that a million times when he was drunk and a couple hundred times when he was sober.

"I was there," he said. "You got to remember this was near the end and there weren't as many people as before. Not nearly as many. But I waited it out. I waited for Jimi."

A few years back, my father packed up the family and the three of us drove to Seattle to visit Jimi Hendrix's grave. We had our photograph taken lying down next to the grave. There isn't a gravestone there. Just one of those flat markers.

Jimi was twenty-eight when he died. That's younger than Jesus Christ when he died. Younger than my father as we stood over the grave.

"Only the good die young," my father said.

"No," my mother said. "Only the crazy people choke to death on their own vomit."

"Why you talking about my hero that way?" my father asked.

"Shit," my mother said. "Old Jesse WildShoe choked to death on his own vomit and he ain't anybody's hero."

I stood back and watched my parents argue. I was used to these battles. When an Indian marriage starts to fall apart, it's even more destructive and painful than usual. A hundred years ago, an Indian marriage was broken easily. The woman or man just packed up all their possessions and left the tipi. There were no arguments, no discussions. Now, Indians fight their way to the end, holding onto the last good thing, because our whole lives have to do with survival.

After a while, after too much fighting and too many angry words had been exchanged, my father went out and bought a motorcycle. A big bike. He left the house often to ride that thing for hours, sometimes for days. He even strapped an old cassette player to the gas tank so he could listen to music. With that bike, he learned something new about running away. He stopped talking as much, stopped drinking as much. He didn't do much of anything except ride that bike and listen to music.

Then one night my father wrecked his bike on Devil's Gap Road and ended up in the hospital for two months. He broke both his legs, cracked his ribs, and punctured a lung. He also lacerated his kidney. The doctors said he could have died easily. In fact, they were surprised he made it through surgery, let alone survived those first few hours when he lay on the road, bleeding. But I wasn't surprised. That's how my father was.

And even though my mother didn't want to be married to him anymore and his wreck didn't change her mind about that, she still came to see him every day. She sang Indian tunes under her breath, in time with the hum of the machines hooked into my father. Although my father could barely move, he tapped his finger in rhythm.

When he had the strength to finally sit up and talk, hold conversations, and tell stories, he called for me.

"Victor," he said. "Stick with four wheels."

After he began to recover, my mother stopped visiting as often. She helped him through the worst, though. When he didn't need her anymore, she went back to the life she had created. She traveled to powwows, started to dance again. She was a champion traditional dancer when she was younger.

"I remember your mother when she was the best traditional dancer in the world," my father said. "Everyone wanted to call her sweetheart. But she only danced for me. That's how it was. She told me that every other step was just for me."

"But that's only half of the dance," I said.

"Yeah," my father said. "She was keeping the rest for herself. Nobody can give everything away. It ain't healthy."

"You know," I said, "sometimes you sound like you ain't even real."

"What's real? I ain't interested in what's real. I'm interested in how things should be."

My father's mind always worked that way. If you don't like the things you remember, then all you have to do is change the memories. Instead of remembering the bad things, remember what happened immediately before. That's what I learned from my father. For me, I remember how good the first drink of that Diet Pepsi tasted instead of how my mouth felt when I swallowed a wasp with the second drink.

Because of all that, my father always remembered the second before my mother left him for good and took me with her. No. I remembered the second before my father left my mother and me. No. My mother remembered the second before my father left her to finish raising me all by herself.

But however memory actually worked, it was my father who climbed on his motorcycle, waved to me as I stood in the window, and rode away. He lived in Seattle, San Francisco, Los Angeles, before he finally ended up in Phoenix. For a while, I got postcards nearly every week. Then it was once a month. Then it was on Christmas and my birthday.

On a reservation, Indian men who abandon their children are treated worse than white fathers who do the same thing. It's because white men have been doing that forever and Indian men have just learned how. That's how assimilation can work.

My mother did her best to explain it all to me, although I understood most of what happened.

"Was it because of Jimi Hendrix?" I asked her.

"Part of it, yeah," she said. "This might be the only marriage broken up by a dead guitar player."

"There's a first time for everything, enit?"

"I guess. Your father just likes being alone more than he likes being with other people. Even men and you."

Sometimes I caught my mother digging through old photo albums or staring at the wall or out the window. She'd get that look on her face that I knew meant she missed my father. Not enough to want him back. She missed him just enough for it to hurt.

On those nights I missed him most I listened to music. Not always Jimi Hendrix. Usually I listened to the blues. Robert Johnson mostly. The first time I heard Robert Johnson sing I knew he understood what it meant to be Indian on the edge of the twenty-first century, even if he was black at the beginning of the twentieth. That must have been how my father felt when he heard Jimi Hendrix. When he stood there in the rain at Woodstock.

Then on the night I missed my father most, when I lay in bed and cried, with that photograph of him beating that National

Guard private in my hands, I imagined his motorcycle pulling up outside. I knew I was dreaming it all but I let it be real for a moment.

"Victor," my father yelled. "Let's go for a ride."

"I'll be right down. I need to get my coat on."

I rushed around the house, pulled my shoes and socks on, struggled into my coat, and ran outside to find an empty driveway. It was so quiet, a reservation kind of quiet, where you can hear somebody drinking whiskey on the rocks three miles away. I stood on the porch and waited until my mother came outside.

"Come on back inside," she said. "It's cold."

"No," I said. "I know he's coming back tonight."

My mother didn't say anything. She just wrapped me in her favorite quilt and went back to sleep. I stood on the porch all night long and imagined I heard motorcycles and guitars, until the sun rose so bright that I knew it was time to go back inside to my mother. She made breakfast for both of us and we ate until we were full.

SCENES FROM A LIFE

Thirty-one years ago, just after I'd graduated from college, I had sex with a teenage Indian boy. I was twenty-three and the boy was seventeen. In the State of Washington, the age of consent is sixteen, but since I was more than five years older than him and in a supervisory position, I was guilty of sexual misconduct, though my crime was never discovered.

I don't think I was a predator. It was only the third time I'd slept with somebody, but the boy told me he'd already had sex with twelve different girls.

"I'm a champion powwow fancydancer," he said. "And fancydancers are the rock stars of the Indian world. We have groupies."

Please don't think I'm trying to justify my actions. But I'm fairly certain that I didn't hurt that Indian boy, either physically or spiritually. At least, I hope that he remembers me with more fondness than pain.

I was a middle-class white girl who'd volunteered to spend a summer on an Indian reservation. Any Indian reservation. I foolishly thought that Indians needed my help. I was arrogant enough to think they deserved my help.

My Indian boy was poor and learning-disabled, and he could barely read, but he was gorgeous and strong and kind and covered his mouth when he laughed, as if he were embarrassed to be enjoying the world. I was slender and pretty, and eager to lift him out of poverty, and so ready to save his life, but ended up naked in a wheat field with him.

The sex didn't last long. And I cried afterward.

"Your skin is so pretty and pale," he said. "Thank you for letting me touch you."

He was a sweet and poetic boy for somebody so young. We held each other tightly and didn't let go even as the ants crawled on us.

"It's okay," he said. "They won't bite us."

And they didn't.

I'm not a Catholic but I would still like to make this official confession: I feel great shame for what I did to that boy. But do you know what makes it worse? I don't remember his name.

*　*　*

Three years ago, I was living in a prefurnished corporate apartment in Phoenix, Arizona. You've heard of the company I work for. You probably own many of its products.

It was July and the sand invaded my apartment and car and mouth. All day long, I swigged and gargled water to clean the grit from between my teeth.

My coworkers didn't get sand in their teeth so they thought I was imagining it. They teased me and wondered if the heat was driving me crazy. I wondered if they were correct.

I was born and grew up on Washington's Olympic Peninsula between a rain forest and a saltwater strait. My parents loved the place so much that they named me BlueGrouse, a bird only found in our rain forest. Lucky me. So, of course, as soon as I turned eighteen, I legally changed my first name to Melissa, the second most common one in the United States that year. In partial honor of my parents, I did keep Blue, but lopped off Grouse, as my middle name.

In any event, a woman originally named for a slug-eating bird doesn't belong in the desert.

One morning late in July, the temperature was already over 100 degrees at dawn. And, minute by minute, it was only getting hotter. I could have hidden in the air-conditioned apartment, but I'd felt the need to challenge myself. I wanted to see how long I could endure that heat.

I was dizzy after a few minutes. And I was so thirsty that everything—the buildings, cars, and mountains—glistened like bottles of water.

And then I saw it.

To the east of the city. And approaching fast.

A massive wave of sand.

It stretched hundreds of feet into the air. And it was at least thirty miles wide.

All around me, my neighbors—none of whom I knew but who must have been watching the morning news—had stepped out onto their decks to stare.

"What is that?" one neighbor shouted to nobody in particular.

"A haboob," somebody else shouted.

"What's a haboob?"

"It's Arabic."

"Okay, it's Arabic, but what does it mean?"

"The rough translation is 'big fucking sandstorm.'"

As it rolled closer, the haboob swallowed the city. I wondered if it was strong enough to destroy buildings. Could the sand be propelled with such force that it stripped metal from cars and skin from humans?

I imagined that a million people—sudden skeletons—were buried and would remain so until an archaeologist discovered them centuries from now.

My neighbors fled back into their apartments, but I remained on my deck and waited for the storm. I welcomed it. But as the wind blew down power lines and exploded a few transformers, I was forced to retreat and watch the storm through the sliding glass door until a fine layer of dust obscured my view.

Later, after the skies had cleared and the electricity had been restored, and the mayor had announced that the city had sustained only minor damage, I remained in my dark apartment and stared at the sliding door. The dust had rearranged itself into ambiguous shapes and lines. It seemed to have formed letters of a strange alphabet. I wondered if God was punishing me by sending a message that I couldn't read.

I've been a member of eleven book clubs in the last twenty years. I've read approximately one hundred novels during that time and I've enjoyed maybe half of them.

While reading books, I write notes in the page margins and I circle and memorize certain lines and passages. The people in each book might be different, but the plotline is basically the same: Somebody is unhappy and they do dangerous and foolish things trying to become happy.

I've been married and divorced twice. No kids. I'm quite positive that I'll marry and divorce the next man who whispers my name.

Like I said, dangerous and foolish.

In my thirties, I made documentaries.

Or rather, I was the script supervisor for many documentary filmmakers. I kept things organized. I kept track of camera angles, dialogue errors, and continuity. If an actor picked up an apple in the first take, then I made sure she picked up an apple in each subsequent take.

In the old days, they called them script girls. These days, the script supervisors are still mostly women. But nobody comments on that. Not aloud.

I didn't get paid much, but I enjoyed the privilege of traveling the country.

One autumn, I worked with a director making a short film about cranberry bogs in Wisconsin. He was a soft-spoken white man and he spent most of his time and budget interviewing the Indians who worked the bogs.

"What is the magic in cranberries?" he asked the Indians again and again. And they'd laugh at him. Or they'd say, "There's nothing magical. It's just a good job, if you don't mind getting wet." One old Indian woman said, "Aren't cranberries supposed to muscle up your bladder so you pee good?" The director, desperately hoping for a new answer, would rephrase his question in a dozen different ways.

In bed, after good sex, he'd stare at the ceiling and chastise the Indians and himself.

"They don't trust me," he said. "I'm just another white guy with a camera. If I were an Indian, I wouldn't trust me. Do you trust me?"

"Of course not," I said. He was married and had three kids. I've never understood why mistresses fall in love with their married lovers. And I really don't understand those mistresses who steal away husbands from their wives and children. Why would you want to destroy marriages and families and friendships? I've always thought the hottest thing about affairs was the secrecy.

"But I know these Indians think cranberries are magical," the director said. "They just don't want to share the magic. But I respect the magic. I want the world to respect the magic."

He was a calm and kind man. He never lost his temper, but he so desperately wanted the Indians to answer his questions with spiritual force. He wanted the Indians to think of themselves as more than just blue-collar workers.

But they were blue-collar workers, and they were strong and scarred, and many of them made passes at me. I was tempted by a few of them, especially this muscular man with long black braids. His skinny butt looked great in his Wrangler jeans. But I politely declined all offers because I knew I couldn't hop into bed with an Indian man without thinking of that Indian boy from my past. Even though I'm what the prigs would call promiscuous, I believe in making love to one man at a time. I didn't want to have a threesome with a real person and a ghost.

On the last day of shooting, the director gathered up all of the Indian bog workers—a few dozen men and women—and organized them for a group shot. Just as he was about to film them waist-deep in a bog, they started laughing. No, they were giggling. And that made me giggle, too. I don't think there's anything funnier than a crowd of big Indians giggling so hard that they cry.

The director didn't understand what was happening. I'm not quite sure that I understood.

"What's so funny?" the director asked.

One of the Indians, a woman, stopped giggling long enough to speak.

"We're laughing," she said, "because white people always want to take photos of Indians. But you're taking a picture of us at work. It might be the first photo ever taken of Indians working."

And then she and the others laughed. They laughed so hard that the director realized he was finally capturing a spontaneous moment. He filmed the Indians laughing and slapping one another on the backs and shoulders. He filmed the Indians as they grew weak-kneed and weak-backed from laughter. He filmed them as, one by one, they had to flee the bog to avoid drowning due to hilarity. He kept filming until the only Indian left was that sexy guy with the long braids. He hadn't laughed as hard as the others, but he was smiling with all of his teeth.

I lived with my second husband in Malibu.

One August, we stood on the roof of our house and fought a wildfire with garden hoses.

Can you believe the madness?

All my life, I'd promised myself that I would never become the kind of person who'd risk her life for material possessions.

Houses can be rebuilt. Your entire fucking life can be rebuilt if you don't die first.

I'm not even sure that I loved that house. Or that husband.

We'd gotten married with the agreement that it would be open. We had explicit and implicit permission to pursue sexual partners outside of our marriage.

The only rule: Don't fall in love.

But how could such a rule ever be enforced? How could anybody make such an unrealistic promise?

In any case, our open marriage was only slightly ajar.

Despite all his best efforts, my husband had only gone to bed with an older woman from work. She was a talkative lady who was bad with money and couldn't retire, so she'd have to keep answering phones until the moment she died.

And while I could have had sex with many men—every woman can have all the men she wants if she lowers her standards a bit—I'd only made out with three guys while dancing in crowded bars. It wasn't fun. And it was with great relief that we closed the marriage. Hell, we slammed it shut.

So, newly faithful, my second husband and I defeated a wildfire.

We won.

We saved our house.

Our barn.

Our three horses.

Three months later, my husband left me for that near-elderly receptionist. She was sixty and he was forty-two. I was happy for him. And I was especially happy for her. Old men always have young girlfriends, but how often does an old woman land a young guy? And my husband was rich, too. That elderly receptionist was living in a goddamn fairy tale. How could I not be happy with that romance?

We conjured up a no-fault divorce. And my dear husband honored the prenuptial agreement.

He kept the horses; I kept the house.

My first husband died in a motorcycle wreck. We lived in a state that didn't require helmets so he split open his skull on the windshield of a Toyota Corolla.

I loved him so much that, twenty years later, I still keep a photo of him in my wallet. I don't talk about him with anybody.

Though I'll dance with almost any man in a crowd, I prefer to grieve alone.

I've slept with thirty-two men in my life. I suppose that's a high number. My male friends give me high fives for my carnal productivity, but my female friends think it's too many.

"You're just trying to fill up all the emptiness inside you," said my best friend. "You're just trying to not be lonely."

"You're right," I said. "But I fail to see why feeling that way should prevent me from trying not to feel that way."

I remember all of my lovers' names. I write them down in a book with the *Titanic* painted on the cover. But, on the front page, I've only sketched a nameless portrait of that Indian boy fancydancer, who made love to me in a wheat field that had been left fallow that season.

On my computer, the bathroom mirror, the front door, and the refrigerator are sticky notes that share the same message: "I'll respect your various hungers if you respect mine."

Two hundred and sixty-six days after I had sex with that Indian boy, I gave birth to our daughter.

"Who's the father?" my parents asked me.

"I'm not going to tell you," I said.

I never held my baby. I didn't want to touch her. I thought it would hurt too much. So they took her away before I could change my mind about the adoption.

It was my choice to give her away. I felt that I deserved the punishment. I needed to serve a lifetime sentence in a jail of my own making.

My daughter was black of hair and brown of skin. It was strange to see such a dark shadow slide out of my white body.

Strangers adopted and raised my daughter. I don't know her history. Sometimes, I think about searching for her. In this Internet age, with its invasions of privacy and wholesale distribution of all the information in the world, I would guess it's easy to find people, especially those who have no reason to hide.

My daughter would be thirty-one now. I'm sure she is dark, pretty, and slender. I wonder if she, like her father, covers her mouth when she laughs.

I wonder if I would recognize her if I saw her on the street.

"Hey," I'd say. "It's you. It's you. I always knew I'd find you. I always knew I'd recognize you."

But I never see her. Or rather, I always see her. Every other woman in Los Angeles is dark, slender, and pretty. And it seems like half of them cover their mouths when they laugh.

I sometimes stop those women and ask them if they recognize me. I love it when they take me seriously and study my face. But they always smile with regret and rue, and say, "I'm sorry, but I don't know you."

BREAKFAST

The son cracked an egg, expecting yolk and egg, but instead dropped his father's impossibly small corpse into the mixing bowl. The son was only mildly surprised. His father had died eleven years earlier, so grief had become a predictable clown.

But what should the son have done with his father's body? He couldn't recycle it or toss it into the trash or compost bin. And he didn't want to wear it around his neck like jewelry or hang it from the rearview mirror like a dream catcher.

The son wondered what advice his father would have given him.

He would have said, "Don't embarrass me."

240

He would have said, "What kind of warrior are you?"

He would have said, "Put on the war paint, you faggot, and ride your pony into battle."

So, like his father would have done, the son added onions, green peppers, diced ham, and egg yolks and whites into the bowl, folded his father into the mix, poured it into the oiled frying pain, and cooked it golden.

One would have expected the omelet to taste bitter, but the son only thought that it needed salt—more salt—tons of salt—all the salt in the world.

NIGHT PEOPLE

Across the street from my apartment there is a twenty-four-hour manicure joint. This is only possible in New York City. Amazingly enough, there are a few other twenty-four-hour salons in town, but those are modernist little palaces. The joint across the street looks more like a 7-Eleven—brightly lit, inadequately mopped, and likely to be robbed soon. When it first opened, I was convinced that it was a front for a drug and/ or prostitution ring. But, night after night, I sat on my minuscule terrace (I fit into it like it was a bathtub) and watched through the large picture windows as women—and men dressed as women and/ or on their way to becoming women—arrived in the middle of the night to get their fingers and toenails done. Who knew there were so many insomniac transsexuals and transvestites?

The manicurists were all Asian women, most of them older than fifty and battered by their graveyard-shifted lives. But there was one twenty-something woman who fascinated me. She was plain-featured and plain of dress, but she gave the appearance of beautiful without being beautiful. I wasn't the only male fascinated with her confident mirage. My building's night doorman, a polite and quiet man otherwise, shouted street poetry at her and tried to find every rhyme and half rhyme for "Japanese," though I'm pretty sure she was Korean. She'd always smile and wave, but would not acknowledge his advances in any other way. I don't know if she ever looked up from my doorman to see me watching her from my third-floor terrace. Could I be seen in the dark?

And so I watched her ply her trade. While her coworkers labored with a silent hostility that I could feel from across the street, she was animated. She seemed to enjoy her customers. She laughed often and made them laugh as well. What kind of person can be that charming at 3:33 A.M.?

After months of this surveillance, I decided that I needed to see the woman up close. I needed to speak to her. I needed to get a manicure, though I knew I could never get a pedicure. A manicure seemed like a public act but a pedicure felt like something private, even sexual. I felt like I'd be cheating on my girlfriend if I got my toes done. But I had a bigger problem than podiatric infidelity. I'm a nail biter. A nail chewer and eater. I was too embarrassed to walk into a manicure place with disfigured nails. So I gave myself an amateurish manicure, worried that my clipping and sanding would wake my girlfriend, and then left my apartment and walked across the street for a professional one.

"Hello, sir," the receptionist said. "How can we help you?"

"I want her," I said, and pointed at the subject of my affections.

She saw me pointing at her, smiled, and waved me over. Her name tag told me that her name was Saundra. Underrated how name tags give a man permission to briefly study a woman's breasts.

"Hello, Saundra," I said. "Can you fix these?"

She took my hand and carefully studied my nails.

"You just cut your nails?" she asked.

"Yes," I said.

Her voice was teen pop culture American with a hint of Queens.

"You sanded them, too?" she asked.

"Yes," I said.

"Like, two minutes ago, right?" she asked.

"Yes," I said.

"You're a nail biter," she said.

"Yeah, how'd you know?" I asked.

"We get them all the time," she said. "I'm a biter, too. That's how I fell into this job. To stop biting. I started getting really expensive manicures. I figured I wouldn't chew on my nails if I'd paid a hundred bucks to make them look good."

"Did it work?"

"No," she said. "So I started coming to cheap places like this one."

"And how's that going?"

"Still chewing my nails. But I've got a job."

Saundra placed my fingers in a warm, soapy liquid. And as I soaked, she prepared her tools.

"We use a cold bath on these," she said. "Kills everything."

I imagined a tiny freezer filled with nail clippers and files.

"The subzero is better than heat," she said. "I think dentists use them, too. Dentists and manicurists. Dirty, dirty jobs."

"You're funny," I said, instead of just laughing, which was, I admit, pretty damn weird. But she didn't seem to notice. She took my hands from the soaking bowl and began her work. It felt amazing. It had been months since I'd been touched with any real kindness. And even that slight, professional intimacy was exhilarating.

"You must get some bizarre folks in here, right?" I asked.

"Not as many as you'd think," she said. "I think even the crazy people are kind of freaked out that we're open all night."

"Even crazy people have standards," I said.

"You're funny," she said, also without laughing. Then there was that quiet, charged moment in which a relationship's romantic possibilities become clear.

"So what do you do for a living?" she asked.

"I do lighting for stage plays," I said.

"For Broadway?" she asked. She was obviously excited by the thought of Broadway. Most people are. But they were thinking of the people in the spotlights, not the guys working in the rafters.

"I work Broadway sometimes," I said. "But mostly for off-off-off-Broadway stuff. If it involves naked people dancing with puppets, then I'm probably lighting it."

"Does that pay well?" she asked.

"Not enough to live in New York."

"Nobody can afford to live here," she said.

"And yet, there are millions of us poor bastards," I said.

She pushed back my cuticles. She buffed my nails. She massaged some oil into my fingers.

"We get actors in here all the time," she said. "Lot of night people in show business, huh?"

"There's a lot of time between jobs," I said. "So you have to fill it up. And a lot of us fill it with lonely."

"Tough to sleep when you're lonely," she said.

"How long have you been insomniac?" I asked.

"I was a good sleeper until I took this job. And now, it feels like I'm always awake."

"Me too."

She massaged my hands. Her fingertips on my palms. It felt so good that I closed my eyes and kept them closed.

"I live in this one-room apartment," she said. "I grew up there with my parents and three brothers. Six of us in one room. But my parents bought it. They owned it. Amazing, huh?"

"I've got friends who have a bathtub in the middle of their kitchen," I said. "They throw a thick slab of wood over it and use it as a table."

"Crazy. But that place is all mine now. My family moved back to Korea. Even my brothers. They were born here and lived their whole lives here, but they moved back."

"Restless," I said. "Everybody's restless."

"When I can't sleep, I just walk around the edges of my apartment like I was in solitary confinement, you know? I've got this Murphy bed but I never pull it out of the wall. I keep this big couch pushed up against it. And I've got two other little couches. Three couches in a studio? I'm crazy, right? I just move from couch to couch. One couch after another. Trying to sleep."

"Lucky couches," I said.

"You're a flirt," she said. "How does your girlfriend feel about that?"

"How do you know I have a girlfriend?" I asked.

"All you flirts have girlfriends."

I opened my eyes.

"You're a flirt, too," I said. "Do you have a boyfriend?"

"Of course," she said. "But he hardly ever stays at my place. He sleeps too easy. He can even sleep while I'm pacing around the room. Pisses me off."

"Have you ever lived with another insomniac?"

"No," she said. "Have you?"

"If two insomniacs fell in love, you know there'd be a murder-suicide."

"That's sad," she said.

"Sorry," I said. "It's not going too well with my girlfriend. She falls asleep two seconds after she closes her eyes. I hate it."

"My boyfriend ignores me. And I keep auditioning for his attention. Maybe you should come over and light me up all pretty."

"Mine teaches community college out on Long Island," I said. "I never see her. Except when she's sleeping and I'm not."

Saundra rubbed some other kind of moisturizer into my hands.

"My boyfriend and I haven't had sex in five years," she said.

"Wow," I said. "Wow."

I thought he had to be a gay man hiding in the closet behind the closet. Or maybe he'd been molested as a kid and couldn't deal with it. Or maybe he was just a drone, one of those strange and lucky people whose engines are not completely powered by various body fluids.

"My girlfriend and I haven't done it in six months," I said. "And it was three months before that. I get sex twice a year, like Catholics who only go to Mass on Christmas and Easter."

She laughed and slapped the table. And spilled a bowl of soapy water. As she cleaned up the mess, she blinked back tears.

"Why don't you leave her?" she asked.

"Why don't you leave yours?" I asked.

Neither of us had the answer.

I suppose I stayed with my girlfriend because I hoped we'd fall in love with each other's bodies again. I wanted her to lust for me again. In bed, I wanted her to crawl on top of me and grind so hard that her sweat fell into my mouth. But I couldn't say such things to her after so many years of honor and respect. I was too damn polite to tell her what I wanted. She might say no. She might laugh. And I was more afraid of being rejected by her than I was of dying.

"And now you're done," she said.

She meant that my manicure was finished.

"I live across the street," I said

"Oh, that's subtle," she said.

"No, I didn't mean it that way," I said. "Or maybe I did. I don't know."

"You have that creepy doorman, right?" she asked.

"He's okay," I said. "Except when it comes to you. Then he gets creepy."

She looked confused.

"I've heard him talking to you," I said. "I've been watching you for months."

"Okay," she said. "So you're the creepy one."

She rolled her chair back.

"You're not a stalker, are you?" she asked.

"No," I said. "I'm a night watchman."

She didn't say anything. She studied me, looking for signs of real danger, I suppose. I knew I wasn't dangerous. And I think she knew it, too.

"Okay," she said. "You can pay the receptionist. Tips are happily accepted."

"Don't worry," I said. "I won't come back. And I'll stop watching you."

She just nodded her head.

I wanted to say something profound to her—give a name to our separate loneliness, a metaphor that described the abysses that can grow between people in love. But I had only my most basic desire.

"If I could only sleep," I said.

"Yeah," Saundra said. "I know."

I paid for my manicure and walked back toward my building. As I noticed that my doorman was absent, I also realized that I'd forgotten my keys in the apartment. I'd have to wake my girlfriend. And she'd be angry that I'd gone missing and jealous that I'd been talking to another woman. My girlfriend wouldn't fuck me but she didn't want anybody else fucking me, either. After the inevitable argument, she and I would lie in the dark, with her worried that she'd be too tired to teach well later that day and me too terrified to reach across the bed and touch her.

I wanted none of that to happen. I didn't want anything to happen. So I stopped in the middle of the street. Amazing how quiet eight million people can be. I wondered if I should just walk over to that twenty-four-hour deli on Canal and wait for sunrise. But then I looked up toward my apartment and saw my girlfriend standing on our little terrace. I could see her through the dark. I wondered how long she'd been watching me. I wondered if she wanted me to walk toward her or to walk away.

BREAKING AND ENTERING

Back in college, when I was first learning how to edit film—how to construct a scene—my professor, Mr. Baron, said to me, "You don't have to show people using a door to walk into a room. If people are already in the room, the audience will understand that they didn't crawl through a window or drop from the ceiling or just materialize. The audience understands that a door has been used—the eyes and mind will make the connection—so you can just skip the door."

Mr. Baron, a full-time visual aid, skipped as he said, "Skip the door." And I laughed, not knowing that I would always remember his bit of teaching, though of course, when I tell the story now, I turn my emotive professor into the scene-eating lead of a Broadway musical.

"Skip the door, young man!" Mr. Baron sings in my stories —my lies and exaggerations—skipping across the stage with a top hat in one hand and a cane in the other. "Skip the door, old friend! And you will be set free!"

"Skip the door" is a good piece of advice—a maxim, if you will—that I've applied to my entire editorial career, if not my entire life. To state it in less poetic terms, one would say, "An editor must omit all unnecessary information." So in telling you this story—with words, not film or video stock—in constructing its scenes, I will attempt to omit all unnecessary information. But oddly enough, in order to skip the door in telling this story, I am forced to begin with a door: the front door of my home on Twenty-seventh Avenue in the Central District neighborhood of Seattle, Washington.

One year ago, there was a knock on that door. I heard it, but I did not rise from my chair to answer. As a freelance editor, I work at home, and I had been struggling with a scene from a locally made film, an independent. Written, directed, and shot by amateurs, the footage was both incomplete and voluminous. Simply stated, there was far too much of nothing. Moreover, it was a love scene—a graphic sex scene, in fact—and the director and the producer had somehow convinced a naive and ambitious local actress to shoot the scene full frontal, graphically so. This was not supposed to be a pornographic movie; this was to be a tender coming-of-age work of art. But it wasn't artistic, or not the kind of art it pretended to be. This young woman had been exploited—with her permission, of course—but I was still going to do my best to protect her.

Don't get me wrong. I'm not a prude—I've edited and enjoyed sexual and violent films that were far more graphic—but I'd spotted honest transformative vulnerability in that young actress's performance. Though the director and the producer thought she'd just been acting—had created her fear and shame through technical skill—I knew better. And so, by editing out the more gratuitous nudity and focusing on faces and small pieces of dialogue—and by paying more attention to fingertips than to what those fingertips were touching—I was hoping to turn a sleazy gymnastic sex scene into an exchange that resembled how two people in new love might actually touch each other.

Was I being paternalistic, condescending, and hypocritical? Sure. After all, I was being paid to work with exploiters, so didn't that mean I was also being exploited as I helped exploit the woman? And what about the young man, the actor, in the scene? Was he dumb and vulnerable as well? Though he was allowed—was legally bound—to keep his penis hidden, wasn't he more exploited than exploiter? These things are hard to define. Still, even in the most compromised of situations, one must find a moral center.

But how could I find any center with that knocking on the door? It had become an evangelical pounding: *Bang, bang, bang, bang!* It had to be the four/four beat of a Jehovah's Witness or a Mormon. *Bang, cha, bang, cha!* It had to be the iambic pentameter of a Sierra Club shill or a magazine sales kid.

Trust me, nobody interesting or vital has ever knocked on a front door at three in the afternoon, so I ignored the knocking and kept at my good work. And, sure enough, my potential guest stopped the noise and went away. I could hear feet pounding down the stairs and there was only silence—or, rather, the relative silence of my urban neighborhood.

But then, a few moments later, I heard a window shatter in my basement. Is shatter too strong a verb? I heard my window break. But break seems too weak a verb. As I visualize the moment—as I edit in my mind—I add the sound track, or rather I completely silence the sound track. I cut the sounds of the city—the planes overhead, the cars on the streets, the boats on the lake, the televisions and the voices and the music and the wind through the trees—until one can hear only shards of glass dropping onto a hardwood floor.

And then one hears—feels—the epic thump of two feet landing on that same floor.

Somebody—the same person who had knocked on my front door to ascertain if anybody was home, had just broken and entered my life.

Now please forgive me if my tenses—my past, present, and future—blend, but one must understand that I happen to be one editor who is not afraid of jump cuts—of rapid flashbacks and flash-forwards. In order to be terrified, one must lose all sense of time and place. When I heard those feet hit the floor, I traveled back in time—I de-evolved, I suppose—and became a primitive version of myself. I had been a complex organism—but I'd turned into a two-hundred-and-two pound one-celled amoeba. And that amoeba knew only fear.

Looking back, I suppose I should have just run away. I could have run out the front door into the street, or the back door onto the patio, or the side door off the kitchen into the alley, or even through the door into the garage—where I could have dived through the dog door cut into the garage and made my caninelike escape.

But here's the salt of the thing: though I cannot be certain, I believe that I was making my way toward the front door—after all, the front door was the only place in my house where I could be positive that my intruder was *not* waiting. But in order to get from my office to the front door, I had to walk past the basement door. And as I walked past the basement door, I spotted the baseball bat.

It wasn't my baseball bat. Now, when one thinks of baseball bats, one conjures images of huge slabs of ash wielded by steroid-fueled freaks. But that particular bat belonged to my ten-year-old son. It was a Little League bat, so it was comically small. I could easily swing it with one hand and had, in fact, often swung it one-handed as I hit practice grounders to the little second baseman of my heart, my son, my Maximilian, my Max. Yes, I am a father. And a husband. That is information you need to know. My wife, Wendy, and my son were not in the house. To give me the space and time I needed to finish editing the film, my wife had taken our son to visit her mother and father in Chicago; they'd been gone for one week and would be gone for another. So, to be truthful, I was in no sense being forced to defend my family, and I'd never been the kind of man to defend his home, his property, his shit. In fact, I'd often laughed at the news footage of silly men armed with garden hoses as they tried to defend their homes from wildfires. I always figured those men would die, go to hell, and spend the rest of eternity having squirt-gun fights with demons.

So with all that information in mind, why did I grab my son's baseball bat and open the basement door? Why did I creep down the stairs? Trust me, I've spent many long nights awake, asking myself those questions. There are no easy answers. Of course, there are many men—and more than a few women—who believe I was fully within my rights to head down those stairs and confront my intruder. There are laws that define—that frankly encourage—the art of self-defense. But since I wasn't interested in defending my

property, and since my family and I were not being directly threatened, what part of my self could I have possibly been defending?

In the end, I think I wasn't defending anything at all. I'm
an editor—an artist—and I like to make connections; I am paid
to make connections. And so I wonder. Did I walk down those
stairs because I was curious? Because a question had been asked
(Who owned the feet that landed on my basement floor?) and I,
the editor, wanted to discover the answer?

So, yes, slowly I made my way down the stairs and through
the dark hallway and turned the corner into our downstairs family
room—the man cave, really, with the big television and the pool
table—and saw a teenaged burglar. I stood still and silent. Standing
with his back to me, obsessed with the task—the crime—at hand,
he hadn't yet realized that I was in the room with him.

Let me get something straight. Up until that point I hadn't
made any guesses as to the identity of my intruder. I mean, yes, I
live in a black neighborhood—and I'm not black—and there had
been news of a series of local burglaries perpetrated by black teenagers, but I swear none of that entered my mind. And when I saw
him, the burglar, rifling through my DVD collection and shoving
selected titles into his backpack—he was a felon with cinematic
taste, I guess, and that was a strangely pleasing observation—I
didn't think, There's a black teenager stealing from me. I only
remember being afraid and wanting to make my fear go away.

"Get the fuck out of here!" I screamed. "You fucking
fucker!"

The black kid was so startled that he staggered into my
television—cracking the screen—and nearly fell before he caught
his balance and ran for the broken window. I could have—would
have—let him make his escape, but he stopped and turned back

toward me. Why did he do that? I don't know. He was young and scared and made an irrational decision. Or maybe it wasn't irrational at all. He'd slashed his right hand when he crawled through the broken window, so he must have decided the opening with its jagged glass edges was not a valid or safe exit—who'd ever think a broken window was a proper entry or exit—so he searched for a door. But the door was behind me. He paused, weighed his options, and sprinted toward me. He was going to bulldoze me. Once again, I could have made the decision to avoid conflict and step aside. But I didn't. As that kid ran toward me I swung the baseball bat with one hand.

I often wonder what would have happened if that bat had been made of wood. When Max and I had gone shopping for bats, I'd tried to convince him to let me buy him a wooden one, an old-fashioned slugger, the type I'd used when I was a Little Leaguer. I've always been a nostalgic guy. But my son recognized that a ten-dollar wooden bat purchased at Target was not a good investment.

"That wood one will break easy," Max had said. "I want the lum-a-lum one."

Of course, he'd meant to say *aluminum*; we'd both laughed at his mispronunciation. And I'd purchased the lum-a-lum bat.

So it was a metal bat that I swung one-handed at the black teenager's head. If it had been cheap and wooden, perhaps the bat would have snapped upon contact and dissipated the force. Perhaps. But this bat did not snap. It was strong and sure, so when it made full contact with the kid's temple, he dropped to the floor and did not move.

He was dead. I had killed him.

I fell to my knees next to the kid, dropped my head onto his chest, and wept.

I don't remember much else about the next few hours, but I called 911, opened the door for the police, and led them to the body. And I answered and asked questions.

"Did he have a gun or knife?"

"I don't know. No. Well, I didn't see one."

"He attacked you first?"

"He ran at me. He was going to run me over."

"And that's when you hit him with the bat?"

"Yes. It's my son's bat. It's so small. I can't believe it's strong enough to—is he really dead?"

"Yes."

"Who is he?"

"We don't know yet."

His name was Elder Briggs. Elder: such an unusual name for anybody, especially a sixteen-year-old kid. He was a junior at Garfield High School, a B student and backup point guard for the basketball team, an average kid. A good kid, by all accounts. He had no criminal record—had never committed even a minor infraction in school, at home, or in the community—so why had this good kid broken into my house? Why had he decided to steal from me? Why had he made all the bad decisions that had led to his death?

The investigation was quick but thorough, and I was not charged with any crime. It was self-defense. But then nothing is ever clear, is it? I was legally innocent, that much is true, but was I morally innocent? I wasn't sure, and neither were a significant percentage of my fellow citizens. Shortly after the police held the press conference that exonerated me, Elder's family—his mother, father, older brother, aunts, uncles, cousins, friends, and priest—organized a protest. It was small, only forty or fifty people, but how truly small can a protest feel when you are the subject—the object—of that protest?

257

I watched the live coverage of the event. My wife and son, after briefly returning from Chicago, had only spent a few days with me before they fled back to her parents. We wanted to protect our child from the media. An ironic wish, considering that the media were only interested in me because I'd killed somebody else's child.

"The police don't care about my son because he's black," Elder's mother, Althea, said to a dozen different microphones and as many cameras. "He's just another black boy killed by a white man. And none of these white men care."

As Althea continued to rant about my whiteness, some clever producer—and his editor—cut into footage of me, the white man who owned a baseball bat, walking out of the police station as a free man. It was a powerful piece of editing. It made me look pale and guilty. But all of them—Althea, the other protesters, the reporters, producers, and editors—were unaware of one crucial piece of information: I am not a white man.

I am an enrolled member of the Spokane Tribe of Indians. Oh, I don't look Indian, or at least not typically Indian. Some folks assume I'm a little bit Italian or Spanish or perhaps Middle Eastern. Most folks think I'm just another white guy who tans well. And since I'd just spent months in a dark editing room, I was at my palest. But I grew up on the Spokane Indian Reservation, the only son of a mother and father who were also Spokane Indians who grew up on our reservation. Yes, both of my grandfathers had been half-white, but they'd both died before I was born.

I'm not trying to be holy here. I wasn't a traditional Indian. I didn't dance or sing powwow or speak my language or spend my free time marching for Indian sovereignty. And I'd married a white woman. One could easily mock my lack of cultural connection, but one could not question my race. That's not true, of course.

People, especially other Indians, always doubted my race. And I'd always tried to pretend it didn't matter—I was confident about my identity—but it did hurt my feelings. So when I heard Althea Briggs misidentify my race—and watched the media covertly use editing techniques to confirm her misdiagnosis—I picked up my cell phone and dialed the news station.

"Hello," I said to the receptionist. "This is George Wilson. I'm watching your coverage of the protests and I must issue a correction."

"Wait, what?" the receptionist asked. "Are you really George Wilson?"

"Yes, I am."

"Hold on," she said. "Let me put you straight through to the producer."

So the producer took the call and, after asking a few questions to further confirm my identity, he put me on live. So my voice played over images of Althea Briggs weeping and wailing, of her screaming at the sky, at God. How could I have allowed myself to be placed into such a compromising position? How could I have been such an idiot? How could I have been so goddamn callous and self-centered?

"Hello, Mr. Wilson," the evening news anchor said. "I understand you have something you'd like to say."

"Yes." My voice carried into tens of thousands of Seattle homes. "I am watching the coverage of the protest, and I insist on a correction. I am not a white man. I am an enrolled member of the Spokane Tribe of Indians."

Yes, that was my first official public statement about the death of Elder Briggs. It didn't take clever editing to make me look evil; I had accomplished this in one take, live and uncut.

I was suddenly the most hated man in Seattle. And the most beloved. My fellow liberals spoke of my lateral violence and the destructive influence of colonialism on the indigenous, while conservatives lauded my defensive stand and lonely struggle against urban crime. Local bloggers posted hijacked footage of the most graphically violent films I'd edited.

And finally, a local news program obtained rough footage of the film I'd been working on when Elder Briggs broke into my house. Though I had, through judicious editing, been trying to protect the young actress, a black actress, the news only played the uncut footage of the obviously frightened and confused woman. And when the reporters ambushed her—her name was Tracy—she, of course, could only respond that, yes, she felt as if she'd been violated. I didn't blame her for that; I agreed with her. But none of that mattered. I could in no way dispute the story—the cleverly edited series of short films—that had been made about me. Yes, I was a victim, but I didn't for one second forget that Elder Briggs was dead. I was ashamed and vilified, but I was alive.

I spent most of that time alone in my basement, in the room where I had killed Elder Briggs. When one spends that much time alone, one ponders. And when one ponders, one creates theories—hypotheses, to explain the world. Oh, hell, forget rationalization; I was pissed, mostly at myself for failing to walk away from a dangerous situation. And I was certainly pissed at the local media, who had become as exploitative as any pornographic moviemaker. But I was also pissed at Althea and Elder Briggs.

Yes, the kid was a decent athlete; yes, the kid was a decent student; yes, the kid was a decent person. But he had broken into my house. He had smashed my window and was stealing my DVDs and, if I had not been home, would have stolen my computer and television and stereo and every other valuable thing in my house. And his mother, Althea, instead of explaining why her good and decent son had broken and entered a stranger's house, committing a felony, had instead decided to blame me and accuse me of being yet another white man who was always looking to maim another black kid—had already maimed generations of black kids—when in fact I was a reservation Indian who had been plenty fucked myself by generations of white men. So, Althea, do you want to get into a pain contest? Do you want to participate in the Genocidal Olympics? Whose tragic history has more breadth and depth and length?

Oh, Althea, why the hell was your son in my house? And oh, my God, it was a *Little League* baseball bat! It was only twenty inches long and weighed less than three pounds. I could have hit one hundred men in the head—maybe one thousand or one million—and not done anything more than given them a headache. But on that one day, on that one bitter afternoon, I took a swing—a stupid, one-handed, unlucky cut—and killed a kid, a son, a young man who was making a bad decision but who maybe had brains and heart and soul enough to stop making bad decisions.

Oh, Jesus, I murdered somebody's potential.

Oh, Mary, it was self-defense, but it was still murder. I confess: I am a killer.

How does one survive these revelations? One just lives. Or, rather, one just finally walks out of his basement and realizes that the story is over. It's old news. There are new villains and heroes, criminals and victims, to be defined and examined and tossed aside.

Elder Briggs and I were suddenly and equally unimportant.

My life became quiet again. I took a job teaching private-school white teenagers how to edit video. They used their newly developed skills to make documentaries about poor brown people in other countries. It's not oil that runs the world, it's shame. My Max was always going to love me, even when he began to understand my limitations. I didn't know what my wife thought of my weaknesses.

Weeks later, in bed, after lovemaking, she interrogated me.

"Honey," she said.

"Yes," I said.

"Can I ask you something?"

"Anything."

"With that kid, did you lose your temper?"

"What do you mean?" I asked.

"Well, you have lost your temper before."

"Just one time."

"Yes, but you broke your hand when you punched the wall."

"Do you think I lost my temper with Elder Briggs?" I asked.

My wife paused before answering, and in that pause I heard all her doubt and fear. So I got out of bed, dressed, and left the house. I decided to drive to see a hot new independent film—a gory war flick that pretended to be antiwar—but first stepped into a mini-mart to buy candy I could smuggle into the theater.

I was standing in the candy aisle, trying to decide between a PayDay and a Snickers, when a group of young black men walked into the store. They were drunk or high and they were cursing the world, but in a strangely friendly way. How is it that black men can make a word like *motherfucker* sound jovial?

There are people—white folks, mostly—who are extremely uncomfortable in the presence of black people. And I know plenty of Indians—my parents, for example—who are also uncomfortable around black folks. As for me? I suppose I'd always been the kind of nonblack person who celebrated himself for not being uncomfortable around blacks. But now, as I watched those black men jostle one another up and down the aisles, I was afraid—no, I was nervous. What if they recognized me? What if they were friends of Elder Briggs? What if they attacked me?

Nothing happened, of course. Nothing ever really happens, you know. Life is infinitesimal and incremental and inconsequential. Those young black men paid for their energy drinks and left the store. I paid for my candy bar, walked out to my car, and drove toward the movie theater.

One block later, I had to hit my brakes when those same black guys jaywalked across the street in front of me. All of them stared me down and walked as slowly as possible through the crosswalk. I'd lived in this neighborhood for years and I'd often had this same encounter with young black men. It was some remnant of the warrior culture, I suppose.

When it had happened before, I had always made it a point to smile goofily and wave to the black men who were challenging me. Since they thought I was a dorky white guy, I'd behave like one. I'd be what they wanted me to be.

But this time, when those black men walked in slow motion in front of me, I did not smile or laugh. I just stared back at them. I knew I could hit the gas and slam into them and hurt them, maybe even kill them. I knew I had that power. And I knew that I would not use that power. But what about these black guys? What power did they have? They could only make me wait at an intersection. And so I waited. I waited until they walked around the corner and out of my vision. I waited until another driver pulled up behind me and honked his horn. I was supposed to move, and so I went.

DO YOU KNOW
WHERE I AM?

Sharon and I were college sweethearts at St. Jerome the
Second University in Seattle, or, as it is affectionately
known, St. Junior's. We met at the first mixer dance of our fresh-
man year and soon discovered we were the only confirmed Native
American Roman Catholics within a three-mile radius of campus,
so we slept together that inaugural night, in open defiance of Pope
Whomever, and kept sleeping together for the next three years. It
was primary love: red girl and red boy on white sheets.

Sharon was Apache, and I was Spokane, but we practiced
our tribal religions like we practiced Catholicism: We loved all of the
ceremonies but thought they were pitiful cries to a disinterested god.

My white mother, Mary, bless her soul, raised me all by herself in Seattle because my Indian daddy, Marvin, died of stomach cancer when I was a baby. I never knew him, but I spent half of every summer on the Spokane Reservation with his mother and father, my grandparents. My mother wanted me to keep in touch with my tribal heritage, but mostly, I read spy novels to my grandfather and shopped garage sales and secondhand stores with my grandmother. I suppose, for many Indians, garage sales and trashy novels are highly traditional and sacred. We all make up our ceremonies as we go along, right? I thought the reservation was ordinary and magical, like a sedate version of Disneyland. All told, I loved to visit but loved my home much more. In Seattle, my mother was a corporate lawyer for old-money companies and sent me to Lakeside Upper School, where I was a schoolmate of Bill Gates and Paul Allen, who have become the new-money kings of the world.

Sharon went to St. Therese's School for Girls. Her parents, Wilson and Pauline, were both architects; they helped build three of the tallest skyscrapers in downtown Seattle. If Zeus ate a few million pounds of glass, steel, and concrete, his offal would look something like those buildings. However fecal, those monstrosities won awards and made Wilson and Pauline very popular and wealthy. They lived in a self-designed home on Lake Washington that was lovely and tasteful in all ways except for its ridiculously turquoise exterior. I don't know whether they painted the house turquoise to honor the sacred stone of the Southwest or if they were being ironic: *Ha! We're Apache Indians from the desert, and this is our big blue house on the water! Deal with it!*

Sharon and I were Native American royalty, the aboriginal prince and princess of western Washington. Sure, we'd been thoroughly defeated by white culture, but dang it, we were conquered and assimilated National Merit Scholars in St. Junior's English honors department.

Sharon and I were in love and happy and young and skinny and beautiful and hyperliterate. We recited Shakespeare monologues as foreplay: *To be or not to be, take off your panties, oh, Horatio, I knew him well, a fellow of infinite jest, I'm going to wear your panties now.* All over campus, we were known as Sharon-and-David-the-Bohemian-Indians. We were inseparable. We ate our meals together and fed each other. Risking expulsion for moral violations, we sneaked into each other's dorm rooms at night and made love while our respective roommates covered their heads with pillows. Sharon and I always tried to take the same classes and mourned the other's absence whenever we couldn't. We read the same books and discussed them while we were naked and intertwined. Oh Lord, we were twins conjoined at the brain, heart, and crotch.

I proposed to Sharon on the first day of our senior year, and she accepted, and we planned to secretly elope on the day after our graduation.

In June, the day before graduation, Sharon and I were taking one last walk along the path beside the anonymous creek that ran through the middle of campus. We were saying good-bye to a good place. Overgrown with fern and blackberry thickets, the creek had been left wild and wet.

"'Whose woods these are I think I know,'" I said.

"Robert Frost wrote the poem," said Sharon. We were playing Name the Poet, a game of our own invention.

"'Know' and 'poem,'" I said. "A clumsy rhyme, don't you think?"

"You stink," she said and laughed too loudly. Her joy was always rowdy, rude, and pervasive. I laughed with her and pulled her close to me and pressed my face into her hair and breathed in her scent. After the first time we'd made love, she'd said, *Now I know what you smell like, and no matter what else happens to us, I'm always going to know what you smell like.*

"Hey," I said as we walked the creek. "How about we climb into the bushes and I get you a little wild and wet?"

We kissed and kissed until she pulled away.

"Do you hear that?" she said.

"What?"

"I think it's a cat. Can you hear it meowing?"

I listened and heard nothing.

"You're imagining things," I said.

"No, it's a cat. I can hear it. It sounds pitiful."

"There must be a hundred cats around here. City cats. They're tough."

"No, it sounds hurt. Listen."

I listened and finally heard the faint feline cry.

"It's down there in the creek somewhere," she said.

We peered over the edge and could barely see the water through the thick and thorny overgrowth.

"I'm sure it's hunting rats or something," I said. "It's okay."

"No, listen to it. It's crying. I think it's stuck."

"What do you want me to do? It's just a dumb-ass cat."

"Can you go find it?"

I looked again at the jungle between that cat and me.

"I'd need a machete to get through there," I said.

"Please," said Sharon.

"I'm going to get all cut up."

"'All in green went my love riding,'" she whispered in that special way, "'on a great horse of gold into the silver dawn.'"

"Cummings wrote the poem, and I'm in love and gone," I said and made my slow way down the creek side. I didn't want to save the cat; I wanted to preserve Sharon's high opinion of me. If she hadn't been there to push me down the slope, I never would have gone after that cat. As it was, I cursed the world as I tripped over ferns and pushed blackberry branches out of the way. I was cut and scraped and threatened by spiders and wasps, all for a dumb cat.

"It's like *Wild Kingdom* down here," I said.

"Do you see him?" she said, more worried about the cat. I could hear the love in her voice. I was jealous of that damn cat!

I stopped and listened. I heard the cry from somewhere close.

"He's right around here," I said.

"Find him," she said, her voice choking with fierce tears.

I leaned over, pushed aside one last fern, and saw him, a black cat trapped in blackberry branches. He was starved, too skinny to be alive, I thought, but his eyes were bright with fear and pain.

"Man," I said. "I think he's been caught in here for a long time."

"Save him, save him."

I reached in, expecting the cat to bite or claw me, but he remained gratefully passive as I tore away the branches and freed him. I lifted and carried him back up the bank. He was dirty and smelly, and I wanted all of this to be over.

"Oh my God," said Sharon as she took him from me. "Oh, he's so sad, so sad." She hugged him, and he accepted it without protest.

"What are we going to do with him?" I asked.

"I don't know."

"We can't keep him," I said. "Let's let him go here. He's free now. He'll be okay."

"What if he gets stuck again?"

"Then it'll be natural selection. Come on, he doesn't have a tag or anything. He's just a stray cat."

"No, he's tame, he's got a home somewhere." She stared the cat in the eyes as if he could tell us his phone number and address.

"Oh, wait, wait," she said. "I remember, in the newspaper, last week or something, there was a lost cat ad. It said he was black with white heart-shaped fur on his belly."

Sharon had a supernatural memory; she could meet a few dozen new people at a party and rattle off their names two days later. During an English department party our sophomore year, she recited by memory seventy-three Shakespeare sonnets in a row. It was the most voluminous display of erudition any of us had ever witnessed. Tenured English professors wept. But I was the one who enjoyed the honor and privilege of taking her home that night and making her grunt in repetitive monosyllables.

Beside the creek, Sharon gently turned the cat over, and we both saw the white heart. Without another word, Sharon ran back to her dorm room, and I followed her. She searched for the newspaper in her desk but couldn't find it, and none of her floormates had a copy of the old paper, either, so she ran into the basement and climbed into the Dumpster. I held the cat while she burrowed into the fetid pile of garbage.

"Come on," I said. "You're never going to find it. Maybe you imagined the whole thing. Let's take him to the shelter. They can take care of him."

She ignored me and kept searching. I felt like throwing the cat into the wall.

"This is it," she said and pulled a greasy newspaper out of the mess. She flipped to the classifieds, found the lost cat ad, and shouted out the phone number. She jumped out of the Dumpster, grabbed the cat, ran back to her room, and quickly dialed.

"Hello," said Sharon over the telephone. "We have your cat. Yes, yes, yes. We found him by the creek. At St. Junior's. We'll bring him right over. What's your address? Oh God, that's really close."

Sharon ran out of the dorm; I ran after her.

"Slow down," I called after her, but she ignored me. Maybe Sharon wasn't a good Apache or Catholic, but she was religious when she found the proper mission.

We sprinted through a residential neighborhood, which may or may not have been a good idea for two brown kids, no matter how high our grade-point averages. But it felt good to run fast, and I dreamed about being a superhero. Fifteen minutes later and out of breath, Sharon knocked on the front door of a small house. An old couple opened the door.

"Lester," shouted the old man and took the cat from Sharon. The old woman hugged the man and the cat. All three cried to one another.

"How'd you find him?" asked the old man, weeping hard now, barely able to talk, but unashamed of his tears. "He's been gone for a month."

"I heard him crying," I said (I lied) and stepped into the doorway. Sharon stood behind me and peered over my shoulder.

"Oh, thank you, bless you," said the old woman.

"I pulled him out of some blackberry thorns," I said. "And then I remembered your ad in the newspaper, and I found the paper in the garbage, and I called you, and here I am."

The old man and woman hugged me, holding the cat between us, all of us celebrating the reunion, while Sharon stood silently by. I think I lied because I wanted to be briefly adored by strangers, to be remembered as a handsome and kind man, a better man, more complete, even saintly. But it was Orwell who wrote that "saints should be always judged guilty until they are proved innocent."

All during this time, Sharon never spoke. I can only guess at her emotions, but I imagine she was shocked and hurt by my disloyalty. Standing in the presence of such obvious commitment between two people and their damn cat, she must have lost faith in me and, more importantly, in herself.

"How can we ever repay you?" asked the old woman.

"Nothing," I said. "We need nothing."

"Here, here," said the old man as he opened his wallet and offered me a twenty.

"No, no," I said. "I don't need that. I just wanted to be good, you know?"

He forced the money into my hand; I accepted it.

"You're a good man," said the old woman.

I shook my head, took Sharon's hand, and walked away, leaving those grateful strangers to their beloved pet.

"Why did you do that?" Sharon asked as we walked.

271

"I needed to," I said. That was the best answer I could give her. It wasn't enough.

"You lied to me, you lied to them, and you took their money," she said. "How could you do that?"

"I don't know," I said.

Sharon broke away from me and ran.

I didn't see her that night as I got ready for graduation, and I didn't see her the next morning.

"Where's Sharon?" asked my mother as she adjusted my cap and gown.

"She's with her parents," I said, which was a true statement, I suppose, but hardly close to the truth.

I went through the ceremony alone; Sharon went through the ceremony alone; we sat ten chairs apart.

The day after graduation, Sharon was still missing. I didn't know where she was. When my mother asked me about her absence, I said she was on a spiritual retreat.

"One month of silence," I said, lying to my mother, to another woman who loved me. "After a big event, like a graduation or birth, the Apaches leave for a month. It's an Apache thing."

"I wish I could do that," she said. "I think everybody should do that. Make it a law. Once a year, everybody has to be silent for a month. We'd all rotate, you know? You have to be quiet during your birth month."

"It's a good idea, Mom, I'm sure it would go over well."

"Sarcasm is a sin, honey."

After another day of unceremonial silence, I assumed Sharon had left me forever, and I finally confessed my fears to my mother.

"Mom," I said. "I love Sharon and I destroyed her."

Was I overreacting to Sharon's overreaction? I'd told such a small lie, had taken credit and reward for such a small act of heroism. But then I wondered if Sharon had always had her doubts about my character, and perhaps had always considered me an undependable braggart. What if she'd been gathering evidence against me all along, and I'd finally committed the last unpardonable crime?

"You have to go find her," my mother said.

"I can't," I said, and it was true and cowardly.

My mother turned away from me and cried while she fixed dinner. Later that night, while she washed dishes and I dried, my mother told me how much she still missed my father.

"He's been gone twenty-two years," she said. "But I can still feel him right here in the room with us. I can still smell him, his hair, his skin."

My mother didn't call my father by name because she wanted the dead to stay dead; I wanted to learn magic and open a twenty-four-hour supermarket that sold resurrection and redemption.

The next morning, Sharon came to see me. I was so grateful for her presence that I leaned against the wall to keep from falling down. My mother hugged Sharon until they both cried. Then Sharon asked my mother to give us some privacy. After my mother left, Sharon took my face in her hands.

"You're a liar," Sharon said. "I'm going to marry a liar."

I didn't want to ask her why she came back. We were so fragile, I worried that one wrong word could completely break us.

For the next twenty-nine years, we lived as wife and husband, as the mother and father of four kids (Sarah, Rachael, Francis, and Joshua) who suddenly grew into adults and became wives and husbands and mothers and fathers. During our long marriage, Sharon and I buried her mother and father and my mother, all of our grandparents, and many of our aunts, uncles, and cousins. I covered high school sports and reviewed movies for the local alternative weekly; an odd pair of beats, I suppose, but I enjoyed the appearance of being odd while living a sedate life. Sharon ran her own coffee shop and wrote lyric odes she never published. We paid our taxes, owned a modest home, and made love an average of three times a week. We didn't have nearly as much money as our parents, and that could be viewed as our failure, but we felt successful. We weren't triumphant, by any means, but we lived a good and simple life, and I often wondered if I deserved it.

All during those years, at every house party, group dinner, family gathering, and company picnic, Sharon told the story of the lost cat.

"My husband, the liar," she always called me. At first, she told the story to hurt me, then she told it out of habit, and then she told it because she'd turned it into a wildly funny and exaggerated adventure: *And then he fell in the creek!* She loved to make people laugh, and so they laughed at my small sins. I wanted the laughter to absolve me, but I'm not sure if that was its purpose. I never asked to be forgiven, and Sharon never offered her forgiveness. We never talked about the lost cat in private; it was our most public secret.

But there were other secrets, of course. Sharon kept most of hers, and I kept most of mine. Those kept secrets were small and ordinary, having to do with broken diets and hidden pornography, and they were of little consequence, but one evening, a decade into our marriage, Sharon confessed to an extramarital affair.

"I don't love him," she said. "It's over now. I only slept with him three times. To be fair, you can ask me three questions about it, and I'll answer them as honestly as possible, and then I don't ever want to talk about it again."

I was hurt by the frankness of her words, by her deal-making, but she cried, and her voice trembled as she spoke, and she'd never been one to feign emotion or cry for dramatic purposes, so I was lost in her contradictions.

"How could you do that to me?" I asked.

"Is that a real question?" she asked. "Or is it rhetorical?"

I panicked. I didn't want to waste my three questions. I wanted to know details, the facts and figures, and not emotional states. But which particular details did I want to know? And which questions would elicit the most information? I needed to be a brutally efficient interrogator. I couldn't believe I was participating in this horrible transaction.

"Listen," I said, "this is ridiculous. Let's talk this out like normal people."

"That's the problem," she said. "Everything is so normal. You didn't used to be normal. I didn't marry normal."

She was a thirty-two-year-old woman with four young kids, and she owned and managed a small business. So she was one of those notorious superwomen. I knew she was always exhausted, but what could I do to help her? I could never tell her she worked too hard, and I certainly couldn't tell her she should spend more time with the kids. I couldn't ask her to choose between her work life and her home life. As a man, I would never be asked to make a similar choice. I spent most Friday and Saturday nights watching other people's children play football, basketball, and volleyball. What kind of father was I? I could best be described as cordially absent on weekends and lovingly distracted on weekdays. What kind of husband was I? Apparently, I was the kind of husband whose wife needed to sleep with at least one other man and an untold number of others who might be waiting in line. There are millions of those clueless husbands, aren't there? Wasn't I yet another cuckolded husband, slightly distinguished by knowing how to self-define with an Old English word? I was eight hundred years old. I was historic, predictable, and planned. I was normal.

"Who is he?" I asked.

"His name is Michael Joyce," she said. "He's a regular at the shop. I've asked him to never come back. He agreed. He's a good man."

I was surprised to discover I wanted to hit my wife. I wanted to punch her in the stomach and make her fall to the floor. I wanted to see her gasping with physical pain. I would never hurt her that way—I hadn't struck another human being since the third grade—but the violent impulse was there, and I was frightened and exhilarated by it. My wife had no idea how dangerous I could be. I felt better knowing I could hurt her far more than she'd hurt me. And then I was revolted. How could I love a person and want to hurt her so much? How could I look at my wife, the mother of my children, and feel only the need for revenge? I paced around the room, ran my fingers roughly through my hair, because I needed to move. I needed to find another space in which to exist. I studied the details of the living room: the antique lamps purchased for full price and the end tables rescued from garage sales and refurbished; the brown leather couch and black leather recliner; the Monet and Kahlo prints on the walls; the bookshelves stuffed with novels and sports histories; and the coffee tables adorned with art books. All of it was tasteful and beautiful and appropriate and hard-earned and useless.

Sharon wore a red blouse and blue jeans. Her feet were bare and needed a pedicure. Once a month, her feet were scrubbed clean and polished by a Vietnamese woman whose name and exact place of business I would never know. Sharon wore a fake pearl necklace her mother had given her for some birthday, and real pearl earrings I'd given her on our fifth anniversary. The fake pearls were prettier than the real ones. I don't know why I noticed her physical details, but it seemed important to take note of all I could. I felt the insistent need to be exact. Since it was laundry day, I knew she'd be wearing her oldest brassiere, and would never initiate lovemaking while wearing it, but would gladly receive my advances after first dashing into the bathroom to quickly remove the tattered bra. How many times had she emerged topless from the bathroom and run laughing toward me? Who keeps accurate count of such wonderful moments? Wouldn't a better husband know that number by heart?

"I'm a bad husband," I said. Why was I apologizing?

She turned away and sat on the couch as far away from me as possible. I kept pacing around the room.

"He's white," she said, volunteering the information, and I was strangely relieved. My emotions were changing and shifting randomly. If I'd been an actor in a musical, I would have broken into song for no apparent reason. I would have tap-danced to the primal 4/4 beat of betrayal. I would have leaped over the couch where she was sitting and rewon her heart with my grace and strength. What a dream life I have, and how instantly I can immerse myself in it! Can you believe I was happy to hear she'd slept with only a white man? I would have been tortured to hear she'd slept with another Indian man. Considering her beauty, ambition, and intelligence, I could conceive of an amazing white man or black man who might love her and be loved in return, but I doubted another Indian man of my particular talents existed out there in the world. Call it a potent mix of arrogance and self-hatred, but

I was certain I was the one Indian man who was good enough for my Indian wife.

I believed I was being rational, but who can be rational in such a painful situation? Wouldn't my wife and I hold entirely different standards for what made a man good or great? What if she'd slept with a plumber or a construction worker? What if she'd slept with a supermarket graveyard-shift worker or a high school dropout? I couldn't stand the thought of my wife sleeping with a blue-collar man who'd read fewer books than I had. I wanted to believe my wife slept with another man because she needed to be loved in a new way, a more educated and intellectual way, and not because she wanted to hurt me. I didn't understand what I was feeling, and I didn't know what to do, and I couldn't ask her to help me, because that might qualify as my second question and would leave me with only one.

"Don't look at me that way," she said.

"What way?" I asked.

"Like this is inconceivable. Like I'm the Loch Ness Monster."

"I don't know what I'm thinking, feeling, or seeing."

"That's the problem. You've been blind for years."

I sat on the couch beside her. I tried to take her hand, but she pulled it away.

"No," she said. "You don't get to comfort me. And I don't get to comfort you. You have two questions. Ask them."

I was struck with the terrible fear that she'd had sex with Michael Joyce in our house, in our bed.

"Where did it happen?" I asked.

"The first time was in a hotel," she said. "The Westin downtown. A suite. Early. Eight in the morning. I got the kids off to school, opened up the shop. Jody ran the register and Rick made the coffee and Christy waited tables. I told them I had a dentist appointment."

"You told me you had a dentist appointment," I said.

"Yes," she said. "I lied to you directly. I never wanted to do that. I knew I was lying to you indirectly, but I hated to look you in the eyes and lie to you. I hated it."

"The Westin is a decent hotel," I said. Jesus, I sounded like a travel agent.

"The second time was in his car. We parked down on Lake Washington. You were down in Tacoma, covering the football championships."

"I called home that night," I said. "Sara was watching the kids. She said you had an emergency at the shop. The espresso maker was overheating."

"She didn't know I was lying. She thought I was at the shop."

Once or twice a month, I ran the path alongside Lake Washington. I knew I would never run it again. How can I survive this? I thought. How many more of my routines will I have to change? Again I tried to take my wife's hand. This time she let me. We interlaced our fingers. A small moment of intimacy, but enough to keep me from running out of the room and house and fleeing down the street.

"The third time was in his apartment," she said. "In his bed. Lunchtime. I fell asleep with him. I hated that. That's why I ended it. Falling asleep with him felt like the worst thing I could do. I never felt evil until I fell asleep with him."

She leaned over and kissed my forehead. I felt her heat. I didn't want to feel her heat. I didn't want to smell her scent. I didn't want to taste her. And it felt like time squared and cubed and then exploded exponentially. Days and months and years passed before I would find enough stupid courage to ask my third question.

"What did you do with him?"

"What do you mean?" she asked.

"I mean, into which parts of you did he put it?"

She flinched so painfully that I might as well have punched her in her chest. I was briefly happy about that.

"Do you really want to know that?" she asked.

"Yes."

She stood and walked away from me. I assume she was afraid I might really punch her.

"We," she said. "He—I mean, we—did everything."

"Say it exactly."

"I don't want to."

"You have to. It's part of the deal."

"I can't. It hurts too much."

"You don't get to feel as much pain as me. Now say it. Tell me exactly."

She closed her eyes and moaned like some tortured animal, like she was the first animal feeling the first pain. I heard that sound again when she buried her mother and, thirteen months later, her father.

"Tell me," I said. "Exactly."

She couldn't speak. Instead, she pointed at her mouth, her vagina, and her ass. She looked like a pornographic mime. I started laughing. I lay down on the couch and laughed. I couldn't stop laughing. She stared at me like I was crazy. Then she started laughing with me. Softly at first, but soon she had to sit down laughing on the floor so she wouldn't fall down laughing on the floor. She crawled across the floor and climbed onto the couch with me. We held each other and laughed. Then, as suddenly as it started, it stopped. We held each other in the silence.

"If you still love me," she said, "please, please, build me a time machine."

She sounded like a little girl talking to her father. I didn't know what to say. But we lay there together for hours until the kids came home from school and surprised us.

"Mommy and Daddy were doing it!" the four of them chanted and danced around the living room. "Mommy and Daddy were doing it!"

Sharon and I danced with our children. We danced the family dance, three quick spins, two hops, and a scream at the ceiling, and then Sharon and I made dinner, and we ate with our kids and gossiped about their school days and played *Chutes and Ladders* and watched *The Lion King* and made them brush their teeth and wash their faces and forced them into their pajamas and pushed them down the hallways into their beds and read them *Curious George* and Go, *Dog, Go!* and turned off the lights and told them good night and gave them our love, and we sat in the kitchen across from each other and drank coffee and added up our wins and our losses and decided to stay married.

It was Emily Dickinson who wrote, "After great pain, a formal feeling comes." So Sharon and I formally rebuilt our marriage. And it was blue-collar work, exhausting and painful. We didn't argue more often than before, but we did live with longer and greater silences. There were times when both of us wanted to quit, but we always found the strength to get up in the morning and go back to the job. And then, one winter night two years after her confession, after eating a lovely dinner at a waterfront restaurant and slow-dancing in the parking lot while a small group of tourists cheered for us, she read a book in bed while I stood at our bedroom window and stared out into the dark. We were comfortable in the silence. A day or week or month or year before, I would have felt the need to end such a wonderful evening by making love to her, by proving I could share our bed and her body with ghosts. But I felt no such need that night, and I realized we'd completed the rebuilding project, we'd constructed a brand-new marriage, a new home, that sat next to the old marriage and its dusty and shuttered house. Standing at the window, I could almost see our old house out there in the dark, and I missed it. I often thought of it as we continued with our lives.

Suddenly, Sharon and I were forty. For my birthday that year, she and the kids all pitched in together and gave me a T-shirt that read LOST CAT on the front and DO YOU KNOW WHERE I AM? on the back.

I laughed and wore that shirt as pajamas. For two years, Sharon fell asleep next to me wearing that shirt.

"Oh, Lord," I said to Sharon on the day I finally tossed the ragged T-shirt into the trash. "With every new day comes a new monument to our love and pain."

"Who wrote that?" she asked.

"I did."

"It's free verse," she said. "I hate free verse."

We laughed and kissed and made love and read books in bed. We read through years of books, decades of books. There were never enough books for us. Read, partially read, and unread, our books filled the house, stacked on shelves and counters, piled into corners and closets. Our marriage became an eccentric and disorganized library. Whitman in the pantry! The Brontë sisters in the television room! Hardy on the front porch! Dickinson in the laundry room! We kept a battered copy of Native Son in the downstairs bathroom so our guests would have something valuable to read!

How do you measure a marriage? Three of our children still lived in Seattle and taught high school English, history, and Spanish respectively, while the fourth managed a homeless shelter in Portland, Oregon. Maybe Sharon and I had never loved each other well enough, but our kids were smart and talented and sober. They made less money than we did, as we made less than our parents did. We were going the wrong way on the social-class map! How glorious!

Every Sunday night, we all gathered for dinner (Joshua drove up from Portland with his partner, Aaron, and their son) and told one another the best stories of our weeks. We needed those small ceremonies. Our contentment was always running only slightly ahead of our dissatisfaction.

Was it enough? I don't know. But we knew enough not to ask ourselves too often. We knew to ask ourselves such questions during daylight hours. We fought hard for our happiness, and sometimes we won. Over the years, we won often enough to develop a strong taste for winning.

And then suddenly and mortally, Sharon and I were sixty-six years old.

On her birthday that year, surrounded by her husband, daughters, sons, and six grandkids, Sharon blew out the candles on her cake, closed her eyes, and made some secret wish.

One year later, after chemotherapy, radiation, organic food, acupuncture, and tribal shaman, Sharon lay on her deathbed in Sacred Hope Hospital. Our children had left their children to gather around Sharon, and it was good-bye Sarah! Good-bye Rachael! Good-bye Francis! Good-bye Joshua! She asked our children to give us some privacy. They cried and hugged her and left us alone.

"I'm going to die soon," Sharon said.

"I know," I said.

"I'm okay with it."

"I'm not. Because I love you so much," I said, "I would fistfight Time to win back your youth."

"You're a liar," she said and smiled, too tired to laugh.

"I lied to you once," I said. "But I haven't lied to you since."

"Is that the truth?"

"Yes," I said.

INDIAN EDUCATION

First Grade

My hair was too short and my U.S. Government glasses were horn-rimmed, ugly, and all that first winter in school, the other Indian boys chased me from one corner of the playground to the other. They pushed me down, buried me in the snow until I couldn't breathe, thought I'd never breathe again.

They stole my glasses and threw them over my head, around my outstretched hands, just beyond my reach, until someone tripped me and sent me falling again, facedown in the snow.

I was always falling down; my Indian name was Junior Falls

Down. Sometimes it was Bloody Nose or Steal-His-Lunch. Once, it was Cries-Like-a-White-Boy, even though none of us had seen a white boy cry.

Then it was a Friday morning recess and Frenchy SiJohn threw snowballs at me while the rest of the Indian boys tortured some other *top-yogh-yaught* kid, another weakling. But Frenchy was confident enough to torment me all by himself, and most days I would have let him.

But the little warrior in me roared to life that day and knocked Frenchy to the ground, held his head against the snow, and punched him so hard that my knuckles and the snow made symmetrical bruises on his face. He almost looked like he was wearing war paint.

But he wasn't the warrior. I was. And I chanted *It's a good day to die, it's a good day to die*, all the way down to the principal's office.

Second Grade

Betty Towle, missionary teacher, redheaded and so ugly that no one ever had a puppy crush on her, made me stay in for recess fourteen days straight.

"Tell me you're sorry," she said.

"Sorry for what?" I asked.

"Everything," she said and made me stand straight for fifteen minutes, eagle-armed with books in each hand. One was a math book; the other was English. But all I learned was that gravity can be painful.

For Halloween I drew a picture of her riding a broom with a scrawny cat on the back. She said that her God would never forgive me for that.

Once, she gave the class a spelling test but set me aside and gave me a test designed for junior high students. When I spelled all the words right, she crumpled up the paper and made me eat it.

"You'll learn respect," she said.

She sent a letter home with me that told my parents to either cut my braids or keep me home from class. My parents came in the next day and dragged their braids across Betty Towle's desk.

"Indians, indians, indians." She said it without capitalization. She called me "indian, indian, indian."

And I said, *Yes, I am. I am Indian. Indian, I am.*

Third Grade

My traditional Native American art career began and ended with my very first portrait: *Stick Indian Taking a Piss in My Backyard.*

As I circulated the original print around the classroom, Mrs. Schluter intercepted and confiscated my art.

Censorship, I might cry now. *Freedom of expression*, I would write in editorials to the tribal newspaper.

In third grade, though, I stood alone in the corner, faced the wall, and waited for the punishment to end.

I'm still waiting.

Fourth Grade

"You should be a doctor when you grow up," Mr. Schluter told me, even though his wife, the third grade teacher, thought I was crazy beyond my years. My eyes always looked like I had just hit-and-run someone.

"Guilty," she said. "You always look guilty."

"Why should I be a doctor?" I asked Mr. Schluter.

"So you can come back and help the tribe. So you can heal people."

That was the year my father drank a gallon of vodka a day and the same year that my mother started two hundred different quilts but never finished any. They sat in separate, dark places in our HUD house and wept savagely.

I ran home after school, heard their Indian tears, and looked in the mirror. *Doctor Victor*, I called myself, invented an education, talked to my reflection. *Doctor Victor to the emergency room.*

Fifth Grade

I picked up a basketball for the first time and made my first shot. No. I missed my first shot, missed the basket completely, and the ball landed in the dirt and sawdust, sat there just like I had sat there only minutes before.

But it felt good, that ball in my hands, all those possibilities and angles. It was mathematics, geometry. It was beautiful.

At that same moment, my cousin Steven Ford sniffed rubber cement from a paper bag and leaned back on the merry-go-round. His ears rang, his mouth was dry, and everyone seemed so far away.

But it felt good, that buzz in his head, all those colors and noises. It was chemistry, biology. It was beautiful.

* * *

Oh, do you remember those sweet, almost innocent choices that the Indian boys were forced to make?

Sixth Grade

Randy, the new Indian kid from the white town of Spring-dale, got into a fight an hour after he first walked into the reservation school.

Stevie Flett called him out, called him a squawman, called him a pussy, and called him a punk.

Randy and Stevie, and the rest of the Indian boys, walked out into the playground.

"Throw the first punch," Stevie said as they squared off.

"No," Randy said.

"Throw the first punch," Stevie said again.

"No," Randy said again.

"Throw the first punch!" Stevie said for the third time, and Randy reared back and pitched a knuckle fastball that broke Stevie's nose.

We all stood there in silence, in awe.

That was Randy, my soon-to-be first and best friend, who taught me the most valuable lesson about living in the white world: *Always throw the first punch.*

Seventh Grade

I leaned through the basement window of the HUD house and kissed the white girl who would later be raped by her foster-parent father, who was also white. They both lived on the reservation, though, and when the headlines and stories filled the papers later, not one word was made of their color.

Just Indians being Indians, someone must have said somewhere and they were wrong.

But on the day I leaned through the basement window of the HUD house and kissed the white girl, I felt the good-byes I was saying to my entire tribe. I held my lips tight against her lips, a dry, clumsy, and ultimately stupid kiss.

But I was saying good-bye to my tribe, to all the Indian girls and women I might have loved, to all the Indian men who might have called me cousin, even brother.

I kissed that white girl and when I opened my eyes, she was gone from the reservation, and when I opened my eyes, I was gone from the reservation, living in a farm town where a beautiful white girl asked my name.

"Junior Polatkin," I said, and she laughed.

After that, no one spoke to me for another five hundred years.

Eighth Grade

At the farm town junior high, in the boys' bathroom, I could hear voices from the girls' bathroom, nervous whispers of anorexia and bulimia. I could hear the white girls' forced vomiting, a sound so familiar and natural to me after years of listening to my father's hangovers.

"Give me your lunch if you're just going to throw it up," I said to one of those girls once.

I sat back and watched them grow skinny from self-pity.

* * *

Back on the reservation, my mother stood in line to get us commodities. We carried them home, happy to have food, and opened the canned beef that even the dogs wouldn't eat.

But we ate it day after day and grew skinny from self-pity.

There is more than one way to starve.

Ninth Grade

At the farm town high school dance, after a basketball game in an overheated gym where I had scored twenty-seven points and pulled down thirteen rebounds, I passed out during a slow song.

As my white friends revived me and prepared to take me to the emergency room where doctors would later diagnose my diabetes, the Chicano teacher ran up to us.

"Hey," he said. "What's that boy been drinking? I know all about these Indian kids. They start drinking real young."

Sharing dark skin doesn't necessarily make two men brothers.

Tenth Grade

I passed the written test easily and nearly flunked the driving, but still received my Washington State driver's license on the same day that Wally Jim killed himself by driving his car into a pine tree.

No traces of alcohol in his blood, good job, wife and two kids.

"Why'd he do it?" asked a white Washington State trooper.

All the Indians shrugged their shoulders, looked down at the ground.

"Don't know," we all said, but when we look in the mirror, see the history of our tribe in our eyes, taste failure in the tap water, and shake with old tears, we understand completely.

Believe me, everything looks like a noose if you stare at it long enough.

Eleventh Grade

Last night I missed two free throws which would have won the game against the best team in the state. The farm town high school I play for is nicknamed the "Indians," and I'm probably the only actual Indian ever to play for a team with such a mascot.

This morning I pick up the sports page and read the headline: INDIANS LOSE AGAIN.

Go ahead and tell me none of this is supposed to hurt me very much.

Twelfth Grade

I walk down the aisle, valedictorian of this farm town high school, and my cap doesn't fit because I've grown my hair longer than it's ever been. Later, I stand as the school board chairman recites my awards, accomplishments, and scholarships.

I try to remain stoic for the photographers as I look toward the future.

*   *   *

Back home on the reservation, my former classmates graduate: a few can't read, one or two are just given attendance diplomas, most look forward to the parties. The bright students are shaken frightened, because they don't know what comes next.

They smile for the photographer as they look back toward tradition.

The tribal newspaper runs my photograph and the photograph of my former classmates side by side.

Postscript: Class Reunion

Victor said, "Why should we organize a reservation high school reunion? My graduating class has a reunion every weekend at the Powwow Tavern."

GENTRIFICATION

A month ago, my next-door neighbors tossed a horribly stained mattress onto the curb in front of their house. I suppose they believed the mattress would be collected on our next regular garbage day. But the city charges thirty dollars to dispose of bulky items and you have to go online and schedule the pickup. Obviously, my neighbors had not bothered to schedule such an appointment. I'd thought the city, once they'd learned of the abandoned mattress, would have collected it anyway and automatically added the charge, plus a fine, to my neighbors' utility bill.

But four garbage collection days passed and nothing happened. The mattress, dank and dirty to begin with, had begun to mold. There were new holes in the fabric that I assumed were made by rats. We live in a large waterfront city so there are millions of rodents. It's an expected, if rather unwelcome, part of urban life. In every city in the world, there are more rats than people. But one doesn't throw a potential home for them onto the curb in front of one's house. That mattress was an apartment building for rats. Or at least a vacation home.

I'd thought to call the city and tell them about the mattress, but I doubted that I would have remained anonymous.

I am the only white man living on a block where all of my neighbors are black. Don't get me wrong. My neighbors are like any other group of neighbors I've ever had. They are the same self-appointed guardians, social directors, friendly alcoholics, paranoid assholes, overburdened parents, sullen teenagers, flirty housewives, elderly misers, amateur comedians, and hermits that exist in every neighborhood of every city in the country. They are people, not black people; and I am a person, not a white person. And that is how we relate to one another, as people. I'm not treated as the white guy on the block, at least not overtly or rudely, and I do not treat my neighbors as if they are some kind of aliens. We live as people live, aware of racial dynamics but uninterested in their applications as it applies to our neighborhood.

My next-door neighbors, an older couple with two adult sons living at home, are kind. All four of them often sit on their front porch, sharing snacks and drinks, and greeting everybody who walks past. But they'd been sitting only a few feet away from the mattress they'd so haphazardly tossed onto the curb. How could they have continued to live as if creating such a mess were normal? I wanted to ask them what they planned to do about the mattress, though I wasn't even sure of the older son's name. It's something ornately African-sounding that I hadn't quite understood when I'd first met him, and it was too late, a year later, to ask for the proper pronunciation. And that made me feel racist. If his name were something more typical, like Ron or Eddie or Vlad or Pete or Carlos or Juan, then I would have remembered it later. The simple names are easier to remember. So, in this regard, perhaps I am racist.

And, frankly, it felt racist for me to look out my front window at that abandoned mattress and wonder about the cultural norms that allowed my neighbors, so considerate otherwise, to create a health hazard. And why hadn't my other neighbors complained? Or maybe they had complained and the city had ignored the mattress because it was a black neighborhood? Who was the most racist in that situation? Was it the white man who was too terrified to confront his black neighbors on their rudeness? Was it the black folks who abandoned the mattress on their curb? Was it the black people who didn't feel the need to judge the behavior of their black neighbors? Was it the city, which let a mattress molder on the street in full view of hundreds, if not thousands, of people? Or was it all of us, black and white, passively revealing that, despite our surface friendliness, we didn't really care about one another?

In any case, after another garbage day had passed, I rented a U-Haul truck, a flatbed with enough room to carry the mattress, and parked it—hid it, really—two blocks away. I didn't want to embarrass or anger my neighbors so I set my alarm for three A.M. I didn't turn on the lights as I donned gloves, coveralls, and soft-soled shoes. Perhaps I was being overcautious. But it was fun, too, to be on a secret mission.

I slowly opened my front door, worried the hinges might creak, and took step after careful step on the porch, avoiding the loose boards. Then I walked across my lawn rather than on the sidewalk. A dog barked. It was slightly foggy. A bat swooped near a streetlight. For a moment, I felt like I'd walked into a werewolf movie. Then I wondered what the police would do if they discovered a clean-cut white man creeping through a black neighborhood.

"Buddy," the cops would say. "You don't fit the profile of the neighborhood."

I almost laughed out loud at my joke. That would have been a stupid way to get caught.

Then I stood next to the mattress and realized that I hadn't figured out how I was supposed to carry that heavy, awkward, water-logged thing two blocks to the truck.

Given more time, I probably could have rigged up a pulley system or a Rube Goldberg contraption that would have worked. But all I had that night was brute strength, without the brute.

I kicked the mattress a few times to flush out any rats. Then I grabbed the mattress's plastic handles—thank God they were still intact—and tried to lift the thing. It was heavier than I expected, and smelled and felt like a dead dolphin.

At first I tried to drag the mattress, but that made too much noise. Then I tried to carry it on my back, but it kept sliding from my grip. My only option was to carry the mattress on my head, like an African woman gracefully walking with a vase of water balanced on her head, except without her grace.

Of course, the mattress was too heavy and unbalanced to be carried that way for long. It kept slipping off my head onto the sidewalk. It didn't make much noise when it fell; I was more worried that my lung-burning panting would wake everybody.

It took me twenty minutes to carry that mattress to the truck and another ten to slide it into the flatbed. Then I got behind the wheel and drove to the city's waste disposal facility in the Fremont neighborhood. But it wouldn't open for another two hours so I parked on the street, lay across the seat, and fell asleep in the truck.

I was awakened by the raw noise of recycling and garbage trucks. I wiped my mouth, ran my fingers through my hair, and hoped that I wouldn't offend anybody with my breath. I also hoped that the facility workers wouldn't think that filthy mattress was mine. But I shouldn't have worried. The workers were too busy to notice one bad-breathed man with one rat-stained mattress.

They charged me forty bucks to dispose of the mattress, and it was worth it. Then I returned the truck to the U-Haul rental site and took a taxi back to my house.

I felt clean. I felt rich and modest, like an anonymous benefactor.

When I stepped out of the taxi I saw my neighbors— mother, father, and two adult sons—sitting in the usual places on their porch. They were drinking Folgers instant coffee, awful stuff they'd shared with me on many occasions.

I waved to them but they didn't wave back. I pretended they hadn't noticed me and waved again. They stared at me. They knew what I had done.

"You didn't have to do that," said the son with the African name. "We can take care of ourselves."

"I'm sorry," I said.

"You think you're better than us, don't you?"

I wanted to say that, when it came to abandoned mattresses, I was better.

"Right now, I feel worse," I said.

I knew I had done a good thing, so why did I hurt so bad? Why did I feel judged?

"You go home, white boy," the son said. "And don't you bother us anymore."

I knew the entire block would now shun me. I felt pale and lost, like an American explorer in the wilderness.

FAME

You've seen the viral video of the zoo lion, in its enclosure, trying to eat a toddler girl through the observation glass, right?

I was there, at the zoo, and watched it live.

Three million people think it's the cutest thing ever. And the toddler's mother, as she filmed the scene, laughed and laughed.

I didn't think it was funny. I kept thinking, Shit, that lion wants to eat that kid's face. But, yeah, yeah, laugh at the lion. Laugh at the apex predator trapped behind glass.

I was only at the zoo because I was trying to impress a woman who made balloon animals. She worked part-time near the primate enclosure, but I met her when she worked my niece's birthday party at the local community center.

Her giraffes were great; her elephants were passable; her tarantulas looked like tarantulas so nobody wanted them.

She made fifty bucks for each party she worked. The zoo paid her minimum wage plus commission. But who comes to the zoo for balloon animals? If you're going to buy something for a kid at the zoo, then you're going to get a stuffed animal.

So she was a beautiful woman with an eccentric skill that was financially unsustainable.

I liked her well enough to think about being in love with her. We'd been on two dates.

Later that afternoon, over coffee, halfway through our third date, she told me I had a great face but weighed thirty pounds too much.

Get skinny, she said, like we could wear each other's jeans, and then maybe I'll have sex with you.

I knew I'd never be thin enough. So we dumped our coffees and I walked her home. We didn't talk. What needed to be said? I probably should have let her walk home alone, but I faintly hoped she'd change her mind about me.

It was a security building, and she didn't revise her opinion of me, so I said goodbye on the sidewalk.

She apologized for rejecting me.

I said, Apologies offered and accepted are what make us human.

She laughed and walked into her building. Through the lobby window, I watched her step into her elevator and disappear behind the closing doors.

I knew she was rising away from me.

I wasn't angry. I was lonely. I was bored. And I half-remembered a time when I'd been feared.

Nostalgic, I pressed my mouth against the glass and chewed.

If somebody had filmed me and posted it online then I would have become that guy with the teeth. I would have become a star.

FAITH

Afew months ago, my wife, Sarah, and I went to a dinner party at Aaron's house. He's a longtime friend of Sarah's. They were counselors at a summer Bible camp in the '70s. I suspected they fell in love, but I doubt they'd consummated that teenage infatuation. Or maybe they did it in a boathouse and felt elated and guilty. I never asked them. Who wants to know such a thing? Both of them had grown up in strict Evangelical families. Aaron was still a Jesus freak, but Sarah had become an American Catholic. Like me, she was disinterested in the Pope and in love with Eucharist, that glorious metaphoric cannibalism of our Messiah. We had baptized our daughter, Jessica, but she hadn't been confirmed. And we only went to Mass on Easter and Christmas and maybe three other random Sundays during the year.

Aaron's dinner party was less about pot roast and more about group prayer. He'd called for a gathering of his old and new Evangelical friends. And he'd invited Sarah despite her conversion to my religion. I've always hated any party, but was especially wary of one that included conservative Christians. My wife had an Evangelical streak that surfaced when she was around Jesus freaks, and I thought it was ugly and unsexy.

"If they start faith-healing," I said to Sarah, "I am out of there."

"It's just dinner," she said.

Five minutes after we arrived at the party, and one minute into a conversation with a couple we'd just met, a fifty-something blonde said, "I have an artificial leg." Just like that. Boom. After somebody says that, you have to work hard to *not* look down and try to figure out which leg was which. And if I'd been in any other environment except for that bunch of repressed Christians, I would have said, "Cool. Which one?" And probably asked to touch it. But all I could do was sort of stammer. She was wearing a knee-length black skirt, black stockings, and long black boots, so it was impossible to tell which leg was which. I suspected she'd often tried to shock people with sudden announcements about her prosthetic limb. Perhaps she was self-conscious about it. Or maybe she was just funny. Maybe she used humor, consciously or subconsciously, to gain power over the situation. Fair enough.

Carefully balancing my plate, I sat next to her on the couch during the dinner party and kept taking quick glances at her legs.

I could not contain my curiosity. She had great legs, by the way, both very shapely, so I thought, Damn, that is an awesome artificial leg. And then I wondered if it was okay to call it an artificial leg. She used it in all the ways that a person uses a leg, right? And she was so natural, so practiced, that her two legs seemed to work in exactly the same ways. So wasn't the prosthetic leg, philosophically speaking, as real as the other one?

Anyway, she eventually caught me staring, and while it's not unusual for a woman to catch a man staring at some part of her, this particular moment wasn't about passion. She was a very attractive woman, but I wasn't looking at her legs out of sexual interest. I mean, while I noticed the shapeliness of her legs and of her in general, I was only interested in solving the mystery of which leg was made of plastic and metal. But my glances had become longer and more obvious, so she defensively crossed her legs, and then I felt sure the right one was flesh-bone-and-blood because it moved in ways that I assumed you can't move a prosthetic. I looked up at her eyes. I wanted to apologize, but I couldn't exactly blurt out at a dinner party, "Hey, I'm really sorry for objectifying you there, and I do respect you as a human being, even if you are a crazy fundamentalist Christian, and if you want to stare at my legs or any other part of me, that's okay, because men love to be objectified." But instead of being, you know, insane, I decided it was best to have a normal conversation with her.

"So what do you do?" I asked.

"I'm a guidance counselor at an elementary school in Rainier Valley," she said. Rainier Valley was the most ethnically diverse neighborhood in Seattle—actually, the only ethnically diverse neighborhood—and therefore had the most poor people and/or first-generation immigrants.

"That must be pretty tough," I said.

"Yeah," she said. "Education isn't always the first priority. And there is a lot of poverty, as you know. And drug use and domestic violence. And sometimes kids come to school hungry."

"Wow, that must be heartbreaking," I said.

"Sometimes," she said. "But it's good work. Sometimes, you can save a kid's life. Or at least give them a chance to save their own lives. I've had about a dozen kids who've gone on to graduate from college. One of them is a teacher at my school, so that's pretty amazing. Every time I see him, I'm reminded of why I do this work."

Okay, so she had a bit of a Messiah complex, but what Christian doesn't? And, hey, I thought, she's one of those crazy religious people who actually lives up to her ideals, so I liked her all of a sudden. I liked her too suddenly and too much.

"So what do you do?" she asked me.

"I'm a firefighter," I said.

"You ever pull anybody out of a burning house?" she asked.

"A few times," I said.

"Oh, so we have the same jobs," she said, and leaned a bit closer to me. I could smell her perfume and it reminded me of every woman I had ever slept with.

And then she told a series of very funny and entertaining stories about her husband, who was sitting on another couch five feet away from us. She was performing for everybody at the party. Most of the stories were gently mocking—like most of the stories that spouses tell about each other—but there was also a current of cruelty. The basic theme of each story was, "My husband is the omega wolf in any pack." And her short, bald, chubby husband quietly sat there and accepted the abuse.

"Do you know that SkyMall catalogue?" she asked all of us.

Of course we did. Anybody who has ever traveled by airplane has glanced through that catalogue of garden gnomes, quick-drying polyester pantsuits, and cell phone chargers that work in countries no one's ever heard of.

"Have you ever seen that bug vacuum?" she asked.

None of the others remembered it, but I did.

"You mean that red thing with the long tube?" I said.

"Yes," she said, and explained it to the others. "You put the nozzle over the bugs, hit the go button, and it sucks them up. And it has these extender tubes that are, like, thirty feet long. You can reach the top of a church to vacuum up bugs. And you can supposedly dump them outside, still alive."

We all laughed.

"My husband bought one of those things," she said. "Right from the airplane. He went on the in-flight Wi-Fi and ordered it at thirty thousand feet."

"I've never heard of anyone buying anything from Sky-Mall." I said. "It's so goofy."

And then I realized that I'd called her husband goofy. I wanted to pretend that I did it by accident, but no, I was competing for his wife's attention. They'd been married for decades and I was flirting with her in front of his friends. And I was also doing it in front of my wife, whom I hadn't even thought of since I'd sat down beside that woman. I glanced over at her husband and he was staring down at his open hands. I wondered if he wanted to make fists.

"Yeah, so my dear husband buys this bug vacuum," she said. "And has it shipped overnight to our house. Overnight! And he opens it right away, puts it together, and goes looking for bugs. Like he's on safari."

"Was he wearing khaki?" I asked.

"He should have been," she said. "He could have ordered that from SkyMall, too."

More laughter from the gathered Christians.

"So he finds this big spider in his man cave in the basement," she said. "One of those scary ones that look like a piece of popcorn. It's on the ceiling, but the ceiling is low, seven feet high, so my husband puts on the extenders. He's standing thirty feet away from the spider. Thirty!"

The Christians howled.

"So he sucks that thing up. And runs to the front door, flings it open with one hand, and runs out to the street. I follow him out and I see him trying to reverse the vacuum so it shoots that spider out instead of sucking it in. But he does something wrong, so the whole thing falls apart. The extensions drop off and the storage chamber thing is open and the spider comes roaring out and jumps onto his shirt."

Her husband smiled. It wasn't real.

"And he starts screaming. This high-pitched wail that sounds like a nine-year-old girl. And he's jumping around trying to knock that spider off his shirt. He's slapping his chest trying to smash it. And then it crawls up onto his neck and his face. And, there he is, my tough husband, slapping his own face trying to kill a spider. And then he gets it. So he has giant dead popcorn spider all over his chin."

The Christians applauded. I wondered how often she told stories that humiliated her husband. And I realized that her mean-ness made her more attractive. It was my turn to cross my legs.

"Can you believe my husband?" she asked. "Afraid of spiders."

She laughed, shook her head, and put her hand on my thigh. Women often touch other people during conversation. Women enjoy that slight affection but it's always a touch to a safe area: knee, elbow, shoulder. Touching a joint is a polite way to establish connection. There are fewer nerves. If you want to stay friendly, touch the place with the fewest nerves. But that woman touched my thigh with her whole hand and squeezed just a bit, and it was high enough up my thigh to be on the border between "Friendly Female Gesture" and "Do You Want a Hand Job?"

I looked around the room, but nearly everybody, my wife included, was too busy laughing to have noticed the thigh grab. Of course, the husband had noticed. And he stared at me with such a blank look, I couldn't read him. I didn't know what he was thinking. But I immodestly knew I'd always been the alpha male in any room and he'd probably always been the omega. His wife had chosen to flirt with me and insult her husband. And I still hadn't bothered to look at my wife. Jesus, I felt like I was having a swift and very public affair.

And then, I saw real emotion in the husband. A flash of pain. Male vanity is so sad because it goes against our macho train-ing and does not receive much sympathy from anybody. I bully myself when I am in periods of male vanity.

And now the other folks began to tell stories, none of them particularly interesting or cruel, and they prayed together.

I opened my eyes and stared at the woman. I fought the urge to reach out and touch her prosthetic limb. I wanted to prove to her that I wasn't afraid of her disability, that I could be affectionate about it. I wanted to whisper in her ear and tell her that her thigh touch had made me shudder, and that if she had moved her hand ever so slightly, I would have orgasmed.

And I kept thinking such sinful thoughts until they ended their prayer.

"Oh, wait," she said to me. "We're having a career day for the third graders at my school next week. You have to come. Every kid loves a fireman. Give me your e-mail address so I can send you an official invitation. To come speak."

But it felt like an official invitation to commit adultery. Or maybe I was just fooling myself. Maybe she was just a flirt. Maybe she was one of those repressed Christian women who are blind to their own sexuality. Maybe she wasn't aware that she'd touched my thigh.

I looked at my wife for the first time but she was talking to another woman and there were no signs that she felt threatened, that she'd even been aware of what was (or wasn't) happening.

"Will you come to my school?" the wife asked. "You have to come."

"I'm kind of an asshole," I said. "I'm really not appropriate for third graders."

Then, because I'd driven myself to the party, straight from work, I made excuses that I had to fill in for a sick guy and work the graveyard shift.

"It's a firefighter's life," I said. "Always on call."

My wife looked at me and smiled. She knew I was lying about work, but I assumed she thought I was just fleeing the fundamentalists. I don't think she was aware that I was fleeing temptation. She was unaware that I was being an iron husband, strong and faithful.

I said my goodbyes and hurried out the door and into my car. But I took the long way, around the lake, so I could think more about that woman. I promised myself that I'd only think about sex with her as long as it took me to get home. And I have mostly kept that promise. Mostly.

So, damn.

SALT

I wrote the obituary for the obituaries editor. Her name was Lois Andrews. Breast cancer. She was only forty-five. One in eight women get breast cancer, an epidemic. Lois's parents had died years earlier. Dad's cigarettes kept their promises. Mom's Parkinson's shook her into the ground. Lois had no siblings and had never been married. No kids. No significant other at present. No significant others in recent memory. Nobody remembered meeting one of her others. Some wondered if there had been any others. Perhaps Lois had been that rarest of holy people, the secular and chaste nun. So, yes, her sexuality was a mystery often discussed but never solved. She had many friends. All of them worked at the paper.

I wasn't her friend, not really. I was only eighteen, a summer intern at the newspaper, moving from department to department as need and boredom required, and had only spent a few days working with Lois. But she'd left a note, a handwritten will and testament, with the editor in chief, and she'd named me as the person she wanted to write her obituary.

"Why me?" I asked the chief. He was a bucket of pizza and beer tied to a broomstick.

"I don't know," he said. "It's what she wanted."

"I didn't even know her."

"She was a strange duck," he said.

I wanted to ask him how to tell the difference between strange and typical ducks. But he was a humorless white man with power, and I was a reservation Indian boy intern. I was to be admired for my ethnic tenacity but barely tolerated because of my callow youth.

"I've never written an obituary by myself," I said. During my hours at her desk, Lois had carefully supervised my work.

"It may seem bureaucratic and formal," she'd said. "But we have to be perfect. This is a sacred thing. We have to do this perfectly."

"Come on," the chief said. "What did you do when you were working with her? She taught you how to write one, didn't she?"

"Well, yeah, but—"

"Just do your best," he said and handed me her note. It was short, rather brutal, and witty. She didn't want any ceremony. She didn't want a moment of silence. Or a moment of indistinct noise, either. And she didn't want anybody to gather at a local bar and tell drunken stories about her because those stories would inevitably be romantic and false. And she'd rather be forgotten than inaccurately remembered. And she wanted me to write the obituary.

It was an honor, I guess. It would have been difficult, maybe impossible, to write a good obituary about a woman I didn't know. But she made it easy. She insisted in her letter that I use the standard fill-in-the-blanks form.

"If it was good enough for others," she'd written, "it is good enough for me."

A pragmatic and lonely woman, sure. And serious about her work. But, trust me, she was able to tell jokes without insulting the dead. At least, not directly.

That June, a few days before she went on the medical leave that she'd never return from, Lois had typed *surveyed* instead of *survived* in the obituary for a locally famous banker. That error made it past the copy editors and was printed: *Mr. X is surveyed by his family and friends.*

Mr. X's widow called Lois to ask about the odd word choice.

"I'm sorry," Lois said. She was mortified. It was the only serious typo of her career. "It was my error. It's entirely my fault. I apologize. I will correct it for tomorrow's issue."

"Oh, no, please don't," the widow said. "My husband would have loved it. He was a poet. Never published or anything like that. But he loved poems. And that word, *survey*—well, it might be accidental, but it's poetry, I think. I mean, my husband would have been delighted to know that his family and friends were surveying him at the funeral."

And so a surprised and delighted Lois spent the rest of the day thinking of verbs that more accurately reflected our interactions with the dead.

Mr. X is assailed by his family and friends.

Mr. X is superseded by his family and friends.

Mr. X is superimposed by his family and friends.

Mr. X is sensationalized by his family and friends.

Mr. X is shadowboxed by his family and friends.

Lois laughed as she composed her imaginary obituaries. I'd never seen her laugh that much, and I suspected that very few people had seen her react that strongly to anything. She wasn't remote or strained, she was just private. And so her laughter—her public joy—was frankly erotic. Though I'd always thought of her as a sexy librarian—with her wire-rimmed glasses and curly brown hair and serious panty hose and suits—I'd never really thought of going to bed with her. Not to any serious degree. I was eighteen, so I fantasized about having sex with nearly every woman I saw, but I hadn't obsessed about Lois. Not really. I'd certainly noticed that her calves were a miracle of muscle—her best feature—but I'd only occasionally thought of kissing my way up and down her legs. But at that moment, as she laughed about death, I had to shift my legs to hide my erection.

"Hey, kid," she said, "when you die, how do you want your friends and family to remember you?"

"Jeez," I said. "I don't want to think about that stuff. I'm eighteen."

"Oh, so young," she said. "So young and handsome. You're going to be very popular with the college girls."

I almost whimpered. But I froze, knowing that the slightest movement, the softest brush of my pants against my skin, would cause me to orgasm.

Forgive me, I was only a kid.

"Ah, look at you," Lois said. "You're blushing."

And so I grabbed a random file off her desk and ran. I made my escape. But, oh, I was in love with the obituaries editor. And she—well, she taught me how to write an obituary.

And so this is how I wrote hers:

Lois Andrews, age 45, of Spokane, died Friday, August 24, 1985, at Sacred Heart Hospital.

There will be no funeral service. She donated her body to Washington State University. An only child, Lois Anne Andrews was born January 16, 1940, at Sacred Heart Hospital, to Martin and Betsy (Harrison) Andrews. She never married. She was the obituaries editor at the *Spokesman-Review* for twenty-two years. She is survived by her friends and colleagues at the newspaper.

Yes, that was the story of her death. It was not enough. I felt morally compelled to write a few more sentences, as if those extra words would somehow compensate for what had been a brief and solitary life.

I was also bothered that Lois had donated her body to science. Of course, her skin and organs would become training tools for doctors and scientists, and that was absolutely vital, but the whole process still felt disrespectful to me. I thought of her, dead and naked, lying on a gurney while dozens of students stuck their hands inside of her. It seemed—well, pornographic. But I also knew that my distaste was cultural.

Indians respect dead bodies even more than live ones.

Of course, I never said anything. I was young and frightened and craved respect and its ugly cousin, approval, so I did as I was told. And that's why, five days after Lois's death and a few minutes after the editor in chief had told me I would be writing the obituaries until they found "somebody official," I found myself sitting at her desk.

"What am I supposed to do first?" I asked the chief.

"Well, she must have unfiled files and unwritten obits and unmailed letters."

"Okay, but where?"

"I don't know. It was *her* desk."

This was in the paper days, and Lois kept five tall filing cabinets stuffed with her job.

"I don't know what to do," I said, panicked.

"Jesus, boy," the editor in chief said. "If you want to be a journalist, you'll have to work under pressure. Jesus. And this is hardly any pressure at all. All these people are dead. The dead will not pressure you."

I stared at him. I couldn't believe what he was saying. He seemed so cruel. He was a cruel duck, that's what he was.

"Jesus," he said yet again, and grabbed a folder off the top of the pile. "Start with this one."

He handed me the file and walked away. I wanted to shout at him that he'd said Jesus three times in less than fifteen seconds. I wasn't a Christian and didn't know much about the definition of blasphemy, but it seemed like he'd committed some kind of sin.

But I kept my peace, opened the file, and read the handwritten letter inside. A woman had lost her husband. Heart attack. And she wanted to write the obituary and run his picture. She included her phone number. I figured it was okay to call her. So I did.

"Hello?" she said. Her name was Mona.

"Oh, hi," I said. "I'm calling from the *Spokesman-Review*. About your—uh, late husband?"

"Oh. Oh, did you get my letter? I'm so happy you called. I wasn't sure if anybody down there would pay attention to me."

"This is sacred," I said, remembering Lois's lessons. "We take this very seriously."

"Oh, well, that's good—that's great—and, well, do you think it will be okay for me to write the obituary? I'm a good writer. And I'd love to run my husband's photo—his name was Dean—I'd love to run his photo with the—with his—with my remembrance of him."

I had no idea if it was okay for her to write the obituary. And I believed that the newspaper generally ran only the photographs of famous dead people. But then I looked at the desktop and noticed Lois's neatly written notes trapped beneath the glass. I gave praise for her organizational skills.

"Okay, okay," I said, scanning the notes. "Yes. Yes, it's okay if you want to write the obituary yourself."

I paused and then read aloud the official response to such a request.

"Because we understand, in your time of grieving, that you want your loved one to be honored with the perfect words—"

"Oh, that's lovely."

"—but, and we're truly sorry about this, it will cost you extra," I said.

"Oh," she said. "Oh, I didn't know that. How much extra?"

"Fifty dollars."

"Wow, that's a lot of money."

"Yes," I said. It was one-fifth of my monthly rent.

"And how about running the photograph?" Mona asked.

"How much extra does that cost?"

"It depends on the size of the photo."

"How much is the smallest size?"

"Fifty dollars, as well."

"So it will be one hundred dollars to do this for my husband?"

"Yes."

"I don't know if I can afford it. I'm a retired schoolteacher on a fixed income."

"What did you teach?" I asked.

"I taught elementary school—mostly second grade—at Meadow Hills for forty-five years. I taught three generations." She was proud, even boastful. "I'll have you know that I taught the grandchildren of three of my original students."

"Well, listen," I said, making an immediate and inappropriate decision to fuck the duck in chief. "We have a special rate for—uh, retired public employees. So the rate for your own obituary and your husband's photograph is—uh, let's say twenty dollars. Does that sound okay?"

"Twenty dollars? Twenty dollars? I can do twenty dollars. Yes, that's lovely. Oh, thank you, thank you."

"You're welcome, ma'am. So—uh, tell me, when do you want this to run?"

"Well, I told my daughters and sons that it would run tomorrow."

"Tomorrow?"

"Yes, the funeral is tomorrow. I really want this to run on the same day. Is that okay? Will that be possible?"

I had no idea if it was possible. "Let me talk to the boys down in the print room," I said, as if I knew them. "And I'll call you back in a few minutes, okay?"

"Oh, yes, yes, I'll be waiting by the phone."

We said our good-byes and I slumped in my chair. In Lois's chair. What had I done? I'd made a promise I could not keep. I counted to one hundred, trying to find a cool center, and walked over to the chief's office.

"What do you want?" he asked.

"I think I screwed up."

"Well, isn't that a surprise," he said. I wanted to punch the sarcasm out of his throat.

"This woman—her husband died," I said. "And she wanted to write the obituary and run his photo—"

"That costs extra."

"I know. I read that on Lois's desk. But I read incorrectly, I think."

"How incorrectly?"

"Well, I think it's supposed to cost, like, one hundred dollars to run the obit and the size photo she wants—"

"How much did you tell her it would cost?"

"Twenty."

"So you gave her an eighty-percent discount?"

"I guess."

He stared at me. Judged me. He'd once been a Pulitzer finalist for a story about a rural drug syndicate.

"And there's more," I said.

"Yes?" His anger was shrinking his vocabulary.

"I told her we'd run it tomorrow."

"Jesus," he said. "Damn it, kid."

I think he wanted to fire me, to throw me out of his office, out of his building, out of his city and country. I suddenly realized that he was grieving for Lois, that he was angry about her death. Of course he was. They had worked together for two decades. They were friends. So I tried to forgive him for his short temper. And I did forgive him, a little.

"I'm sorry," I said.

"Well, shit on a rooster," he said, and leaned back in his chair. "Listen. I know this is a tough gig here. This is not your job. I know that. But this is a newspaper and we measure the world by column inches, okay? We have to make tough decisions about what can fit and what cannot fit. And by telling this woman—this poor woman—that she could have this space tomorrow, you have fucked with the shape of my world, okay?"

"Yes, sir," I said.

He ran his fingers through his hair (my father did the same thing when he was pissed), made a quick decision, picked up his phone, and made the call.

"Hey, Charlie, it's me," he said. "Do we have any room for another obituary? With a photo?"

I could hear the man screaming on the other end.

"I know, I know," the chief said. "But this is an important one. It's a family thing."

The chief listened to more screaming, then hung up on the other guy.

"All right," he said. "The woman gets one column inch for the obit."

"That's not much," I said.

"She's going to have to write a haiku, isn't she?"

I wanted to tell him that haikus were not supposed to be elegies, but then I realized that I wasn't too sure about that literary hypothesis.

"What do I do now?" I asked.

"We need the obit and the photo by three o'clock."

It was almost one.

"How do I get them?" I asked.

"Well, you could do something crazy like get in a car, drive to this woman's house, pick up the obit and the photo, and bring them back here."

"I don't have a car," I said.

"Do you have a driver's license?"

"Yes."

"Well, then, why don't you go sign a vehicle out of the car pool and do your fucking job?"

I fled. Obtained the car. And while cursing Lois and her early death, and then apologizing to Lois for cursing her, I drove up Maple to the widow's small house on Francis. A green house with a white fence that was maybe one foot tall. A useless fence. It couldn't keep out anything.

I rang the doorbell and waited a long time for the woman— Mona, her name was Mona—to answer. She was scrawny, thin-haired, dark for a white woman. At least eighty years old. Maybe ninety. Maybe older than that. I did the math. Geronimo was still alive when this woman was born. An old raven, I thought. No, too small to be a raven. She was a starling.

"Hello," she said.

"Hi, Mona," I said. "I'm from the *Spokesman*; we talked on the phone."

"Oh, yes, oh, yes, please come in."

I followed her inside into the living room. She slowly, painfully, sat on a wooden chair. She was too weak and frail to lower herself into a soft chair, I guess. I sat on her couch. I looked around the room and realized that every piece of furniture, every painting, every knickknack and candlestick, was older than me. Most of the stuff was probably older than my parents. I saw photographs of Mona, a man I assumed was her husband, and five or six children, and a few dozen grandchildren. Her children and grandchildren, I guess. Damn, her children were older than my parents. Her grandchildren were older than me.

"You have a nice house," I said.

"My husband and I lived here for sixty years. We raised five children here."

"Where are your children now?"

"Oh, they live all over the country. But they're all flying in tonight and tomorrow for the funeral. They loved their father. Do you love your father?"

My father was a drunken liar.

"Yes," I said. "I love him very much."

"That's good, you're a good son. A very good son."

She smiled at me. I realized she'd forgotten why I was there.

"Ma'am, about the obituary and the photograph?"

"Yes?" she said, still confused.

"We need them, the obituary you wrote for your husband, and his photograph?"

And then she remembered.

"Oh, yes, oh, yes, I have them right here in my pocket."

She handed me the photograph and the obit. And yes, it was clumsily written and mercifully short. The man in the photograph was quite handsome. A soldier in uniform. Black hair, blue eyes. I wondered if his portrait had been taken before or after he'd killed somebody.

"My husband was a looker, wasn't he?" she asked.

"Yes, very much so."

"I couldn't decide which photograph to give you. I mean, I thought I might give you a more recent one. To show you what he looks like now. He's still very handsome. But then I thought, No, let's find the most beautiful picture of them all. Let the world see my husband at his best. Don't you think that's romantic?"

"Yes, you must have loved him very much," I said.

"Oh, yes, he was ninety percent perfect. Nobody's all perfect, of course. But he was close, he was very close."

Her sentiment was brutal.

"Listen, ma'am," I said. "I'm sorry, but I have to get this photograph back to the newspaper if they're going to run on time."

"Oh, don't worry, young man, there's no rush."

Now I was confused. "But I thought the funeral was tomorrow?" I asked.

"Oh, no, silly, I buried my husband six months ago. In Veterans' Cemetery. He was at D-Day."

"And your children?"

"Oh, they were here for the funeral, but they went away."

But she looked around the room as if she could still see her kids. Or maybe she was remembering them as they had been, the children who'd indiscriminately filled the house and then, just as indiscriminately, had moved away and into their own houses. Or maybe everything was ghosts, ghosts, ghosts. She scared me. Maybe this house was lousy with ghosts. I was afraid that Lois's ghost was going to touch me on the shoulder and gently correct my errors.

"Mona, are you alone here?" I asked. I didn't want to know the answer.

"No, no—well, yes, I suppose. But my Henry, he's buried in the backyard."

"Henry?"

"My cat. Oh, my beloved cat."

And then she told me about Henry and his death. The poor cat, just as widowed as Mona, had fallen into a depression after her husband's death. Cat and wife mourned together.

"You know," she said. "I read once that grief can cause cancer. I think it's true. At least, it's true for cats. Because that's what my Henry had, cancer of the blood. Cats get it all the time. They see a lot of death, they do."

And so she, dependent on the veterinarian's kindness and charity, had arranged for her Henry to be put down.

"What's that big word for killing cats?" she asked me.

"Euthanasia," I said.

"Yes, that's it. That's the word. It's kind of a pretty word, isn't it? It sounds pretty, don't you think?"

"Yes."

"Such a pretty word for such a sad and lonely thing," she said.

"Yes, it is," I said.

"You can name your daughter Euthanasia and nobody would even notice if they didn't know what the word meant."

"I suppose," I said.

"My cat was too sick to live," Mona said.

And then she told me how she'd held Henry as the vet injected him with the death shot. And, oh, how she cried when Henry's heart and breath slowed and stopped. He was gone, gone,

gone. And so she brought him home, carried him into the backyard, and laid him beside the hole she'd paid a neighbor boy to dig. That neighbor boy was probably fifty years old.

"I prayed for a long time," she said. "I wanted God to know that my cat deserved to be in Heaven. And I didn't want Henry to be in cat heaven. Not at all. I wanted Henry to go find my husband. I want them both to be waiting for me."

And so she prayed for hours. Who can tell the exact time at such moments? And then she kneeled beside her cat. And that was painful because her knees were so old, so used—like the ancient sedan in the garage—and she pushed her Henry into the grave and poured salt over him.

"I read once," she said, "that the Egyptians used to cover dead bodies with salt. It helps people get to Heaven quicker. That's what I read."

When she poured the salt on her cat, a few grains dropped and burned in his eyes.

"And let me tell you," she said. "I almost fell in that grave when my Henry meowed. Just a little one. I barely heard it. But it was there. I put my hand on his chest and his little heart was beating. Just barely. But it was beating. I couldn't believe it. The salt brought him back to life."

Shit, I thought, the damn vet hadn't injected enough death juice into the cat. Shit, shit, shit.

"Oh, that's awful," I said.

"No, I was happy. My cat was alive. Because of the salt. So I called my doctor—"

"You mean you called the vet?"

"No, I called my doctor, Ed Marashi, and I told him that it was a miracle, that the salt brought Henry back to life."

I wanted to scream at her senile hope. I wanted to run to Lois's grave and cover her with salt so she'd rise, replace me, and be forced to hear this story. This was her job; this was her responsibility.

"And let me tell you," the old woman said. "My doctor was amazed, too, so he said he'd call the vet and they'd both be over, and it wasn't too long before they were both in my home. Imagine! Two doctors on a house call. That doesn't happen anymore, does it?"

It happens when two graceful men want to help a fragile and finite woman.

And so she told me that the doctors went to work on the cat. And, oh, how they tried to bring him back all the way, but there just wasn't enough salt in the world to make it happen. So the doctors helped her sing and pray and bury her Henry. And, oh, yes—Dr. Marashi had sworn to her that he'd tried to help her husband with salt.

"Dr. Marashi said he poured salt on my husband," she said. "But it didn't work. There are some people too sick to be salted."

She looked around the room as if she expected her husband and cat to materialize. How well can you mourn if you continually forget that the dead are dead?

I needed to escape.

"I'm really sorry, ma'am," I said. "I really am. But I have to get back to the newspaper with these."

"Is that my husband's photograph?" she asked.

"Yes."

"And is that his obituary?"

"Yes," I said. "It's the one you wrote."

"I remember, I remember."

She studied the artifacts in my hands.

"Can I have them back?" she asked.

"Excuse me?"

"The photo, and my letter, that's all I have to remember my husband. He died, you know?"

"Yes, I know," I said.

"He was at D-Day."

"If I give you these back," I said. "I won't be able to run them in the newspaper."

"Oh, I don't want them in the newspaper," she said. "My husband was a very private man."

Ah, Lois, I thought, you never told me about this kind of death.

"I have to go now," I said. I wanted to crash through the door and run away from this house fire.

"Okay, okay. Thank you for visiting," she said. "Will you come back? I love visitors."

"Yes," I said. I lied. I knew I should call somebody about her dementia. She surely couldn't take care of herself anymore. I knew I should call the police or her doctor or find her children and tell them. I knew I had responsibilities to her—to this grieving and confused stranger—but I was young and terrified.

So I left her on her porch. She was still waving when I turned the corner. Ah, Lois, I thought, are you with me, are you with me? I drove the newspaper's car out of the city and onto the freeway. I drove for three hours to the shore of Soap Lake, an inland sea heavy with iron, calcium, and salt. For thousands of years, my indigenous ancestors had traveled here to be healed. They're all gone now, dead by disease and self-destruction. Why had they believed so strongly in this magic water when it never protected them for long? When it might not have protected them at all? But you, Lois, you were never afraid of death, were you? You laughed and played. And you honored the dead with your brief and serious prayers.

Standing on the shore, I prayed for my dead. I praised them. I stupidly hoped the lake would heal my small wounds. Then I stripped off my clothes and waded naked into the water.

Jesus, I don't want to die today or tomorrow, but I don't want to live forever.

ASSIMILATION

Regarding love, marriage, and sex, both Shakespeare and Sitting Bull knew the only truth: treaties get broken. Therefore, Mary Lynn wanted to have sex with any man other than her husband. For the first time in her life, she wanted to go to bed with an Indian man only because he was Indian. She was a Coeur d'Alene Indian married to a white man; she was a wife who wanted to have sex with an indigenous stranger. She didn't care about the stranger's job or his hobbies, or whether he was due for a Cost of Living raise, or owned ten thousand miles of model railroad track. She didn't care if he was handsome or ugly, mostly because she wasn't sure exactly what those terms meant anymore and how much relevance they truly had when it came to choosing sexual partners. Oh, she'd married a very handsome man, there was no doubt about that, and she was still attracted to her husband, to his long, graceful fingers, to his arrogance and utter lack of fear in social situations—he'd say anything to anybody—but lately, she'd been forced to concentrate too hard when making love to him. If she didn't focus completely on him, on the smallest details of his body, then she would drift away from the bed and float around the room like a bored angel. Of course, all this made her feel like a failure, especially since it seemed that her husband had yet to notice her growing disinterest. She wanted to be a good lover, wife, and partner, but she'd obviously developed some form of sexual dyslexia or had picked up a mutant, contagious, and erotic strain of Attention Deficit Disorder. She felt baffled by the complications of sex. She haunted the aisles of bookstores and desperately paged through every book in the self-help section and studied every diagram and chart in the human sensuality encyclopedias. She wanted answers. She wanted to feel it again, whatever *it* was.

A few summers ago, during Crow Fair, Mary Lynn had been standing in a Montana supermarket, in the produce aisle, when a homely white woman, her spiky blond hair still wet from a trailer-house shower, walked by in a white T-shirt and blue jeans, and though Mary Lynn was straight—having politely declined all three lesbian overtures thrown at her in her life—she'd felt a warm breeze pass through her DNA in that ugly woman's wake, and had briefly wanted to knock her to the linoleum and do beautiful things to her. Mary Lynn had never before felt such lust—in Montana, of all places, for a white woman who was functionally illiterate and underemployed!—and had not since felt that sensually about any other woman or man.

Who could explain such things, these vagaries of love? There were many people who would blame Mary Lynn's unhappiness, her dissatisfaction, on her ethnicity. God, she thought, how simple and earnest was that particular bit of psychotherapy! Yes, she was most certainly a Coeur d'Alene—she'd grown up on the rez, had been very happy during her time there, and had left without serious regrets or full-time enemies—but that wasn't the only way to define her. She wished that she could be called Coeur d'Alene as a description, rather than as an excuse, reason, prescription, placebo, prediction, or diminutive. She only wanted to be understood as eccentric and complicated!

Her most cherished eccentricity: when she was feeling her most lonely, she'd put one of the Big Mom Singers's powwow CDs on the stereo (*I'm not afraid of death, hey, ya, hey, death is my cousin, hey, ya, ha, ha*) and read from Emily Dickinson's poetry (*Because I could not stop for Death— / He kindly stopped for me—*).

Her most important complication: she was a woman in a turbulent marriage that was threatening to go bad, or had gone bad and might get worse.

Yes, she was a Coeur d'Alene woman, passionately and dispassionately, who wanted to cheat on her white husband because he was white. She wanted to find an anonymous lover, an Indian man who would fade away into the crowd when she was done with him, a man whose face could appear on the back of her milk carton. She didn't care if he was the kind of man who knew the punch lines to everybody's dirty jokes, or if he was the kind of man who read Zane Grey before he went to sleep, or if he was both of those men simultaneously. She simply wanted to find the darkest Indian in Seattle—the man with the greatest amount of melanin—and get naked with him in a cheap motel room. Therefore, she walked up to a flabby Lummi Indian man in a coffee shop and asked him to make love to her.

"Now," she said. "Before I change my mind."

He hesitated for a brief moment, wondering why he was the chosen one, and then took her by the hand. He decided to believe he was a handsome man.

"Don't you want to know my name?" he asked before she put her hand over his mouth.

"Don't talk to me," she said. "Don't say one word. Just take me to the closest motel and fuck me."

The obscenity bothered her. It felt staged, forced, as if she were an actress in a three-in-the-morning cable-television movie. But she was acting, wasn't she? She was not an adulteress, was she?

Why exactly did she want to have sex with an Indian stranger? She told herself it was because of pessimism, existential-ism, even nihilism, but those reasons—*those words*—were a func-tion of her vocabulary and not of her motivations. If forced to admit the truth, or some version of the truth, she'd testify she was about to go to bed with an Indian stranger because she wanted to know how it would feel. After all, she'd slept with a white stranger in her life, so why not include a Native American? Why not practice a carnal form of affirmative action? By God, her infidelity was a political act! Rebellion, resistance, revolution!

In the motel room, Mary Lynn made the Indian take off his clothes first. Thirty pounds overweight, with purple scars criss-crossing his pale chest and belly, he trembled as he undressed. He wore a wedding ring on his right hand. She knew that some Europeans wore their wedding bands on the right hand—so maybe this Indian was married to a French woman—but Mary Lynn also knew that some divorced Americans wore rings on their right hands as symbols of pain, of mourning. Mary Lynn didn't care if he was married or not, or whether he shared custody of the sons and daughters, or whether he had any children at all. She was grateful that he was plain and desperate and lonely.

Mary Lynn stepped close to him, took his hand, and slid his thumb into her mouth. She sucked on it and felt ridiculous. His skin was salty and oily, the taste of a working man. She closed her eyes and thought about her husband, a professional who had his shirts laundered. In one hour, he was going to meet her at a new downtown restaurant.

She walked a slow, tight circle around the Indian. She stood behind him, reached around his thick waist, and held his erect penis. He moaned and she decided that she hated him. She decided to hate all men. Hate, hate, hate, she thought, and then let her hate go.

She was lovely and intelligent, and had grown up with Indian women who were more lovely and more intelligent, but who also had far less ambition and mendacity. She'd once read in a book, perhaps by Primo Levi or Elie Wiesel, that the survivors of the Nazi death camps were the Jews who lied, cheated, murdered, stole, and subverted. You must remember, said Levi or Wiesel, that the best of us did not survive the camps. Mary Lynn felt the same way about the reservation. Before she'd turned ten, she'd attended the funerals of seventeen good women—the best of the Coeur d'Alenes—and had read about the deaths of eighteen more good women since she'd left the rez. But what about the Coeur d'Alene men—those liars, cheats, and thieves—who'd survived, even thrived? Mary Lynn wanted nothing to do with them, then or now. As a teenager, she'd dated only white boys. As an adult, she'd only dated white men. God, she hated to admit it, but white men—her teachers, coaches, bosses, and lovers—had always been more dependable than the Indian men in her life. White men had rarely disappointed her, but they'd never surprised her either. White men were neutral, she thought, just like Belgium! And when has Belgium ever been sexy? When has Belgium caused a grown woman to shake with fear and guilt? She didn't want to feel Belgian; she wanted to feel dangerous.

In the cheap motel room, Mary Lynn breathed deeply. The Indian smelled of old sweat and a shirt worn twice before washing. She ran her finger along the ugly scars on his belly and chest. She wanted to know the scars' creation story—she hoped this Indian man was a warrior with a history of knife fighting—but she feared he was only carrying the transplanted heart and lungs of another man. She pushed him onto the bed, onto the scratchy comforter. She'd once read that scientists had examined a hotel-room comforter and discovered four hundred and thirty-two different samples of sperm. God, she thought, those scientists obviously had too much time on their hands and, in the end, had failed to ask the most important questions: Who left the samples? Spouses, strangers? Were these exchanges of money, tenderness, disease? Was there love?

"This has to be quick," she said to the stranger beside her.

Jeremiah, her husband, was already angry when Mary Lynn arrived thirty minutes late at the restaurant and he nearly lost all of his self-control when they were asked to wait for the next available table. He often raged at strangers, though he was incredibly patient and kind with their four children. Mary Lynn had seen that kind of rage in other white men when their wishes and desires were ignored. At ball games, in parking lots, and especially in airports, white men demanded to receive the privileges whose very existence they denied. White men could be so predictable, thought Mary Lynn. She thought: O, Jeremiah! O, season ticket holder! O, monthly parker! O, frequent flyer! She dreamed of him out there, sitting in the airplane with eighty-seven other white men wearing their second-best suits, all of them traveling toward small rooms in the Ramadas, Radissons, and sometimes the Hyatts, where they all separately watched the same pay-per-view porno that showed everything except penetration. What's the point of porno without graphic penetration? Mary Lynn knew it only made these lonely men feel all that more lonely. And didn't they deserve better, these white salesmen and middle managers, these twenty-first century Willy Lomans, who only wanted to be better men than their fathers had been? Of course, thought Mary Lynn, these sons definitely deserved better—they were smarter and more tender and generous than all previous generations of white American men—but they'd never receive their just rewards, and thus their anger was justified and banal.

"Calm down," Mary Lynn said to her husband as he continued to rage at the restaurant hostess.

Mary Lynn said those two words to him more often in their marriage than any other combination of words.

"It could be twenty, thirty minutes," said the hostess. "Maybe longer."

"We'll wait outside," said Jeremiah. He breathed deeply, remembering some mantra that his therapist had taught him.

Mary Lynn's mantra: I cheated on my husband, I cheated on my husband.

"We'll call your name," said the hostess, a white woman who was tired of men no matter what their color. "When."

Their backs pressed against the brick wall, their feet crossed on the sidewalk, on a warm Seattle evening, Mary Lynn and Jeremiah smoked faux cigarettes filled with some foul-tasting, overwhelmingly organic herb substance. For years they had smoked unfiltered Camels, but had quit after all four of their parents had simultaneously suffered through at least one form of cancer. Mary Lynn had called them the Mormon Tabernacle Goddamn Cancer Choir, though none of them was Mormon and all of them were altos. With and without grace, they had all survived the radiation, chemotherapy, and in-hospital cable-television bingo games, with their bodies reasonably intact, only to resume their previously self-destructive habits. After so many nights spent in hospital corridors, waiting rooms, and armchairs, Mary Lynn and Jeremiah hated doctors, all doctors, even the ones on television, especially the ones on television. United in their obsessive hatred, Mary Lynn and Jeremiah resorted to taking vitamins, eating free-range chicken, and smoking cigarettes rolled together and marketed by six odoriferous white liberals in Northern California.

As they waited for a table, Mary Lynn and Jeremiah watched dozens of people arrive and get seated immediately.

"I bet they don't have reservations," he said.

"I hate these cigarettes," she said.

"Why do you keep buying them?"

"Because the cashier at the health-food store is cute."

"You're shallow."

"Like a mud puddle."

Mary Lynn hated going out on weeknights. She hated driving into the city. She hated waiting for a table. Standing outside the downtown restaurant, desperate to hear their names, she decided to hate Jeremiah for a few seconds. Hate, hate, hate, she thought, and then she let her hate go. She wondered if she smelled like sex, like indigenous sex, and if a white man could recognize the scent of an enemy. She'd showered, but the water pressure had been weak and the soap bar too small.

"Let's go someplace else," she said.

"No. Five seconds after we leave, they'll call our names."

"But we won't know they called our names."

"But I'll feel it."

"It must be difficult to be psychic and insecure."

"I knew you were going to say that."

Clad in leather jackets and black jeans, standing inches apart but never quite touching, both handsome to the point of distraction, smoking crappy cigarettes that appeared to be real cigarettes, they could have been the subjects of a Schultz photograph or a Runnette poem.

The title of the photograph: "Infidelity."

The title of the poem: "More Infidelity."

Jeremiah's virtue was reasonably intact, though he'd recently been involved in a flirtatious near-affair with a coworker. At the crucial moment, when the last button was about to be unbuttoned, when consummation was just a fingertip away, Jeremiah had pushed his potential lover away and said I can't, I just can't, I love my marriage. He didn't admit to love for his spouse, partner, wife. No, he confessed his love for marriage, for the blessed union, for the legal document, for the shared mortgage payments, and for their four children.

Mary Lynn wondered what would happen if she grew pregnant with the Lummi's baby. Would this full-blood baby look more Indian than her half-blood sons and daughters?

"Don't they know who I am?" she asked her husband as they waited outside the downtown restaurant. She wasn't pregnant; there would be no paternity tests, no revealing of great secrets. His secret: he was still in love with a white woman from high school he hadn't seen in decades. What Mary Lynn knew: he was truly in love with the idea of a white woman from a mythical high school, with a prom queen named *If Only* or a homecoming princess named *My Life Could Have Been Different*.

"I'm sure they know who you are," he said. "That's why we're on the wait list. Otherwise, we'd be heading for McDonald's or Denny's."

"Your kinds of places."

"Dependable. The Big Mac you eat in Hong Kong or Des Moines tastes just like the Big Mac in Seattle."

"Sounds like colonialism to me."

"Colonialism ain't all bad."

"Put that on a bumper sticker."

This place was called Tan Tan, though it would soon be trendy enough to go by a nickname: Tan's. Maybe Tan's would become T's, and then T's would be identified only by a slight turn of the head or a certain widening of the eyes. After that, the downhill slide in reputation would be inevitable, whether or not the culinary content and quality of the restaurant remained exactly the same or improved. As it was, Tan Tan was a pan-Asian restaurant whose ownership and chefs—head, sauce, and line—were white, though most of the waitstaff appeared to be one form of Asian or another.

"Don't you hate it?" Jeremiah asked. "When they have Chinese waiters in sushi joints? Or Korean dishwashers in a Thai noodle house?"

"I hadn't really thought about it," she said.

"No, think about it, these restaurants, these Asian restaurants, they hire Asians indiscriminately because they think white people won't be able to tell the difference."

"White people can't tell the difference."

"I can."

"Hey, Geronimo, you've been hanging around Indians too long to be white."

"Fucking an Indian doesn't make me Indian."

"So, that's what we're doing now? Fucking?"

"You have a problem with fucking?"

"No, not with the act itself, but I do have a problem with your sexual thesaurus."

Mary Lynn and Jeremiah had met in college, when they were still called Mary and Jerry. After sleeping together for the first time, after her first orgasm and his third, Mary had turned to Jerry and said, with absolute seriousness: If this thing is going to last, we have to stop the end rhyme. She had majored in Milton and Blake. He'd been a chemical engineer since the age of seven, with the degree being only a matter of formality, so he'd had plenty of time to wonder how an Indian from the reservation could be so smart. He still wondered how it had happened, though he'd never had the courage to ask her.

Now, a little more than two decades after graduating with a useless degree, Mary Lynn worked at Microsoft for a man named Dickinson. Jeremiah didn't know his first name, though he hoped it wasn't Emery, and had never met the guy, and didn't care if he ever did. Mary Lynn's job title and responsibilities were vague, so vague that Jeremiah had never asked her to elaborate. She often worked sixty-hour weeks and he didn't want to reward that behavior by expressing an interest in what specific tasks she performed for Bill Gates.

Waiting outside Tan Tan, he and she could smell ginger, burned rice, beer.

"Are they ever going to seat us?" she asked.

"Yeah, don't they know who you are?"

"I hear this place discriminates against white people."

"Really?"

"Yeah, I heard once, these lawyers, bunch of white guys in Nordstrom's suits, had to wait, like, two hours for a table."

"Were those billable hours?"

"It's getting hard for a white guy to find a place to eat."

"Damn affirmative action is what it is."

Their first child had been an accident, the result of a broken condom and a missed birth control pill. They named her Antonya, Toni for short. The second and third children, Robert and Michael, had been on purpose, and the fourth, Ariel, came after Mary Lynn thought she could no longer get pregnant.

Toni was fourteen, immature for her age, quite beautiful and narcissistic, with her translucent skin, her long blond hair, and eight-ball eyes. Botticelli eyes, she bragged after taking an Introduction to Art class. She never bothered to tell anybody she was Indian, mostly because nobody asked.

Jeremiah was quite sure that his daughter, his Antonya, had lost her virginity to the pimply quarterback of the junior varsity football team. He found the thought of his daughter's adolescent sexuality both curious and disturbing. Above all else, he believed that she was far too special to sleep with a cliché, let alone a junior varsity cliché.

Three months out of every year, Robert and Michael were the same age. Currently, they were both eleven. Dark-skinned, with their mother's black hair, strong jawline, and endless nose, they looked Indian, very Indian. Robert, who had refused to be called anything other than Robert, was the smart boy, a math prodigy, while Mikey was the basketball player.

When Mary Lynn's parents called from the reservation, they always asked after the boys, always invited the boys out for the weekend, the holidays, and the summer, and always sent the boys more elaborate gifts than they sent the two girls.

When Jeremiah had pointed out this discrepancy to Mary Lynn, she had readily agreed, but had made it clear that his parents also paid more attention to the boys. Jeremiah never mentioned it again, but had silently vowed to love the girls a little more than he loved the boys.

As if love were a thing that could be quantified, he thought.

He asked himself: What if I love the girls more because they look more like me, because they look more white than the boys?

Towheaded Ariel was two, and the clay of her personality was just beginning to harden, but she was certainly petulant and funny as hell, with the ability to sleep in sixteen-hour marathons that made her parents very nervous. She seemed to exist in her own world, enough so that she was periodically monitored for incipient autism. She treated her siblings as if they somehow bored her, and was the kind of kid who could stay alone in her crib for hours, amusing herself with all sorts of personal games and imaginary friends.

Mary Lynn insisted that her youngest daughter was going to be an artist, but Jeremiah didn't understand the child, and despite the fact that he was her father and forty-three years older, he felt inferior to Ariel.

He wondered if his wife was ever going to leave him because he was white.

When Tan Tan's doors swung open, laughter and smoke rolled out together.

"You got another cigarette?" he asked.

"Quit calling them cigarettes. They're not cigarettes. They're more like rose bushes. Hell, they're more like the shit that rose bushes grow in."

"You think we're going to get a table?"

"By the time we get a table, this place is going to be very unpopular."

"Do you want to leave?"

"Do you?"

"If you do."

"We told the baby-sitter we'd be home by ten."

They both wished that Toni were responsible enough to baby-sit her siblings, rather than needing to be sat along with them.

"What time is it?" she asked.

"Nine."

"Let's go home."

Last Christmas, when the kids had been splayed out all over the living room, buried to their shoulders in wrapping paper and expensive toys, Mary Lynn had studied her children's features, had recognized most of her face in her sons' faces and very little of it in her daughters', and had decided, quite facetiously, that the genetic score was tied.

We should have another kid, she'd said to Jeremiah, so we'll know if this is a white family or an Indian family.

It's a family family, he'd said, without a trace of humor.

Only a white guy would say that, she'd said.

Well, he'd said, you married a white guy.

The space between them had grown very cold at that moment, in that silence, and perhaps one or both of them might have said something truly destructive, but Ariel had started crying then, for no obvious reason, relieving both parents of the responsibility of finishing that particular conversation. During the course of their relationship, Mary Lynn and Jeremiah had often discussed race as a concept, as a foreign country they occasionally visited, or as an enemy that existed outside their house, as a destructive force they could fight against as a couple, as a family. But race was also a constant presence, a houseguest and permanent tenant who crept around all the rooms in their shared lives, opening drawers, stealing utensils and small articles of clothing, changing the temperature.

Before he'd married Mary Lynn, Jeremiah had always believed there was too much talk of race, that white people were all too willing to be racist and that brown people were just as willing and just as racist. As a rational scientist, he'd known that race was primarily a social construct, illusionary, but as the husband of an Indian woman and the father of Indian children, he'd since learned that race, whatever its construction, was real. Now, there were plenty of white people who wanted to eliminate the idea of race, to cast it aside as an unwanted invention, but it was far too late for that. If white people are the mad scientists who created race, thought Jeremiah, then we created race so we could enslave black people and kill Indians, and now race has become the Frankenstein monster that has grown beyond our control. Though he'd once been willfully blind, Jeremiah had learned how to recognize that monster in the faces of whites and Indians and in their eyes.

Long ago, Jeremiah and Mary Lynn had both decided to challenge those who stared by staring back, by flinging each other against walls and tongue-kissing with pornographic élan.

Long ago, they'd both decided to respond to any questions of why, how, what, who, or when by simply stating: Love is Love. They knew it was romantic bullshit, a simpleminded answer only satisfying for simpleminded people, but it was the best available defense.

Listen, Mary Lynn had once said to Jeremiah, asking somebody why they fall in love is like asking somebody why they believe in God.

You start asking questions like that, she had added, and you're either going to start a war or you're going to hear folk music.

You think too much, Jeremiah had said, rolling over and falling asleep.

Then, in the dark, as Jeremiah slept, Mary Lynn had masturbated while fantasizing about an Indian man with sundance scars on his chest.

After they left Tan Tan, they drove a sensible and indigenous Ford Taurus over the 520 bridge, back toward their house in Kirkland, a five-bedroom rancher only ten blocks away from the Microsoft campus. Mary Lynn walked to work. That made her feel privileged. She estimated there were twenty-two American Indians who had ever felt even a moment of privilege.

"We still have to eat," she said as she drove across the bridge. She felt strange. She wondered if she was ever going to feel normal again.

"How about Taco Bell drive-thru?" he asked.

"You devil, you're trying to get into my pants, aren't you?"

Impulsively, he dropped his head into her lap and pressed his lips against her black-jeaned crotch. She yelped and pushed him away. She wondered if he could smell her, if he could smell the Lummi Indian. Maybe he could, but he seemed to interpret it as something different, as something meant for him, as he pushed his head into her lap again. What was she supposed to do? She decided to laugh, so she did laugh as she pushed his face against her pubic bone. She loved the man for reasons she could not always explain. She closed her eyes, drove in that darkness, and felt dangerous.

Halfway across the bridge, Mary Lynn slammed on the brakes, not because she'd seen anything—her eyes were still closed—but because she'd felt something. The car skidded to a stop just inches from the bumper of a truck that had just missed sliding into the row of cars stopped ahead of it.

"What the hell is going on?" Jeremiah asked as he lifted his head from her lap.

"Traffic jam."

"Jesus, we'll never make it home by ten. We better call."

"The cell phone is in the glove."

Jeremiah dialed the home number but received only a busy signal.

"Toni must be talking to her boyfriend," she said.

"I don't like him."

"He doesn't like you."

"What the hell is going on? Why aren't we moving?"

"I don't know. Why don't you go check?"

Jeremiah climbed out of the car.

"I was kidding," she said as he closed the door behind him.

He walked up to the window of the truck ahead of him.

"You know what's going on?" Jeremiah asked the truck driver.

"Nope."

Jeremiah walked farther down the bridge. He wondered if there was a disabled car ahead, what the radio liked to call a "blocking accident." There was also the more serious "injury accident" and the deadly "accident with fatality involved." He had to drive this bridge ten times a week. The commute. White men had invented the commute, had deepened its meaning, had diversified its complications, and now spent most of the time trying to shorten it, reduce it, lessen it.

In the car, Mary Lynn wondered why Jeremiah always found it necessary to insert himself into every situation. He continually moved from the passive to the active. The man was kinetic. She wondered if it was a white thing. Possibly. But more likely, it was a Jeremiah thing. She remembered Mikey's third-grade-class's school play, an edited version of *Hamlet*. Jeremiah had walked onto the stage to help his son drag the unconscious Polonius, who had merely been clubbed over the head rather than stabbed to death, from the stage. Mortally embarrassed, Mikey had cried himself to sleep that night, positive that he was going to be an elementary-school pariah, while Jeremiah vainly tried to explain to the rest of the family why he had acted so impulsively.

I was just trying to be a good father, he had said.

Mary Lynn watched Jeremiah walk farther down the bridge. He was just a shadow, a silhouette. She was slapped by the brief, irrational fear that he would never return.

Husband, come back to me, she thought, and I will confess.

Impatient drivers honked their horns. Mary Lynn joined them. She hoped Jeremiah would recognize the specific sound of their horn and return to the car.

Listen to me, listen to me, listen to me, she thought as she pounded the steering wheel.

Jeremiah heard their car horn, but only as one note in the symphony of noise playing on the bridge. He walked through that noise, through an ever-increasing amount of noise, until he pushed through a sudden crowd of people and found himself witnessing a suicide.

Illuminated by headlights, the jumper was a white woman, pretty, wearing a sundress and good shoes. Jeremiah could see that much as she stood on the bridge railing, forty feet above the cold water.

He could hear sirens approaching from both sides of the bridge, but they would never make it through the traffic in time to save this woman.

The jumper was screaming somebody's name.

Jeremiah stepped closer, wanting to hear the name, wanting to have that information so that he could use it later. To what use, he didn't know, but he knew that name had value, importance. That name, the owner of that name, was the reason why the jumper stood on the bridge.

"Aaron," she said. The jumper screamed, "Aaron."

In the car, Mary Lynn could not see either Jeremiah or the jumper, but she could see dozens of drivers leaving their cars and running ahead.

She was suddenly and impossibly sure that her husband was the reason for this commotion, this emergency. He's dying, thought Mary Lynn, he's dead. This is not what I wanted, she thought, this is not why I cheated on him, this is not what was supposed to happen.

As more drivers left their cars and ran ahead, Mary Lynn dialed 911 on the cell phone and received only a busy signal.

She opened her door and stepped out, placed one foot on the pavement, and stopped.

The jumper did not stop. She turned to look at the crowd watching her. She looked into the anonymous faces, into the maw, and then looked back down at the black water.

Then she jumped.

Jeremiah rushed forward, along with a few others, and peered over the edge of the bridge. One brave man leapt off the bridge in a vain rescue attempt. Jeremiah stopped a redheaded young man from jumping.

"No," said Jeremiah. "It's too cold. You'll die too."

Jeremiah stared down into the black water, looking for the woman who'd jumped and the man who'd jumped after her.

In the car, or rather with one foot still in the car and one foot placed on the pavement outside of the car, Mary Lynn wept. Oh, God, she loved him, sometimes because he was white and often despite his whiteness. In her fear, she found the one truth Sitting Bull never knew: there was at least one white man who could be trusted.

The black water was silent.

Jeremiah stared down into that silence.

"Jesus, Jesus," said a lovely woman next to him. "Who was she? Who was she?"

"I'm never leaving," Jeremiah said.

"What?" asked the lovely woman, quite confused.

"My wife," said Jeremiah, strangely joyous. "I'm never leaving her." Ever the scientist and mathematician, Jeremiah knew that his wife was a constant. In his relief, he found the one truth Shakespeare never knew: gravity is overrated.

Jeremiah looked up through the crossbeams above him, as he stared at the black sky, at the clouds that he could not see but knew were there, the invisible clouds that covered the stars. He shouted out his wife's name, shouted it so loud that he could not speak in the morning.

In the car, Mary Lynn pounded the steering wheel. With one foot in the car and one foot out, she honked and honked the horn. She wondered if this was how the world was supposed to end, with everybody trapped on a bridge, with the black water pushing against their foundations.

Out on the bridge, four paramedics arrived far too late. Out of breath, exhausted from running across the bridge with medical gear and stretchers, the paramedics could only join the onlookers at the railing.

A boat, a small boat, a miracle, floated through the black water. They found the man, the would-be rescuer, who had jumped into the water after the young woman, but they could not find her.

Jeremiah turned from the water and walked away from the crowd. He knew that people could want death as much as they wanted anything else. What did Jeremiah want? Did he want his wife? Did she want him? After all these years how much could they still want each other? Mary Lynn waited for him. She could see him walking toward her. She could hear the waves riddling the bridge. She felt the spray of the water. She felt a chill. When Jeremiah returned to her, she was going to hold his face in her hands and ask him, "Who do you think you are?" And she hoped that the answer would surprise her.

OLD GROWTH

In 1989, while hunting on the Spokane Indian Reservation, I saw a quick flash of movement on the ridge above me, spun, aimed high, and fired my rifle. I'd been hunting deer since childhood and had shot and missed twenty-seven times over the years. I was widely recognized as the worst hunter in reservation history. But, on that day, I didn't miss. At the advanced age of twenty-six, I thought I'd killed my first deer and was extremely excited as I climbed that ridge to claim my kill. But I hadn't shot a deer. I'd shot and killed a white guy who'd been tending to the field of marijuana he'd planted deep in the reservation woods. White guys did that because the reservation cops never ventured off the paved roads and federal agents didn't want to deal with the complicated laws surrounding tribal sovereignty and police jurisdiction.

I kneeled beside the man's body. I couldn't believe what I'd done. I'd killed a man—by accident, yes, but it was still murder. I'd shot him in the back of the head. The bullet had torn through his brain and exited out his face, exploding it into a bloody maw. He was unrecognizable.

I'd never been a cruel man but I'd often been drunk and stupid. I'd spent two years in jail for robbing a bowling alley with a water pistol that looked like a gun and six months for stealing a go-cart from an amusement park and crashing it into a police car in the parking lot. I wasn't exactly a criminal mastermind and nobody, not even the cop in the police cruiser that I'd slightly dented, would have ever considered me dangerous.

But now, I had killed a man and I knew I would spend real time in a real prison for it. Probably not for murder but certainly for manslaughter. So I did what I thought I should do to save myself. I dragged that man's body back to his pot field and buried him in the middle of it. If he was ever discovered, I figured the police would think that he was killed by his partners or by a rival pot-growing operation.

After I buried him, I walked the two miles back to my truck and drove the twelve miles back to the house that I shared with my brother.

"How'd it go?" he asked.

"One shot," I said. "And one miss."

For the next year, I was terrified that the body would be discovered. I scanned the newspapers for news of missing men. Missing criminals. Missing drug dealers. And, sure, a few bad guys disappeared, as they always do, but they also disappeared from the news pretty quickly.

After a few more years, it began to feel like the event had never happened. It felt like a movie that I must have watched at three in the morning in a motel next to a freeway.

Then, twenty-one years after I'd killed the man, I went to the tribal clinic with a bad cough and discovered that I had terminal cancer. My body was a museum of cancer; there was a tumor exhibition in every nook and cranny.

"Three months if you're unlucky," the doctor said. "Six months if you bump into a miracle."

So what does a dying man do about the worst sin of his life? I didn't confess. I was still too cowardly to do that. And I didn't want to spend my last days in court or jail.

But I felt the need to atone.

So, in my weakened state, I drove along that familiar logging road, and slowly climbed back to that ridge where I'd shot and killed a man. The pot field had grown wild and huge. How had it survived winter and freezing temperatures? And how fast does pot grow? How many generations of the plants can live and die in a two-decade span? I didn't know, but I had to crawl through a pot jungle to the spot where I'd buried that white guy.

And, bit by bit, handful by handful, I dug up his body.

His tattered clothes were draped over brown bones. His skull was a collapsed sinkhole. I was surprised that animals hadn't dug him up and spread the remains far and wide. I stared at him for a long time.

Then I sang a death song for him. And an honor song for the family and friends who never knew what had happened to him.

Then I took his skull, carefully wrapped it in newspaper, slid it into my backpack, crawled out of the pot garden, and walked back to my truck.

It was late when I returned to my house. My brother had long ago married a Lakota woman and moved to South Dakota. I was alone in the world. And I would soon be dead. I stripped naked and carried the dead man's skull into the shower with me. I cleaned my body and the dead man's skull.

Then I put on my favorite T-shirt and sweatpants and set the skull on the TV in my bedroom. I lay on the bed and stared at that crushed face.

I wanted to be haunted. But that skull did not speak to me. I wanted that skull to be more than a dead man's skull. I wanted it to be a hive abandoned by its wasps, or a shell left behind by its insect, or a husk peeled from its vegetable, or a planet knocked free of its orbit, or the universe collapsing around me.

But the skull was only the reminder that I had killed a man. It was proof that I had lived and would die without magnificence. God, I wanted to be forgiven, but an apology offered to a dead man is only a selfish apology to yourself.

EMIGRATION

The hummingbirds swarmed my garden, randomly at first, but then hovered and formed themselves into midair letters. It took seventeen hummingbirds to make an "A" and twenty-eight to make a "W." In this way, feather by feather, letter by letter, the hummingbirds spelled my mother's full name.

I hadn't called her for at least a month, so it was obvious these birds had come to remind me of family duties.

"Hello, Mother," I said.

"Who is this?" she asked. "The voice is so familiar, but I can't quite place it."

"It's me," I said.

"I'm sorry. Who is this again?"

"It's your son."

"Which son?" she asked.

"The distant one," I said.

"It took you long enough," she said. "I sent those hummingbirds last Friday."

"They flew in maybe fifteen minutes ago."

"Damn hummingbirds," she said. "How can animals that quick always be so late?"

"You could have just used the phone."

"And you would have let it go to voice mail. Like you always do."

"Okay, okay," I said. "You've got my full attention now. What's up?"

"You promised you'd send my granddaughters' school photos."

"Oh, shit, Mom, I forgot again. I'll mail them out today."

"You said that the last time."

"I know, I know," I said. "It would be so much easier if you got a computer. Then I could e-mail them to you."

"Ah, I don't need anything fancy like that," she said. "And I don't understand how they work anyway."

"I'll head to the post office right after I hang up. I'll overnight the photos."

"They better be here," she said. "Or I'm going to send the hornets. And you know how mean and disciplined they are."

"And what are you going to make them spell for me?"

"They're just going to swarm your house and spell the word 'guilt' everywhere. Those hornets are going to be like miniature Catholic priests. And they're going to sting, sting, sting."

I laughed; she laughed. I mailed the photos twenty minutes after I got off the phone with her. But she still sent a few dozen hornets. They didn't arrive angry. Instead, they settled on my shoulders and murmured something that I couldn't quite hear.

So, yes, as you might imagine, I am jealous of my mother's magic. And I am jealous of my three daughters. They can make the tallest pine trees lean close, pick them up with their branches, and lift them high into the city sky.

As the years have passed, my daughters have spent more and more time up among the highest branches. They are soon going to leave me as I long ago left my mother. But I fled my family on foot. My daughters will be carried by trees back to my reservation to live with my mother, their grandmother. And our people will celebrate. The trees that transported my daughters will happily accept flame. And they will burn. And their smoke will rise into the dark and spell words from the tribal language that I never learned to speak.

THE SEARCH ENGINE

On Wednesday afternoon in the student union café, Corliss looked up from her American history textbook and watched a young man and younger woman walk in together and sit two tables away. The student union wasn't crowded, so Corliss clearly heard the young couple's conversation. He offered her coffee from his thermos, but she declined. Hurt by her rejection, or feigning pain—he always carried two cups because well, you never know, do you?—he poured himself one, sipped and sighed with theatrical pleasure, and monologued. The young woman slumped in her seat and listened. He told her where he was from and where he wanted to go after college, and how much he liked these books and those teachers but hated those movies and these classes, and it was all part of an ordinary man's list-making attempts to seduce an ordinary woman. Blonde, blue-eyed, pretty, and thin, she hid her incipient bulimia beneath a bulky wool sweater. Corliss wanted to buy the skeletal woman a sandwich, ten sandwiches, and a big bowl of vanilla ice cream. Eat, young woman, eat, Corliss thought, and you will be redeemed! The young woman set her backpack on the table and crossed her arms over her chest, but the young man didn't seem to notice or care about the defensive meaning of her body language. He talked and talked and gestured passionately with long-fingered hands. A former lover, an older woman, had probably told him his hands were artistic, so he assumed all women would be similarly charmed. He wore his long blond hair pulled back into a ponytail and a flowered blue shirt that was really a blouse; he was narcissistic, androgynous, lovely, and yes, charming. Corliss thought she might sleep with him if he took her home to a clean apartment, but she decided to hate him instead. She knew she judged people based on their surface appearances, but Lord Byron said only shallow people don't judge by surfaces. So Corliss thought of herself as Byronesque as she eavesdropped on the young couple. She hoped one of these ordinary people might say something interesting and original. She believed in the endless nature of human possibility. She would be delighted if these two messy humans transcended their stereotypes and revealed themselves as mortal angels.

"Well, you know," the young man said to the young woman, "it was Auden who wrote that no poem ever saved a Jew from the ovens."

"Oh," the young woman said. She didn't know why he'd abruptly paraphrased Auden. She wasn't sure who this Auden person was, or why his opinions about poetry should matter to her, or why poetry itself was so important. She knew this coffee-drinking guy wanted to have sex with her, and she was considering it, but he wasn't improving his chances by making her feel stupid.

Corliss was confused by the poetic non sequitur as well. She thought he might be trying to prove how many books he'd skimmed. Maybe he deserved her contempt, but Corliss realized that very few young men read poetry at Washington State University. And how many of those boys quoted, or misquoted, the poems they'd read? Twenty, ten, less than five? This longhaired guy enjoyed a monopoly on the poetry-quoting market in the southeastern corner of Washington, and he knew it. Corliss had read a few poems by W. H. Auden but couldn't remember any of them other than the elegy recited in that Hugh Grant romantic comedy. She figured the young man had memorized the first stanzas of thirty-three love poems and used them like propaganda to win the hearts and minds of young women. He'd probably tattooed the opening lines of Andrew Marvell's "To His Coy Mistress" on his chest: "Had we but world enough, and time, / This coyness, Lady, were no crime." Corliss wondered if Shakespeare wrote his plays and sonnets only because he was trying to get laid. Which poet or poem has been quoted most often in the effort to get laid? Most important, which poet or poem has been quoted most successfully in the effort to get laid? Corliss needed to know the serious answers to her silly questions. Or vice versa. So she gathered her books and papers and approached the couple.

"Excuse me," Corliss said to the young man. "Was that W. H. Auden you were quoting?"

"Yes," he said. His smile was genuine and boyish. He had displayed his intelligence and was being rewarded for it. Why shouldn't he smile?

"I didn't recognize the quote," Corliss said. "Which poem did it come from?"

The young man looked at Corliss and at the young woman. Corliss knew he was choosing between them. The young woman knew it, too, and she decided the whole thing was pointless.

"I've got to go," she said, grabbed her backpack, and fled.

"Wow, that was quick," he said. "Rejected at the speed of light."

"Sorry about that," Corliss said. But she was pleased with the young woman's quick decision and quicker flight. If she could resist one man's efforts to shape and determine her future, perhaps she could resist all future efforts.

"It's all right," the young man said. "Do you want to sit down, keep me company?"

"No thanks," Corliss said. "Tell me about that Auden quote."

He smiled again. He studied her. She was very short, a few inches under five feet, maybe thirty pounds overweight, and plain-featured. But her skin was clear and dark brown (like good coffee!), and her long black hair hung down past her waist. And she wore red cowboy boots, and her breasts were large, and she knew about Auden, and she was confident enough to approach strangers, so maybe her beauty was eccentric, even exotic. And exoticism was hard to find in Pullman, Washington.

"What's your name?" he asked her.

"Corliss."

"That's a beautiful name. What does it mean?"

"It means Corliss is my name. Are you going to tell me where you read that Auden quote or not?"

"You're Indian, aren't you?"

"Good-bye," she said and stood to leave.

"Wait, wait," he said. "You don't like me, do you?"

"You're cute and smart, and you've gotten everything you've ever asked for, and that makes you lazy and dangerous."

"Wow, you're honest. Will you like me better if I'm honest?"

"I might."

"I've never read Auden's poems. Not much, anyway. I read some article about him. They quoted him on the thing about Jews and poems. I don't know where they got it from. But it's true, don't you think?"

"What's true?"

"A good gun will always beat a good poem."

"I hope not," Corliss said and walked away.

Back in Spokane, Washington, Corliss had attended Spokane River High School, which had contained a mirage-library. Sure, the books had looked like Dickens and Dickinson from a distance, but they turned into cookbooks and auto-repair manuals when you picked them up. As a poor kid, and a middle-class Indian, she seemed destined for a minimum-wage life of waiting tables or changing oil. But she had wanted a maximum life, an original aboriginal life, so she had fought her way out of her underfunded public high school into an underfunded public college. So maybe, despite American racism, sexism, and classism, Corliss's biography confirmed everything nearly wonderful and partially meritorious about her country. Ever the rugged individual, she had collected aluminum cans during the summer before her junior year of high school so she could afford the yearlong SAT-prep course that had astronomically raised her scores and won her a dozen academic scholarships. At the beginning of every semester, Corliss had called the history and English teachers at the local prep school she couldn't afford, and asked what books they would be reading in class, and she had found those books and lived with them like siblings. And those same teachers, good white people whose whiteness and goodness blended and separated, had faxed her study guides and copies of the best student papers. Two of those teachers, without having met Corliss in person, had sent her graduation gifts of money and yet more books. She'd been a resourceful thief, a narcissistic Robin Hood who stole a rich education from white people and kept it.

In the Washington State University library, her version of Sherwood Forest, Corliss walked the poetry stacks. She endured a contentious and passionate relationship with this library. The huge number of books confirmed how much magic she'd been denied for most of her life, and now she hungrily wanted to read every book on every shelf. An impossible task, to be sure, Herculean in its exaggeration, but Corliss wanted to read herself to death. She wanted to be buried in a coffin filled with used paperbacks.

She found W. H. Auden's *Collected Poems* on a shelf above her head. She stood on her toes and pulled down the thick volume, but she also pulled out another book that dropped to the floor. It was a book of poems titled *In the Reservation of My Mind*, by Harlan Atwater. According to the author's biography on the back cover, Harlan Atwater was a Spokane Indian, but Corliss had never heard of the guy. Her parents, grandparents, and great-grandparents were all born and raised on the Spokane Indian Reservation. And the rest of her ancestors, going back a dozen generations, were born and raised on the land that would eventually be called the Spokane Indian Reservation. Her one white ancestor, a Russian fur trapper, had been legally adopted into the tribe, given some corny Indian name she didn't like to repeat, and served on the tribal council for ten years. Corliss was a Spokane Indian born in Sacred Heart Hospital, only a mile from the Spokane River Falls, the heart of the Spokane Tribe, and had grown up in the city of Spokane, which was really an annex of the reservation, and thought she knew or knew of every Spokane. Demographically and biologically speaking, Corliss was about as Spokane as a Spokane Indian can be, and only three thousand other Spokanes of various Spokane-ness existed in the whole world, so how had this guy escaped her attention? She opened the book and read the first poem:

The Naming Ceremony

No Indian ever gave me an Indian name
So I named myself.
I am Crying Shame.
I am Takes the Blame.
I am the Four Directions:
South, A Little More South,
Way More South, and All the Way South.
If you are ever driving toward Mexico

And see me hitchhiking, you'll know me
By the size of my feet.
My left foot is named Self-Pity
And my right foot is named Born to Lose.

But if you give me a ride, you can call me
And all of my parts any name you choose.

Corliss recognized the poem as a free-verse sonnet whose
end rhymes gave it a little more music. It was a funny and clumsy
poem desperate to please the reader. It was like a slobbery puppy
in an animal shelter: Choose me! Choose me! But the poem was
definitely charming and strange. Harlan Atwater was making fun
of being Indian, of the essential sadness of being Indian, and so
maybe he was saying Indians aren't sad at all. Maybe Indians are just
big-footed hitchhikers eager to tell a joke! That wasn't a profound
thought, but maybe it was an accurate one. But can you be accurate
without profundity? Corliss didn't know the answer to the question.

She carried the Atwater and Auden books to the front
desk to check them out. The librarian was a small woman wearing khaki pants and large glasses. Corliss wanted to shout at her:
Honey, get yourself some contacts and a pair of leather chaps!
Fight your stereotypes!

"Wow," the librarian said as she scanned the books' bar
codes and entered them into her computer.

"Wow what?" Corliss asked.

"You're the first person who's ever checked out this book."
The librarian held up the Atwater.

"Is it new?"

"We've had it since 1972."

Corliss wondered what happens to a book that sits unread
on a library shelf for thirty years. Can a book rightfully be called a
book if it never gets read? If a tree falls in a forest and gets pulped
to make paper for a book that never gets read, but there's nobody
there to read it, does it make a sound?

"How many books never get checked out?" Corliss asked the librarian.

"Most of them," she said.

Corliss had never once considered the fate of library books. She'd never wondered how many books go unread. She loved books. How could she not worry about the unread? She felt like a disorganized scholar, an inconsiderate lover, an abusive mother, and a cowardly solider.

"Are you serious?" Corliss asked. "What are we talking about here? If you were guessing, what is the percentage of books in this library that never get checked out?"

"We're talking sixty percent of them. Seriously. Maybe seventy percent. And I'm being optimistic. It's probably more like eighty or ninety percent. This isn't a library, it's an orphanage."

The librarian spoke in a reverential whisper. Corliss knew she'd misjudged this passionate woman. Maybe she dressed poorly, but she was probably great in bed, certainly believed in God and goodness, and kept an illicit collection of overdue library books on her shelves.

"How many books do you have here?" Corliss asked.

"Two million, one hundred thousand, and eleven," the librarian said proudly, but Corliss was frightened. What happens to the world when that many books go unread? And what happens to the unread authors of those unread books?

"And don't think it's just this library, either," the librarian said. "There's about eighteen million books in the Library of Congress, and nobody reads about seventeen and a half million of them."

"You're scaring me."

"Sorry about that," the librarian said. "These are due back in two weeks."

Corliss carried the Auden and Atwater books out of the library and into the afternoon air. She sat on a bench and flipped through the pages. The Auden was worn and battered, with pen and pencil notes scribbled all over the margins. Three generations of WSU students had defaced Auden with their scholarly graffiti, but Atwater was stiff and unmarked. This book had not been exposed to direct sunlight in three decades. W. H. Auden didn't need Corliss to read him—his work was already immortal—but she felt like she'd rescued Harlan Atwater. And who else should rescue the poems of a Spokane Indian but another Spokane? Corliss felt the weight and heat of destiny. She had been chosen. God had nearly dropped Atwater's book on her head. Who knew the Supreme One could be so obvious? But then again, when has the infallible been anything other than predictable? Maybe God was dropping other books on other people's heads, Corliss thought. Maybe every book in every library is patiently waiting for its savior. Ha! She felt romantic and young and foolish. What kind of Indian loses her mind over a book of poems? She was that kind of Indian, she was exactly that kind of Indian, and it was the only kind of Indian she knew how to be.

Corliss lived alone. She supposed that was a rare thing for a nineteen-year-old college sophomore, especially a Native American college student living on scholarships and luck and family charity, but she couldn't stand the thought of sharing her apartment with another person. She didn't want to live with another Indian because she understood Indians all too well. If she took an Indian roommate, Corliss knew she'd soon be taking in the roommate's cousin, little brother, half uncle, and long-lost dog, and none of them would contribute anything toward the rent other than wispy apologies. Indians were used to sharing and called it tribalism, but Corliss suspected it was yet another failed form of communism. Over the last two centuries, Indians had learned how to stand in lines for food, love, hope, sex, and dreams, but they didn't know how to step away. They were good at line-standing and didn't know if they'd be good at anything else. Of course, all sorts of folks made it their business to confirm Indian fears and insecurities. Indians hadn't invented the line. And George Armstrong Custer is alive and well in the twenty-first century, Corliss thought, though he kills Indians by dumping huge piles of paperwork on their skulls. But Indians made themselves easy targets for bureaucratic skull-crushing, didn't they? Indians took numbers and lined up for skull-crushing. They'd rather die standing together in long lines than wandering alone in the wilderness. Indians were terrified of being lonely, of being exiled, but Corliss had always dreamed of solitude. Since she'd shared her childhood home with an Indian mother, an Indian father, seven Indian siblings, and a random assortment of Indian cousins, strangers, and party crashers, she cherished her domestic solitude and kept it sacred. Maybe she lived in an academic gulag, but she'd chosen to live that way. She furnished her apartment with a mattress on the floor, one bookshelf, two lamps, a dining table, two chairs, two sets of plates, cups, and utensils, three pots, and one frying pan. Her wardrobe consisted of three pairs of blue jeans, three white blouses, one pair of tennis shoes, three pairs of cowboy boots, six white T-shirts, thirteen pairs of socks, and a week's worth of underwear. Her only luxuries (necessities!) were books. There were hundreds of them stacked around her apartment. She'd never met one human being more interesting to her than a good book. So why would she live with an uninteresting Indian when she could live with John Donne, Elizabeth Bishop, and Langston Hughes?

Corliss didn't want to live with a white roommate, either, no matter how interesting he or she might become. Hell, even if Emily Dickinson were resurrected and had her reclusive-hermit-unrequited-love-addict gene removed from her DNA, Corliss wouldn't have wanted to room with her. White people, no matter how smart, were too romantic about Indians. White people looked at the Grand Canyon, Niagara Falls, the full moon, newborn babies, and Indians with the same goofy sentimentalism. Being a smart Indian, Corliss had always taken advantage of this romanticism, but that didn't mean she wanted to share the refrigerator with it. If white folks assumed she was serene and spiritual and wise simply because she was an Indian, and thought she was special based on those mistaken assumptions, then Corliss saw no reason to contradict them. The world is a competitive place, and a poor Indian girl needs all the advantages she can get. So if George W. Bush, a man who possessed no remarkable distinctions other than being the son of a former U.S. president, could also become president, then Corliss figured she could certainly benefit from positive ethnic stereotypes and not feel any guilt about it. For five centuries, Indians were slaughtered because they were Indians, so if Corliss received a free coffee now and again from the local free-range lesbian Indiophile, who could possibly find the wrong in that? In the twenty-first century, any Indian with a decent vocabulary wielded enormous social power, but only if she was a stoic who rarely spoke. If she lived with a white person, Corliss knew she'd quickly be seen as ordinary, because she was ordinary. It's tough to share a bathroom with an Indian and continue to romanticize her. If word got around that Corliss was ordinary, even boring, she feared she'd lose her power and magic. She knew there would come a day when white folks finally understood that Indians are every bit as relentlessly boring, self-ish, and smelly as they are, and that would be a wonderful day for human rights but a terrible day for Corliss.

Corliss caught the number 7 home from the library. She wanted to read Harlan Atwater's book on the bus, but she also wanted to keep it private. The book felt dangerous and forbidden. At her stop, she stepped off and walked toward her apartment, and then ran. She felt giddy, foolish, and strangely aroused, as if she were running home to read pornography. Once alone, Corliss sat on the floor, backed into a corner, and read Harlan Atwater's book of poems. There were forty-five free-verse sonnets. Corliss found it interesting that an Indian of his generation wrote sonnets, while other Indians occupied Alcatraz and Wounded Knee. Most of the poems were set in and around the Spokane Indian Reservation, so Corliss wondered again why she'd never heard of this man. How many poetry lovers were among the Spokanes? Fifty, thirty, fewer than twenty? And how many Spokanes would recognize a sonnet when they saw it, let alone be able to write one? Since her public high school teachers had known how much Corliss loved poetry, and had always loved it, why hadn't one of them handed her this book? Maybe this book could have saved her years of shame. Instead of trying to hide her poetry habit from her friends and family, and sneaking huge piles of poetry books into her room, maybe she could have proudly read a book of poems at the dinner table. She could have held that book above her head and shouted, "See, look, it's a book of poems by another Spokane, what are you going to do about that?" Instead, she'd endured endless domestic interrogations about her bookish nature.

During one family reunion, her father sat around the living room with his three brothers. That was over twelve hundred pounds of Spokane Indian sharing a couch and a bowl of tortilla chips. Coming home from school, Corliss tried to dash across the room and make her escape, but one uncle noticed the book under her arm.

"Why you always reading?" he asked.

"I like stories," she said. It seemed to be the safest answer. Indians loved to think of themselves as the best storytellers in the world, and maybe they were, but did they need to be so sure of it?

"She's reading those poems again," her father said. "She's always reading those poems."

She loved her father and uncles. She loved how they filled a room with their laughter and rank male bodies and endless nostalgia and quick tempers, but she hated their individual fears and collective lack of ambition. They all worked blue-collar construction jobs, not because they loved the good work or found it valuable or rewarding but because some teacher or guidance counselor once told them all they could work only blue-collar jobs. When they were young, some authority figure had told them to pick up a wrench, and so they picked up the wrench and never once considered what would happen if they picked up a pencil or a book. Her father and uncles never asked questions. How can you live a special life without constantly interrogating it? How can you live a good life without good poetry? She knew her family feared poetry, but they didn't fear it because they were Indian. The fear of poetry was multicultural and timeless. So maybe she loved poetry precisely because so many people feared it. Maybe she wanted to frighten people with the size of her poetic love.

"I bet you're reading one of those white books again, enit?" the first uncle asked.

"His name is Gerard Manley Hopkins," Corliss said. "He wrote poems in the nineteenth century."

"White people were killing Indians in the nineteenth century," the second uncle said. "I bet this Hopkins dude was killing Indians, too."

"I don't think so," Corliss said. "He was a Jesuit priest."

Her father and uncles cursed with shock and disgust.

"He was a Catholic?" her father asked. "Oh, Corliss, those Catholics were the worst. Your grandmother still has scars on her back from when a priest and a nun whipped her in boarding school. You shouldn't be reading that stuff. It will pollute your heart."

"What do you think those white people can teach you, anyway?" the third uncle asked.

She wanted to say, "Everything." She wanted to scream it. But she knew she'd be punished for her disrespect of her elders. Because she was Indian, she'd been taught to fear and hate white people. Sure, she hated all sorts of white people—the arrogant white businessmen in their wool suits, the illiterate white cheerleaders in their convertibles, the thousands of flannel-shirted rednecks who roamed the streets of Spokane—but she knew they represented the worst of whiteness. It was easy to hate white vanity and white rage and white ignorance, but what about white compassion and white genius and white poetry? Maybe it wasn't about whiteness or redness or any other color. Corliss wasn't naive. She knew racism, tribalism, and nationalism were encoded in human DNA, and we'd all save our own child from a burning building even if it meant a thousand strangers would die, and we'd all kill in defense of our wives, husbands, brothers, sisters, parents, and children. However, she also wanted to believe in human goodness and mortal grace. She was contradictory and young and confused and smart and unformed and ambitious. How could she tell her father and uncles she read Hopkins precisely because he was a white man and precisely because he was a Jesuit priest? Maybe Hopkins had been an Indian killer, or a supporter of Indian killers, but he'd also been a sad and lonely and lovely man who screamed to God for comfort, answers, sleep, and peace. Since Corliss rarely found comfort from her family and friends, and never found it in God, but continued to want it and never stopped asking for it, then maybe she was also a Jesuit priest who found it in poetry. How could she tell her family that she didn't belong with them, that she was destined for something larger, that she believed she was supposed to be eccentric and powerful and great and all alone in the world? How could she tell her Indian family she sometimes felt like a white Jesuit priest? Who would ever believe such a thing? Who would ever understand how a nineteen-year-old Indian woman looked in the mirror and sometimes saw an old white man in a white collar and black robe?

"I've got to go," Corliss said. "I've got homework."

"Give me that book," the second uncle said. He took the book from her, opened it at random, and read, "'Glory be to God for dappled things— / For skies of couple-colour as a brinded cow.'"

All of the men laughed.

"What the hell does that mean?" the third uncle asked.

"It's a poem about a cow," her father said. "She's always reading poems about cows."

"You can't write a poem about a cow, can you?" the first uncle asked. "They're ugly and stupid. I thought poems were supposed to be pretty and smart."

373

"Yeah, Corliss," the second uncle said. "You're pretty and smart, why are you wasting your time with poems? You should be studying science and math and law and politics. You're going to be rich and famous. You're going to be the toughest Indian woman around."

How could these men hate poetry so much and respect her intelligence? Sure, they were men raised in a matriarchal culture, but they lived in a patriarchal country. Therefore, they were kind and decent and sensitive and stupid and sexist and unpredictable. These husbands were happily married to wives who earned more money than they did. These men bragged about their spouses' accomplishments: *Ha, my woman just got a raise! My honey makes more money than your honey! My wife manages the whole dang Kmart, and then she comes home and manages us! She's a twenty-first-century woman! Nah, I ain't threatened by her! I'm challenged!* Who were these Indian men? What kind of warriors were they? Were Crazy Horse and Geronimo supportive of their wives? Did Sitting Bull sit with his wife for weekly chats about the state of their relationship? Did Red Cloud proudly send his daughter out to fight the enemy? Corliss looked at her father and saw a stranger, a loving stranger, but a stranger nonetheless.

"And I'll tell you what," her father said. "After Corliss graduates from college and gets her law degree, she's going to move back to the reservation and fix what's wrong. We men have had our chances, I'll tell you what. We'll send all the tribal councilmen to the golf courses and let the smart women run the show. I'll tell you what. My daughter is going to save our tribe."

Yes, her family loved and supported her, so how could she resent them for being clueless about her real dreams and ambitions? Her mother and father and all of her uncles and aunts sent her money to help her through college. How many times had she opened an envelope and discovered a miraculous twenty-dollar bill? The family and the tribe were helping her, so maybe she was a selfish bitch for questioning the usefulness of tribalism. Here she was sitting in a corner of her tiny apartment, pretending to be alone in the world, the one poetic Spokane, and she was reading a book of poems, of sonnets, by another Spokane. How could she ever be alone if Harlan Atwater was somewhere out there in the world? Okay, his poems weren't great. Some of them were amateurish and trite, and others were comedic throwaways, but there were a few poems and a few lines that contained small bits of power and magic:

The Little Spokane

My river is not the same size as your river.
My river is smaller and colder.
My river begins in the north
And rushes to find me.
My river calls to me.
I swim it because it is water.
Water doesn't care about anybody
But this water cares about me.

Or maybe it doesn't care about me.
Maybe the river thinks I'm driftwood
Or a rubber tire or a bird or a dead dog.
Maybe the river is not a river.
Maybe the river is my father.
Maybe he's smaller and colder than your father.

Corliss had swum the Little Spokane River. She'd floated down the river in a makeshift raft. She'd drifted beneath bridges and the limbs of trees. She'd been in the physical and emotional places described in the poem. She'd been in the same places where Harlan Atwater had been, and that made her sad and happy. She felt connected to him and wanted to know more about him. She picked up the telephone and called her mother.

"Hey, Mom."

"Corliss, hey, sweetie, it's so good to hear your voice. I miss you."

Her mother was a loan officer for Farmers' Bank. Twenty years earlier, she'd started as a bank teller and had swum her way up the corporate fish ladder.

"I miss you, too, Mom. How is everybody?"

"We're still Indian. How's school going?"

"Good."

All of their conversations began the same way. The mother-daughter telephone ceremony. Corliss knew her mother would soon become emotional and tell her how proud the family was of her accomplishments.

"I don't know if we tell you this enough," her mother said. "But we're so proud of you."

"You tell me every time we talk."

"Oh, well, you know, I'm a mother. I'm supposed to talk that way. It's just, well, you're the first person from our family to ever go to college."

"I know, Mom, you don't need to tell me my résumé."

"You don't need to get smart."

Corliss couldn't help herself. She loved her mother, but her mother was a bipolar storyteller who told lies during her manic phases and heavily exaggerated during her depressed times. Those lies and exaggerations were often flattering to Corliss, so it was hard to completely resent them. According to the stories, Corliss had already been accepted to Harvard Medical School but had declined because she didn't feel Harvard would respect her indigenous healing methods. You couldn't hate a mother full of such tender and flattering garbage, but you could certainly view her with a large measure of contempt.

"I'm sorry, Mom. Listen, I picked up this book of poems—"

"Corliss, you know how your father feels about those poems."

"They're poems, Mom, not crack."

"I know you love them, honey, but how are you going to get a job with poems? You go to a job interview, and they ask you what you did in college, and you say 'poems,' then what are your chances?"

"Maybe I'll work in a poem factory."

"Don't get smart."

"I can't help it. I am smart."

Corliss knew she was smart because her mother was smart, but she also knew she'd inherited a little bit of her mother's crazies as well. Why else would she be calling to talk about a vanished Indian poet? The crazy mother–crazy daughter telephone ceremony!

"So did you call to break my heart," her mother said, "or do you have some other reason?"

"I called about this book of poems."

"Okay, so tell me about your book of poems."

"It's written by this guy called Harlan Atwater. It says he's a Spokane. Do you know him?"

Her mother was the unofficial historian of the urban Spokane Indians. Corliss figured "historian" and "pathological liar" meant the same thing in all cultures and countries.

"Harlan Atwater? Harlan Atwater?" her mother repeated the name and tried to place it. "Nope. Don't know him. Don't know any Spokanes named Atwater."

"His book was published in 1972. It's called *In the Reservation of My Mind*. Do you remember that?"

"I don't read books much."

"Yes, I know, Mom. But you're aware there are inventions called books and inside some of those books they have things called poems."

"I know what books are, smart-ass daughter."

"Okay, then, have you heard of this book?"

"No."

"Are you sure?"

"Yes, I'm sure."

"I thought you knew every Spokane."

"I guess I don't. Have you looked him up on the Internet?"

"How do you know about the Internet?"

"I'm old, Corliss, I'm not stupid."

"Oh, jeez, Mom, I'm sorry. I don't mean to be such a jerk. It's just, this book, is pretty cool. It's getting me all riled up."

"It's okay. You're always riled up. I love that about you."

"I love you, too, Mom. I got to go."

"Okay, bye-bye."

Corliss hung up the telephone, grabbed her backpack and coat, and hurried to the campus computer lab. She was too poor to afford her own computer and was ashamed of her poverty. Corliss talked her way past the work-study student who'd said the computers were all reserved by other poor students. She sat at a Mac and logged on. Her user name was "CrazyIndian," and her password was "StillCrazy." She typed "Harlan Atwater, Native American poet, Spokane Indian" into the search engine and found nothing. She didn't find him with any variations of the search, either. She couldn't find his book on Amazon.com, Alibris.com, or Powells.com. She couldn't find any evidence that Harlan Atwater's book had ever existed. She couldn't find the press that had published his book. She couldn't find any reviews or mention of the book. She sent e-mails to two dozen different Indian writers, including Simon Ortiz, Joy Harjo, Leslie Marmon Silko, and Adrian C. Louis, and those who responded said they'd never heard of Harlan Atwater. She paged through old government records. Maybe he'd been a criminal and had gone to prison. Maybe he'd been married and divorced. Maybe he'd died in a spectacular car wreck. But she couldn't find any mention of him. The library didn't have any re-cord of where or when the book had been purchased. The Spokane Tribal Enrollment Office didn't have any records of his existence. According to the enrollment secretary, who also happened to be Corliss's second cousin, there'd never been an enrolled Spokane Indian named Atwater. Corliss was stumped and suspicious. Every moment of an Indian's life is put down in triplicate on government forms, collated, and filed. Indians are given their social security numbers before the OB/GYN sucks the snot and blood out of their throats. How could this Harlan Atwater escape the government? How could an Indian live and work in the United States and not leave one piece of paper to mark his passage? Corliss thought Harlan Atwater might be a fraud, a white man pretending to be an Indian, seeking to make a profit, to co-opt and capitalize. Then again, what opportunistic white man was stupid enough to think he could profit from pretending to be a Spokane Indian? Even Spo-kane Indians can't profit from being Spokane! How many people had ever heard of the Spokane Tribe of Indians? Corliss felt like a literary detective, a poetic gumshoe, Sam Spade with braids. She worked for hours and days, and finally, two weeks after she first came across his book, she found an interview printed in *Radical Seattle Weekly*:

Harlan Atwater grew up in Wellpinit, Washington, on the Spokane Indian Reservation in eastern Washington State. His work has appeared in *Experimental Rice, Seattle Poetry Now!*, and *The Left Heart of Love*. The author of a book of poems, *In the Reservation of My Mind*, he lives in Seattle and is currently a warehouse supply clerk during the day while writing and performing his poems long into the night.

How did you start writing?
    Well, coming from a culture where the oral tradition is so valued, and where storytelling is an everyday and informal part of life, I think I was born and trained to tell stories, in some sense. Of course, this country isn't just Indian, is it? And it's certainly the farthest thing from sacred. I am the child and grandchild of poor Indians, and since none of them ever put pen to paper, it never occurred to me I could try to be a poet. I didn't know any poets or poems. But a few years ago, I took a poetry class with Jenny Shandy. She was on this sort of mission to teach poetry to the working class. She called it "Blue Collars, White Pages, True Stories," and I was

the only one who survived the whole class. There were ten of us when the class started. Ten weeks later, I was the last one. Jenny just kept giving me poetry books to read. I read over a hundred books of poems that year. That was my education. Jenny was white, so she gave me mostly white classical poets to read. I had to go out and find the Indian poets, the black poets, the Chicanos, you know, all the revolutionaries. I loved it all, so I guess I'm trying to combine it all, the white classicism with the dark-skinned rebellion.

How do your poem ideas come to you?

Well, shoot, everything I write is pretty autobiographical, so you could say I'm only interested in the stuff that really happens. There's been so much junk written about Indians, you know? So much romanticism and stereotyping. I'm just trying to be authentic, you know? If you look at my poems, if you really study them, I think you're going to find I'm writing the most authentic Indian poems that have ever been written. I'm trying to help people understand Indians. I'm trying to make the world a better place, full of more love and understanding.

How do you know when an idea is worth pursuing?

Well, I don't mean to sound hokey, but it's all about the elders, you know? If I think the tribal elders would love the idea, then to me, it's an idea worth turning into a poem, you know?

What is your process like for working on a poem?

It's all about ceremony. As an Indian, you learn about these sacred spaces. Sometimes, when you're lucky and prepared, you find yourself in a sacred space, and the poems come to you. Shoot, I'm putting ink to paper, you could say, but I don't always feel like I'm the one writing the poem. Sometimes my whole tribe is writing the poem with me. And I feel best about the poems when I look out in the audience and see a bunch of Indian faces. I mean, the best thing to me is when Indians come up to me and say, "Hey, man, that poem was me, that was my life." That's when I feel like I'm doing the best work.

What writers have influenced your work, and whom do you admire now?

Well, I could name a dozen writers, a hundred poets, I love and respect. But I guess I am most influenced by the natural rhythms of the world, you know? Late at night, I go outside and listen to the wind. That's all the wisdom I need. I mean, I love books, but shoot, most of the world's wisdom is not contained in books.

There is a lot of humor in your poems, often in the face of tragedy. Where does your sense of humor come from?

My grandmother was the funniest person I've ever known and the most traditional. She was a sacred person in our tribe and told the dirtiest jokes, you know? So, obviously, I grew up with the idea the sacred and profane are linked, you know? I guess you'd say my sense of humor is genetic.

Do you consider yourself a radical?

I believe in the essential goodness of human beings, and if that's being radical, then I guess I'm a radical. I believe human beings would rather hop in bed with each other and do tender things to each other than run through the jungle and shoot each other. If that's a radical thought, then I'm a radical. I believe that poetry can save the world. And shoot, that one has always been a radical thought, I guess. So maybe I am a radical, you know?

What do you think will happen to American Indians in the future?

Well, shoot, my grandfather, he was a sha-man, he used to tell me that tribal stories foretold the coming of the white man. "Grandson," he'd say to me, "we always knew the white man was coming. We knew the exact date. We knew he'd eat all the food in the house and poop on the liv-ing room carpet." My grandfather was so funny, you know? And he'd tell me that the tribal stories also foretold the white man's leaving. "Grandson," he'd say, "we always knew the white man was com-ing, and we've always known he was leaving." So,

what's the future of Indians? Well, someday soon,
I think we're going to have a lot more breathing
room.

Corliss was puzzled by the interview. Harlan Atwater
seemed to be an immodest poet who claimed to be highly sacred
and traditional and connected to his tribe, but his tribe had never
heard of him. He seemed peacefully unaware of his arrogance and
pretension. Most important, Corliss's mother had never heard of
him. No Spokane Indian had ever known him. Exactly who were
this mythical grandmother and grandfather who'd lived on the
reservation? Who was Harlan Atwater? And where was he? He
must be a fraud, and yet he was funny and hopeful, so maybe he
was a funny, hopeful, and self-absorbed fraud.

Corliss kept searching for more information about Atwater.
She found him listed in the 1971 edition of *Who's Who Among
American Writers*. There was a Seattle address and phone number.
Corliss picked up the phone and dialed the number. Naturally, it
was pointless. That number was thirty-three years old. The phone
rang a dozen times. What kind of American doesn't have an answering machine or voice mail? But after ten more rings, as Corliss
wondered why in the hell she let it ring so long, she was surprised
to hear somebody answer.

"Hello," a man said. He was tired or angry or both or didn't
have any phone manners. He sounded exactly like a man who
wouldn't have an answering machine or voice mail.

"Yes, hello, my name is Corliss Joseph, and I—"

"Is this a sales call?"

She knew he'd hang up if she didn't say the exact right
thing.

"Are you in the reservation of your mind?" she asked and heard silence from the other end. He didn't hang up, so she knew she'd asked the right question. But maybe he was calling the police on another phone line: *Hello, Officer, I'm calling to report a poetry stalker. Yes, I'm serious, Officer. I'm completely serious. I am a poet, and a lovely young woman is stalking me. Stop laughing at me, Officer.*

"Hello?" she asked. "Are you there?"

"Who are you?" he asked.

"I'm looking for, well, I found this book by a man named Harlan Atwater—"

"Where'd you find this book?"

"In the Washington State University library. I'm a student here."

"What the hell do you want from me?"

Excited, she spoke quickly. "Well, this used to be Harlan Atwater's phone number, so I called it."

"It's still Harlan Atwater's phone number," the man said.

"Wow, are you him?"

"I used that name when I wrote poems."

Corliss couldn't believe she was talking to the one and only Harlan Atwater. Once again, she felt she'd been chosen for a special mission. She had so many questions to ask, but she knew she needed to be careful. This mysterious man seemed to be fragile and suspicious of her, and she needed to earn his trust. She couldn't interrogate him. She couldn't shine a bright light in his face and ask him if he was a fraud.

"Your poems are very good," she said, hoping flattery would work. It usually worked.

"Don't try to flatter me," he said. "Those poems are mostly crap. I was a young man with more scrotum than common sense."

"Well, I think they're good. Most of them, anyway."

"Who the hell are you?"

"I'm a Spokane Indian. I'm an English literature major here."

"Oh, God, you're an Indian?"

"Well, mostly. Fifteen sixteenths, to be exact."

"So, fifteen sixteenths of you is studying the literature of the other one sixteenth of you?"

"I suppose that's one way to put it."

"Shoot, it's been a long time since I talked to an Indian."

"Really? Aren't you Indian?"

"I'm of the urban variety, bottled in 1947."

"You're Spokane, enit?"

"That's what I was born, but I haven't been to the rez in thirty years, and you're the first Spokane I've talked to in maybe twenty years. So if I'm still Spokane, I'm not a very good one."

Self-deprecating and bitter, he certainly talked like an Indian. Corliss liked him.

"I've got so many things I want to ask you," she said. "I don't even know where to begin."

"What, you think you're going to interview me?"

"Well, no, I'm not a journalist or anything. This is just for me."

"Listen, kid, I'm impressed you found my book of poems. Shoot, I only printed up about three hundred of them, and I lost most of them. Hell, I'm flattered you found me. But I didn't want to be found. So, listen, I'm really impressed you're in college. I'm proud of you. I know how tough that is. So, knock them dead, make lots of money, and never call me again, okay?"

He hung up before Corliss could respond. She sat quietly for a moment, wondering why it had ended so abruptly. She'd searched for the man, found him, and didn't like what had happened. Corliss was confused, hurt, and angry. Long ago, as part of the passage into adulthood, young Indians used to wander into the wilderness in search of a vision, in search of meaning and definition. Who am I? Who am I supposed to be? Ancient questions answered by ancient ceremonies. Maybe Corliss couldn't climb a mountain and starve herself into self-revealing hallucinations. Maybe she'd never find her spirit animal, her ethereal guide through the material world. Maybe she was only a confused indigenous woman negotiating her way through a colonial maze, but she was one Indian who had good credit and knew how to use her Visa card.

Eighteen hours later, Corliss stepped off the Greyhound in downtown Seattle and stared up at the skyscrapers. Though it was a five-hour drive from Spokane, Corliss had never been to Seattle. She'd never traveled farther than 110 miles from the house where she grew up. The big city felt exciting and dangerous to her. Great things happened in big cities. She could count on one hand the amazing people who'd grown up in Spokane, but hundreds of superheroes had lived in Seattle. Jimi Hendrix! Kurt Cobain! Bruce Lee! What about Paris, Rome, and New York City? You could stand on Houston Street in Lower Manhattan, throw a rock in some random direction, and hit a great poet in the head. If human beings possessed endless possibilities, then cities contained exponential hopes. As she walked away from the bus station through the rainy, musty streets of Seattle, Corliss thought of Homer: "Tell me, O Muse, of that ingenious hero who traveled far and wide after he sacked the famous town of Troy." She was no Odysseus, and her eight-hour bus ride hardly qualified as an odyssey. But maybe Odysseus wasn't all that heroic, either, Corliss thought. He was a drug addict and thief who abused the disabled. That giant might have been tall and strong, Corliss thought, but he still had only one eye. It's easy to elude a monster with poor depth perception. Odysseus cheated on his wife, and disguised himself as a potential lover so he could spy on her, and eventually slaughtered all of her suitors before he identified himself. He was also a romantic fool who believed his wife stayed faithful during the twenty years he was missing and presumed dead. Self-serving and vain, he sacrificed six of his men so he could survive a monster attack. In the very end, when all of his enemies had massed to kill him, Odysseus was saved by the intervention of a god who had a romantic crush on him. If one thought about it, and Corliss had often thought about it, the epic poem was foremost a powerful piece of military propaganda. Homer had transformed a lying colonial asshole into one of the most admired literary figures in human history. So, Corliss asked, what lessons could we learn from Homer? To be considered epic, one needed only to employ an epic biographer. Since Corliss was telling her own story, she decided it was an autobiographical epic. Hell, maybe she was Homer. Maybe she was Odysseus. Maybe everybody was a descendant of Homer and Odysseus. Maybe every human journey was epic.

As she walked and marveled at the architecture, at the depth and breadth and width of the city, Corliss saw a homeless man begging for change outside a McDonald's and decided he could be epic. He was dirty and had wrapped an old blanket around his shoulders for warmth, but his eyes were bright and impossibly blue, and he stood with a proud and defiant posture. This handsome homeless man was not defeated. He was still fighting his monsters, and maybe he'd someday win. If he won, maybe he'd write an epic poem about his journey back from the darkness. Okay, so maybe I'm romantic, Corliss thought, but somebody is supposed to be romantic. Some warrior is supposed to go to war against the imperial forces of cynicism and irony. I am a sentimental soldier, Corliss thought, and I am going to befriend this homeless man, no matter how crazy he might be.

"Hello," she said to him.

"Hey," he said. "You got any spare change?"

"All I've got is a credit card and hope," she said.

"Having a credit card means somebody knows you're alive. Somebody cares if you keep on living."

He smelled like five gallons of cheap wine and hard times.

"Listen," Corliss said. "McDonald's takes credit cards. I'll buy you a Super Value Meal if you tell me where I can find this address."

She showed him the paper on which she'd written down Harlan Atwater's last known place of residence.

"Okay," he said. "I'll tell you where that is. You don't have to buy me no lunch."

"You give me directions out of the goodness of your heart. And I'll buy you lunch out of the goodness of my heart."

"That sounds like a safe and sane human interaction."

Inside, they both ordered Quarter Pounders, french fries, and chocolate shakes, and shared a small table at the front window. A homeless old man and a romantic young woman! A strange couple, but only if you looked at the surface, if you used five senses. Because she was Indian, displaced by colonial rule, Corliss had always been approximately homeless. Like the homeless, she lived a dangerous and random life. Unlike landed white men, she didn't need to climb mountains to experience mystic panic. All she needed was to set her alarm clock for the next morning, wake when it rang, and go to class. College was an extreme sport for an Indian woman. Maybe ESPN2 should send a camera crew to cover her academic career. Maybe she should be awarded gold medals for taking American history and not shooting everybody during the hour and a half in which they covered five hundred years of Indian history. If pushed, Corliss knew she could go crazy. She was a paranoid schizophrenic in waiting. Maybe all the crazy homeless Indians were former college students who'd heard about manifest destiny one too many times.

Corliss and the homeless white man ate in silence. He was too hungry to talk. She didn't know what to say.

"Thank you," he said after he'd finished. "Thank you for the acknowledgment of my humanity. A man like me doesn't get to be human much."

"Can I ask you a personal question?" she asked.

"You can ask me a human question, yes."

"How'd you end up homeless? You're obviously a smart man, talking the way you do. I know smart doesn't guarantee anything, but still, what happened?"

"I just fell out of love with the world."

"I understand how that goes. I'm not so sure about the world myself, but was there anything in particular?"

"First of all, I am nuts. Diagnosed and prescribed. But there's all sorts of nutcases making millions and billions of dollars in this country. That Ted Turner, for example, is a crazy rat living in a gold-plated outhouse. But I got this particular kind of nuts, you know? I got a pathological need for respect."

"I've never heard of that condition."

"Yeah, ain't no Jerry Lewis running a telethon for my kind of sickness. The thing is, I should have been getting respect. I was an economics professor at St. Jerome the Second University here in Seattle. A fine institution of higher education."

"That's why you're so smart."

"Knowing economics only means you know numbers. Doesn't mean you know people. Anyway, I hated my job. I hated the kids. I hated my colleagues. I hated money. And I felt like none of them respected me, you know? I felt their disrespect growing all around me. I felt suffocated by their disrespect. So one day, I just walked out in the campus center, you know, right there on the green, green Roman Catholic grass, and started shouting."

Corliss could feel the heat from this man's mania. It was familiar and warm.

"What did you shout?" she asked.

"I kept shouting, 'I want some respect! I want some respect!' I shouted it all day and all night. And nobody gave me any respect. I was asking directly for it, and people just kept walking around me. Avoiding me. Not even looking at me. Not even acknowledging me. Hundreds of people walked by me. Thousands. Then finally, twenty-seven hours after I started, one of my students, a young woman by the name of Melissa, a kind person who was terrible with numbers, came up to me, hugged me very close, and whispered, 'I respect you, Professor Williams, I respect you.' I started crying. Weeping. Those tears that start from your bowels and roar up through your stomach and heart and lungs and out of your mouth. Do you know the kind of tears of which I'm speaking?"

"Yes, yes," she said. "Of course I do."

"Yes. So I started crying, and I kept crying, and I couldn't stop crying no matter how hard I tried. They tell me I cried for two weeks straight, but all I remember is that first day. I took a leave of absence from school, sold my house, and spent my money in a year, and now I'm here, relying, as they say, on the kindness of strangers."

"I am kind because you are kind. Thank you for sharing your story."

"Thank you for showing me some respect. I need respect."

"You're welcome," she said. She knew this man would talk to her for days. She knew he'd fall in love with her and steal everything she owned if given the chance. And she knew he might be lying to her about everything. He might be an illiterate heroin addict with a gift for gab. But he was also a man who could and would give her directions.

"Listen," she said. "I'm sorry. But I really have to get moving. Can you tell me where this address is?"

"I'm sorry you have to leave me. But I understand. I was born to be left and bereft. Still, I made a human promise to you, and I will keep it, as a human. This address is on the other side of the Space Needle. Walk directly toward the Space Needle, pass right beneath it, keep walking to the other side of the Seattle Center, and you'll find this address somewhere close to the McDonald's over there."

"You know where all the McDonald's are?"

"Yes, humans who eat fast food feel very guilty about eating it. And guilty people are more generous with their money and time."

Corliss bought him a chicken sandwich and another chocolate shake and then left him alone.

She walked toward the Space Needle, beneath it, and beyond it. She wondered if the homeless professor had sent her on a
wild-goose chase, or on what her malaproping auntie called a dumb-
duck run. But she saw that second McDonald's and walked along
the street until she found the address she was looking for. There, at
that address, was a tiny, battered, eighty-year-old house set among
recently constructed condominiums and apartment buildings. If
Harlan Atwater had kept the same phone number for thirty-three
years, Corliss surmised, then he'd probably lived in the same house
the whole time, too. She wasn't searching for a nomad who had
disappeared into the wilds. She'd found a man who had stayed in
one place and slowly become invisible. If a poet falls in a forest,
and there's nobody there to hear him, does he make a metaphor or
simile? Corliss was afraid of confronting the man in person. What
if he was violent? Or worse, what if he was boring? She walked into
the second McDonald's, ordered a Diet Coke, and sat at the window
and stared at Harlan Atwater's house. She studied it.

Love Song

I have loved you during the powwow
And I have loved you during the rodeo.
I have loved you from jail
And I have loved you from Browning, Montana.
I have loved you like a drum and drummer
And I have loved you like a holy man.
I have loved you with my tongue
And I have loved you with my hands.

But I haven't loved you like a scream.
And I haven't loved you like a moan.

And I haven't loved you like a laugh.
And I haven't loved you like a sigh.
And I haven't loved you like a cough.
And I haven't loved you well enough.

After two more Diet Cokes and a baked apple pie, Corliss walked across the street and knocked on the door. A short, fat Indian man answered.

"Who are you?" he asked. He wore thick glasses, and his black hair needed washing. Though he was a dark-skinned Indian, one of the darker Spokanes she'd ever seen, he also managed to look pasty. Dark and pasty, like a chocolate doughnut. Corliss was angry with him for being homely. She'd hoped he would be an indigenous version of Harrison Ford. She'd wanted Indiana Jones and found Seattle Atwater.

"Are you just going to stand there?" he asked. "If you don't close your mouth, you're going to catch flies."

He was fifty or sixty years old, maybe older. Old! Of course he was that age. He'd published his book thirty years ago, but Corliss hadn't thought much about the passage of time. In her mind, he was young and poetic and beautiful. Now here he was, the Indian sonneteer, the reservation bard, dressed in a Seattle SuperSonics T-shirt and sweatpants.

"Yo, kid," he said. "I don't have all day. What do you want?"

"You're Harlan Atwater," she said, hoping he wasn't.

He laughed. "Dang," he said. "You're that college kid. You don't give up, do you?"

"I'm on a vision quest."

"A vision quest?" he asked and laughed harder. "You flatter me. I'm just a smelly old man."

"You're a poet."

"I used to be a poet."

"You wrote this book," she said and held it up for him.

He took it from her and flipped through it. "Man," he said.
"I haven't seen a copy of this in a long time."

He remembered. Nostalgia is a dangerous thing.

"You don't have one?" she asked.

"No," he said and silently read one of the sonnets. "Dang,
I was young when I wrote these. Too young."

"You should keep that one."

"It's a library book."

"I'll pay the fine."

"This book means more to you than it means to me. Otherwise, you wouldn't have found me. You should keep it and pay
the fine."

He handed the book back to her. He laughed some more.

"I'm sorry, kid," he said. "I'm not trying to belittle you. But
I can't believe that little book brought you here."

"I've never read a book of Indian poems like that."

She started to cry and furiously wiped her tears away. She
cried too easily, she thought, and hated how feminine and weak
it appeared to be. No, it wasn't feminine and weak to cry, not
objectively speaking, but she still hated it.

"Nobody's cried over me in a long time," he said.

"You know," she said, "I came here because I thought you
were something special. I read your poems, and some of them are
really bad, but some of them are really good, and maybe I can't
always tell the difference between the good and the bad. But I know
somebody with a good heart wrote them. Somebody lovely wrote
them. And now I look at you, and you look terrible, and you sound

terrible, and you smell terrible, and I'm sad. No, I'm not sad. I'm pissed off. You're not supposed to be like this. You're supposed to be somebody better. I needed you to be somebody better."

He shook his head, sighed, and looked as if he might cry with her.

"I'm sorry, kid," he said. "But I am who I am. And I haven't written a poem in thirty years, you know? I don't even remember what it feels like to write a poem."

"Why did you quit writing poems?" she asked. She knew she sounded desperate, but she was truly desperate, and she couldn't hide it. "Nobody should ever quit writing poems."

"Jesus, you're putting me in a spot here. All right, all right, we'll have a talk, okay? You've come this far, you deserve to hear the truth. But not in my house. Nobody comes in my house. Give me fifteen minutes, and I'll meet you over to the McDonald's."

"I've already been in that McDonald's."

"So?"

"So, I don't like to go to the same place twice in the same day. Especially since I was just there."

"That's a little bit crazy."

"I'm a little bit crazy."

He liked that.

"All right," he said. "I'll meet you down to the used-book store. You can see it there at the corner."

"You read books?"

"Just because I quit writing doesn't mean I quit reading. For a smart kid, you're kind of dumb, you know?"

That pleased her more than she'd expected. He was still a smart-ass, so maybe he was still rowdy enough to write poems. Maybe there was hope for him. She felt evangelical. Maybe she could save him. Maybe she'd pray for him and he'd fall to his knees in the bookstore and beg for salvation and resurrection.

"All right?" he asked. "About fifteen minutes, okay?"

"Okay," she said.

He closed the door. For a moment, she wondered if he was tricking her, if he needed a way to close the door on her. Well, he'd have to call the cops to get rid of her. She'd camp on his doorstep until he came out. She'd wait in the bookstore for exactly seventeen minutes, and if he was one second later, she'd break down his front door and interrogate him. He was an out-of-shape loser and she could take him. She'd teach him nineteen different ways to spell matriarchy.

She hurried to the bookstore and walked inside. An elderly woman was crocheting behind the front desk.

"Can I help you?" the yarn woman asked.

"I'm just waiting for somebody," Corliss said.

"A young man, perhaps?"

Why were young women always supposed to be waiting for young men? Corliss didn't like young men all that much. Or old men, either. She was no virgin. She'd slept with three boys and heavily petted a dozen more, but she'd also gone to bed with one woman and French-kissed the holy-moly out of another, and hey, maybe that was the way to go. Maybe I'm not exactly a lesbian, Corliss thought, but I might be an inexact lesbian.

"Is there a man waiting at home for you?" Corliss asked and immediately felt like a jerk.

"Oh, no," the yarn woman said and smiled. "My husband died twenty years ago. If he's waiting for me, he's all the way upstairs, you know?"

"I'm sorry," Corliss said and meant it.

"It's okay, dear, I shouldn't have invaded your privacy. You go on ahead and look for what you came for."

On every mission, there is a time to be strong and a time to be humble.

"Listen, my name is Corliss Joseph, and I'm sorry for being such a bitch. There's no excuse for it. I'm really angry with the guy I'm supposed to be meeting here soon. He's not my boyfriend, or even my friend, or anything like that. He's a stranger, but I thought I knew him. And he disappointed me. I don't even think I have a right to be angry with him. So I'm really confused about—Well, I'm confused about my whole life right now. So I'm sorry, I really am, and I'm usually a much kinder person than this, you know?"

The yarn woman was eighty years old. She knew.

"My name is Lillian, and thank you for being so honest. When your friend, or whatever he is, arrives, I'll turn off my hearing aids so you'll have privacy."

Who would ever think of such an eccentric act of kindness? An old woman who owned a bookstore!

"Thank you," Corliss said. "I'll just look around until he gets here."

She walked through the bookstore that smelled of musty paper and moldy carpet. She scanned the shelves and read the names of authors printed on the spines of all the lovely, lovely books. She loved the smell of new books, sure, but she loved the smell of old books even more. She thought old books smelled like everybody who'd ever read them. Possibly that was a disgusting thought, and it certainly was a silly thought, but Corliss felt like old books were sentient beings that listened and remembered and passed judgment. Oh, God, I'm going to cry again, Corliss thought, I'm losing my mind in a used-book store. I am my mother's daughter.

And that made her laugh. Hey, she thought, I'm riding in the front car of the crazy-woman roller coaster.

She knew she needed to calm down. And to calm down, she needed to perform her usual bookstore ceremony. She found the books by her favorite authors—Whitman, Shapiro, Jordan, Turcotte, Plath, Lourie, O'Hara, Hershon, Alvarez, Brooke, Schreiber, Pawlak, Offutt, Duncan, Moore—and reshelved them with their front covers facing outward. The other books led with their spines, but Corliss's favorites led with their chests, bellies, crotches, and faces. The casual reader wouldn't be able to resist these books now. Choose me! Choose me! The browser would fall in love at first sight. Corliss, in love with poetry, opened Harlan Atwater's book and read one more sonnet:

Poverty

When you're poor and hungry
And love your dog
You share your food with him.
There is no love like his.
When you're poor and hungry
And your dog gets sick,
You can't afford to take him
To the veterinarian,

So you have to watch him get sicker
And cough blood and cry all night.
You can't afford to put him gently to sleep
So your uncle comes over for free
And shoots your dog twice in the head
And buries him in the town dump.

How could he know such things about poverty and pain if he had not experienced them? Can a poet be that accomplished a liar? Can a poet invent history so well that his audience is completely fooled? Only if they want to be fooled, thought Corliss, knowing she was exactly that kind of literate fool. For her, each great book was the Holy Bible, and each great author was a prophet. Oh, God, listen to me, Corliss thought, I'm a cult member. If Sylvia Plath walked into the bookstore and told her to drink a glass of cyanide-laced grape juice, Corliss knew she would happily do it.

Precisely on time, Harlan Atwater opened the door and stepped into the bookstore. He'd obviously showered and shaved, and he wore a navy blue suit that had fit better ten years and twenty pounds earlier but still looked decent enough to qualify as formal wear. He'd replaced his big clunky glasses with John Lennon wire frames. Corliss felt honored by Harlan's sartorial efforts and was once again amazed by Lillian as she smiled and turned off her hearing aids.

"You look good," Corliss said to Harlan.

"I look like I'm trying to look good," he said. "That's about all I can do right now. I hope it's enough."

"It is. Thank you for trying."

"Well, you know, it's not every day I'm the object of a vision quest."

"Everything feels new today."

He smiled. She didn't know what he was thinking.

"So," he said. "Do you want to hear my story?"

"Yes."

He led her to a stuffed couch in the back of the store. They sat together. He stared at the floor as he talked.

"I'm not really a Spokane Indian," he said.

400

She knew it! He was a fraud! He was a white man with a good tan!

"Well, I'm biologically a Spokane Indian," he said. "But I wasn't raised Spokane. I was adopted out and raised by a white family here in Seattle."

That explained why he knew so much about Spokane Indians but remained unknown by them.

"You're a lost bird," she said.

"Is that what they're calling us now?"

"Yes."

"Well, isn't that poetic? I suppose it's better than calling us stolen goods. Or clueless bastards."

"But your poems, they're so Indian."

"Indian is easy to fake. People have been faking it for five hundred years. I was just better at it than most."

She knew Indians were obsessed with authenticity. Colonized, genocided, exiled, Indians formed their identities by questioning the identities of other Indians. Self-hating, self-doubting, Indians turned their tribes into nationalistic sects. But who could blame us for our madness? Corliss thought. We are people exiled by other exiles, by Puritans, Pilgrims, Protestants, and all of those other crazy white people thrown out of a crazier Europe. We who were once indigenous to this land must immigrate into its culture. I was born one mile south and raised one mile north from the place on the Spokane River where the very first Spokane Indian was ever born, and I somehow feel like a nomad, so Harlan Atwater must feel completely lost.

"Maybe you're faking," she said. "But the poems aren't fake."

"Do you write?" he asked.

"Only academic stuff," she said. "I'm kind of afraid of writing poems."

"Why?"

"No matter what I write, a bunch of other Indians will hate it because it isn't Indian enough, and a bunch of white people will like it because it's Indian. Do you know what I mean? If I wrote poems, I'd feel trapped."

Harlan had been waiting for years to talk about his traps.

"I started writing poems to feel like I belonged," he said. "To feel more Indian. And I started imagining what it felt like to grow up on the reservation, to grow up like an Indian is supposed to grow up, you know?"

She knew. She wasn't supposed to be in college and she wasn't supposed to be as smart as she was and she wasn't supposed to read the books she read and she wasn't supposed to say the things she said. She was too young and too female and too Indian to be that smart. But I exist, she shouted to the world, and my very existence disproves what my conquerors believe about this world and me, but since my conquerors cannot be contradicted, I must not exist.

"Harlan," she said. "I don't even know what Indian is supposed to be. How could you know?"

"Well, that's the thing," he said. "I wrote those poems because I wanted to know. They weren't statements of fact, I guess. They were more like questions."

"But Harlan, that's what poetry is for. It's supposed to be about questions, about the imagination."

"I know, I know. The thing is, I mean, I started reading these poems, asking these questions, around town, you know? At the coffee shops and bookstores and open-mike nights. Late sixties, early seventies, shoot, it was a huge time for poetry. People don't remember it like that, I guess. But poetry was huge. Poets were rock stars. And I was, like, this local rock star, you know? Like a garage-band poet. And people, white people, they really loved my poems, you know? They looked at me onstage, looking as Indian as I do, with my dark skin and long hair and big nose and cheekbones, and they didn't know my poems were just pretend. How could they know? Shoot, half the white people in the crowd thought they were Indian, so why were they going to question me?"

Corliss reached across and took his hand. She hoped he wouldn't interpret it as a sexual gesture. But he didn't seem to notice or acknowledge her touch. He was too involved with his own story. He was confessing; she was his priest.

"Even though my poems were just my imagination," he said, "just my dreams and ideas about what it would've been like to grow up Indian, these white people, they thought my poems were real. They thought I had lived the life I was writing about. They thought I was the Indian I was only pretending to be. After a while, I started believing it, too. How could I not? They wanted me to be a certain kind of Indian, and when I acted like that kind of Indian, like the Indian in my poems, those white people loved me."

July 22, 1973. Seven-twenty-three p.m. Open-mike night at Boo's Books and Coffee on University Way in Seattle. Harlan Atwater walked in with twenty-five copies of *In the Reservation of My Mind*. He'd printed three hundred copies and planned to sell them for five dollars each, fairly expensive for self-published poetry, but Harlan thought he was worth it. He'd considered bringing all three hundred copies to the open mike, but he didn't want to look arrogant. He figured he'd quickly sell the twenty-five copies he had brought, and it would look better to sell out of his current stock than to have huge piles of unsold books sitting about. He didn't need the money, but he didn't want to give the books away. People didn't respect art when it was free.

He was number twelve on the list of twenty readers for the night. That was good placement. Any earlier and the crowds would be sparse. Any later and the crowds would be anxious to split and might take off while you were trying to orate and berate. There were seven women reading. He'd already slept with three of them, and three others had already rejected him, so that left one stranger with carnal possibilities.

Harlan looked good. "Thin and Indian, thin and Indian, thin and Indian," that was his personal mantra. He wore tight jeans, black cowboy boots, and a white T-shirt. A clean and simple look, overtly masculine. He didn't believe women were truly attracted to that androgynous hippie-boy look. He figured women wanted a warrior-poet.

He impatiently listened to eleven poets read their poems, then he read three of his sonnets, enough to make the crowd happy but not enough to bore them, sold all twenty-five of his books, and then he listened to six other poets read. Normally, he would have eased his way out the door after he'd finished performing, but that stranger girl was reading last, and he wanted to know if he could see more of her.

She was a good poet, funny and rowdy, no earth-loving pieties or shallow radical politics for her. She read poems about a police-chief father who loved his hippie daughter only a little more than he hated her. Okay, so she was no Plath or Sexton, but he wasn't Lowell or O'Hara. And she was cute, wearing rainbow-striped pants and a brown leather shirt. Her hair was long and blonde, of course, but she also wore bright red lipstick. Harlan couldn't remember the last time he saw a hippie woman wearing Marilyn Monroe's lips. Shoot, Harlan thought, hippie men were more apt to look like Marilyn Monroe, and that's all right, but it's not always all right.

After she finished reading, Harlan had to hang back as she quickly and politely rejected three other potential suitors, and then he approached her.

"Your poems are good," he said.

"Hey, thanks, man," she said. "You're Harlan Atwater, aren't you?"

She recognized him. That was a good sign.

"Yeah, I'm Harlan. What's your name?"

"I call myself Star Girl," she said. "But you're the real star, man, your poems are good. No, they're the best. You're going to be famous, man."

She was a fan. Things were looking even better for him.

"Hey," he said. "You want to go get a drink or something?"

Two hours later, they were naked in her bed. They hadn't touched or kissed. They'd only read poems to each other. But they were naked. Harlan had played this game before. You took off your clothes to prove how comfortable you were with your body, and how comfortable you were with other people's bodies, and how you didn't think of the body as just a sexual tool. If you could get naked with a woman and not touch her, you were a liberated man unafraid of true intimacy. But shoot, men were simpleminded about female nudity, despite how complicated naked women wanted na-ked men to be. Throughout human history, Harlan thought, men have been inventing ways to get women naked, and this hippie thing seemed to be the most effective invention of all time. Harlan knew his chances of sex with Star Girl increased with every passing minute of noncontact nudity. And she was so smart, funny, and beautiful—she'd read Rimbaud, Barnes, and Baraka to him!—he'd stay naked and sexless for six weeks.

"Tell me about your pain," she said.

"What about my pain?" he asked.

"You know, being Indian, man. That has to be a tough gig. The way we treated you and stuff. We broke your hearts, man. How do you deal with all that pain?"

"It's hard," he said. He looked down at his hands as he spoke. "I mean, I grew up so poor on the reservation, you know? We call it the rez, you know? And the thing is, Indian poor is the poorest there is. Indian poor is the basement of the skyscraper called poverty."

"That's sad and beautiful," she said. "You're sad and beauti-ful." She reached over and brushed a stray hair away from his face. Tender gestures.

"I was raised by my grandmother," he said. "My mom and dad, they were killed in a house fire. My two sisters died in the fire, too. I was the only one who lived. I was a baby when the fire happened. Somebody, they don't know whether it was my mom or dad, threw me out a window, and I landed in a tree. At first they thought I'd burned up in the fire with everyone else, but a fireman found me sleeping high up in that tree."

"That's just it, man," she said. "That's how it happens. That's how pain visits, man. You break somebody's heart two hun-dred years ago, and it's like this chain reaction, man. Hearts keep on getting broken. Oh, Harlan, you're breaking my heart."

She hugged him. She kissed him on the cheek. She kissed him on the mouth. He pushed her down and climbed on top of her. She reached down and helped him put his penis inside her. But he felt passive and removed from the act.

"Put your pain into me," she said. "I can take it. I need it. I deserve it."

He didn't know whether to laugh or cry. He knew some folks got off on being punished, on being degraded during sex. But he'd never made love to a woman who wanted him to take revenge against her for hundreds of years of pain she never caused. Who could make love with that kind of historical and hysterical passion? He laughed.

"What is it?" she asked. "What's so funny?"

"I don't know, I'm scared, I'm scared," he said. It was always good to admit your fear, or to pretend you were afraid. Women loved men who confessed their fears and doubts, however real or imaginary they might be.

"It's okay to be afraid," she said. "Give me everything you are."

He couldn't look at her. He didn't want to see the need in her eyes, and he didn't want her to see the deceit in his eyes. So he flipped her over onto her stomach and pushed into her from behind. She moaned loudly, louder than she had before, reached back and under and played with herself while he pumped in and out, in and out. He looked down at the back of her head, her face buried in the pillow, and he understood she could be any white woman. This wasn't a new and exciting position, a bid for a different kind of intimacy, or carnal experimentation. He wanted her to be faceless and anonymous because he was faceless and anonymous. He didn't know her real name, and she didn't know his.

"Give it to me," she said. "I'm here for you, I'm here for you, I'm here for you."

He felt like a ghost watching a man make love to a woman, and he wondered how a man could completely separate his body from his soul. Can women separate themselves like that? Of course they must be able to. They must have to. Star Girl was not making love to him. She was making love to an imaginary man. His body was inside her body, but who was he inside her mind? Am I her father? Am I her brother, her mother, her sister? Or am I only her Indian?

He flipped her over onto her back and penetrated her again. He pushed and pushed and pushed, and she closed her eyes.

"Look at me," he said.

She opened her eyes and looked at him. She smiled. How could she smile? She was a stranger with strange ideas.

"Say my name," he said.

"Harlan," she said.

She was wrong and didn't know she was wrong.

"Say my name," he said again.

"Harlan," she said. "Harlan Atwater."

He pulled out of her and crawled off the bed. He ignored her as he quickly dressed, and then he ran out the door, away from her. He ran to the house he shared with his white parents, grabbed the box filled with his self-printed poetry books, and ran back out into the world. He ran twenty-two blocks to Big Heart's, the Indian bar on Aurora. He threw open the door and strode into the crowded bar like a warrior chief.

"I am a poet!" he screamed to the assembled Indians.

The drunken Indians, those broken men and women, let Harlan be their poet for the night. They let him perform his poems between jukebox songs. They listened and applauded. They hugged and kissed him. They told him his poems sounded exactly like Indian poems were supposed to sound. They recited their poems to him, and asked if their poems were as good as his poems, and he said they were very good, very good, so keep working on them. They all wanted copies of his books. Harlan was so happy he gave them away for free. He autographed 275 books and gave them to 275 different Indians. They all bought him drinks. He didn't need their charity. He had money. But he wanted to be part of their tribe, their collective, so he drank the free drinks, and he laughed and sang and danced and performed his poems again and again. And yes, he could recite all of them by memory because he loved his poems so much. He asked them if he was Indian, and they said he was the best Indian they'd ever known, and he was happy to hear it, so he drank the free drinks and bought drinks for others, and they all drank together, completely forgetting who had paid for what. He drank more, and the lights and faces blurred, and he could see only one bright red light, and then he could see nothing at all.

Harlan woke the next morning in the alley behind the bar. He staggered to his feet, retched, and emptied his stomach onto a pile of his poetry books lying on the dirty cement. Dry-heaving, he knelt, cleaned his vomit off his books, and read the inscriptions inside:

> *To Junior, my new best friend, Love, Harlan*
> *To Agnes! Indian Power! From Harlan!*
> *To Hank, who fought in the Nam and don't give a*
> *   damn, Harlan*
> *To Pumpkin, who always remembers the elders,*
> *   Always, Harlan*
> *To Dee, the rodeo queen, from the rodeo king, Harlan*

Carrying the damp books, Harlan staggered down the alley and onto the street. Sunrise. The street was empty of cars and people, but Harlan could see a dozen of his books lying abandoned on the street. He knew hundreds of others were lying on hundreds of other streets. Harlan dropped the books he carried, let them join the rest of their tribe, and walked home to his parents.

In the used-book store, Corliss covered her face with her hands. She couldn't look at the world where such a sad thing could take place.

"Shoot, that's the thing," Harlan said. "That's why I was so surprised to hear one of my books was in the library. In the end, I didn't write poems. I wrote litter."

He laughed. Corliss wondered how he could laugh. But she laughed with him and didn't know why. What was so funny about the world? Everything! Corliss and Harlan laughed until the hearing-impaired bookstore owner probably felt the floor shake.

"So, what lessons can we learn from this story?" Corliss asked.

"Never autograph books for drunk Indians," he said.

"Never have sex with women named after celestial bodies."

"Never self-publish your poetry."

"Never perform at open-mike nights."

"Never pretend to be an Indian when you're not," he said. He took off his glasses and wiped tears from his eyes. Two Indians crying in the back of a used-book store. Indians are always crying, Corliss thought, but at least we're two Indians crying in an original venue. What kind of ceremony was that? An original ceremony! Every ceremony has to be created somewhere; her Eden was a

410

used-book store. In the beginning, there was the word, and the word was on sale at the local bookstore. That was only natural, she thought, it was apt and justified and ordained. Again, she felt blessed and chosen. She felt young and epic. Can one be young and epic? She didn't know, but she'd gladly be the first such adventurer, or second, or thirty-third, or one millionth. She was Odysseus, and Harlan was Homer. Or vice versa.

"I never wrote another poem after that night," Harlan said. "It seemed indecent."

"I think poetry writing is supposed to feel indecent."

"Well, maybe. You're young. I was young, too. And I made a lot of fuss about some fairly inconsequential poems. It's not like I was famous or rich or talented. I was ordinary, or maybe a little better than ordinary, and I wanted to be more than that, and I couldn't be, and it hurt for a long time. I think writing poems, I think if I would've kept writing them, I would've always been reminded of that, of how ordinary I am."

Corliss wondered what sort of person could continue working jobs that made him feel ordinary. But everybody worked those jobs. Corliss didn't believe there was a huge difference between the average pizza deliveryman's self-esteem and Clint Eastwood's. Or maybe she only wanted to believe there was no real difference. How do small people feel larger? Well, silly, they pretend the large people are smaller. In an ideal world, Corliss thought, everybody weighs 150 pounds!

"Can I ask you a human question?" she asked.

"What's a human question?" he asked.

"A homeless guy taught me the phrase. I think it's a variation on a personal question."

"You're a strange, strange woman," he said.

She couldn't disagree.

"All right," he said. "Go ahead. Ask away."

"What have you been doing all these years?"

"I still drive a forklift down on the waterfront. Nothing spectacular. I'm going to retire at the end of the year. I've got a big pension coming. It's good money, honest work, I guess, as long as I don't think too hard about what's in the boxes, you know?"

Corliss knew about denial.

"And I take care of my folks," he said. "I still live with them in the house. That's why I didn't let you in. They're old and sick. They took care of me then. I take care of them now."

"Were they good parents?" she asked.

"Better than most, I suppose," he said. "But the thing is, shoot, they could have completely ignored me, and it wouldn't have mattered much. Because they saved my life. I mean, I know they're white and I'm Indian, and that's supposed to be such a sad-sack story, but well, they did, they really saved my life."

"What do you mean?" she asked.

"Well, shoot," he said. "I went looking for my real mother once. And it took me a few years, but I found her. She was living alone in Los Angeles. Living in some downtown dive hotel, and she was smoking crack, you know? That's what my real mother was doing the first time I saw her. I was sitting in my car outside that hotel, because it was scary, you know? And I saw this old Indian woman walking down the street, walking with a cane, and her face was all swollen, and her legs were all swollen. And she had all these sores all over her arms and legs and face. And she looked like a zombie, you know? Like Stephen King's nightmare Indian."

"How'd you know it was your mother?" Corliss asked.

"I don't know," he said. "I just knew. I mean, she looked like me. I looked like her. But there was something else, too. I felt connected. And she started coughing. I was parked fifty feet away, but I could hear her coughing so loud. She was retching up stuff and spitting it on the sidewalk. And it was the saddest thing I'd ever seen. And this was my mother. This was the woman who gave birth to me, who'd left me behind. I felt sorry for her and loved her and hated her all at the same time, you know?"

Corliss knew about mothers and their difficult love.

"I opened the door and got out. I was going to walk across the street and stop her and say to her—I'd rehearsed it all—I was going to say, 'Mother, I am your son.' Basic, simple, clean. Nothing dramatic. Still, I thought even that simple statement might kill her. I keep thinking I might shock her into a heart attack, she looked so frail and weak. I'm walking across the street toward her, and she's coughing, and I'm getting closer, and then she reaches into her pocket, pulls out this crack pipe and a lighter, and she lights up right there in the middle of the street. Broad daylight. She lights up and sucks the crap in. And I kept walking right past her, came within a foot of her, you know. I could smell her. She didn't even look at me. She just kept sucking at that pipe. Old Indian woman sucking on a crack pipe. It was sad and ridiculous, but you know the worst part?"

"What?" Corliss asked.

Harlan stood and walked down the aisle away from Corliss. He spoke with his back to her.

"I was happy to see my mother like that," he said. "I was smiling when I walked away from her. I just kept thinking how lucky I was, how blessed, that this woman didn't raise me. I just

413

kept thinking God had chosen me, had chosen these two white people to swoop in and save me. Do you know how terrible it is to feel that way? And how good it feels, too?"

"I don't have any idea how you feel," Corliss said. Her confusion was the best thing she could offer. What could she say to him that would matter? She'd spent her whole life talking. Words had always been her weapon, her offense and defense, and she felt that her silence, her wordlessness, might be the only thing she could give him.

"The thing is," he said, "the two best, the two most honorable and loyal people in my life are my white mother and my white father. So, you tell me, kid, what kind of Indian does that make me?"

Corliss knew only Harlan could answer that question for himself. She knew the name of her tribe, and the name of her archaic clan, and her public Indian name, and her secret Indian name, but everything else she knew about Indians was ambiguous and transitory.

"What's your name?" she asked him. "What's your real name?"

Harlan Atwater faced her. He smiled, turned away, and walked out of the store. She could follow him and ask for more. She could demand to know his real name. She could interrogate him for days and attempt to separate his truth from his lies and his exaggerations from his omissions. But she let him go. She understood she was supposed to let him go. And he was gone. But Corliss sat for hours in the bookstore. She didn't care about time. She was tired and hungry, but she sat and waited. Indians are good at waiting, she thought, especially when we don't know what we're waiting for. But there comes a time when an Indian stops waiting, and when that time came for Corliss, she stood, took Harlan Atwater's book to the poetry section, placed it with its front cover facing outward for all the world to see, and then she left the bookstore and began her small journey back home.

THE VOW

If I get Alzheimer's," he said, "then I want you to put me in a home."

"Indians don't get Alzheimer's," she said.

"Why not?"

"Because our elders continue to be an active part of our culture. With powwows and storytelling and ceremonies."

"That sounds very anecdotal," he said. "And also, you know, like bullshit."

"It sounds true is what it sounds like."

"Everything sounds true if you say it enough."

"It's true for me," she said. "If you get Alzheimer's, I'm going to take care of you. I'll turn the dining room into a hospital room. And I'll get one of those recliners that you can raise and lower. And I'll spoon-feed you sweet potatoes."

"I hate sweet potatoes," he said.

"Carrots, then."

"Why would you take care of me like that? Why would you sacrifice your health for mine?"

"A thing called wedding vows," she said. "Perhaps you remember ours?"

"We need Wedding Vows 2.0," he said.

"How very modern of you."

"I'm an Indian man," he said. "You know I'm going to get sick before you do. If one of us gets Alzheimer's, it's going to be me."

"Self-pity is so sexy."

"No, really," he said, and took her hand. "Promise me."

"Promise you what?"

"Promise me you'll put me in a home if I get Alzheimer's."

"I'm not going to do that. You're still going to be you."

"I can't be me if I don't have my memories. We're made of memories, damn it."

She was not surprised by his sudden anger. And she knew how to mollify him.

"Okay," she said. "You'll lose your memories. I understand. But I'll still have mine. I'll have enough memory for both of us."

"That's beautiful," he said. "And also, you know, more bullshit."

"Maybe. But it's my bullshit."

"Listen," he said. "Just make this promise. When I forget your name—when I forget who you are—then you have to put me in a home."

She tried to picture it. She imagined him staring at her like she was an intruder in their home. It was a terrifying hypothetical, but it felt so possible that she was startled by her grief.

"I don't want to talk about this," she said. "It's not going to happen."

"I love you," he said. "I love you like the earth loves the earth. I need you to promise me this."

"No."

"Promise me you'll put me in a home if I forget who you are."

"No."

He stood from the couch and walked across the room. He paused in the doorway to the kitchen and turned to face her.

"Pretend," he said. "Pretend this space between us is all we have left. Pretend I can't see or hear you across the distance. Pretend I have to introduce myself to you thirty times a day."

Her eyes watered. She didn't want to cry.

"Stop it," she said. "Why are you doing this?"

"Just make the promise," he said. "Quit asking questions. And just make the promise. I need the promise. Just be my wife and don't question my motives this time. Just accept it. Don't you love me enough to just accept something I ask for?"

She hid her face and sobbed. After a few minutes, she stopped. Then, a few minutes after that, she could speak again.

"Okay," she said. "If you can't remember who I am, then I'll put you in a home. But I'm going to visit you every day. I'll introduce myself to you every fucking day for the rest of our lives."

She rarely cursed, so he knew that she was telling the truth.

"Damn you," she said. "Damn you for doing this to me. Damn you for being so fucking sad."

They were both twenty-seven years old and lived in a one-bedroom house in a city. They'd been married for three years. She was pregnant with their second child. They'd known beforehand the gender of the first child, a daughter, but they'd decided to keep the gender of the second one a mystery. She was from the Colville Indian Reservation and he from the Spokane Indian Reservation. Between their tribal lands flowed the Columbia River, the fourth largest in the United States. During their seven years of courtship, he'd drive his car onto the Gifford Ferry and cross the water for her.

O, he'd loved that river since his birth.

O, he'd loved her since the first time he'd seen her shawl-dancing in the powwow twilight.

But he'd always been afraid of his love's volume, and he'd always been more afraid of her love's volume.

When he was nineteen, he'd driven onto the ferry, positive he was going to break up with her and join the Marines. Distraught by his weakness, he stepped out of his car and paced the ferry's small deck. Then he leaned over the railing and saw a herd of deer swimming alongside the ship.

"Holy shit," he said to himself.

"Holy shit," he said again, and counted eleven deer.

"Holy shit," he said for the third time as the largest buck turned its head and looked at him. The deer was judging him.

Amazed, he turned to tell the three other people on the ferry. But he changed his mind. He wanted to keep the deer for himself. It was a sign, he thought. How could he leave a place where he could see miracles like this?

So, instead of leaving her on that day and going to war, he carried his hand drum into her house. And with an audience of three—her and her parents—he sang an honor song to deer. He improvised a song for deer. And as he sang it, he knew that his honor song was also a love song for her. And he'd instantly memorized it.

So, years later, as he stood in the kitchen doorway and watched his wife weeping over his ridiculous amendment of their wedding vows, he tried to comfort her.

"Sweetheart," he said. "Even if I forget your name, I'll still remember that deer song. Every time you come to visit me, I'll sing you that deer song, even if I'm not sure why I'm singing it, and everything will be okay."

He almost believed it. And she almost believed it, too.

BASIC TRAINING

George Mikan was the best basketball donkey that Carter & Sons had ever owned. You could train any donkey to let any human ride it randomly around a basketball court. But George Mikan, named for the bespectacled giant who played pro ball in the '50s, had an affinity for the game. He always trotted directly toward the hoop regardless of the dexterity, intelligence, or size of the person he was carrying. Emery Carter, Jr., mostly known as Deuce, was convinced that George Mikan would have shot the ball if he had opposable thumbs, but Emery Carter, Sr., mostly known as Emery, scoffed at the idea.

"Donkeys got only three talents," Emery said. "Fucking, braying, and shitting."

"What about basketball?" Deuce asked.

"For donkeys, everything is fucking, braying, and shitting."

Deuce wanted to tell his father that all human activity is also about fucking, braying, and shitting, but he knew his father wouldn't appreciate the joke. His father wasn't dumb but he lived in a world that did not include metaphors.

There comes a time in every son's life when he thinks he is smarter than his father. But the truth is that fathers and sons are mostly equal in intelligence. Geniuses beget geniuses and idiots beget idiots. And yet, there also comes a time in a few sons' lives when it can be proven beyond any doubt that they are very much smarter than their fathers. So, yes, Deuce was the Socrates of the Carter clan. But even Deuce knew that wasn't saying much because the Carter clan currently consisted of himself, the elder Emery, and twelve donkeys.

Emery Sr. and Emery Jr. were the president and vice president of Carter & Sons, one of two Donkey Basketball outfits in the Pacific Northwest and one of only ten still operating in the United States. Founded by Edgar Carter in the days after he'd come limping home from WWII, it had, for over four decades, provided solid middle-class employment for Edgar, his wife Eileen, and their three sons, Edgar Jr., Edward, and Emery.

The 1950s through early 1980s were the glory days of Donkey Basketball. Every weekend, the Carters and their donkeys traveled to high schools in Washington, Oregon, and Idaho, and split the gate proceeds 50/50 with the sponsoring organizations. Once in a while, they even found games in Utah, Northern California, Nevada, and western Montana. Donkey Basketball was popular.

Donkey Basketball helped high schools raise money for new football uniforms or new trumpets for the band or typewriters for the business classes. Donkey Basketball helped the Masons and Elks raise money for college scholarships or give out toys to poor kids at Christmas or help a war widow fix the roof on her house. Donkey Basketball wasn't just profitable—it was socially responsible. It was good Christian work, and the Carters happened to be the most dedicated outfit with the most friendly humans and donkeys.

Then came the late '80s and the concept, the romantic poetry, of Animal Rights, and Donkey Basketball was soon viewed in the same way as slaughtering pigs or injecting hepatitis into lab rats or cutting open the skulls of live monkeys and studying their working brains. It wasn't fair. The Carters loved their donkeys. They fed and bathed the donkeys. The Carters, as a family, midwifed the births of at least a hundred donkey babies. Their donkeys weren't just pets. And they weren't just moneymaking employees. They were family.

By 1991, Carter & Sons went Chapter 11 bankrupt. Edgar and Eileen, married for fifty years, died within days of each other. The older boys, Edgar Jr. and Edward, went looking for work in Alaska and never came back. So that left only Emery to care for a barnful of unemployable donkeys and to try and save the family business. And he'd been saving it for twenty years, gaining and losing two wives in the process, but hanging on to a son, a namesake, who was also his best friend.

After dragging the company out of bankruptcy, Emery and Deuce somehow made enough money each year to feed the donkeys and themselves and to pay for the gas to make it to the various towns that still welcomed Donkey Basketball. And once in a while, they had enough cash to rent a motel rather than sleeping in the truck or driving for hours to get back home or to the next game. Though Emery considered himself a Truman Democrat, he discovered that 99 percent of Donkey Basketball fans were now Republicans and/or reservation Indians. He figured Indians loved basketball and animals in equal measure, and he knew those rez people loved to laugh, but he didn't understand why Donkey Basketball had suddenly become a nearly exclusive Republican tradition. He decided not to care. Money was money, after all. And his donkeys didn't give a shit about liberal-vs.-conservative battles, so Emery decided not to care, either. If Emery had thought to own a motto or to issue a mission statement, it would have been: "Donkeys love everybody."

And it was true. Donkeys did love everybody. And Emery loved everybody, too. He was, in an old-fashioned way, a very decent man. One might have thought to call him chivalrous if that word wasn't loaded with a history of pistol duels.

But Deuce hated the donkeys. He'd hated them since he could walk and say the word "donkey." But mostly he hated the fact that he had, through family obligation, dedicated his life to something as inane as Donkey Basketball. He was embarrassed that his job hampered—no, destroyed—his romantic life. After all, what's the third question any woman asks any potential lover?

—What's your name?

—Deuce.

—Where you from?

—North of Spokane. Little town called Chewelah.

—So what do you do for a living?

—I run a Donkey Basketball company.

—Donkey Basketball?

—Uh, yeah.

—So you teach donkeys how to play basketball?

—Well, no, we've trained the donkeys to carry people around the court. The people play basketball while riding the donkeys.

—So it's like wheelchair basketball? Except the donkeys are the wheelchairs?

—Well, no, those wheelchair folks are amazing athletes. We don't usually have athletes in our games. The people are goofs. And the donkeys just wander around the court. Mostly wander. But we got one donkey that's a natural ballplayer.

—Don't donkeys make, you know, a mess on the court?

—Yeah, sometimes. Most times, I guess. It's part of the show. It's funny. People laugh.

—So who cleans up the mess?

—I do. Mostly. My dad has a bad back so the shoveling isn't always too good for him.

—So your name is Deuce and you clean it up when donkeys go number two? You're the Deuce who cleans up the deuce?

—Yeah, I guess.

—Well, um, okay, it was nice to meet you, but I've got some friends waiting for me. I have to go. Bye.

It had been nearly a decade since Deuce hadn't had to pay for sex. He wasn't a bad-looking guy. He was thin and muscular like a slice of beef jerky, and had read a couple thousand books in his life. He was one of those rare men who did not monologue his way through life. Deuce *loved* conversation, but that still did him no good with women, not even the women who liked Donkey Basketball, because those women tended to be farm wives married to their high school sweethearts who were, in turn, in love with their thousand acres of wheat or lentils or some other damn plant. And it wasn't like Deuce didn't try. He always picked the most attractive women—the ones without wedding rings—to ride George Mikan. He wanted to use his most talented donkey as a matchmaker, as a love connection, as an aphrodisiac. But Deuce knew that even the hope of using a donkey as a romantic tool was weird, sad, and doomed.

In fact, it had become so weird, sad, and doomed that Deuce had, without informing his father, enlisted in the Army. After basic training, Deuce, even at the advanced age of thirty-one, was certain to be sent into an active combat zone, but he was desperate enough to believe that getting shot at by angry Muslims was a better deal than refereeing one more game of Donkey Basketball.

The game that very evening had been in Browning, Montana, on the Blackfeet Indian Reservation. They were raising money for the Meals on Wheels program for senior citizens. A damn good cause, so Carter & Sons had volunteered to take a 40 percent cut of the proceeds instead of their usual 50. But it turned out the white woman who organized the event was new to the reservation and hadn't realized it was the same weekend as some special Blackfeet holiday. Deuce hadn't spent any time with Indians outside of Donkey Basketball, but he'd learned that Indians have more holidays than just about any other group of people. This meant that most of the Blackfeet were busy with holiday activities, so that more people rode the donkeys than watched the game from the stands.

As usual, Deuce had given George Mikan to the most attractive single woman in the gym. And, oh, was this Indian woman gorgeous. She was probably six-four, a couple inches taller than Deuce, and her black hair hung down to her knees. All by itself her hair was taller than Emery. She was probably thirty pounds heavier than she should have been but it was thirty pounds placed in exactly the best places. And though you wouldn't think it would be beautiful, her nose was an indigenous work of art that belonged in the Smithsonian. She was pale brown, like maybe one of her parents was white. And her hands—oh, her hands—were long and aerodynamic, like she was carrying ten thin birds around instead of fingers.

"What's your name?" Deuce asked her.

"Carlene," she said.

Carlene! Deuce thought women were named Carlene only in country songs.

"Have you ever ridden a donkey before?"

"I barrel race horses," she said.

"Okay, so you can handle George Mikan. Do you play basketball?"

"Not so much anymore, but I played college hoops at BYU."

"Oh, you're Mormon?"

"No, Mormons make Indians their special mission. Well, Indians are the special mission for a lot of white people, but Mormons are the superstars of trying to save Indians."

"How come you aren't at those holiday ceremonies?"

"Does it look like I can fit in those little ceremony rooms?" she asked.

She was a smart and funny woman. Deuce wondered if Carlene had a thing for white men, or maybe could develop a thing for one particular white man. Maybe her dad was white and mean. If so, then Deuce could potentially take gentle advantage of her father issues.

"Are you married?" he asked.

"Ain't you the bold one?" she said. "No, I'm not married. But if Montana ever makes it legal, I'll marry my girlfriend."

Damn. A tall, smart, athletic, hilarious, horse-riding Indian beauty queen who liked her men to be, well, women.

"Well, I'm happy for you and your girl," Deuce said. "But it's a damn shame for me and mankind in general. I swear I would have killed buffalo for you, or whatever it is an Indian warrior is supposed to do to earn your love."

"Thank you," she said. "Now me and this mule here are going to kick ass, no pun intended."

And so Carlene and George Mikan instantly became the greatest duo in Donkey Basketball history. George didn't trot this time. No, he galloped. And Carlene made basket after basket. Hell, she was hitting long three-point shots from the back of a donkey. George Mikan weaved through the other donkeys, his stablemates, and drove toward the hoop to give Carlene easy lay-ins. And though the crowd was small, they knew they were witness-ing something special—perhaps the greatest Donkey Basketball performance of all time—and so they cheered and hooted and war-whooped so loud that they seemed to turn a mostly empty gym into a crowded arena.

In the end, Carlene scored 42 points and led her team of mostly Blackfeet women to a huge victory over a bunch of mostly white guys who must have worked for the Bureau of Indian Affairs.

Emery thanked the crowd for their attendance and en-thusiasm, handed Carlene one of the cheap little plastic trophies they always gave to the Most Valuable Player, and then Carter & Sons hustled to get the donkeys into the trailer so they could get on the road.

As they loaded the last donkey, Deuce saw Carlene walk-ing through the parking lot with a small white woman. They were holding hands, a pretty bold move in rural Montana, he guessed, but he figured Indians must be more kind toward the eccentric—to Donkey Basketball kingpins and lesbians.

"Hey, MVP," Deuce shouted at Carlene. "I hope I see you down the road somewhere."

She smiled and waved, as did her partner, and Deuce felt a cold, cold Chinook wind barrel race through his heart. Carlene was an honest and good woman, but Deuce knew he'd been keeping a terrible secret from his father.

So it was one in the morning, mid-April, and Emery and Deuce were driving east on Highway 2. They were just a few miles from Cut Bank on their way to a game the next night in Poplar, on the North Dakota border.

In his pocket, Deuce held a one-way Greyhound bus ticket that would carry him from Cut Bank to Tacoma, Washington, where he would take a taxi and report to basic training at Fort Lewis. Deuce knew that it was less a piece of paper than it was an epic betrayal of his father and his family's history. For weeks, he'd tried to tell his father the truth. That it was over. That it was done. That donkeys had become dinosaurs. He'd wanted to tell his father back at the ranch in Chewelah. He'd wanted to maybe just sneak out of the house one night and never return. But he lacked the courage. Instead, he'd decided to abandon his father in the middle of a road trip. It was a cruel and sinful thing to do but Deuce decided that it was his only alternative. He had to break his father's heart in order to break away from the family business. Most folks went into the military out of some sense of honor, but Deuce was dishonorably discharging himself *into* the Army.

"How much money we make tonight?" Emery asked Deuce.

"Fifty bucks," Deuce said. "If we don't make two hundred in Poplar, we're not going to have money to get back home."

"Tomorrow will be all right," Emery said. "Everything will be all right. Donkey Basketball is coming back. With all this new technology shit, people are aching to get back to what really matters. They're hurting to get back to the land. And Donkey Basketball is the land. Donkey Basketball is the good earth. And you and I are the good earth, too. I'm telling you, Deuce, we're going to get rich the old-fashioned way and we're going to get rich because we're doing something old-fashioned."

But Deuce knew that the old-fashioned never became the new thing, especially in this era when people changed their cell phones more often than they changed their pants.

And so in their truck, towing a trailer with twelve donkeys, Deuce, after much pain, self-loathing, and deliberation, told his father the truth about his military enlistment. And the shock of the news gave Emery a spiritual heart attack. He lost control of the steering wheel and sent the truck carrying the men and the trailer carrying the donkeys rolling into a fallow wheat field where both vehicles broke apart and rolled over four times.

Father and son survived the wreck with seemingly minor cuts and bruises and sprained fingers and knees. They crawled out of the broken truck and rushed to the trailer lying on its side fifty feet away.

Six donkeys—Dave Cowens, Tiny Archibald, Tom and Dick Van Arsdale, Artis Gilmore, and Billy Paultz—were obviously dead, torn into parts and pieces.

Four other donkeys—Dr. J, Connie Hawkins, Billy Cunningham, and Bob Cousy—were mortally wounded. Two were screaming somewhere in the wreckage and two were trying to walk away despite their injuries.

One donkey, Bill Laimbeer, seemed to be alive and well and just angry at the situation.

But George Mikan, the greatest basketball donkey in the world, was missing.

Seeing the carnage, and the end of his way of life, Emery attacked his son.

"This is your fault!" he screamed again and again, throwing punch after punch.

Deuce, younger and quicker, dodged most of the blows. In no world would he have struck his father so Deuce just defended himself as best as he could. The father, cursing the world, chased the son around the field until the old man lost his anger and collapsed to his knees and wept.

It was the first time that Deuce had seen his father cry. He kneeled beside him, and though Emery resisted at first, he soon accepted his son's embrace, and they wept together.

"I'm sorry, Dad, I'm so sorry."

After a while, Emery recovered and did the only thing a simple man could do in such a situation.

"We have to take care of the donkeys," he said.

Deuce understood what his father wanted. So he climbed back into the truck, unbolted the rifle from its rack, pulled the box of bullets from the glove compartment, and carried it back to his father. Emery looked at the rifle and bullets.

"You do the first one," he said. "I'm not ready for it yet."

But loading the rifle, Deuce wasn't sure that he could shoot the mortally wounded and suffering donkeys. He realized for the first time that perhaps he did love the animals. Or at least, he loved how much his father loved the donkeys.

"I'll take care of everybody," Deuce said.

"No," Emery said. "Just let me catch my breath. I'll help."

"Half," Deuce said. "We'll each do half."

"Okay, okay," Emery said, and got to his feet.

Such are the compromises of grief.

Carrying the rifle, Deuce walked over to Billy Cunningham, desperately trying to walk on mutilated forelegs. Deuce could see white bone shining through red viscera in both. Billy was a dumb animal but was probably the most affectionate of the herd. Even in great pain, he leaned his head against Deuce's chest.

"I'm sorry, Billy," Deuce said, then stepped back, pressed the rifle against the donkey's skull, and pulled the trigger.

Emery cried out at the gunshot, fell back to his knees, and buried his face in the dirt like a mourning pilgrim. Deuce knew then he'd have to do the entire killing. It was mercy, he guessed, but is there really such a thing as mercy with a bullet?

Connie Hawkins, quite intelligent and aware of what a gunshot meant, tried to run away. And she was moving pretty quickly for an animal whose lower jaw was broken in two and whose ribs were visible through a massive gash in her flank. Deuce, weeping hard again and gasping for breath, had to jog to catch up with Connie. And poor, smart Connie tried to defend herself. She weakly reared up and tried to head-butt Deuce but only tripped herself and fell heavily to the dirt. Deuce stood over Connie, who looked up at him with anger and fear. Deuce wanted to lean over and hug the animal but he knew that Connie might find the strength to hurt him. So Deuce aimed, held his breath, and shot Connie in the head.

Dr. J and Bob Cousy were still trapped in the ruined trailer. A piece of metal had pierced Dr. J's chest, missing her heart, but had likely torn her lungs. She was coughing blood. Deuce could barely see through his tears as he shot the animal.

Deuce went to his knees again and tossed the rifle aside. He knew he couldn't shoot another one of his animals, even though Bob Cousy was screaming beneath a pile of twisted metal. Deuce scuttled his way through the mess and lay down beside the dying donkey. As soon as Deuce held the donkey's face in his hands, Bob Cousy stopped screaming.

Man and donkey had known each other for fifteen years. And they stared into each other's eyes with a man's regret and a donkey's primal pain. But Deuce could see that Bob Cousy wanted to live. Considering how slow and clueless Bob had been as a basketball player, it was surprising to see such strength in him now.

"Just let go, Bob," Deuce said. "Let go. It's okay. Let go. It's okay to let go."

And so Bob took two deep breaths, shuddered, and died.

In that silence, Deuce could hear only his father's quiet weeping. The son had no idea how long he listened to his father. But eventually, he crawled out of the trailer and walked over to his father, lying facedown in the dirt. Deuce rolled his wailing father over and saw that his face was covered with dirt turned to mud from tears.

"Dad, are you hurt? Do you feel anything broken inside you?"

"Where's George Mikan?" Emery asked. "Go find George."

"I will, I will, but are you going to be okay? Are you bleeding inside?"

"I'm okay, I'm okay. Just find George."

But Deuce couldn't leave his father looking that way. So he pulled off his shirt and wiped his father's face clean and pulled off his T-shirt and wrapped that around his father's bloody arm. Then Deuce pulled out his cell phone, but there was no signal.

"Dad, I'm going to have to walk to get us help."

"No, find George."

Deuce scanned the dark horizon. He could see lights out on the plains. Farmhouses, he supposed. Deuce thought he could easily walk close to one of those lights but that it probably wasn't wise for a shirtless, bloody man to knock on a rural Montana door in the middle of the night. He had to walk into Cut Bank.

"Dad, we can find George in the daylight. I have to go get help for you now."

"Goddamn you, goddamn you," Emery said. He weakly punched and kicked at his son. "You do what I say. If it's the last goddamn time, you do what I say. I'm your goddamn father and you're going to obey me. Obey me, you little fucker. Obey me."

Deuce again weathered his father's blows. And then he handed the phone to Emery.

"Dad, keep trying to call for help. I'll go look for George."

Deuce was terrified to leave his father alone.

"Go get George," Emery said. "I've got Bill Laimbeer. He'll take care of me."

Deuce couldn't believe that Bill wasn't as injured as the other donkeys, and that gave him hope that George Mikan was also okay.

"All right, Bill," Deuce said to the donkey. "You watch Dad. I'm going for George."

And so Deuce walked out into the dark. He tried to think like a donkey, like George Mikan, who always trotted for the rim, the goal. So Deuce picked the brightest light in the distance. He figured that George would be traveling toward that light. That light was the hoop and that wheat field was the court.

"Okay, George," Deuce said. "Let's win this game."

He'd walked maybe ten yards when he realized that George might be terribly injured. Deuce understood that he might have to shoot their best donkey. He might have to end that beautiful animal's misery. But he'd been unable to shoot Bob, so how could he shoot George?

And yet, he knew it was his duty. He knew he had to find the strength and grace. The violent kindness. So he walked back to the trailer, picked up the rifle, and then headed again toward the bright light.

Traveling through the dark with his rifle, Deuce realized that he was now some other kind of soldier. This damn donkey business had started at the end of one war and was now dying in the middle of another one.

After half an hour, Deuce had slowed considerably. The adrenaline had dissipated, so that he could feel his sprained ankles and knees, and the hundred different bruises, and the probably broken collarbone. He knew that George had to be injured, too. He understood that George must have been slowing down.

After another half hour, Deuce had to stop. His ribs felt like they were scraping against his lungs. Maybe a busted rib had pierced his lungs. Deuce wondered if he was dying. He wanted to lie down in the cool dirt and rest. Just close his eyes for a few minutes. And then he'd get up and resume the hunt.

Deuce wanted to surrender.

But then he saw George, illuminated by moonlight, standing atop a rise fifty feet away. Soaked with blood and sweat, trembling and ruined, George couldn't possibly survive his injuries.

Deuce thought of his father, lying back there in the dark. Deuce knew that he'd mortally wounded his father's soul.

Deuce knew he was a bad man. But he hoped that he could become a good soldier.

On the rise, George staggered and nearly fell. He brayed and brayed, and it sounded like a prayer, like a plea to be released. Deuce wanted to walk up the rise, stand next to his friend, and end his pain. But he didn't have the strength. Even as he tried to remain standing, Deuce lost his balance and fell again on his knees. Jesus, he thought, give me some strength. But he didn't think he'd ever have strength enough to crawl to George.

So Deuce raised the rifle to his shoulder and aimed at George's head. In the daylight, with full strength, it would have been an easy shot. But on this night, in this dark, he might miss.

Deuce inhaled and exhaled deeply. Then, with shaking hands and with both eyes open, he pulled the trigger.

WHAT YOU PAWN
I WILL REDEEM

Noon

One day you have a home and the next you don't, but I'm not going to tell you my particular reasons for being homeless, because it's my secret story, and Indians have to work hard to keep secrets from hungry white folks.

I'm a Spokane Indian boy, an Interior Salish, and my people have lived within a one-hundred-mile radius of Spokane, Washington, for at least ten thousand years. I grew up in Spokane, moved to Seattle twenty-three years ago for college, flunked out within two semesters, worked various blue- and bluer-collar jobs for many years, married two or three times, fathered two or three kids, and then went crazy. Of course, "crazy" is not the official definition of my mental problem, but I don't think "asocial disorder" fits it, either, because that makes me sound like I'm a serial killer or something. I've never hurt another human being, or at least not physically. I've broken a few hearts in my time, but we've all done that, so I'm nothing special in that regard. I'm a boring heartbreaker, at that, because I've never abandoned one woman for another. I never dated or married more than one woman at a time. I didn't break hearts into pieces overnight. I broke them slowly and carefully. I didn't set any land-speed records running out the door. Piece by piece, I disappeared. And I've been disappearing ever since. But I'm not going to tell you any more about my brain or my soul.

I've been homeless for six years. If there's such a thing as being an effective homeless man, I suppose I'm effective. Being homeless is probably the only thing I've ever been good at. I know where to get the best free food. I've made friends with restaurant and convenience-store managers who let me use their bathrooms. I don't mean the public bathrooms, either. I mean the employees' bathrooms, the clean ones hidden in the back of the kitchen or the pantry or the cooler. I know it sounds strange to be proud of, but it means a lot to me, being trustworthy enough to piss in somebody else's clean bathroom. Maybe you don't understand the value of a clean bathroom, but I do.

Probably none of this interests you. I probably don't interest you much. Homeless Indians are everywhere in Seattle. We're common and boring, and you walk right on by us, with maybe a look of anger or disgust or even sadness at the terrible fate of the noble savage. But we have dreams and families. I'm friends with a homeless Plains Indian man whose son is the editor of a big-time newspaper back east. That's his story, but we Indians are great storytellers and liars and mythmakers, so maybe that Plains Indian hobo is a plain old everyday Indian. I'm kind of suspicious of him, because he describes himself only as Plains Indian, a generic term, and not by a specific tribe. When I asked him why he wouldn't tell me exactly what he is, he said, "Do any of us know exactly what we are?" Yeah, great, a philosophizing Indian. "Hey," I said, "you got to have a home to be that homely." He laughed and flipped me the eagle and walked away. But you probably want to know more about the story I'm really trying to tell you.

I wander the streets with a regular crew, my teammates, my defenders, and my posse. It's Rose of Sharon, Junior, and me. We matter to one another if we don't matter to anybody else. Rose of Sharon is a big woman, about seven feet tall if you're measuring overall effect, and about five feet tall if you're talking about the physical. She's a Yakama Indian of the Wishram variety. Junior is a Colville, but there are about 199 tribes that make up the Colville, so he could be anything. He's good-looking, though, like he just stepped out of some "Don't Litter the Earth" public-service advertisement. He's got those great big cheekbones that are like planets, you know, with little moons orbiting around them. He gets me jealous, jealous, and jealous. If you put Junior and me next to each other, he's the Before Columbus Arrived Indian, and I'm the After Columbus Arrived Indian. I am living proof of the horrible damage that colonialism has done to us Skins. But I'm not going to let you know how scared I sometimes get of history and its ways. I'm a strong man, and I know that silence is the best way of dealing with white folks.

This whole story started at lunchtime, when Rose of Sharon, Junior, and I were panning the handle down at Pike Place

Market. After about two hours of negotiating, we earned five dollars, good enough for a bottle of fortified courage from the most beautiful 7–Eleven in the world. So we headed over that way, feeling like warrior drunks, and we walked past this pawnshop I'd never noticed before. And that was strange, because we Indians have built-in pawnshop radar. But the strangest thing was the old powwow-dance regalia I saw hanging in the window.

"That's my grandmother's regalia," I said to Rose of Sharon and Junior.

"How do you know for sure?" Junior asked.

I didn't know for sure, because I hadn't seen that regalia in person ever. I'd seen only photographs of my grandmother dancing in it. And that was before somebody stole it from her fifty years ago. But it sure looked like my memory of it, and it had all the same colors of feathers and beads that my family always sewed into their powwow regalia.

"There's only one way to know for sure," I said.

So Rose of Sharon, Junior, and I walked into the pawnshop and greeted the old white man working behind the counter.

"How can I help you?" he asked.

"That's my grandmother's powwow regalia in your window," I said. "Somebody stole it from her fifty years ago, and my family has been looking for it ever since."

The pawnbroker looked at me like I was a liar. I understood. Pawnshops are filled with liars.

"I'm not lying," I said. "Ask my friends here. They'll tell you."

"He's the most honest Indian I know," Rose of Sharon said.

"All right, honest Indian," the pawnbroker said. "I'll give you the benefit of the doubt. Can you prove it's your grandmother's regalia?"

Because they don't want to be perfect, because only God is perfect, Indian people sew flaws into their powwow regalia. My family always sewed one yellow bead somewhere on their regalia. But we always hid it where you had to search hard to find it.

"If it really is my grandmother's," I said, "there will be one yellow bead hidden somewhere on it."

"All right, then," the pawnbroker said. "Let's take a look."

He pulled the regalia out of the window, laid it down on his glass counter, and we searched for that yellow bead and found it hidden beneath the armpit.

"There it is," the pawnbroker said. He didn't sound surprised. "You were right. This is your grandmother's regalia."

"It's been missing for fifty years," Junior said.

"Hey, Junior," I said. "It's my family's story. Let me tell it."

"All right," he said. "I apologize. You go ahead."

"It's been missing for fifty years," I said.

"That's his family's sad story," Rose of Sharon said. "Are you going to give it back to him?"

"That would be the right thing to do," the pawnbroker said. "But I can't afford to do the right thing. I paid a thousand dollars for this. I can't give away a thousand dollars."

"We could go to the cops and tell them it was stolen," Rose of Sharon said.

"Hey," I said to her, "don't go threatening people."

The pawnbroker sighed. He was thinking hard about the possibilities.

"Well, I suppose you could go to the cops," he said. "But I don't think they'd believe a word you said."

He sounded sad about that. Like he was sorry for taking advantage of our disadvantages.

"What's your name?" the pawnbroker asked me.

"Jackson," I said.

"Is that first or last?" he asked.

"Both."

"Are you serious?"

"Yes, it's true. My mother and father named me Jackson Jackson. My family nickname is Jackson Squared. My family is funny."

"All right, Jackson Jackson," the pawnbroker said. "You wouldn't happen to have a thousand dollars, would you?"

"We've got five dollars total," I said.

"That's too bad," he said and thought hard about the possibilities. "I'd sell it to you for a thousand dollars if you had it. Heck, to make it fair, I'd sell it to you for nine hundred and ninety-nine dollars. I'd lose a dollar. It would be the moral thing to do in this case. To lose a dollar would be the right thing."

"We've got five dollars total," I said again.

"That's too bad," he said again and thought harder about the possibilities. "How about this? I'll give you twenty-four hours to come up with nine hundred and ninety-nine dollars. You come back here at lunchtime tomorrow with the money, and I'll sell it back to you. How does that sound?"

"It sounds good," I said.

"All right, then," he said. "We have a deal. And I'll get you started. Here's twenty bucks to get you started."

He opened up his wallet and pulled out a crisp twenty-dollar bill and gave it to me. Rose of Sharon, Junior, and I walked out into the daylight to search for nine hundred and seventy-four more dollars.

1:00 P.M.

Rose of Sharon, Junior, and I carried our twenty-dollar bill and our five dollars in loose change over to the 7–Eleven and spent it to buy three bottles of imagination. We needed to figure out how to raise all that money in one day. Thinking hard, we huddled in an alley beneath the Alaska Way Viaduct and finished off those bottles one, two, and three.

2:00 P.M.

Rose of Sharon was gone when I woke. I heard later she had hitchhiked back to Toppenish and was living with her sister on the reservation.

Junior was passed out beside me, covered in his own vomit, or maybe somebody else's vomit, and my head hurt from thinking, so I left him alone and walked down to the water. I loved the smell of ocean water. Salt always smells like memory.

When I got to the wharf, I ran into three Aleut cousins who sat on a wooden bench and stared out at the bay and cried. Most of the homeless Indians in Seattle come from Alaska. One by one, each of them hopped a big working boat in Anchorage or Barrow or Juneau, fished his way south to Seattle, jumped off the boat with a pocketful of cash to party hard at one of the highly sacred and traditional Indian bars, went broke and broker, and has been trying to find his way back to the boat and the frozen north ever since.

These Aleuts smelled like salmon, I thought, and they told me they were going to sit on that wooden bench until their boat came back.

"How long has your boat been gone?" I asked.

"Eleven years," the elder Aleut said.

I cried with them for a while.

"Hey," I said. "Do you guys have any money I can borrow?"

They didn't.

3:00 P.M.

I walked back to Junior. He was still passed out. I put my face down near his mouth to make sure he was breathing. He was alive, so I dug around in his blue-jean pockets and found half a cigarette. I smoked it all the way down and thought about my grandmother.

Her name was Agnes, and she died of breast cancer when I was fourteen. My father thought Agnes caught her tumors from the uranium mine on the reservation. But my mother said the disease started when Agnes was walking back from the powwow one night and got run over by a motorcycle. She broke three ribs, and my mother said those ribs never healed right, and tumors always take over when you don't heal right.

Sitting beside Junior, smelling the smoke and salt and vomit, I wondered if my grandmother's cancer had started when somebody stole her powwow regalia. Maybe the cancer started in her broken heart and then leaked out into her breasts. I know it's crazy, but I wondered if I could bring my grandmother back to life if I bought back her regalia.

I needed money, big money, so I left Junior and walked over to the Real Change office.

4:00 P.M.

"Real Change is a multifaceted organization that publishes a newspaper, supports cultural projects that empower the poor and homeless, and mobilizes the public around poverty issues. Real Change's mission is to organize, educate, and build alliances to create solutions to homelessness and poverty. They exist to provide a voice to poor people in our community."

I memorized Real Change's mission statement because I sometimes sell the newspaper on the streets. But you have to stay sober to sell it, and I'm not always good at staying sober. Anybody can sell the newspaper. You buy each copy for thirty cents and sell it for a dollar and keep the net profit.

"I need one thousand four hundred and thirty papers," I said to the Big Boss.

"That's a strange number," he said. "And that's a lot of papers."

"I need them."

The Big Boss pulled out the calculator and did the math. "It will cost you four hundred and twenty-nine dollars for that many," he said.

"If I had that kind of money, I wouldn't need to sell the papers."

"What's going on, Jackson-to-the-Second-Power?" he asked. He is the only one who calls me that. He is a funny and kind man.

I told him about my grandmother's powwow regalia and how much money I needed to buy it back.

"We should call the police," he said.

"I don't want to do that," I said. "It's a quest now. I need to win it back by myself."

"I understand," he said. "And to be honest, I'd give you the papers to sell if I thought it would work. But the record for most papers sold in a day by one vendor is only three hundred and two."

"That would net me about two hundred bucks," I said.

The Big Boss used his calculator. "Two hundred and eleven dollars and forty cents," he said.

"That's not enough," I said.

"The most money anybody has made in one day is five hundred and twenty-five. And that's because somebody gave Old Blue five hundred-dollar bills for some dang reason. The average daily net is about thirty dollars."

"This isn't going to work."

"No."

"Can you lend me some money?"

"I can't do that," he said. "If I lend you money, I have to lend money to everybody."

"What can you do?"

"I'll give you fifty papers for free. But don't tell anybody I did it."

"Okay," I said.

He gathered up the newspapers and handed them to me. I held them to my chest. He hugged me. I carried the newspapers back toward the water.

5:00 P.M.

Back on the wharf, I stood near the Bainbridge Island Terminal and tried to sell papers to business commuters walking onto the ferry.

I sold five in one hour, dumped the other forty-five into a garbage can, and walked into the McDonald's, ordered four cheese-burgers for a dollar each, and slowly ate them.

After eating, I walked outside and vomited on the sidewalk. I hated to lose my food so soon after eating it. As an alcoholic Indian with a busted stomach, I always hope I can keep enough food in my stomach to stay alive.

6:00 P.M.

With one dollar in my pocket, I walked back to Junior. He was still passed out, so I put my ear to his chest and listened for his heartbeat. He was alive, so I took off his shoes and socks and found one dollar in his left sock and fifty cents in his right sock. With two dollars and fifty cents in my hand, I sat beside Junior and thought about my grandmother and her stories.

When I was sixteen, my grandmother told me a story about World War II. She was a nurse at a military hospital in Sydney, Australia. Over the course of two years, she comforted and healed U.S. and Australian soldiers.

One day, she tended to a wounded Maori soldier. He was very dark-skinned. His hair was black and curly, and his eyes were black and warm. His face with covered with bright tattoos.

"Are you Maori?" he asked my grandmother.

"No," she said. "I'm Spokane Indian. From the United States."

"Ah, yes," he said. "I have heard of your tribes. But you are the first American Indian I have ever met."

"There's a lot of Indian soldiers fighting for the United States," she said. "I have a brother still fighting in Germany, and I lost another brother on Okinawa."

"I am sorry," he said. "I was on Okinawa as well. It was terrible." He had lost his legs to an artillery attack.

"I am sorry about your legs," my grandmother said.

"It's funny, isn't it?" he asked.

"What's funny?"

"How we brown people are killing other brown people so white people will remain free."

"I hadn't thought of it that way."

"Well, sometimes I think of it that way. And other times, I think of it the way they want me to think of it. I get confused."

She fed him morphine.

"Do you believe in heaven?" he asked.

"Which heaven?" she asked.

"I'm talking about the heaven where my legs are waiting for me."

They laughed.

"Of course," he said, "my legs will probably run away from me when I get to heaven. And how will I ever catch them?"

"You have to get your arms strong," my grandmother said. "So you can run on your hands."

They laughed again.

Sitting beside Junior, I laughed with the memory of my grandmother's story. I put my hand close to Junior's mouth to make sure he was still breathing. Yes, Junior was alive, so I took his two dollars and fifty cents and walked to the Korean grocery store over in Pioneer Square.

7:00 P.M.

In the Korean grocery store, I bought a fifty-cent cigar and two scratch lottery tickets for a dollar each. The maximum cash prize was five hundred dollars a ticket. If I won both, I would have enough money to buy back the regalia.

I loved Kay, the young Korean woman who worked the register. She was the daughter of the owners and sang all day.

"I love you," I said when I handed her the money.

"You always say you love me," she said.

"That's because I will always love you."

"You are a sentimental fool."

"I'm a romantic old man."

"Too old for me."

"I know I'm too old for you, but I can dream."

"Okay," she said. "I agree to be a part of your dreams, but I will only hold your hand in your dreams. No kissing and no sex. Not even in your dreams."

"Okay," I said. "No sex. Just romance."

"Good-bye, Jackson Jackson, my love, I will see you soon."

I left the store, walked over to Occidental Park, sat on a bench, and smoked my cigar all the way down.

Ten minutes after I finished the cigar, I scratched my first lottery ticket and won nothing. So I could win only five hundred dollars now, and that would be just half of what I needed.

449

Ten minutes later, I scratched my other lottery ticket and won a free ticket, a small consolation and one more chance to win money.

I walked back to Kay.

"Jackson Jackson," she said. "Have you come back to claim my heart?"

"I won a free ticket," I said.

"Just like a man," she said. "You love money and power more than you love me."

"It's true," I said. "And I'm sorry it's true."

She gave me another scratch ticket, and I carried it outside. I liked to scratch my tickets in private. Hopeful and sad, I scratched that third ticket and won real money. I carried it back inside to Kay.

"I won a hundred dollars," I said.

She examined the ticket and laughed. "That's a fortune," she said and counted out five twenties. Our fingertips touched as she handed me the money. I felt electric and constant.

"Thank you," I said and gave her one of the bills.

"I can't take that," she said. "It's your money."

"No, it's tribal. It's an Indian thing. When you win, you're supposed to share with your family."

"I'm not your family."

"Yes, you are."

She smiled. She kept the money. With eighty dollars in my pocket, I said good-bye to my dear Kay and walked out into the cold night air.

8:00 P.M.

I wanted to share the good news with Junior. I walked back to him, but he was gone. I later heard he had hitchhiked down to Portland, Oregon, and died of exposure in an alley behind the Hilton Hotel.

9:00 P.M.

Lonely for Indians, I carried my eighty dollars over to Big Heart's in South Downtown. Big Heart's is an all-Indian bar. Nobody knows how or why Indians migrate to one bar and turn it into an official Indian bar. But Big Heart's has been an Indian bar for twenty-three years. It used to be way up on Aurora Avenue, but a crazy Lummi Indian burned that one down, and the owners moved to the new location, a few blocks south of Safeco Field.

I walked inside Big Heart's and counted fifteen Indians, eight men and seven women. I didn't know any of them, but Indians like to belong, so we all pretended to be cousins.

"How much for whiskey shots?" I asked the bartender, a fat white guy.

"You want the bad stuff or the badder stuff?"

"As bad as you got."

"One dollar a shot."

I laid my eighty dollars on the bar top.

"All right," I said. "Me and all my cousins here are going to be drinking eighty shots. How many is that apiece?"

"Counting you," a woman shouted from behind me, "that's five shots for everybody."

I turned to look at her. She was a chubby and pale Indian sitting with a tall and skinny Indian man.

"All right, math genius," I said to her and then shouted for the whole bar to hear. "Five drinks for everybody!"

All of the other Indians rushed the bar, but I sat with the mathematician and her skinny friend. We took our time with our whiskey shots.

"What's your tribe?" I asked them.

"I'm Duwamish," she said. "And he's Crow."

"You're a long way from Montana," I said to him.

"I'm Crow," he said. "I flew here."

"What's your name?" I asked them.

"I'm Irene Muse," she said. "And this is Honey Boy."

She shook my hand hard, but he offered his hand like I was supposed to kiss it. So I kissed it. He giggled and blushed as well as a dark-skinned Crow can blush.

"You're one of them two-spirits, aren't you?" I asked him.

"I love women," he said. "And I love men."

"Sometimes both at the same time," Irene said.

We laughed.

"Man," I said to Honey Boy. "So you must have about eight or nine spirits going on inside of you, enit?"

"Sweetie," he said, "I'll be whatever you want me to be."

"Oh, no," Irene said. "Honey Boy is falling in love."

"It has nothing to do with love," he said.

We laughed.

"Wow," I said. "I'm flattered, Honey Boy, but I don't play on your team."

"Never say never," he said.

"You better be careful," Irene said. "Honey Boy knows all sorts of magic. He always makes straight boys fall for him."

"Honey Boy," I said, "you can try to seduce me. And Irene, you can try with him. But my heart belongs to a woman named Kay."

"Is your Kay a virgin?" Honey Boy asked.

We laughed.

We drank our whiskey shots until they were gone. But the other Indians bought me more whiskey shots because I'd been so generous with my money. Honey Boy pulled out his credit card, and I drank and sailed on that plastic boat.

After a dozen shots, I asked Irene to dance. And she refused. But Honey Boy shuffled over to the jukebox, dropped in a quarter, and selected Willie Nelson's "Help Me Make It Through the Night." As Irene and I sat at the table and laughed and drank more whiskey, Honey Boy danced a slow circle around us and sang along with Willie.

"Are you serenading me?" I asked him.

He kept singing and dancing.

"Are you serenading me?" I asked him again.

"He's going to put a spell on you," Irene said.

I leaned over the table, spilling a few drinks, and kissed Irene hard. She kissed me back.

10:00 P.M.

Irene pushed me into the women's bathroom, into a stall, shut the door behind us, and shoved her hand down my pants. She was short, so I had to lean over to kiss her. I grabbed and squeezed her everywhere I could reach, and she was wonderfully fat, and every part of her body felt like a large, warm, and soft breast.

Midnight

Nearly blind with alcohol, I stood alone at the bar and swore I'd been standing in the bathroom with Irene only a minute ago.

"One more shot!" I yelled at the bartender.

"You've got no more money!" he yelled.

"Somebody buy me a drink!" I shouted.

"They've got no more money!"

"Where's Irene and Honey Boy?"

"Long gone!"

2:00 A.M.

"Closing time!" the bartender shouted at the three or four Indians still drinking hard after a long hard day of drinking. Indian alcoholics are either sprinters or marathon runners.

"Where's Irene and Honey Bear?" I asked.

"They've been gone for hours," the bartender said.

"Where'd they go?"

"I told you a hundred times, I don't know."

"What am I supposed to do?"

"It's closing time. I don't care where you go, but you're not staying here."

"You are an ungrateful bastard. I've been good to you."

"You don't leave right now, I'm going to kick your ass."

"Come on, I know how to fight."

He came for me. I don't remember what happened after that.

4:00 A.M.

I emerged from the blackness and discovered myself walking behind a big warehouse. I didn't know where I was. My face hurt. I touched my nose and decided it might be broken. Exhausted and cold, I pulled a plastic tarp from a truck bed, wrapped it around me like a faithful lover, and fell asleep in the dirt.

6:00 A.M.

Somebody kicked me in the ribs. I opened my eyes and looked up at a white cop.

"Jackson," said the cop. "Is that you?"

"Officer Williams," I said. He was a good cop with a sweet tooth. He'd given me hundreds of candy bars over the years. I wonder if he knew I was diabetic.

"What the hell are you doing here?" he asked.

"I was cold and sleepy," I said. "So I laid down."

"You dumb-ass, you passed out on the railroad tracks."

I sat up and looked around. I was lying on the railroad tracks. Dockworkers stared at me. I should have been a railroad-track pizza, a double Indian pepperoni with extra cheese. Sick and scared, I leaned over and puked whiskey.

"What the hell's wrong with you?" Officer Williams asked. "You've never been this stupid."

"It's my grandmother," I said. "She died."

"I'm sorry, man. When did she die?"

"1972."

"And you're killing yourself now?"

"I've been killing myself ever since she died."

He shook his head. He was sad for me. Like I said, he was a good cop.

"And somebody beat the hell out of you," he said. "You remember who?"

"Mr. Grief and I went a few rounds."

455

"It looks like Mr. Grief knocked you out."

"Mr. Grief always wins."

"Come on," he said, "let's get you out of here."

He helped me stand and led me over to his squad car. He put me in the back. "You throw up in there," he said, "and you're cleaning it up."

"That's fair," I said.

He walked around the car and sat in the driver's seat. "I'm taking you over to detox," he said.

"No, man, that place is awful," I said. "It's full of drunk Indians."

We laughed. He drove away from the docks.

"I don't know how you guys do it," he said.

"What guys?" I asked.

"You Indians. How the hell do you laugh so much? I just picked your ass off the railroad tracks, and you're making jokes. Why the hell do you do that?"

"The two funniest tribes I've ever been around are Indians and Jews, so I guess that says something about the inherent humor of genocide."

We laughed.

"Listen to you, Jackson. You're so smart. Why the hell are you on the streets?"

"Give me a thousand dollars, and I'll tell you."

"You bet I'd give you a thousand dollars if I knew you'd straighten up your life."

He meant it. He was the second-best cop I'd ever known.

"You're a good cop," I said.

"Come on, Jackson," he said. "Don't blow smoke up my ass."

"No, really, you remind me of my grandfather."

"Yeah, that's what you Indians always tell me."

"No, man, my grandfather was a tribal cop. He was a good cop. He never arrested people. He took care of them. Just like you."

"I've arrested hundreds of scumbags, Jackson. And I've shot a couple in the ass."

"It don't matter. You're not a killer."

"I didn't kill them. I killed their asses. I'm an ass-killer."

We drove through downtown. The missions and shelters had already released their overnighters. Sleepy homeless men and women stood on corners and stared up at the gray sky. It was the morning after the night of the living dead.

"Did you ever get scared?" I asked Officer Williams.

"What do you mean?"

"I mean, being a cop, is it scary?"

He thought about that for a while. He contemplated it. I liked that about him.

"I guess I try not to think too much about being afraid," he said. "If you think about fear, then you'll be afraid. The job is boring most of the time. Just driving and looking into dark corners, you know, and seeing nothing. But then things get heavy. You're chasing somebody or fighting them or walking around a dark house and you just know some crazy guy is hiding around a corner, and hell yes, it's scary."

"My grandfather was killed in the line of duty," I said.

"I'm sorry. How'd it happen?"

I knew he'd listen closely to my story.

"He worked on the reservation. Everybody knew everybody. It was safe. We aren't like those crazy Sioux or Apache or any of those other warrior tribes. There's only been three murders on my reservation in the last hundred years."

"That is safe."

"Yeah, we Spokane, we're passive, you know? We're mean with words. And we'll cuss out anybody. But we don't shoot people. Or stab them. Not much, anyway."

"So what happened to your grandfather?"

"This man and his girlfriend were fighting down by Little Falls."

"Domestic dispute. Those are the worst."

"Yeah, but this guy was my grandfather's brother. My great-uncle."

"Oh, no."

"Yeah, it was awful. My grandfather just strolled into the house. He'd been there a thousand times. And his brother and his girlfriend were all drunk and beating on each other. And my grandfather stepped between them just like he'd done a hundred times before. And the girlfriend tripped or something. She fell down and hit her head and started crying. And my grandfather knelt down beside her to make sure she was all right. And for some reason, my great-uncle reached down, pulled my grandfather's pistol out of the holster, and shot him in the head."

"That's terrible. I'm sorry."

"Yeah, my great-uncle could never figure out why he did it. He went to prison forever, you know, and he always wrote these long letters. Like fifty pages of tiny little handwriting. And he was always trying to figure out why he did it. He'd write and write and write and try to figure it out. He never did. It's a great big mystery."

"Do you remember your grandfather?"

"A little bit. I remember the funeral. My grandmother wouldn't let them bury him. My father had to drag her away from the grave."

"I don't know what to say."

"I don't, either."

We stopped in front of the detox center.

"We're here," Officer Williams said.

"I can't go in there," I said.

"You have to."

"Please, no. They'll keep me for twenty-four hours. And then it will be too late."

"Too late for what?"

I told him about my grandmother's regalia and the deadline for buying it back.

"If it was stolen," he said, "then you need to file reports. I'll investigate it myself. If that thing is really your grandmother's, I'll get it back for you. Legally."

"No," I said. "That's not fair. The pawnbroker didn't know it was stolen. And besides, I'm on a mission here. I want to be a hero, you know? I want to win it back like a knight."

"That's romantic crap."

"It might be. But I care about it. It's been a long time since I really cared about something."

Officer Williams turned around in his seat and stared at me. He studied me.

"I'll give you some money," he said. "I don't have much. Only thirty bucks. I'm short until payday. And it's not enough to get back the regalia. But it's something."

"I'll take it," I said.

"I'm giving it to you because I believe in what you believe. I'm hoping, and I don't know why I'm hoping it, but I hope you can turn thirty bucks into a thousand somehow."

"I believe in magic."

"I believe you'll take my money and get drunk on it."

"Then why are you giving it to me?"

"There ain't no such thing as an atheist cop."

"Sure there is."

"Yeah, well, I'm not an atheist cop."

He let me out of the car, handed me two fives and a twenty, and shook my hand. "Take care of yourself, Jackson," he said. "Stay off the railroad tracks."

"I'll try," I said.

He drove away. Carrying my money, I headed back toward the water.

8:00 A.M.

On the wharf, those three Aleut men still waited on the wooden bench.

"Have you seen your ship?" I asked.

"Seen a lot of ships," the elder Aleut said. "But not our ship."

I sat on the bench with them. We sat in silence for a long time. I wondered whether we would fossilize if we sat there long enough.

I thought about my grandmother. I'd never seen her dance in her regalia. More than anything, I wished I'd seen her dance at a powwow.

"Do you guys know any songs?" I asked the Aleuts.

"I know all of Hank Williams," the elder Aleut said.

"How about Indian songs?"

"Hank Williams is Indian."

"How about sacred songs?"

"Hank Williams is sacred."

"I'm talking about ceremonial songs, you know, religious ones. The songs you sing back home when you're wishing and hoping."

"What are you wishing and hoping for?"

"I'm wishing my grandmother was still alive."

"Every song I know is about that."

"Well, sing me as many as you can."

The Aleuts sang their strange and beautiful songs. I listened. They sang about my grandmother and their grandmothers. They were lonely for the cold and snow. I was lonely for everybody.

10:00 A.M.

After the Aleuts finished their last song, we sat in silence. Indians are good at silence.

"Was that the last song?" I asked.

"We sang all the ones we could," the elder Aleut said. "All the others are just for our people."

I understood. We Indians have to keep our secrets. And these Aleuts were so secretive that they didn't refer to themselves as Indians.

"Are you guys hungry?" I asked.

They looked at one another and communicated without talking.

"We could eat," the elder Aleut said.

11:00 A.M.

The Aleuts and I walked over to Mother's Kitchen, a greasy diner in the International District. I knew they served homeless Indians who'd lucked in to money.

"Four for breakfast?" the waitress asked when we stepped inside.

"Yes, we're very hungry," the elder Aleut said.

She sat us in a booth near the kitchen. I could smell the food cooking. My stomach growled.

"You guys want separate checks?" the waitress asked.

"No, I'm paying for it," I said.

"Aren't you the generous one," she said.

"Don't do that," I said.

"Do what?" she asked.

"Don't ask me rhetorical questions. They scare me."

She looked puzzled, and then she laughed.

"Okay, Professor," she said. "I'll only ask you real questions from now on."

"Thank you."

"What do you guys want to eat?"

"That's the best question anybody can ask anybody," I said.

"How much money you got?" she asked.

"Another good question," I said. "I've got twenty-five dollars I can spend. Bring us all the breakfast you can, plus your tip."

She knew the math.

"All right, that's four specials and four coffees and fifteen percent for me."

The Aleuts and I waited in silence. Soon enough, the waitress returned and poured us four coffees, and we sipped at them until she returned again with four plates of food. Eggs, bacon, toast, hash-brown potatoes. It is amazing how much food you can buy for so little money.

Grateful, we feasted.

Noon

I said farewell to the Aleuts and walked toward the pawn-shop. I later heard the Aleuts had waded into the saltwater near Dock 47 and disappeared. Some Indians said the Aleuts walked on the water and headed north. Other Indians saw the Aleuts drown. I don't know what happened to them.

I looked for the pawnshop and couldn't find it. I swear it wasn't located in the place where it had been before. I walked twenty or thirty blocks looking for the pawnshop, turned corners and bisected intersections, looked up its name in the phone books, and asked people walking past me if they'd ever heard of it. But that pawnshop seemed to have sailed away from me like a ghost ship. I wanted to cry. Right when I'd given up, when I turned one last corner and thought I might die if I didn't find that pawnshop, there it was, located in a space I swore it hadn't been filling up a few minutes before.

I walked inside and greeted the pawnbroker, who looked a little younger than he had before.

"It's you," he said.

"Yes, it's me," I said.

"Jackson Jackson."

"That is my name."

"Where are your friends?"

"They went traveling. But it's okay. Indians are everywhere."

"Do you have my money?"

"How much do you need again?" I asked and hoped the price had changed.

"Nine hundred and ninety-nine dollars."

It was still the same price. Of course it was the same price. Why would it change?

"I don't have that," I said.

"What do you have?"

"Five dollars."

I set the crumpled Lincoln on the countertop. The pawnbroker studied it.

"Is that the same five dollars from yesterday?"

"No, it's different."

He thought about the possibilities.

"Did you work hard for this money?" he asked.

"Yes," I said.

He closed his eyes and thought harder about the possibilities. Then he stepped into his back room and returned with my grandmother's regalia.

"Take it," he said and held it out to me.

"I don't have the money."

"I don't want your money."

"But I wanted to win it."

"You did win it. Now, take it before I change my mind."

Do you know how many good men live in this world? Too many to count!

I took my grandmother's regalia and walked outside. I knew that solitary yellow bead was part of me. I knew I was that yellow bead in part. Outside, I wrapped myself in my grandmother's regalia and breathed her in. I stepped off the sidewalk and into the intersection. Pedestrians stopped. Cars stopped. The city stopped. They all watched me dance with my grandmother. I was my grandmother, dancing.

ACKNOWLEDGMENTS

For their editorial advice, insults, and friendship, I want to thank Jess Walter, Shann Ferch, and Kevin Taylor.

I also send loving trash talk out to the Thursday and Sunday night basketball boys. You know who you are.

I certainly thank Elisabeth, Deb, Judy, and Morgan for twenty years of joy.

For their support and patience, I extend special thanks to Reagan Arthur and Megan Tinley.

To my agent hero, Nancy Stauffer, I send all the love and respect in the world.

With her brilliant legal mind, Susan Grode has always been way ahead of the rest of the world when it comes to a rapidly changing publishing world. I am lucky to call her my friend and colleague.

To Rosalie Swedlin, I sing an honor song for her guidance.

And, of course, to my mother and siblings for loving my stories even when they probably reveal too many family secrets.

And most of all, I want to thank my wife, Diane, and my sons, Joseph and David. It's hard to live with a writer but they manage to survive me with beauty and grace. I cherish them.